MITCHELL ARCHER

LEGENDS LIVE: VOLUME ONE

★

RISING SON

For all my friends, especially Hoffa, Jeremy and Matt.

For Brandon, who grew up with pictures of Tom on his bedroom walls.

And for M. Edward, who (more than anyone) made sure I did it. Thanks for the push!

CHAPTER ONE

Independence opened his eyes and the dream slipped away. The hero sprawled in the dirt, facedown at the bottom of a shallow crater. For a moment he wasn't sure where he was, how he'd come to be there.

Something had happened. Something had attacked. He remembered flying above the river, stretching his limbs in the morning sun. He'd rolled over in the air to glance at Manhattan. Then, like a housefly, he'd been swatted from the sky.

Raising his head, Independence saw his hands in the dirt. The long blue gloves had been burned and torn; blood stained his knuckles. He looked at it, astonished and a little afraid. He hadn't bled since childhood; he'd forgotten the feeling, forgotten the sting. He'd forgotten what it was like to be vulnerable.

People often called Independence the most powerful man on Earth. But right then, he felt nearly powerless. Weak and dizzy, his bones throbbed, his body ached. Nothing had ever hit him like that. Nothing had ever hurt like this. A bittersweet thought crossed the hero's mind; for the first time in his life, he felt like a man.

So he chose to stand like a man and rose to his feet on the shattered earth. Burns and tears covered his red-and-white costume. A rough slash crossed his chest—cutting right through the star-within-a-circle emblem. Charred tatters were all that remained his famous blue cape.

The morning sun glinted on his metallic golden eyes; he'd come down in the middle of Central Park. He looked south, across Sheep Meadow, toward the memorial at the southern end of the field. Aegis, the first hero—once known throughout the galaxy as the Golden Light—had died on that very spot.

And Independence understood what had happened, why he'd come down in that field. Only one being would have flung him there. Only one being *could* have.

Bloodlust had returned to Earth.

From above, a voice spoke without words, in response to the hero's thoughts. It boomed in his mind and the minds of the millions below—and the billions, around the globe, who knew nothing of the events in New York City. The voice rolled over the world, roaring without language. A terrible power spoke; all humanity heard and trembled.

You have no power, and
you are not a man.
You, a hollow abomination;
you, an empty imitation;
You, I name Nothing;
for you, nothingness I bring.

Independence grimaced and touched the deep connection he shared with Bloodlust—it was impossible to ignore, the call of like to like. Aegis and his murderer had been of the same species, if creatures of living energy can be called a species.

Back in 1947, when Aegis appeared during the Roswell incident, he'd created a human body. He'd gathered atoms, written a code of DNA, formed eukaryotic cells and grew living flesh.

And Independence had been made from that genetic code, those cells, that flesh. He'd been created by the ancient Home and raised by the American government, the clone of Aegis. His nature and substance was identical to the Golden Light.

Bloodlust shared that nature; it was made of the same substance. They were kin, they were equals, and Independence *knew* it. He could fight back.

His eyes began to glow with an intense, golden light. He flared and brightened until he shined like the sun itself.

The memorial statue seemed to look over his shoulder, almost as if Aegis stood there, challenging Bloodlust—but the Golden Light had been dead for thirty-eight years. This was

Independence's day.

He rose into the air, spinning around to face Bloodlust. It hovered above the city, waiting.

It had taken the form of a crude upper body, only vaguely humanoid and perhaps eight feet tall, surrounded by a roiling sphere of plasma and radiation. The legless figure appeared pitch black and dense, like it was carved from coal. Its torso was a blunt wedge; the oversize arms had broad, inhuman hands and long, curved talons. The face resembled a hollow mask with jagged features and a fanged maw; the eyes contained only flame and scorn.

The people of New York watched from below. Their city been attacked before—by fanatical terrorists, alien invaders and Posthuman villains—and they would not cower. Though many stared at the sky, only a few cried out in fear. Others watched Independence rise over Central Park and cheered. Those who had lived through 1961 knew better. They looked on with respectful silence as the hero took flight.

The world had always wondered if Bloodlust would come for Independence, as it had come for Aegis. For his part, Independence had always known the answer. He spent his life waiting for this moment, secretly waiting for it, never admitting his fear.

But now the moment had arrived, and Independence realized that he did not fear the possibility of death. He would fight to stay alive, but he would not run. Better people than him had met worse fates. Death would make him more human than he'd ever been; it was nothing to fear.

Instead, Independence feared for Earth and her children. He feared for this world of precious life. But more than anything, he feared for the woman he loved, whom he could no longer protect.

Bloodlust responded to these thoughts, bellowing in the minds of the people of Earth. The creature did not believe in guile or subtlety; it wanted everyone to understand its intentions.

I will not crumble this world's foundation,
nor end it all in flame.
But punishment for your creation
will be a pleasing game.

Until time's passage brings extinction,
these apes will fear my name.

With that, Bloodlust lowered its face, and death followed its line of sight. Flashes of combustion flickered on the streets as hundreds of people died by pressure and heat. The victims lived long enough to feel their flesh disintegrate; their shrieking deaths echoed in the doomsday silence of Manhattan's streets.

Independence immediately hurtled across the sky; Bloodlust shot forward and met him in the air. The force of the collision shattered windows across the city and threw the combatants apart. They immediately looped around and raced toward each other again. The hero struck with a powerful, two-handed ram, sending the monster over the horizon.

But Bloodlust rocketed back and launched Independence to the edge of space with a blast of raw force. The hero returned within seconds and rammed the monster at hypersonic speed. The burning plasma engulfed Independence, as he pierced Bloodlust's raging aura. They arced, dipped and whirled high, locked together like a contact binary star—bound by physics, hostility and fate.

At the heart of the inferno, Independence grappled with Bloodlust. He held the fiend's left arm in his right hand; its right claw wrapped around the hero's left forearm. They wheeled through the air, neither one able to overcome the other.

Independence felt a surge of hope; their powers were evenly matched. Spiraling around their common center, they soared into the sky.

Then Bloodlust leaned in, locked eyes with the hero and roared. An afterburner blast of plasma rolled over Independence's face. He winced as the energy flowed over his eyes.

That brief flinch was all Bloodlust needed.

Independence's left arm snapped with a rifle's crack. The ulna and radius burst through flesh midway down his forearm.

Independence screamed as Bloodlust twisted the hideously fractured arm. It pulled with monstrous strength, wrenching and tugging until the forearm ripped free. Blood spewed into the superheated air, igniting like a flamethrower's stream until the wound cauterized.

Bloodlust dropped the blackened remains of Independence's hand and reached for the hero's throat. Two searing fingers wrapped around Independence's neck and darkness crawled across his field of vision.

They fell together, tracing a line of fire between the skyscrapers. They crashed again in Central Park; the skyline swayed as if the blow staggered the city.

The meteoric descent uprooted half of the park's trees— limbs, brush and leaves were consumed by the unnatural heat—and left a hundred-foot crater at the end of Sheep Meadow. Radioactive flame tainted the earth and sent deadly ash on the wind; a small mushroom cloud blossomed over Manhattan.

Independence couldn't see any of that. He didn't see the blackened crater, or the ruins of the Aegis memorial. He did not see Bloodlust. His unfocused eyes aimed up, toward thick smoke and patches of brilliant sky, but his mind perceived other things.

He saw soft light over a green field; he saw a gentle day in a place of peace. He saw his friends—so many friends. And in the middle of the field stood his beloved; she carried the future in her arms.

His spine had been shattered, his skull split open, and he had a dozen other mortal wounds. Nearly every bone in his body had been splintered by the impact; nearly every organ was smashed, ruptured and failing. He lay in a twisted tangle of limbs, blood and dirt, and the shimmering aura began to flicker and dim.

His mind retreated from reality; he no longer felt pain, fear, or much of anything, really. He did not notice as Bloodlust doubled in size and picked up the broken statue of Aegis. He did not see the fiend raise the sculpture overhead, a club in its monstrous fist.

Independence held her in his arms. He felt the warmth of her skin against his lips. He realized that he was dying but wasn't troubled by the thought. He felt only slightly regretful. At least he got to see her one last time, even if only in a dream. He looked at the future and made one last wish.

The statue came down. Then it came down again. And again.

✪   ✪   ✪

Tom's eyes snapped open in the early morning darkness. He wasn't sure whether he'd screamed or not, but it felt like he had. Throwing back the sheets, he sat up and swung his feet to the floor. The clock said six-twenty; almost time to get out of bed anyway.

"What the fuck," muttered the boy. He was sixteen and had never experienced a dream like that. So real, so terrifying. He closed his eyes and tried to push it away. But he still saw Bloodlust, surrounded by flame, holding the statue high.

"Tom? Are you okay?" came his mother's voice. Her knuckles rapped on his bedroom door before it opened. Light rushed in from the hall.

"Yeah, I guess I kind of had a nightmare."

"Really? You haven't had one of those in a while." Her voice was soft and comforting. Tom thought she'd always been the best mom on Earth; he was lucky to have her and knew it. Lots of kids have pretty shitty parents. Tom only had his mother but couldn't ask for more. She walked closer and put a hand on his shoulder. "What was it about?"

Tom shook his head. He didn't want to tell her, but she was too persistent for that. So he just shrugged and tried to sound casual. "Independence and Bloodlust. Weird, huh?"

"Independence ... and Bloodlust?" She shuddered.

Tom cringed. He felt like a heel. His father, Adam Washington, had been killed the same day as Independence, along with over two million people worldwide. Bloodlust had lived up to its word, punishing humanity for cloning Aegis. Adam had simply been another victim of the attack.

But that had been half-a-year before Tom's birth; the boy had grown up without a father, in a world with no heroes.

"Did he look at you?" Her voice dropped to a whisper.

Tom turned toward his mother. "Independence?"

"Bloodlust. Did he notice you? Did he say anything to you?"

"No. It was like watching a movie. I wasn't really there. Why?"

She shook her head and gave a dismissive wave. "Just trying to figure out why you'd dream about them. Go take a shower, and

I'll cook breakfast."

"Okay. Thanks Mom."

"I love you, Tom."

"I love you, too."

She left his room and went down stairs. Tom looked out the window; their home was on the edge of Westburg, Virginia, surrounded by dense forest that stretched all the way to Kentucky. The mountains were black under the predawn sky, but it wasn't too early to wake up. Tom had a nice long school day to look forward to, followed by another two years minimum of life in hillbilly country. Despite growing up in rural Appalachia, Tom wanted to live in a city. He wanted to see the world. He'd like to go to New York, maybe visit the new memorial for Aegis and Independence. His mother had never taken him to New York and claimed to prefer country life.

She retired after Adam's death to raise their son in a small town, probably because she'd grown up in Chicago. Her name was Megan Fuson, and she'd been some kind of scientist before Tom's birth. He googled her once but didn't learn very much, and she always avoided answering questions. Laboratory work, she'd always say, nothing very exciting. She didn't talk about the past too much. Considering what happened to his father, Tom didn't blame her.

Dreaming about Bloodlust had been bad enough.

CHAPTER TWO

Nikki and her big brother David walked underground, into the Dust Bin, the only bar they had ever visited. They were both under twenty-one, but the owner was like family, and they'd been more times than either one could remember. And the bar wasn't exactly a legally authorized establishment.

It had been carved into solid rock decades ago, a small part of the Paragon Patrol's secret headquarters. The legendary California Girl had claimed ownership, sealed off the rest of the subterranean complex, and turned a few rooms into the Bin. It was the Posthuman watering hole, a haven for hero and villain alike.

It was a shrine to the old age of heroes, the Seventies through the Nineties, and every wall was covered in memorabilia. Photographs hung everywhere, along with newspaper clippings and souvenirs. Weapons, gizmos and costume pieces decorated the room. Mister Moment's onyx staff had been given a prominent place. A probot from the Carnivore Invasion hovered in a corner.

Posthumans didn't really have that many places to hang out, and the Dust Bin was always open. It had to be. Uncle Sam had been after the Posties for over fourteen years, since Daytona Beach's destruction and the assassination of the President by a superhuman madman in 2002. That was back at the beginning of the War on Terror, less than a year after 9/11 and two years after the death of Independence. The American people just couldn't handle any more tragedies.

A new intragovernmental agency—similar to the then-newborn Department of Homeland Security—was formed. Instead of hunting terrorists or other enemies of the state, the Department of Public Safety was charged with handling the Posthuman problem.

All public displays of superhuman abilities were declared illegal throughout the United States. Posties were hazardous to the public. They were required by law to submit to indefinite confinement, while Doctor Angus and the scientists of the American Biological Research Agency sought a method of counteracting the Aegis virus. Even Postie employees of the government, like Milk, were not exempt. Anyone found hiding a Postie was guilty of aiding and abetting a fugitive.

Of course, that's exactly why the Dust Bin existed. It had been made to aid and abet. California Girl, Milk and the rest of the bigwigs used the bar as home base for the underground railroad. Runaways and refugees could show up at any time. It was as a place to relax in a hostile world. Nearly every Postie was welcome, though only a few knew the way.

Most people could only get to the bar by calling Rodrigo Mendez, the legendary outlaw hero from Mexico City known as Portero. He'd open a door for anyone who asked; California Girl paid him very well for the service.

But Nikki and David didn't need one of Portero's doors. They'd always known how to get to the Dust Bin.

The well-polished bar stood on the right side of the room; a row of booths lined the left wall. Tables filled most of the space, except for the dance floor in back. But there were only thirteen people in sight. The room was practically empty.

Six guys were playing poker in the middle of the room, and five shady figures huddled at one of the rearmost tables. The other two people were employees.

One of them sat alone in the closest booth. He was a rather short man with Asian features, a clean-shaven head and no eyes. His name was Quietus; he was telepathic and didn't need eyes. He was the Bin's head bouncer and usually kept peace among the superhuman clientele without resorting to combat, but everyone said he could outfight anybody. And Quietus said never said a thing. He'd never been known to speak at all.

The last person in the Dust Bin sat in a chair behind the bar, napping. His name was Curt Talmadge. Back in the day, people called him Lockdown. He used to be a hero. He even helped form the East Coast Alliance, the largest hero team in the world, but that was long ago. Curt had recently turned sixty-two and looked it. He practically lived at the Bin, sometimes worked behind the bar. Nobody cared if he fell asleep on the job.

"God, this place is dead," muttered Nikki. She was sixteen years old and right around five feet tall, with warm brown skin, dark eyes and an athletic but curvy figure. She drew the gaze of most of the males in the room, all of whom were way too old.

"What'd you expect, Nik? It's Monday morning." David walked behind her, trying to size up the patrons without being obvious. He was only nineteen but considered himself a trained professional, ready for anything. He traded nods with Quietus, knowing the bald man could see just fine in his own way.

"Well, I was hoping Aunt Jacqui would be here or at least someone worth talking to."

"*I'm* worth talking to, sugar," said a tall, skinny white guy, one of the poker players. He had a smarmy mustache and a gap-toothed leer that made David's skin crawl.

Nikki, of course, wasn't fazed by the creep. She may have been young, but she was more than used to unwanted attention from dubious men. "I doubt it. I'm way out of your league."

"Nobody's out of my league, sweetheart. I'm Will Russell, the Stealer. I'm *sure* you've heard of me." He leaned back in the chair and puffed out his narrow chest.

Most Posties claim a new name after popping, even fifteen years after the Public Safety Act. There were no more heroes or villains, but comic-book names were ingrained parts of Postie culture. Evidently Will Russell liked to steal. Nikki was not impressed.

"Sorry," she said. "I don't keep track of lowlifes."

The bar erupted in snickers. David shook his head and walked around the bar, trying to not disturb old Curt's sleep. He grabbed a can of Coke for Nikki and a bottle of water for himself. David rolled his eyes when Will cashed out of the game and walk toward his sister.

"Lowlife? C'mon, doll baby, give me a chance and I'll show you the high life."

"I bet that's not the first time you've had to use that line, is it?" Nikki raised an eyebrow, took the can from David and began to walk, with Will, toward the back of the room. Her brother followed, but not too closely.

"I never use lines, baby. I only speak from the heart."

David sighed and started to say something, but a glance from Nikki silenced him. He looked at Quietus who sat, totally relaxed, with a slight smirk on his ambiguous face. David thought a question to the bouncer. *Does he know who we are?*

Quietus shook his head, and his smile broadened.

"I doubt your heart has much to do with this conversation." Nikki slid into the rearmost booth. Will sat down across from her. David kept his distance, pretending to examine the bric-a-brac on the walls.

"Just give me a chance, will ya? It's not every day that an angel walks into a bar."

"An angel, huh?" Nikki pursed her lips. "You sure I'm not one of the fallen variety?"

"Oh, no. You don't seem very fallen to me. And if you are, well, let me put you back on top of the pedestal where you belong, baby."

"That one wasn't too bad, *Stealer*, but still a little over the top. Does this kind of stuff ever actually work?" Nikki looked past Will and caught her brother's eye.

David made a face; he couldn't believe she was giving that creep so much of her time. She subtly shrugged; she was just trying to amuse herself. She must be even more bored than he realized. The perils of being home schooled.

The mustachioed man winked. "I don't know, baby. I'll tell you tomorrow."

Nikki laughed, "I doubt that. I don't go home with strangers. Besides, I think I'm a little too young for you."

"Shh," Will waved a hand. "Age ain't nothing but a number, baby. And we're all outlaws here. What have I got to worry about? Unless your big brother—he is your brother, right? You two look a lot alike." Nikki nodded. "Well unless he has an objection, we've got nothing to worry about. But I think you're big enough to take care of yourself."

"I certainly am. What about you? How good are you at taking care of yourself, big boy?"

Will's gap-toothed grin spread wider. "Just fine, baby. I can take care of you even better."

"Oh, really? And what is it you do, Mister Stealer?"

"Lots and lots of things. See?" He raised a pencil-thin arm and a bottle of Jack floated from the bar, crossing the room smoothly and landing in his open hand. The lid unscrewed itself and plopped onto the table. He took a swig and offered the bottle to her.

"No thanks. Too early to drink," she replied, not bothering to mention that the entire bottle wouldn't even give her a buzz. "Telekinesis, huh? That must be pretty nifty. So what are you, a burglar?"

He laughed a bit, "I prefer to think of myself as a connoisseur of the finer things in life. Fast cars, big houses, fine dining. They call me the Stealer cause I can get anything I want. I'm really surprised you never heard of me."

"Well, I guess you could say I've been kind of sheltered. So tell me, what do you want right now?"

"Right now? I'd like to get out of this dump and head some place where we can get to know each other better. My door's set to open in Maui. Tell me, baby, you ever been to Hawaii?"

"No, I haven't. I live on a farm, actually."

"Really? You don't strike me as a farmer's daughter. You're just made for a tropical paradise. We can take a long walk on the beach, maybe dip in the water for a while. Where's your door go? Back to the farm?"

Nikki shook her head. "No. We didn't need Portero's help getting here. But I guess you were too busy playing cards to notice that the door didn't flash for us."

Will's eyes narrowed. "Really? I didn't think anybody knows how to get here."

Nikki gave him her most coy pout. "Not too many people do. You could say I'm special."

"You certainly are, baby. I'd love to get a chance to find out."

"You just might," she said, draining her Coke and crushing the can. She began to slide from her seat. "Well, it's been fun, but this place is dead. I think it's time to leave."

She took two steps and felt an invisible force squeezing her body, stopping her dead in her tracks. The Stealer held her in a telekinetic grip. She pressed out, but not too hard. There was a little give. The pressure was firm, but didn't feel terribly strong. She wasn't worried. She was pissed.

This skinny, pale-ass dipshit thought he could manhandle *her*?

"C'mon, baby. You can't just walk away like that," said Will, rising from the booth. He noticed David looking at him and extended an arm, locking Nikki's brother in place, too. Then he flicked a wrist, and Nikki spun around. She glared at him, seething.

Quietus watched, but did not move. The poker players all looked at him, expecting the bouncer to intervene. The eyeless man just shook his head.

That should have clued Will into the fact that something was very wrong, but he was apparently not a very deep thinker. "Now don't none of you interfere, this is between me and the girl."

"Your funeral," David whispered, not caring if the thin man could hear.

"Girl?" hissed Nikki. "*Girl!*" Her eyes narrowed and her skin flushed even darker. Her full, pouting lips twisted into a snarl of wrath. "You worthless piece of shit!"

Then she flexed, her arms pressing against Will's telekinesis. He raised his hands to focus the power, but she planted her feet on the stone floor. The muscles of her thighs and back rippled. She didn't know the strength of his ability, but she knew one thing: it wasn't strong enough.

She sneered and pushed hard against his grip and shattered

the telekinetic force with her titanic might.

Will stumbled backward and Nikki leaped forward. She grabbed the front of his shirt, pulled him off his feet, and hopped to the tabletop. She held him, helpless in the iron grasp of her small, powerful hand. She raised him high as she could, until his feet dangled and the color drained from his weaselly face.

"You must think you're something special, don't you, Stealer? You're so fucking full of yourself that you didn't even bother to ask my name. Is that how you treat a lady? No wonder you have to hit on goddamn teenagers! Well ask me now."

He opened his mouth but the only noise was a gasping sputter.

"Ask me!" she roared. Old Curt jerked awake and knocked over a bottle of Chartreuse. Everyone in the bar stared in silence; the only sounds were terrified panting from Will, angry breathing from Nikki and a soft laugh from David. "Ask me *now*!"

With his eyes tightly clenched, Will muttered, "What. Huh. Whuhsa ... Whuhsa name?"

"My name is Nikki Young. Nicole. Marie. *Young*." She pulled him closer and growled. "I *know* you've heard about the Young family."

Will's eyes shot open. He knew about the Youngs. Every Postie knew about the Youngs; Charles and Gloria Young, Milk and Shockwave. Milk was the *first* Posthuman, a soldier turned superhuman, the second hero—after Aegis, before Independence— and the strongest man alive. And *Milk* had married Shockwave, another one of the A-list. They helped run the railroad that kept Posties out of ABRA City. They lived on the lam and supposedly had two or three kids.

Oh, shit, thought Will, realizing how much he'd screwed up.

Nikki dropped him to the floor and kicked him—hard enough to knock him back a few feet but not hard enough to really hurt. David covered his mouth and stifled a chuckle. Quietus finally rose from his seat but waited for Nikki to step away. He bent down and placed a calming hand on Will's shoulder.

Nikki walked over to her brother, still steaming with fury. "Come on, Davy. Let's get out of here."

"Sure thing, Nik. Where do you want to go?"

"I don't know. How about Maui? I've always wanted to visit Hawaii."

David laughed, "Right on, sis. Been a while since I ran across the Pacific. You'll love it."

They walked through the door—which did not flash, as it would have for almost anyone else—and made their way to the surface. The bar was silent for a long time, as Quietus tried to comfort the quivering Stealer.

Eventually things returned to normal. Curtis poured a round for everybody, and the poker game continued without missing more than a few beats.

CHAPTER THREE

Tom stepped through the heavy doors of Westburg High School into the bright autumn sun. The long, boring school day was finally over. It hadn't been a bad one, just more of the same; boring lessons, easy work and pointless teen drama.

The only notable event was that the history teacher, Mister Willis, handed out a stack of heavy envelopes, right at the end of class; about half of the students received one, including Tom. Each envelope had been marked with two official seals — the American Biological Research Agency and the Department of Public Safety's official logos — and contained semi-customized form letters. Tom needed to give it to his mother and bring it back signed tomorrow.

The annual genetic screening had been rescheduled to the end of the week. The Postie test, people usually called it. Normally it happened after spring break, but it had been moved back six months this year. Everyone who'd turned sixteen since the last test was legally required to submit to the examination. Medical-type people would swab the students' mouths for cell samples, take fingerprints and personal information for filing and then send the teens on their way. The samples would then be sent to a regional laboratory for testing; a test every student sane wanted to fail.

Coming up positive meant you were a Posthuman, and that meant being sent to Alaska for the foreseeable future. Tom wasn't worried; he wasn't a Postie. He knew how rare infection by the

Aegis virus was; his mother told him that it affected less than one out of a million people. Tom had never caught the random flu-like illness that indicated infection, and neither of his parents were Posties. His father had been a soldier, not a superhero. Tom wasn't worried about the genetic screening. If anything, it was good news. He'd get to skip a class, maybe even two; hopefully one of them would be Geometry.

"Tom! Thomas Effing Fuson!" called a familiar voice.

Tom stopped at the sound of his name, and spun around, tossing a nod at his approaching friend, Marcus, who was at the back of the mass of students. His locker was on the ass-end of school, slowing escape each day. Marcus wasn't a big guy, but he was stout and stubborn; he doggedly pushed through the crowd and walked to his friend's side.

"What's up, bro?" Tom grinned, and they bumped fists in greeting. The young men were generally inseparable and usually walked home together. Marcus lived down the street from the Fuson house, a quarter mile behind the school, and the boys had known each other as far back as they could remember. They'd been best friends for just as long.

"The usual," Marcus grunted and shoved his envelope in front of Tom's face. "Fascist pigs, taking over. Hell, they already took over. What do you think of this shit?"

"Who cares? It would have happened next spring, anyway." Tom shrugged. He thought Marcus had become too obsessed with politics lately and way too angry about it. But he wouldn't say that to his best friend. Instead, he said, "It's not like we're Posties or anything."

Marcus narrowed his eyes. "That's not the point. Besides, I might be a Postie. You might be. Anyone could be ... so they run their tests, and then you're hauled off by the man. Never seen again. We're minors for fuck's sake!"

The sidewalk ended just beyond the school, where Main Street intersected a narrow, two-lane road. It was the way home, and they turned to walk along the right shoulder. A truck drove by—a few other kids from school. They honked and yelled as they swerved, honked and burned rubber. Marcus shot them the bird in return.

Tom said, "Posties are dangerous, man, even if they don't mean to be. Joey the Exploder proved that. And some of them *do* mean to be. King Kaos killed President Wallace on live TV, for fuck's sake. Think about psychos like Flamechylde or the Behemoth of the Bay. We don't have to worry about them anymore."

Marcus replied, "Lee Harvey Oswald was a white dude with a gun. Should all white, male gun owners get arrested?"

"That's totally different."

"Is it? I bet that white dudes with guns have killed way more people than Posties ever will. Besides, some of them were heroes. Think about *Milk*, man."

"What about him? Milk ran away when we were in diapers. What was it he said before he left? Oh, yeah, that's right. He said, 'Fuck you, too.'"

"Yeah, well ... he's right. He'd worked for the country his whole life, and they made him a criminal. He had to run ... or let himself get thrown in a concentration camp with the rest of the Posties."

"Come on, Marcus, ABRA City isn't a concentration camp. It's like a small town," said Tom, unconvinced by his friend's outrage. Everyone had seen pictures and movies about the Alaskan prison city. The prisoners wore normal clothes, lived in decent apartments and didn't even have to work. Tom didn't think it looked all that bad.

"Except that nobody leaves," Marcus added. "Ever."

"At least we don't kill them like they do in some places. We're not the bad guys. We're still America, man."

"Yeah, land of the free," Marcus kicked a small rock down the road. "Unless you test positive for the Aegis virus, then ... so much for independence."

"Independence is dead, man." Tom thought about his dream, about Bloodlust gloating in the sky.

"I didn't mean him," Marcus sighed. "I meant—"

"I know what you meant. And I see your point. But sometimes you have to do things to protect yourself."

"'Those who would give up essential liberty to purchase a

little temporary safety deserve neither liberty nor safety,'" Marcus said, obviously quoting something.

"Is that Jefferson?" Tom guessed; it sounded like a Founding Father.

"No. Benjamin Franklin."

"Oh." Tom adjusted the strap of his backpack. "I just don't know. Maybe things would be different if Independence hadn't been killed."

"That's the thing," Marcus said. "If there were somebody like Independence, they'd want to control him, too. They'd have him tossing governments, bagging Posties. Whatever. A damned army of one."

"Just like Independence," agreed Tom. The late hero was generally regarded as a good man, practically a saint, but *everyone* knew the military had kept him on a short leash.

"Damn straight. Aegis never worked for them, so they made sure Independence would. Maybe they aren't bad guys, maybe they're just afraid, but that doesn't make it right. They'll do anything to control the Posties … and anybody *else* who can change the world."

The boys walked on in silence for a few minutes. Marcus seemed to be calming down, and Tom had a lot of things on his mind.

"You look just like him," Marcus said suddenly, staring straight ahead. He seemed to be lost in thought. "Independence, I mean. You look just like him."

"Yeah, I know." The long-dead hero had been taller and much more muscular, but they had the same blondish hair, the same short, narrow nose, the same broad forehead and strong jaw. Tom's face was rounder, younger and softer, but the resemblance was strong. He squinted up at the golden sun. "Everyone says that. Except Mom."

"Oh? She doesn't think you look like him?"

"No. She says…" Tom trailed off into silence and said no more. He just shook his head, as if dismissing the question.

"What does she say?" Marcus tugged on the strap of his backpack and glanced at Tom.

"She says I look like my father."

❂   ❂   ❂

"Hey, sweetie," said Megan, as Tom walked into the living room. "How was school?"

The tall boy shrugged. The conversation with Marcus still spun around in his mind.

Megan raised an eyebrow. "That bad?"

"Nah, Mom. It wasn't bad. Here," Tom removed his backpack and held it in front. He unzipped it, reached inside and pulled out the envelope. "They moved the screening to Friday."

Megan looked confused until she took the envelope. Her eyes swelled briefly as she saw the agencies' logos. She read the letter twice, with burning intensity and narrowed eyes.

"Thomas." Her expression looked carved in stone, her lips paled. She crumpled the paper in a fist and lowered her face. Again she said, "Thomas."

"Mom?" An icy weight formed in Tom's stomach, growing swiftly to swallow his heart. Something was wrong, obviously. Very wrong. "What is it, Mom?"

"I've lied to you, Tom. I ... I've *always* been lying to you. I couldn't tell the truth to you, back when you were little. I couldn't risk it." She looked up, but didn't quite meet her son's eyes. "And lately ... I didn't want to ruin your life. I wanted to give you as much time ... as much of a life ... I wanted you to be happy for as long as possible. I'd planned to tell you over Christmas break. I've been planning it for years."

"Planning what?" whispered Tom. His mind raced, trying to understand her meaning.

"We were going to take a vacation this winter so I could tell you ... so you could meet ... everyone. So we could tell you..." Her voice trailed off. She looked away. "So *I* could tell you ... about your father."

"My father?" Tom's jaw clenched, and he understood. His father was a Postie; *that's* what his mother was talking about. She'd been hiding the truth for his entire life, but had planned to reveal it over the winter holiday. The rescheduled genetic screening had forced her hand.

No wonder Mom lied, he thought. *Because if my father was a Postie ... so am I.*

He looked at his mother and cocked his head to the side. "So my father ... he was really a Postie?"

Silence, for a long moment, and then she replied, "No, Tom." She hesitated, opened her mouth but didn't speak. Then she took a deep breath and said, "He wasn't a Posthuman. Not exactly."

Tom stared but could not reply. *Not a Posthuman*, he thought, *not exactly.*

He heard the memory-voice of Marcus say, *You look just like him. Independence, I mean.*

And Tom figured out everything, just like that. He knew what his mother's lies had been and the reasons for them. He understood the meaning behind her words, and he knew the identity of his father.

Not exactly a Posthuman? Neither was the clone of Aegis.

Tom looked at his mother and said, "Independence. You're telling me that my father was Independence?"

"Yes, Tom. Adam, your father ... he was Independence."

Tom nodded but said nothing. He blinked a few times and looked away.

They'd have to run, he realized. He could think of no other way to avoid the DNA test or a life sentence at ABRA City. They were going to run, and the Department of Public Safety was going to hunt them. One way or another, his life in Westburg was over. Tom thought about his friends, especially Marcus. He wondered if they'd get to say goodbye. He wondered if they'd ever see each other again.

Megan reached over and took his hand. She whispered, "I'm sorry, Tom, so sorry. I hope you can forgive me."

"Mom, I... Of course I forgive you," Tom replied, putting an arm around her shoulders. "I'm not mad. I ... I get it. It's a lot to take in, but I understand why you never told me. You did it to protect me. It was the right thing to do."

"I'm so proud of you." She wrapped her arms around her

son. "I love you, Tom. I love you more than I could ever say. Thank you."

"I love you, too, Mom."

They hugged for a long moment. Megan let down her guard and began to quietly weep. Tears rolled down Tom's cheeks, too, but he didn't speak. He merely held his mother close and tried to wrap his mind around the truth.

Eventually they let go of each other. Megan was still crying a bit, and snatched a box of tissues from a corner table to wipe her eyes and blow her nose.

Tom wiped his own eyes and gently squeezed his mother's shoulder. "Honestly, it's pretty freaking cool. Independence is my father, the greatest hero ever. I can't be mad about that, Mom. It's the coolest thing ever."

Megan laughed and said, "I hope you always feel that way, Tommy. Be proud of who you are. There is nobody else like you … anywhere."

Nodding, Tom scratched his head. "So does this mean I have superpowers? When did he get his powers?"

"Adam always had powers," Megan explained. "At least since the age of four or five … before I ever met him. But from what I understand, it did take a trigger. They exposed him to radiation and shocked him with electricity until his body learned to use it for fuel. Once Adam started channeling power, he just couldn't stop. He was always trying to figure out new tricks, though. People liked to say that he could do anything that any Postie could do, but I don't know how much of that you'll get. You're not the child of a Postie, Tom. Nobody knows how it will work with you. I've been worried for years that something would happen, but so far…"

She did not finish her sentence; she didn't need to. So far, Tom had shown no signs of being anything other than an average guy.

They remained silent for a while. Tom was lost in his own mind, and his mother appeared to be thinking deeply.

Eventually she said, "Now you know why you can't get the DNA test."

"Yeah, but it's mandatory. What can we do about it?"

"Well, some of my friends help Posthumans hide from the DPS and ABRA. They helped hide you, so to speak, when you were a baby. They were going to help us with this too, but the test wasn't scheduled to happen until April, not Friday for God's sake. We were supposed to have plenty of time."

"So what can we do? We'll have to run, won't we?"

"Probably," admitted Megan. "I need to make a couple of calls. Just wait in here."

"Okay." Tom hugged his mother again.

"You look just like him, you know."

"Marcus just said that." Tom thought about his friend. He had to talk to Marcus about this, about everything; Tom could trust his best friend to keep the secret. A part of him wondered if Marcus already knew. Was that why he was so obsessed with Postie politics? But Marcus wasn't the only person to notice Tom's resemblance to the late hero. "Everyone says I look like him. You're the one that always said I don't."

"Well, I lied about that, too. I'm sorry. I love you, Tom." Megan squeezed his hand, then turned and walked upstairs to call her mysterious friends.

Tom settled down and hopped on the computer. His mind raced, though, and he couldn't focus. He didn't check his email or Facebook. Instead, he googled for pics of Independence.

Discounting the previous night's dream, it had been a long time since he'd thought about the hero, even longer since he'd looked at pictures. Many of them were familiar magazine covers or famous photos.

Tom looked at a very low-budget website, showing Independence rescuing people from a train accident in India during the mid-Nineties. There were hundreds of sites dedicated to old villain brawls. Tom clicked through a gallery of Independence and Flamechylde fights; the old villainess had been one of the hero's more persistent opponents. There were plenty of similar galleries, showing fights with the Behemoth or Saurus Rex or Mister Moment and the Children of Man. Obviously, there were a ton of photos from the last day of the Carnivore War, back in 1975, the day Independence was revealed to the world.

There were magazine covers, newspaper photos, low-quality videos from twenty or thirty years ago and thousands of clips from news programs. Tom clicked through all of it, his eyes dancing on the screen, and he whispered, "Hi ... Dad."

Suddenly a tremendous noise echoed in the woods—a distant thud followed by crashing trees. Tom stood on shaky legs and swallowed hard, his mouth surprisingly dry.

Then a *boom* in the back yard shook the entire house and broke at least a few dishes.

Megan hurried down the stairs as Tom ran to the door. Something kneeled at the base of the steps, something bright white and simply enormous.

"Holy shit!" exclaimed Tom, as the huge figure rose to its feet.

"Thomas!"

"Sorry, Mom."

Megan pushed past her son and opened the door, a glowing smile on her face. "Charles!"

In the yard stood a horned giant, the first Posthuman, a legendary hero, the indomitable Milk.

CHAPTER FOUR

Larger than life took on a whole new meaning around Milk. The hero was unmistakable; nine feet tall, five feet wide and three feet *thick*, with massive, curling horns and snow-white skin.

Like many super-strong Posties, Milk had odd proportions; he was extremely muscled, and his upper body looked too large, even for such an immense figure. His arms were about five-and-a-half feet long with ludicrously huge hands. His pinkies alone were bigger than Tom's entire hand.

Thick, coiled, ram-like horns sprouted from Milk's temples and looped back, parallel to the curve of his hairless scalp. They curled down behind his ears and then forward, finally, in spirals that came up past his cheeks and narrowed to sharp points just below his eyes.

Milk's black-and-white boots were made of advanced ceramics, reinforced plastics and top-secret alloys. They left yard-long footprints in Megan's garden. But the boots were the only part of his old uniform in sight. The rest of his outfit consisted of a tarp-sized black tank top and the largest pair of blue jeans the world had ever seen.

Tom couldn't help but wonder, *Where the hell does he buy his clothes?*

Megan smiled and said, "Charles! I never expected you of all people."

"Hello there, Megan," Milk replied in his bone rattling voice. "It's been a long time."

"Too long," She agreed and stepped into the back yard. Milk kneeled down on one knee to be closer to eye level. She walked up and hugged the giant; he patted her back gently with a hand the size of her torso. "I just got off the phone with Jacqui. How did you get here so fast?"

"Ever meet Kobar, the spy from Assbackwardstan?" he asked; Megan shook her head. Milk shrugged and explained, "He's an old friend, a teleporter. He's been on the run since the Soviet Union fell. They forced him to work for them after the invasion. Once he got away, he wasn't going to work for nobody ever again."

Megan just nodded, "How do you know him?"

"He works for me."

Tom opened his mouth, "But you just—"

Milk cut him off, "Anyway, Kobar dropped me off a couple of miles away. I'm going to take you and the kid back to him, then we're gonna go some place safe. Maybe to see the Old Man."

"Why didn't this Kobar come with you?" Tom asked. "Or teleport inside the house or something?"

Milk turned his large brown eyes toward Tom and said, "Too risky. The Feds could've been inside with you for all we knew. We gotta to get you two out of here; the Old Man says Uncle Sam is coming after you tonight."

"Tonight?" exclaimed Megan. "How did they find us?"

"Old man? What old man?" Tom asked.

"You're not exactly undercover, Megan. You're the one who didn't want to 'live like criminals' remember? I always said they just gotta see a picture of your son to put two and two together." The pale giant shook his head. "Doesn't matter. All that's done and done. They know now, for sure. The intel is solid, Megan. They've brought in some serious hardware. The Old Man says that's why they moved the test to Friday—they're trying to get you to run. They're watching you right now."

"Won't they notice you?" asked Tom.

"Listen, kid," Milk said, leaning down so that his gigantic face was mere inches from Tom. "They know what you are, and they *will* come after you. If they see me, they might get second thoughts."

"Are you sure?" Tom asked.

"Of course I'm sure," he answered and stood, towering over Tom. "I'm Milk, the strongest man on Earth. Didn't you catch the PBS special?"

Tom wanted to reply but didn't have the time. A rocket flew out of the woods behind the house and slammed into the back of Milk's massive, horned head. The last thing Tom saw was the fireball coming right at his face.

Tom's ears were ringing. His entire body hurt. He heard gunfire and screaming men. He heard an engine—no, two or three engines. But the noise seemed distant, muffled. The ground trembled beneath his face.

He raised his head and saw Milk facing a group of soldiers—if they *were* soldiers. They could have been mercenaries or robots for all Tom knew. They wore combat fatigues and boots, all sorts of gear and what looked like motorcycle helmets with smaller visors. All black. Even the vehicles were black. All of the soldiers were shooting at Milk. Bullets tore through his tank top and bounced off his pale hide. There were more than a dozen soldiers— as well as a pair of Humvees and an honest-to-God Walker tearing up Tom's mother's garden.

One of the Humvees had a flat, oversize dish swiveling on its roof—an Active Denial System. Those things fired microwaves, but were supposedly not lethal, just very, very painful. Tom once watched a documentary about them, but never thought he'd actually see one.

The second Humvee was armed with something Tom had never seen—a footlocker-size black box on a swiveling turret, with dull metal trim and a small, screen-covered opening at one end. It could be anything, maybe it wasn't weapon at all, or maybe it was a death ray. Tom had no idea and felt too afraid to be curious.

But neither of the wheeled vehicles was as frightening as the

Walker.

It was a big Scarab-class model, a heavily armored, two-person cockpit surrounded by guns and missiles. Tom thought it looked like a helicopter's body on four multi-jointed robot legs. Walkers are faster than most people think, and this one constantly moved around the perimeter of the fight, keeping its weapons trained on Milk while remaining out of his reach.

Then Tom noticed his mother laying prone, a few feet to his right. She wasn't moving.

He pushed himself to his knees and crawled toward her. He called for her, but she did not respond. Tom could see wisps of smoke rising from her scalp, and he smelled burnt hair.

Suddenly Milk grabbed the boy and tucked him under his right arm like a football.

"No! Let me go! You fucking asshole! Mom!" Tom kicked and wailed and reached for his far-too-still mother. It was futile; Tom was helpless in Milk's unyielding grip.

"Kid ... Thomas. Tom ... I'm sorry. Megan, she's ... your mother is gone, son. She's gone. The explosion. There's nothing ... nothing we can do. Stay strong kid. You're the son of Independence. And we don't have time to cry just yet."

Tom screamed incoherently, wordlessly. He thrashed and tried to break free, pounding his fists on Milk's impervious hide. He was unaware of anything that happened over the next few minutes. The battle-sounds faded to distant flashes and muted rumbles. The universe withdrew, leaving Tom alone with despair.

His mother was dead. Just like that, she was gone.

Milk still held Tom firmly under the crook of his arm, when the boy regained his senses. The soldiers had stopped firing their weapons but kept them ready.

"Drop the child," demanded an amplified order. Whether from one of the black-clad soldiers or one of the vehicles Tom couldn't tell. His ears were still ringing. "Sergeant Charles Young, you are under arrest. Place your hands in the air and surrender.

Surrender now."

"Like hell," Milk sneered. "You shoot at me, you might hit the kid! Waste of damn bullets anyway. You know you can't hurt me!"

"Drop the child and surrender, or we will open fire!"

"Do it then, you little punks," Milk growled then looked down at Tom. "Hold on kid, this is gonna get nasty."

Suddenly the small black turret on the second Humvee swiveled around and a shrieking, clanging noise ripped through the night. The box fired a focused, high-pitched sound—louder than the roar of a dozen jet engines—directly at Milk's head. Tom covered his ears to no avail. The noise pierced his eardrums and drove spikes into his head.

Milk bellowed and *squeezed* tightly for a split-second. Tom's spine popped, and his ribs creaked. The huge hero dropped the boy and fell to his knees.

Tom landed with a thud that knocked the wind out of him. His body ached, and his head felt like it was in a vice. He screamed but couldn't hear his own voice over the weaponized noise. He struggled to crawl away as the soldiers advanced, some toward Milk, some toward him, all with guns aimed and ready.

Then Milk launched forward, bowled over a group of soldiers and slammed into the attacking Humvee. The horrible screech droned to silence, and the surrounding soldiers stood dumbfounded as Milk pulled the occupants from the now-totaled vehicle and proceeded to tear its metal body apart with his huge hands.

One of the men landed near Tom—so the boy ran over and grabbed the soldier's rifle. He wasn't really thinking at that point; he felt an urge to join the fight, to strike against his mother's killers, to make them pay.

But the soldiers saw him. The tall, flat dish of the Active Denial System turned in his direction. Invisible heat scorched his skin. Tom dropped the gun and screamed, but the roasting pain did not stop. He was burning alive, or at least that's how it felt.

Then he heard Milk's booming words, *Stay strong kid. You're the son of Independence.*

All he could think was, *I am the son of Independence. I am the son of Independence.*

And the pain stopped. He still felt the heat sinking into skin, but it no longer hurt. In fact, his skin tingled with something like pleasure. His entire body felt a vigorous thrill, like hot breath on the nape of his neck.

Tom opened his eyes and could *see* the microwaves pouring over him, into him.

There is no word for the color of microwaves. There doesn't need to be, since only a very few people can see them. Tom would describe them as related to brown but shining, dark but illuminating, like a black light.

He raised his arms and they glowed. His entire body glowed. He shined with a warm, golden light — the light of Aegis, the light of Independence.

I am the son of Independence.

Tom smiled then, a cold, bitter sneer. A chill raced down his spine, his hair drifted up from static, tiny sparks popped and fizzled all over his body. A golden blast of light, heat and electromagnetic force erupted from his hands, blasting the Humvee. The heavy vehicle tumbled end over end into the trees.

Milk turned, gaping, but said nothing. Tom was too stunned to move. He looked at his hands, shocked and exhausted by this first show of power. He felt heavy and tired, weakened by the exertion, drained of so much energy.

The golden aura wavered and vanished.

A soldier on the ground tried to scoot away from the boy. Tom turned toward him, and the soldier pulled out a pistol, aiming it with trembling hands. He had seen what Tom had just done, and it scared him.

Tom raised his hands and opened his mouth to speak, but another rocket from the Walker exploded on the indestructible Milk. Both the soldier and the boy jumped, startled by the blast.

Tom didn't even hear the gunshot.

He felt a sharp pain in his chest, on the right side, just below the nipple. His back hurt, too. A lot. Dizzily, he touched the wound. Hot, slippery blood gushed over his fingertips.

The soldier's pistol was still raised. A strand of smoke drifted up from the barrel and dissipated in the wind.

Tom's chest rattled with each breath. He still couldn't look down, didn't want to see how bad it really was. It felt like a hole blasted all the way through. He could feel the wind, tickling and stinging. He coughed and tasted blood, like a penny, that taste of hot copper in his mouth.

And he fell, face-first in the dirt. His mother was a few feet to his right. He heard the soldiers yell, heard Milk roar. The ground was shaken by multiple explosions. Gunfire filled the air. Then everything went dark again and Tom knew no more.

CHAPTER FIVE

Jeremiah James Joyce was sitting in a lawn chair on his apartment building's roof when the sirens began to shriek. Spotlights blazed across the Wall, the city's rooftops and up into the night sky, illuminating the gentle snowfall overhead. The snow drifted lazily in the wind but would never reach the prison. A Class Three force field covered ABRA City, loot from the Carnivore invasion. Consequently, the gulag maintained pleasant temperatures throughout the year, despite its location just outside the Bering Land Bridge National Preserve on the Seward Peninsula in Alaska.

The seventeen-year-old Postie removed his baseball cap and groggily scratched his head. He stretched, yawned, looked up at the overhead force field and grumbled, "Man, I'm trying to relax up here."

JJ spent a lot of time on the roof; he'd claimed the spot over two months ago. It was a good place to chill and hang out with his friends. He'd originally tried to use the basement, but crates of cold-weather clothing and emergency supplies were piled everywhere down there, and JJ hated being cooped up. The roof felt open and more private. Yeah, he couldn't see over the Wall, and the guard towers were just a few hundred feet away, but anywhere indoors was guaranteed to be bugged. That's just life in ABRA City.

JJ always told people that he was used to it. The place wasn't too bad, he'd say. Besides, life had never really cared about his feelings. He said he was used to *that*, too.

He had been orphaned on his eleventh birthday, though he rarely mentioned it. A drunk plowed into the car on the way home from his party. He didn't remember the wreck; some things are better off forgotten. His last memory was leaving the restaurant, with a pile of presents in his arms. Then he opened his eyes in a hospital bed, with a cast on his leg and no more family.

The next four years had been spent in a string of foster homes. JJ thought of those days as his first imprisonment, back when he was just a skinny little guy with an oversize baseball cap, crammed in unfamiliar houses with other troubled, damaged kids and strange, demanding adults. Compared to *that*, being locked up in ABRA's bullshit prison town wasn't all that bad. That's what he told people, if they asked.

But the foster home couldn't hold him forever. Shortly after his fifteenth birthday, JJ got sick. It was nothing serious, just a bit of a fever, cold chills and a queasy stomach. Everyone thought he'd caught the flu, even the doctor did nothing but write a prescription and send him home. That turned out to be a lucky break, since the illness wasn't a normal flu; it was the Aegis virus inserting itself into his genome, but nobody caught on. If the doc had run any blood tests, JJ would've ended up in ABRA City before his powers even developed.

It took about two weeks for JJ to realize that he was a Postie. He was sitting in the back yard when it happened, avoiding the other kids, daydreaming about his old life. He thought about his family's house with its big yard and the old chestnut tree on the hill. Home was more than sixty miles away, but suddenly JJ seemed to *feel* the distance, like a rubber band stretched tightly between the two places. Without really thinking about it, he wished that the two ends of the rubber band would fly together, connecting here and there. And then his wish came true.

A rippling swirl formed in the air, a two-dimensional vortex, hovering perpendicular to the ground. With a firecracker pop, it opened and became a thin ring, about ten feet wide. And through the ring, clear as day, he saw the old tree, with spiked burrs littered on his family's former yard.

JJ jumped through the portal without a second thought, breathing in the sweet air of his home town. From that moment until his capture, he had been free.

He was the ultimate runaway, able to go anywhere, anytime, and no one could stop him. He roamed the world for over a year and a half, until the Department of Public Safety lucked out and discovered him in North Carolina.

JJ had been living in Charlotte for a month or so, working as a courier for some weed dealers. He wouldn't touch harder drugs or weapons or anything like that, but he had to make cash somehow. Transporting marijuana let him earned the money to live, party hard and keep a mostly clear conscience. He stayed under the radar, and thought he was being careful, but the DPS somehow tracked him down.

JJ was walking to the laundromat of the ghetto hotel on the south end of Tryon Street when a sniper nailed him with a tranquilizer dart. Next thing he knew, he was in Alaska, trapped under a force field that blocked his wormholes, trapped inside the Wall.

The Posthuman prison consisted of six city blocks and looked like a tiny town, except for the goddamn Wall. The colossal barricade was a hundred feet high, made of heavy steel plating over reinforced concrete, with concertina wire coiled tightly between twelve squat towers and dozens of guards on patrol. There was only one gate, and it was probably the most secure passageway in the world.

Half of the prison was the residential area, with four red brick apartment buildings, a small collection of phony storefronts and boring recreational facilities.

The area beside the gate was fenced off from the rest. It was the military part of town, where the guards lived and kept their toys; the hospital was between the two sections, so that everyone had easy access to medical care.

Headquarters stood at the center of the complex, a nine-story tower, a little higher than the Wall. HQ had to be taller than anything else, since it housed the force field emitter that kept the

Alaskan cold outside and, more importantly, kept the residents inside.

Cameras were everywhere, guards were everywhere else, and flying drones circled in the sky like vultures. Heavily-armed Walkers patrolled the streets. Worst of all, every inmate had a tracking implant bolted to the bone behind their left ear. The Posties were tagged like animals and re-tagged every week with a fresh tracker.

JJ always said that he was used to it. That's what he told his friends. He'd been inside for months and the whole Big Brother thing seemed normal. Living in a bubble didn't bother him anymore. That's what he always said.

But it was a lie, every single time.

He wasn't used to it; he hated it. But what could he do? The residents knew better than to cause trouble; the ones that didn't know better simply disappeared and were never seen again. Posties that put up a fight never survived, and JJ wasn't a fighter anyway. He thought about escaping constantly, but knew that trying would be suicide. He needed an edge, something that could tip the balance in his favor. Sometimes, he thought he'd do anything to get out of the shit hole.

He hated the bullshit prison and its fake little town. He hated the fake shopping center, fake food court and fake movie theater. He hated the cameras, the drones, the bubble and the Wall. He even hated his crummy little apartment. JJ was far more comfortable on the roof.

At least, he'd been comfortable until the alarms started to blare.

JJ stood, stretched again, and walked over to the edge of the roof. Soldiers were running and yelling on the Wall. Lots of people were moving among the barracks, armories and garages. Other residents were looking through the windows of their apartments, but none of them were outside. More spotlights pierced the sky, these on the roof of the hospital. The helipad.

"I thought you were up here!" Vanessa Martinez shrieked as she stepped onto the roof behind JJ. The young Hispanic woman from southern California lived down the hall and was something of a prima donna. She was hot, though, and sometimes even friendly, so he tried to overlook her bad attitude. "What the hell's going on, JJ?"

"Like I know," He shrugged and gestured toward the hospital. "Looks like they're flying someone in."

"Or out," came a gravelly voice from the stairwell behind Vanessa. "Could be one of the staff got sick. Maybe someone got hurt down below."

The voice belonged to Solomon Beck, an incredibly stocky man—barely five feet tall, but weighing over two hundred pounds—with bushy, white-blond hair, an extraordinarily large Van Dyke beard and bright blue eyes.

Sol was maybe ten years older than JJ, but the two had become best friends over the past few months. They shared the same taste in movies, video games, music and herb; it was like they'd known each other for years. The stout blond man stepped up beside JJ and Vanessa just as the public address system clicked on and an emotionless, efficient voice filled the night.

"Attention residents," announced the voice. "In a few moments, the containment field will be briefly deactivated. Any attempted escape will be met with immediate lethal force. Flying residents are to remain grounded until the containment field is restored. Any attempt to interfere or disturb the peace will be met with immediate lethal force. Thank you and have a pleasant evening."

JJ snickered, "Nothing like immediate lethal force to ensure a pleasant evening, huh?"

Sol chortled; Vanessa merely sniffed.

Then, with a flash, the force field vanished. The temperature instantly dropped by fifty degrees as howling arctic wind rushed inside.

Vanessa touched JJ's shoulder to get his attention. She said something he couldn't hear over the wind, but made a circular motion with her hands, tapped the small tracking implant behind her ear and shook her head. It took him a second to realize that she was warning him not to use his power to run away.

He gave her a nod and pointed at his own implant—he

hadn't even considered fleeing, but it was nice of her to warn him like that. Maybe she wasn't so bad after all. She nodded, said something else, turned around and went back inside.

Sol stepped a bit closer to JJ, and they both looked up as the snow drifted down. JJ tilted his head back, opened his mouth and caught a flake on his tongue. Sol laughed and did the same.

At that moment, a sonic boom blasted over ABRA City, followed by an unnatural roar, far louder than the wind. An aircraft came into view almost too fast to see.

It was, unmistakably, an alien spaceship of Carnivore design — long and blocky, made of red and gray metal with rotating thrusters and swiveling weapons. On the sides were stenciled English letters, a string of numbers and an Air Force logo. The Invasion had ended in 1975 after the public debut of Independence, so the military had been using Squid technology for over forty years, but JJ had never heard of them actually flying an alien spacecraft.

The spaceship stopped on a dime above the helipad. The ear-splitting engines fell silent, as the vessel touched down on the hospital roof. JJ and Sol gaped and simultaneously exclaimed, "Whoa!"

Hospital staff and guards charged through the door, onto the helipad. A circular hatch spiraled open on the side of the ship, and a narrow ramp extended. Two men walked out (soldiers in black, not giant cephalopods) followed by two medics and a self-propelled gurney. The prison hospital staff quickly surrounded the gurney and rushed it inside.

The soldiers immediately turned and reentered the alien vehicle; the ramp retracted, and the hatch spun closed. With another tooth-rattling howl, the alien spaceship shot straight up at incredible speed, breaking the sound barrier as it vanished in the darkness.

The force field reactivated seconds later, a circular pulse of light in the air above HQ that flashed down to the top of the Wall. Nearly invisible energy once again blocked the falling snow, but it would take hours for warmth to return to the city streets.

"What the hell was that?" Solomon gasped, shivering.

"Not a clue, Sol," JJ replied through chattering teeth. "Not a fucking clue. But I think we can find out. Come on."

JJ walked inside and Sol followed. ABRA City seemed empty, except for the guards on the Wall and the Walkers on patrol.

CHAPTER SIX

Marcus Alexander and Omar Griggs stood on a tree-covered hill, looking through crappy binoculars at the ruins of Tom Fuson's home. The old house had been demolished within ninety minutes of the incident. Three large shipping containers held the broken remains.

"Yeah," Omar whispered, stating the obvious. "They bulldozed the whole place."

"The trucks are gone," said Marcus. "So are the Feds, DPS, ABRA and whoever else was here. No guards. They must know nothing important is in the house."

"Shit, Marcus, they're going to take it away tomorrow. They're even taking the trees. You think there might be some kind of radiation?" Omar was nervous and sweating.

"Who cares? I just want to know what happened to Tom."

They hiked back to Omar's car and drove back to town.

The official statement was that a Posthuman terrorist cell pulled a home invasion on the Fusons. The government had been too late to save the day. The Fusons were dead. There would be a funeral in a couple of days. Closed casket. The story made headlines across the country mere hours after the event itself.

Posthuman Terror in Small-Town America.

"Maybe it's just like they said," Omar suggested as they sat in the car next to Conner's Gas on the edge of what passed for downtown Westburg. "Maybe Tom was just a random victim. They're cleaning up the mess."

Marcus disagreed but didn't voice his opinion. He merely grunted and watched the road. He had good reasons for being suspicious of Tom's fate, but he wouldn't tell Omar about that. Omar was a close friend, but it was too big of a secret to tell anyone.

In fact, Marcus never *had* told anyone, not even Tom.

One day, when they were in eighth grade, Marcus had ridden his bike to Tom's house. It turned out that his friend wasn't home and wouldn't return for at least forty-five minutes, but Ms. Fuson had offered Marcus a cold glass of lemonade and a sandwich. He couldn't refuse, so he thanked her and waited in the living room.

She'd been looking through a photo album when he arrived and left it on the coffee table, closed. Marcus opened it out of simple curiosity and discovered a secret that changed everything.

Within the album were old pictures, apparently from Ms. Fuson's days as a scientist—and prominent in these pictures was a tall, blond man, with oddly familiar features. Young Ms. Fuson and this tall man were obviously in love, and they seemed to be very happy together.

Marcus realized that the man had to be Tom's father, the long-dead Adam Washington. The guy certainly looked like Tom— or rather, the boy looked like the man.

Actually, thought Marcus, *Tom's dad looks a lot like Independence.*

And then he realized that the man *was* Independence— without a doubt. Marcus had seen that face a thousand times before. He flipped through the album and found magazine articles, old newspaper clippings and photos of the hero in all his star-spangled glory. There was that famous *Time* magazine cover with the Capitol building behind a floating Independence, and the picture *Voyager 2* had taken of the hero in front of Jupiter.

Marcus closed the album, leaned back in the chair, and tried to calm down. Ms. Fuson returned with the snack; she casually picked up the book and carried it away. She told him to enjoy his snack. He somehow hid his anxiety. They even talked a little bit, and Marcus managed to keep his cool.

He was only fourteen years old back then, but he was a smart one. Marcus immediately understood the magnitude of his discovery. Nobody knew that Independence had a son.

Tom might not even know, Marcus had thought. He imagined that Tom could not have kept such a secret. A couple of days later he asked Tom about it in a roundabout way.

"What did your Dad look like?"

Tom had shrugged, "I don't really know. Mom doesn't have any pictures. She says I look a lot like him."

Tom was telling the truth, at least what he knew of it. He'd always been a terrible liar.

So Marcus stayed quiet. He never told Tom about the photo album, though he really wanted to. And sometimes he wanted to talk to Ms. Fuson about it but couldn't work up the courage. Sometimes he nearly broke down and confessed the whole thing to his parents.

But he never had.

He understood that Ms. Fuson had good reason to hide it from Tom. Hell, the Department of Public Safety and ABRA were enough reasons. Marcus wasn't stupid.

He knew that it wasn't his job to tell Tom about the secret. But it *was* his job to protect his best friend. So he swore to do just that—even if that meant keeping a secret that could change the world.

Now, more than two years later, Tom had been killed or kidnapped, and the quiet little town of Westburg had been shattered by superhuman powers and military might. Marcus knew that there was more to the story than meets the eye.

"What are you thinking, man?" asked Omar.

"Doesn't matter. Just can't believe he's gone."

Eighty-thousand miles overhead, an alien probe kept watch on Earth from its usual orbit in cislunar space. It was a nearly featureless object, made of dark, dull metal, invisible to humanity's satellites and orbital weapons. The probe was a prolate spheroid, much like an American football, a bit smaller than an average minivan. Its subtly ribbed skin showed no obvious detail, antennae or propulsion, but it had monitored the blue planet for more than half a century.

The probe was an appendage of the Union of Knowledge, one of countless extensions of the galaxy-spanning consciousness of that ancient mechanical mind. The Union's purpose was to learn all that could be learned. It had been created for that very reason, more than two hundred sixty million Earth years ago, by a species long since lost to extinction. The Union existed to study the cosmos, to learn everything. It had come to Earth many times over the course of eons, and this particular probe had arrived in the early Fifties to observe the Golden Light.

Calling himself Aegis, the Golden Light had taken an organic form and seemingly surrendered much of his power to live among the primitive, carbon-based life of Earth. The machine intelligence viewed this as a unique opportunity to uncover the secrets of the Golden Light's enigmatic species.

Aegis and his race of incorporeal reality-manipulating life forms had been mysterious for millions of years—and the Union cannot abide mystery. From where did they originate? What were the limits of their perceptions and powers? What role did they play in course of cosmic history? The Union was desperate to learn.

In 1954, it attacked; thousands of probes were dispatched to capture the Golden Light. Humanity called that event the First Invasion of Earth, although it barely lasted a day. Aegis proved far too powerful, despite the frailty of his new flesh. He gave the machine the first defeat of its long existence. Hundreds of units had been destroyed, so much data lost forever. The Union had simply underestimated the power of the godlike being. It withdrew and returned to the stars.

Only this one unit remained behind, and the single probe continued to monitor the small planet. Through it, the Union witnessed the Golden Light's destruction at the hands of the Great Destroyer and felt something like grief at the wasting of such knowledge and power.

Later on, the Union had been delighted, in its own way, to

discover that humanity had replicated their hero. It observed the young clone with fascination, curiosity ... and patience. It watched the four-year-long Carnivore Invasion and the emergence of the Posthuman race. It saw the clone become a man, the heroic Independence.

Then came a day when Independence rescued the crew of a damaged Soviet spacecraft, and the Union made its move. Dozens of units attacked the clone, and they managed to disable and abduct him. Independence awoke dozens of light years from Earth and destroyed the units. He escaped the Union's grasp, although it took months for the hero to return home.

The Union of Knowledge abandoned its plans to capture Independence, but it continued to watch Earth until the fateful day of the Destroyer's return. Once more the Golden Light had been extinguished by the creature called Bloodlust.

Now, sixteen point eight two four six solar orbits after the termination of Independence, the probe had seen the battle in Virginia. It recognized the unique energy pattern and realized that there existed yet another copy of the Golden Light. The signature was unmistakable, although it was weak, newborn, and far more vulnerable than either of its predecessors.

The Union analyzed the data and chose to investigate the source of this energy. Intricate calculations flowed within the galaxy-spanning entirety of its trillion-bodied essence. Solutions arrived before the problems had even been formed, as the Union began to arrange the ponderous gathering of its forces. This time, it would be prepared.

Amassing the necessary number of units would require two point four seven revolutions of the Earth around Sol, a very brief span for the Union's ancient mind. The time for action would come soon enough; now was the time to compile data.

The probe dropped out of orbit and fell like a stone to Earth.

CHAPTER SEVEN

"Look, Mom! A shooting star!" Sean pointed out the window and hopped up into the chair for a better look. He was eight years old, the runt of the litter; short for his age and very skinny—all elbows and knees. Sean's head also looked too large for his frame but that was mostly due to the horns—they were short cones, thick with blunt tips, and had yet to begin curling like his father's.

"Oh, I missed it," hissed Gloria, who was busy making four meat loaves, two pots of green beans, three tubs of mashed potatoes, two gallons of gravy, twelve ears of corn and three pans of biscuits. You could say that her family had a rather large appetite. You could say a lot of things about the Young family.

Gloria Louise Stewart-Young was the wife of Milk and mother of their three children (no jokes, please; she's heard them all). She thanked God every day that little Sean hadn't been *born* with the horns—of the children, only he had taken after their father. David and Nikki could pass for normal, whatever *that* means. "Normal" is a very subjective word around the Young house.

They lived on a farm, with no neighbors for miles, in Niobrara County, Wyoming. They stayed under the radar as much as possible, especially Milk, one of the world's most wanted and recognizable men. To be honest, Gloria assumed the government knew the family's location but had decided against attacking. The rewards weren't worth the risk.

The family was a special bunch, for sure. Gloria was happy with life and filled with love for her children, her husband and the land that sustained them.

The Youngs were the first family of heroes. Gloria had been one of the original "wild" Posties. She caught the Aegis virus mere weeks after it began to spread in late 1974. Shortly after popping, she had taken on the name Shockwave, the World's Quickest Woman, and became one of the most renowned heroes on Earth. Milk fell in love with her quick wit, impulsive bravery and wicked green eyes; she fell in love with the tender heart in his massive chest. He was a big softy, as pretty much everyone knew, in spite of his intimidating size and bullish demeanor.

Gloria listened to the news, where clueless talking heads jabbered about the murder of Thomas Fuson and his mother by a group of Posthuman terrorists. She frowned, sniffed and blinked away the tears. She'd known Megan for over forty years. They were more than friends; they were family, like all the early Patrollers. Thanks to Uncle Sam and the DPS, it had been years since they'd spent time together and now Megan was gone. Gloria forced herself to bury the grief, anger and regret, if only for Sean's benefit.

She hadn't spoken with her husband since just after the attack. He had called to tell her the sad true story, before she could hear about it on the news, and to let her know that he was going to see the Old Man with help from Kobar. He'd be home after sundown.

So she went about the daily business of domestic life, preparing the night's meal for her largely absent family. Not only was Milk on the other side of the globe, but David and Nikki were God knows where. Like always.

Once David discovered that he shared his mother's speed, the two of them began running all over the world. Literally. It was stupid and dangerous, in Gloria's very vocal opinion. They were just asking to be captured and sent to ABRA's concentration camp for the rest of their lives.

David, in particular, had discovered a unique way of rebelling—being a hero. He tried to walk in his parents' footsteps, helping people here and there, while moving too fast to be seen. And he'd begun to use the name Shockwave—which, admittedly, was a very special compliment to his mother. Gloria wouldn't be surprised if Nikki had come up with a name, too.

Teenagers are exactly the same, no matter the parents.

"Hey Mom, is it true that Dad got in a fight?" asked Sean as he walked to the refrigerator for some water.

"Yes, Sean," Gloria heaved one of the pans of biscuits out of the oven. "But just a little one. You don't need to worry about him."

Sean just laughed, "I'm *not* worried about Dad! He's the toughest one there is."

"Yes, son. Your father is that."

"Am I gonna get big like him?" Sean asked; it was his favorite line of questioning. "I've got horns."

"Well, you might," Gloria responded as always. "But you've got my eyes, and you're not an albino."

Milk, of course, was snow white, and Gloria was a pale redhead of Anglo-Irish descent, but their children all had deep brown skin and thick, black hair. David and Nikki had dark brown eyes, but Sean's were greenish, like his mother, and shocking against his dark skin. Milk never stopped reminding people that, despite his pigmentation, he was a black man. His children were the ultimate proof of that.

"Hmm," groaned Sean. "I wanna be big as a house."

"Where would you sleep, Half-Pint?" David asked as he suddenly walked into the kitchen, followed by his sister.

"Don't call me Half-Pint!" Sean yelled and ran at David, head down in a ramming pose, but David just picked his little brother off the ground and flipped him upside down. Sean kicked helplessly and struggled to escape.

"Half-Pint goes down," David declared. "Shockwave is the winner!"

"Hey, put me down! Put me down now, Davy!"

"Who's the greatest?" David tickled his inverted little brother. "Who's the greatest?"

"Shockwave!" Sean shouted and laughed. "Shockwave's the greatest!"

"Well, that was easy," said David, lowering the boy to the floor. "Too easy."

Sean backed away from his big brother and exclaimed, "I meant Mom, not you! Mom's the real Shockwave! You're just a ... just a sidekick!"

Sean stuck out his tongue and scampered from the kitchen. David started to run after his little brother—when suddenly Gloria appeared in front of him, her hand on his chest.

"No speed in the house, young man."

David glanced at the stove, then back at his mother and started to point out that she must have used *her* speed to catch him before he ran out of the room. Her no-nonsense expression stopped him from saying a thing.

"That's right, son, listen to your mother," Milk boomed, walking in the front door.

He couldn't fit in the kitchen; it was a big house—and structurally reinforced—but still not quite up to his level. He was restricted to the living room, the dining room and the master bedroom, all on the first floor. He couldn't fit on the stairs, even if they could take the strain of his mass, which they could not.

"Daddy!" Nikki squealed and ran to her father. The teen looked absolutely tiny compared to her big old dad.

"Heya, Goober," Milk's arms enveloped his daughter. He squeezed her with a hard hug; she was tough enough to take it. "Where have you been?"

"Oh, we went to see Aunt Jacqui, but she wasn't working."

"You've been gone all day," Gloria said. "Where else have you been?"

"Well..." Nikki shot an imploring look at her big brother.

He shook his head; David knew better than to lie to his parents. "Miami. New York. Um, Maui."

"*Maui?* We've told you to watch the long-distance travel," Milk grumbled sternly.

Nikki rolled her big brown eyes. "I know, Dad, but jeez ... it's not like anyone can catch us."

"*I* can catch you," Gloria stated flatly. "So can our friend Mr. Kobar. Do you think Uncle Sam can't catch you? Besides *you* aren't all that fast, young lady."

Nikki scowled but lacked a comeback; her mother was right. She was fast but topped out at a few hundred miles an hour—unlike her mother or older brother, who could run hundreds of miles in a *minute*. David had inherited Gloria's powers—unmatched speed, lightning reflexes, enhanced regeneration and more speed—but Nikki had a mix of her parents' abilities.

She was quick, but only a fraction as swift as the Shockwaves. She was also incredibly strong, but far below her father's level. Nikki could bench press buses; Milk could throw *tanks*. She was tough, though she didn't know exactly how tough. She could take a wipeout at supersonic speed—David had proved *that* in an accidental spill a few months earlier—but she doubted that she was as durable as her father. Nikki loved her abilities and viewed them as having the best of both worlds—her father's might and her mother's quickness. She called herself Powerhouse, though Mom and Dad weren't supposed to know about that.

She shrugged and looked at her father. "I say let them try. They didn't have much luck with you tonight, Dad."

Milk shook his head and frowned, "Don't make light, Goober. We lost a good friend tonight. She was a brave woman, a genius and one of the best people I ever met. I lost Tom, too, and that's a very bad thing. And *he* lost his mother. It wasn't a walk in the park."

Nikki lowered her eyes, ashamed. For all her bluster, her heart was usually in the right place. "I'm sorry, Dad. I wasn't thinking."

"It's okay, Goober. Just try to think next time. Actions—especially our actions—have repercussions. Don't beat yourself up, though. I didn't think about much at your age, either."

"Except chasing women," Gloria interjected.

"Exactly," laughed Milk. "Now all I think about is chasing women ... and a whole lot of other, less fun things."

Gloria threw a towel at her husband, while Nikki and David began to set the table.

✪   ✪   ✪

Milk sat on the front porch, with Sean on his right knee, teaching his younger son the names of the constellations. Gloria was inside with David and Nikki as they cleaned the kitchen and washed the dishes.

"You don't gotta hover, Mom," Nikki complained over her shoulder.

Gloria harrumphed, "I don't hover. I run very, very fast. I knew a guy who could hover. Poor thing could only float around at walking speed. And he couldn't land. He just bobbed along all day, trying to not be blown away by the breeze. He went to the beach once and got caught by a gust. Took him straight up to ten thousand feet! The witnesses lost sight of him in the clouds. He was never seen again, poor guy."

David snickered and handed a plate to his sister. Nikki took the plate, shoved it in the water and said, "You know what I mean, Mom."

"Yes, I do, and *yes*, I do. You two are doing the dishes. And you will do the dishes at normal, sane, slow speed. Last thing I need is to have to buy new dishes. Again."

Nikki sighed and glanced at her big brother. David shrugged and took the bait, "You don't trust us, Mom? That's not very nice."

Gloria laughed, "I love you both, and take great comfort knowing that you are such fine, polite, well-behaved young adults — as I am just *sure* you both are — but don't think for a second that you can pull the wool over your dear mother's eyes. Do I trust you? Not on your life, kiddo."

David and Nikki both let out groans of youthful agony, and began to protest, but the telephone began to ring, cutting off their retorts.

"I'll get it. You two be good," winked their mother, turning to leave the kitchen.

Milk, still on the porch, motioned for Sean to be silent, and they listened as Gloria answered the phone.

"Hello," Gloria said cheerfully. "I plead the Fifth, who is this?"

Then, there was only silence for several seconds.

"Mister..." Gloria whispered, with a suddenly chilly and bitter tone. "How did you get this number? Well, *obviously*. Fine, thank you. Yourself? Good." Her voice dripped with frigid disdain; she obviously didn't like whoever had called. "Yes, of course. Hold on for a ... for a *moment* while I find him."

She sat the phone on the arm of the couch and walked toward the front of the house. Milk was already at the door. He cocked his head to the side and raised an eyebrow at his wife. Her face was kind of pale, her eyes wide with shock.

"You wouldn't believe me if I told you," she whispered, then took Sean by the hand. "Come on Half-Pint, we're going down to the creek for a bit."

Milk walked to the couch and picked up the receiver, which was far too small for him. He held it with only his thumb and forefinger and the receiving end reached no lower than his cheekbone—but his voice was loud enough to carry, so that didn't really matter. His biggest worry was accidentally crushing the fragile plastic body of the thing.

"Hello? Who is this?" Milk's voice rumbled like an unstable glacier. Whoever was on the other end had upset Gloria—that much was obvious. And Milk *hated* when anyone upset his wife.

"Good evening, Charles. It is such a pleasure to speak with you again," said the crisp, refined voice on the other end—deep, but nowhere near Milk's inhuman timbre, with just the slightest hint of a French accent. Milk knew the voice very well, although he'd not heard it in nearly two decades.

"Mister Moment," Milk growled—spat—the name. The devious cult leader was one of the hero's most dangerous, most hated enemies. "What the hell do you think you are doing, calling my house? You better not even *think* about my kids. Do you hear me, Moment?"

"I think about your lovely children often, my friend," remarked that smiling voice. "I wish them long lives, much happiness and peace for all their days. Do not be hasty, Charles, please. I have called to offer assistance ... and a little advice."

"Why on Earth do you think I'd want your goddamned help,

Moment?"

"Because the future of the human race—and *our* race—is hanging in the balance. Or is the survival of all the Earth not important enough of an occasion to reunite old friends, such as ourselves?"

"We were never friends, Moment. What's your game?"

"No games, Charles, we no longer have time for the playing of games," Moment replied with total seriousness. He sighed and continued, "You have suffered enough tonight, so please do forgive my attempt at banter. I am calling on behalf of the boy, the one who has tonight lost his beloved mother. It is not good for him to be staying with his cruel *uncle*, and my darling Sarah has seen that the uncle will indeed be cruel. But that is merely the beginning; the worst is coming soon. So I ask you this: Will you help the boy? Will you try to save the world as you once so often did? Will you at least listen to what I have to say? *Then* you may decide whether or not you might wish to trust an old enemy when he comes as a new friend."

Milk said nothing. His hatred for the Frenchman went all the way back to Vietnam. It would take more than a few words to make Milk trust that old bastard, *especially* when he came as a friend.

But Milk thought about Tom, orphaned, shot and in the custody of ABRA. The boy was the son of two of his closest friends, and potentially one of the most important people on Earth. The horned hero would do almost anything to protect young Tom. So in a way, his decision had already been made.

"Start talking. Guess I'll give you a *moment* after all."

CHAPTER EIGHT

Marcus clipped the Mini Maglite to his belt and dumped the contents of his backpack on the bed. He locked the bedroom door, crawled out the window and hopped on his bike. He tightened the pack's straps, zipped up his jacket and rode down the pitch-black street to Tom's house. The hills were dark and empty; the only sounds came from far-away dogs and lonely night birds.

Police tape hung from metal posts surrounding the property. The house's foundation was exposed, a rectangular pit in the dirt. Marcus parked the bike, turned on the flashlight and looked around. All of the action seemed to have taken place in the back yard, so he walked that way. The first thing he saw was a white outline of a body painted on the ground. Ms. Fuson, from the looks of it; her size, her build, an indication of her long hair in the outline.

Marcus tried to wipe away the tears with the back of his hand. He tried to calm down and pay attention to his surroundings. He tried to focus on the details. He'd always been good at that; he believed the smallest detail is usually the most important.

The backyard and the woods beyond had been torn to shreds. There were tire tracks, Walker marks and the biggest footprints Marcus had ever seen. The wreckage of at least two Humvees and a Walker had been piled up and covered by camouflage tarps. The vehicles were nothing but twisted metal. Hand prints and knuckle marks had been pressed into the heavy armor.

He looked at the freight containers loaded with the remains of the Fuson house. Lumber and drywall poked up from the top. It was like the government was trying to erase all traces of the Fusons.

Marcus believed that whatever happened here had something to do with Tom's father. Had the DPS discovered Tom's secret and come after him? That's what Marcus thought. How else did they get that kind of hardware down here so fast? There sure weren't any Walkers at the local National Guard armory.

Who did the giant feet belong to?

That was a curiosity. There must have been a real Posthuman here, maybe even a Postie terrorist, like the news said. Maybe that's what happened. Maybe some Posties discovered Tom and came after him. Then the military had come after *them*, and the Fusons got caught in the crossfire.

But there were no other outlines. Nobody else had died here. *Tom is still alive. Where is he?*

Marcus climbed into one of the large shipping containers and began to search the remains of the Fuson house. It was hazardous work, but he dug through the rubble, tenacious and fearless. He didn't know what he was looking for until he found it — Ms. Fuson's photo album.

He held the flashlight with teeth, flipped through the album and found the pictures he'd seen two years earlier. He saw newspaper clippings of Independence's career and photos that he hadn't noticed the first time, including several of the hero's funeral in New York. Ms. Fuson was there — not showing her pregnancy yet — sitting between Doctor Angus and the legendary Milk.

Milk.

Marcus thought about the giant footprints in the mud and decided they had probably been made by Milk. The horned hero had been on the run since the Public Safety Act passed; he was a "Posthuman terrorist" according to the government. It would be just like them to twist the truth like that. Milk had probably come to protect the Fusons from the attack.

Marcus realized that he was jumping to conclusions, but he just couldn't shake the feeling that his friend wasn't dead. The government was lying and the media was wrong. Tom was still alive. He *had* to be alive.

There were photographs of Ms. Fuson during her pregnancy and Tom as an infant. There were some pictures of other people that Marcus didn't recognize; a smiling brunette who might have been an unmasked Melusine, two well-dressed men who looked like Arabian princes, an incredibly old Asian man standing before a rustic shack and dozens more.

Marcus tucked the album under his arm and started to climb out of the container. It wasn't as easy as he imagined it would be, and it took him a few minutes to haul himself over the lip and climb safely to the ground. It was tiring, sweaty work; he removed his jacket, wrapped it around the album and put them both in the backpack.

He looked around the yard, thinking of all of the times that he'd come here to see Tom. He'd practically grown up at the Fuson house. He remembered burning ants with a magnifying glass not ten feet from where he stood—five, maybe even six years earlier—then feeling bad about it. Tom had confessed that he, too, regretted it. Marcus thought about his best friend and how none of this was his fault. Not Tom's fault at all. He didn't deserve whatever happened here.

Marcus walked over to his bike and picked it up, his head low as he thought about his friend, gone forever. *Nothing in life is fair, and that's the truth. And*, he realized, *I'll probably never know the truth.*

He sniffed the breeze; there was a bitter, sharp scent, like ozone, like electricity. Then he heard a low hum, barely louder than the wind.

A chill raced up his spine, and his fist clenched reflexively. He felt a sudden certainty that something was behind him, mere yards away. Something watched from the pitch-black forest. He stood still for a moment, and the hum grew louder.

Whatever it was, it was coming closer. Slowly, inevitably, it approached. Marcus did the only sensible thing he could; he hopped onto his bike and pedaled into the night.

He rode hard but could still hear the whispering buzz of the watcher in the woods. Sweat dripped from his goose-pimpled flesh; his hands trembled. But he maintained control of himself, despite the adrenaline. He rode the bike through the dark and made no mistakes; he had no time for mistakes.

They got me. They're going to take me like they took Tom, Marcus thought. *Nah, they'll just kill me. I'm not important enough to abduct.*

He rode through the woods, on a path that he knew as well as the street in front of his home. It would lead him to his own back yard, almost as fast as the road. The bumps, rocks and other hazards were welcome, familiar, and oddly calming in his time of panic.

Left turn up ahead in three, two…

He followed the curve of the path and gripped the handlebars. His fear-white knuckles practically glowed in the night. His breathing grew rapid and shallow; he wondered if he was hyperventilating. The backpack weighed heavily with its cargo of memories and truth.

Now the big old root.

Marcus gained some airtime from hitting the gnarled half-buried root, but he hit it at just the proper angle and landed perfectly in line for the next bit of straightaway.

He realized that the humming buzz had stopped. Maybe his pursuer had given up, but he doubted it. The thing in the woods had sounded mechanical; it was probably a flying drone, an eye in the sky. Uncle Sam loves his drones. Marcus was sure that the government was already watching him; he was Tom's best friend, after all. He wasn't important by any definition, but Big Brother had to see him as some kind of security risk, right?

Now they'd watched him explore the ruins and steal some treasure. It was only a matter of time before they beat down his door and did whatever they were going to do. He hoped that Uncle Sam wouldn't kill his parents. He decided to tell them everything as soon as he returned home. Maybe he could convince them to run.

Up ahead lay the Graffiti Boulder and the hard right turn that would take him home. The huge rock was a flat-faced slab of granite, defaced by decades of penis drawings, bad jokes and proclamations of adolescent romance (including "J. A. loves L. H."

placed by his own father, back when his parents were high school sweethearts). Marcus thought about slowing down, but began to pump the pedals harder instead. He tapped the brakes and pulled the bike into a hard slide. The wheels slammed to a stop at the base of the boulder—his back door was only a few dozen yards up ahead.

He pushed on the pedals—and went nowhere. The back wheel spun freely, as if the bike was suspended above the ground.

What the hell?

Marcus looked down. The bike *was* suspended, floating in the air, glowing a faint electric blue. The ground was two feet below. All of the hairs on his body stood on end; he felt a charge in the air itself. Crackling static crawled over the bike, on his clothes and in his ears. He heard the deep hum and smelled ozone again.

Suddenly the bike flew forward. He flipped head over heels, as the invisible force yanked it out of his hands. Marcus landed on his stomach with a thud that emptied his lungs.

He rolled onto his back, half-sitting thanks to the backpack. He saw the cold, white stars in the night sky and the leaves fluttering in the wind, black on black. For a few seconds all he could think was, *It sure is lonely out here in the big black nothing.*

Then Marcus stood and realized that he wasn't alone at all.

The alien probe floated down, like a car-sized metal football hanging in air. There were no lights on the thing, but the stars and distant streetlights reflected dimly on its dark hull. It was floating between Marcus and his home.

It hovered for a long moment. Marcus recognized it as belonging to the extraterrestrial AI, the Union of Knowledge. He'd seen video of the Invasion of Fifty-Four, same as everybody. He knew what the alien machine could do to a human being. But his terror began to turn into rage, and he decided to run with it.

Fear can be crippling, in his opinion, but anger can be fuel.

"Do something, you piece of shit!" He looked around for a weapon, any kind of weapon, and saw a nice fist-sized stone maybe two feet to the right. He bent down, still watching the probe—it continued to hang in the air, motionless—and picked up the rock.

It was at that moment the probe turned on a light. Marcus raised his left hand in front of his eyes and stood, with the rock in his right fist.

"Come on," he growled. "Do something or leave!" He threw the rock, and it clanged against the probe, loud but harmless.

Then the light changed. Marcus suddenly felt very warm. He gasped as the bones in his left hand became visible, his flesh made translucent by the painful brightness. He stared at the black metacarpals against a pure white background, like the negative of an x-ray.

He couldn't move. He couldn't even speak. The white light erased all things, and—with the first sting of pain—Marcus felt it erasing *him*. A trillion pinpricks erupted on and within his body, like his cells were bursting. His eyes dried, cracked and burned. He felt the approach of death, though he didn't understand how or why. He wondered if the machine was disintegrating him; it sure felt that way.

And, just like that, Marcus was gone. The probe's light deactivated as the corpse fell to the ground.

In the morning, his parents would find the charred body and curiously unburned clothing. They would find the Fuson's album, too, and tell the world about their neighbor, the son of a hero, and how their boy had died to reveal the truth.

The Union knew none of this, of course; its probe returned to orbit within minutes of killing Marcus Alexander. It had not recognized the photo album—such things are unimaginably primitive—nor would it have cared anyway. The album could tell the Union nothing. But from the boy, it had learned many things. Soon it would have the son of Independence, the half-mortal child named Tom.

CHAPTER NINE

Madison Doyle rubbed her eyes and answered the door to her apartment. The petite twenty year old had short black hair and looked good to JJ despite her apparent exhaustion and rumpled pajamas. He still had a little crush on her—even though she'd made it clear that she wasn't into dudes—but they'd become friends, and he was happy with that.

"Hey, guys," she mumbled sleepily. "What's going on? What was all that racket?"

"UFO or something," Solomon said. "Landed right on the hospital."

"Say what now?" Madi cocked her head to the side then glanced at JJ. "A UFO?"

JJ shrugged, "Looked like a Squiddie interceptor, but it had human pilots. They dropped off somebody at the hospital—"

"Looked major," Solomon interjected. "Like every doc in the city got called in."

"A UFO ambulance?" Madison's fine black eyebrows drew together inquisitively; JJ and Sol both nodded. She made a motion with her right hand. "Well come on in. I guess the whole town's already up. Did anyone else see this?"

"Everyone with a view of the hospital, I'd imagine." Solomon marched inside and sat on the couch. Every resident had a fully furnished apartment, and they all looked the same. A combo living room-kitchen, and between one and three bedrooms—there were several families among ABRA City's Posthuman detainees. Sol pulled a lighter and small glass pipe from the pocket of his jacket. "Yo, Jay, pass me the goods."

JJ removed a small baggy from the right front pocket of his jeans and tossed it to Sol. "Careful with that," he said with a grin. "Stuff's dangerous."

"Counting on it, dude," Sol said and began to pack the bowl of his pipe.

JJ sat in the chair and Madi joined Sol on the couch. Sol flicked his lighter and took a hard hit of the fresh green. Blue, pungent smoke filled the small apartment. Sol coughed slightly, a little red-faced, and handed the pipe to Madi.

"Well, thanks for the hookup," Madi said. "But I get the feeling this ain't really free." She took a drag, and held it long enough to bring tears to her big brown eyes. "You want me to listen, dontcha? Want me to try and find out what the spaceship was doing here?"

JJ raised his hands, palms up, and then leaned forward to take the pipe from the young woman. "If you don't mind. It had to be something big." He took a hit and said, "You're the only one who can help."

"I guess I can do that. If you can get me a little more of the bud," she replied. "Don't know how long it'll take, though."

"That's fine, sugar," Sol took the pipe from JJ and winked at Madi. "I'm happy keep you company tonight."

She gave him a playful shove and made a face. "You're too hairy for me, Sol. Besides you wouldn't have much fun watching me listen to the radio."

"It's always fun to watch you, Madi." Sol lit the pipe again. He shot her a sideways glance. "Not that I spy on you or anything."

"*Often*," added JJ. Then he stood and looked at Madi. "Can you listen right now? I mean ... they might be talking about it since it just happened and all. Here, I'll hook you up."

He extended his right hand and suddenly the air rippled; perfect circles of distortion expanded, fading like ripples in a pond, with a whirlpool at the center. The waves warped the air, and the spiral spun open, blocking JJ from view. Madi rose from the couch and walked around for a better look. She gasped and then giggled at the sight.

From the side, JJ looked like an amputee; half of his arm had simply vanished into the portal. Then he pulled the hand back — like a magic trick — and showed off a wrinkled paper bag. The distortion vanished as he turned to hand over the bag. Madi just stood there, with a wide smile on her face. JJ found himself grinning back. This was the first she'd seen him use his power, and she was impressed. Cool.

She opened the bag and inhaled the potent, dank scent. "Wow, thanks!" She gave JJ a hug, and then sat back down on the couch — taking the pipe from Sol again. "Where do you even get this stuff?" Madi asked between draws. "We're in a prison for fuck's sake."

"Trade secret, ma'am," JJ replied, still grinning. "I never reveal my sources."

In truth, he didn't know where the weed came from; he got it from Lucy Dressler, one of the older residents of ABRA City, who ran what passed for a black market in the prison town. He helped Lucy hide and move her goods — his abilities worked just fine within the city; he just couldn't penetrate the force field — and in return she gave him copious amounts of ganja. He didn't have a clue how she got anything through the bubble.

"If you say so," said Madi. "That's gotta be nearly an ounce."

"I do what I can."

Madi smiled at JJ and shook her head when Sol offered her the pipe again. "Well, I guess I'll do what I can, too. What are those bastards talking about tonight?"

"Thanks, Madi, I really appreciate it." JJ said, relieved and oddly nervous. He couldn't explain it, but he felt like something important had just happened, and he had seen it. Now he wanted — needed — to understand it.

Madi pulled her legs up to sit lotus-style on the couch. She placed her elbows on her knees and leaned forward, resting her face in her hands, eyes closed. She didn't need to do this, but it helped shut out the rest of her senses and focus on low end of the electromagnetic spectrum. Radio and microwaves were her playthings; she could absorb, generate, manipulate and sense them. Her pixie face screwed into a pout as she focused on the flood of signals that rushed over, around and through her mind.

"Whoa, lots of chatter tonight, guys," she said. Usually the only wireless broadcasts around ABRA City were status updates from the guards and whatever the drones beamed down from above. Tonight there was a lot more. Security had been ramped up; extra guards manned the Wall, more drones than usual circled overhead. HQ had numerous lines open to the outside world, but exterior communications were encrypted, and Madi understood none of that gibberish. She could decode it, but doing so would take time, and she figured that it'd be faster just to eavesdrop on unguarded communications.

JJ watched the movement under her eyelids. He remained standing in the middle of the room—too tense and energetic to sit— but resisted the urge to pace. Instead he watched the way she cocked her head to the side, like she was straining to make out a distant sound.

He wondered what it was like to "hear" radio. His powers didn't give him much in the way of extrasensory perception—he could detect gravity, sense the shape of the world and the tug of the moon—but those were tactile sensations, like his sense of touch could stretch around the planet. He wondered how Madi sorted through the signals. Picking through all the broadcasts had to be like trying to hear one person whisper while standing in the middle of a crowd. He wasn't far from the truth, but Madi was very skilled at using her gifts.

She shifted her focus to conversations within the Wall, between guard posts and HQ, between Walkers and monitoring stations. She usually didn't bother to spy on the guards since their conversations were ordinarily dull military speak—these days her abilities were mostly used to reheat coffee or listen to satellite radio.

She knew better than to try to send any signals outside of the prison; the guards would notice the transmissions and throw her in solitary confinement for a week or a month. She had "called" her family more than once right her arrival nearly four years earlier and had no desire to return to the dark, radio-proof isolation cells. But mere listening was passive and couldn't be detected. Madi discovered that there was plenty to hear on that particular night.

And everyone was talking about the exact same thing.

"Omigod!" Her dark eyes shot open and her pink cheeks grew pale as she gaped at JJ while Solomon took another hit of the weed and raised an eyebrow.

"What? What is it?" JJ asked, kneeling down in front of her. "What did you hear? What's happening?"

Madi only looked at the younger man, as if unsure what to say. She licked her lips and glanced over at Sol—who tried to comfort her by gently patting her back.

"Independence had a son," she said quietly. "They shot him."

CHAPTER TEN

Doctor Angus stood at the Operating Room door with his weathered, ancient face nearly pressed against the window. The slow exhalations from his long nose left two asymmetrical cones of fog on the glass. On the other side, a dozen surgeons and nurses had gathered around the boy, and the operating room was a riot of frenzied motion, mirroring the chaotic emotions within the old man. He was careful to hide these emotions from his subordinates—and everyone in ABRA City was subordinate to the legendary Doctor Angus, Chief Administrator of the American Biological Research Agency, creator of Independence and the Posthuman subspecies.

Phillip Angus felt helpless and simply hated it. He was one hundred and twelve years old on that dark October night— although he looked like a healthy eighty-year-old thanks to the Golden Home's renewal process, a gift it had given to certain respected humans, including poor Megan, Doctor Banks and Tom Lehrer. This was only the second time in his long adult life that he could recall being powerless and at the mercy of forces beyond his control.

The first time had been nearly seventeen years earlier, when the living inferno called Bloodlust returned to Earth and murdered Adam. The doctor knew that his creation was doomed when he heard the first reports. Bloodlust had killed Aegis, after all. And Adam, for all of his power, was newborn compared to the Golden

Light. Angus watched the fight on television in the fallout shelter beneath the old ABRA building in San Diego. He watched, helpless, as his creation was slaughtered.

And now the son of Adam lay on a table, injured and dying while Angus stood helpless, angry and afraid.

He looked down at his large hands and remembered the infant Adam grasping them with pudgy baby fingers. Angus recalled gripping Adam's shoulder and looking into the newly-adult man's eyes with pride after he first donned the Independence uniform. He remembered shaking Adam's hand on that last day, the day of the Second Coming of Bloodlust.

Angus raised his eyes and stared at the bright red blood staining the bed and the gloved hands of the busy surgeons – the blood of Thomas Fuson, the blood of Adam and Megan – dear, impulsive Megan.

Angus closed his eyes and held his breath for a moment. He saw Megan, only twenty-six years old as she stepped off the helicopter and onto the heavenly streets of the Golden Home. He saw the wonder in her sky-blue eyes as she stared at the soaring, alien towers and the white expanse of ice far below. He saw the awe on her face when the Golden Home introduced itself. And Angus saw the woman meet the child Adam for the first time; the simplest of events, but it had likely changed the world forever.

Adam matured himself to adulthood less than a year later. Angus clearly recalled Megan's anger at that event – and at Adam's refusal to revert himself to childhood. Thanks to recent intelligence, the doctor knew that the couple's relationship began a decade later, during the mid-Eighties, but he wondered how it had developed. Did she intentionally wait until Adam passed the age of eighteen or was that a coincidence? How long had it taken her to fall in love with the hero? How could they have kept their love secret from him?

He'd never suspected such a thing and was astonished to learn that they had a child together. True, Megan had retired after Bloodlust killed Adam, but that had not been suspicious. Many of their associates did the same. The hero's death – coupled with the rising storm of rogue Posthumans and human terrorists in those wild days – had made all of their work into a cynical joke.

And now trigger-happy soldiers had killed Megan and severely wounded the boy — during a botched operation that should never have taken place.

Angus had argued with the directors of DPS, DHS and the NSA. He had argued with the Joint Chiefs and the President herself. Using force to abduct the boy was foolish, dangerous and self-defeating. But his colleagues had panicked after an anonymous tip led to the discovery of Thomas Fuson.

"Let me speak to them," Angus had said, although he knew that the decision had already been made. "I know Doctor Fuson. Let me speak to her. Would it not be better to at least give them a chance to cooperate? Do you really want to make an enemy of *him*?"

His appeal was denied. The bureaucrats and officers felt that Megan had nearly seventeen years to cooperate. It was obvious, they insisted, that she was unconcerned with the law and the greater good. The DPS soldiers would attempt to arrest the Fusons peacefully but were prepared to kill both woman and child if they did not surrender. Thomas was potentially dangerous, to say the least. He could not be allowed to live free of supervision.

Doctor Angus had left that meeting with the taste of bile in his mouth, but even then he had not felt powerless. The boy would be sent to ABRA City after the raid; Angus would have control of his legacy once again. The old scientist had not believed that they would use lethal force against the son of Independence; he had not believed that Megan would resist. He should have known better.

The brilliant woman had always followed her own path — that's what had made her such a wonderful addition to his team on the Golden Home. Once, Angus had imagined that she would become the steward of his legacy. He found bitter irony in the fact that she had been the steward after all, in an utterly unimaginable way.

And now she was dead. She had been his student, his coworker and perhaps even his friend. Megan was dead and her son wasn't too far behind. All that remained of the legacy lay on that operating table, fragile and fading.

It was becoming obvious that the gunshot wound had been mortal. Angus could see the desperation and fear in the eyes and sweat-beaded brows of the straining doctors. The boy would die. One of the surgeons muttered something about needing a miracle.

Doctor Angus did not believe in miracles. There had been no miracle to save Adam. No miracle had allowed them to create another Aegis clone during the past fifteen years. No miracle would save this boy.

The old man cursed the fate that brought his legacy back to life—only to see it ruined by a single bullet. The soldiers said that the boy had demonstrated powers—even the golden glow that was the signature of his bloodline—but his abilities were too weak, too new to save his life.

A mere bullet would never have injured Adam, but *his* powers had been nurtured from infancy with exposure to radiation and other energy.

Angus raised his widening eyes to the window and heard his old heart drumming. *My God ... it's so obvious.*

He turned and walked briskly out of the observation room. Doctor Angus smiled to himself, no longer helpless.

"I strongly advise against this, sir," Doctor Leon Ng stated in his trademarked brusque, yet respectful manner. The square-jawed surgeon had to work to keep pace with his taller companions as they walked down the hallway.

"So do I," said Captain John Holly, the hulking head of ABRA City Security. "We have no idea what this might do."

"You will likely kill him," added Ng, the concern in his voice would have been touching for most listeners. Not for Doctor Angus, whose interests ran far deeper than mere empathy.

"Your objections have been noted and overruled," said Angus as they approached the elevator door. "I have made my decision."

Captain Holly growled with a near-subsonic rumble, "Lieutenant Gabriel said that fifteen seconds under an Active Denial System gave the boy enough power to destroy—"

"I have read the report, Captain. Thank you," Angus

snapped. The elevator door opened and the three men filed in. Doctor Angus faced the door, with his back to the soldier and the physician. As far as Angus was concerned, this conversation was finished.

Captain Holly apparently disagreed, "Sir, if this boy has a fraction of Independence's power then he is a danger to this facility. We can't afford to let a Postie freak like him—"

Angus wheeled around, and the sudden wrath stamped on his ancient face silenced the linebacker-sized captain. Angus hissed, "Thomas Fuson is *not* a Posthuman, Captain! He is the one hope that we have of recreating the greatest soldier the United States has *ever* produced. If you have issues with my orders, you are free to leave. The same goes for you, Ng. We do not have time to let you surgeons blunder about until he dies. I *will* save this child, with or without the pair of you. You work for me."

Angus turned back toward the door and said nothing for the rest of the ride. Doctor Ng and Captain Holly looked at each other— Ng's eyes quivered with nervousness while Holly's burned with anger—but neither man spoke.

They stepped out of the elevator one hundred feet beneath the hospital, at the main underground security checkpoint. The four guards wore chrome-plated, two-ton suits of robotic power armor— Armored Personal Exoskeletons—and could reputedly go toe-to-toe with all but the strongest of Posthumans. The suits were usually referred to as APEs. Angus thought that they did strongly resemble robotic gorillas, so the acronym was quite fitting.

He ignored the soldiers and turned right toward maintenance instead of heading left to MegaMax. Ng followed closely, looking ever more uncomfortable, but Captain Holly stopped to converse with the guards for a brief moment before double-timing it to catch up to the doctors.

Five members of the reactor crew met the three men in the maintenance corridor. They saluted and introduced themselves, but Angus did not catch their names. He had more important matters on his mind. The enlisted men spent a few minutes speaking with Captain Holly, while Angus grimaced impatiently, and Ng squirmed with trepidation. Then they heard the sound.

The eight men all looked down the hallway as loud, slow and *heavy* footsteps approached. The technicians gasped and stepped back. Angus heard Doctor Ng mutter something under his breath. The overhead lighting seemed to grow darker, and a massive form filled the hall.

The huge Posthuman walked on his knuckles, hunched over like a gorilla, and his head still nearly reached the ceiling. He weighed more than ten thousand pounds, a once-human golem of living rock. His flesh had transformed into an incredibly dense, brown-gray, stone-like substance; his cells were suspended in a mineral matrix. His broad, cylindrical head had minimal features — no lips, no visible nose and simple holes for ears — only his large, brown eyes retained their humanity. His name was a mystery, and no one knew if he even remembered it. For fourteen years, he had gone by the nickname Tank.

"H'lo, Doc-ta," Tank rumbled, his voice so deep and slow that it reminded everyone of a foghorn — one could *feel* that voice as much as hear it.

"Hello, Tank. How are you today?" Angus approached the megalithic figure without fear and placed one hand on Tank's broad forearm.

"Ah'm ow-kay, Doc-ta."

Nobody knew exactly how intelligent Tank really was. Staff psychologists constantly debated the question. Some felt that he had the mind of a young child. Others thought that he was intelligent, but perhaps fell on the autism spectrum.

In any case, Tank was harmless and easily managed. He was invariably friendly and polite, but swiftly grew disinterested in conversation. He could obey even complicated orders and would, without complaint, but he preferred to sit quietly and required neither companionship nor entertainment. Despite his inhuman appearance and incredible power, he wasn't dangerous and would never try to escape. He was only kept in MegaMax to help the guards deal with certain dangerous inmates. That night he had been summoned to serve a different function.

"Follow us, Tank. I need your assistance." Angus turned and began to head deeper into maintenance.

"Ow-kay, Doc-ta."

Doctor Ng and the five techs crowded close to the large Captain Holly, crammed as they were between their imperious boss and the stone giant. Angus kept his back to the men; he did not want them to see his enjoyment of their discomfort. The only sounds were the rhythmic thuds of Tank's feet and fists on the reinforced steel floor — and the barely controlled, rapid breathing from the six frightened men.

Captain Holly knew better than to be disturbed by Tank. He glared at Ng and the petty officers but remained silent.

They reached the freight elevator just as it descended to their level. Four medics and a doctor were already on the platform, surrounding a gurney that carried the comatose Thomas Fuson. They were trying their best to keep him alive with the limited portable equipment and were obviously flustered by their orders. However, they were focused on their patient and barely raised eyebrows at Tank; Angus admired their professionalism.

Everyone stepped onto the elevator, which immediately began to descend. Angus ignored the nervous glances of the others; he could feel their fear at sharing an elevator with the five-ton Postie. Their concerns were baseless; ABRA's underground facilities had been designed with Tank's bulk in mind. In fact, he had helped with the construction — or at least he'd helped bring in the heavy equipment.

Angus bent over the pale, blond boy. Thomas really did look like his father, although the old scientist had never seen Adam this gray-faced and frail. The doctor had also never seen Independence at this age; the clone had gone from child to man in mere moments. The boy was several inches shorter than his father and far less muscular, but the features were incredibly similar. Thomas Fuson was undoubtedly the son Adam.

Angus laid his palm on the boy's cool, damp forehead and then felt for a pulse. It was weak but there. Thomas breathed shallowly and bubbles of blood occasionally rose from his lips.

"We're not even sure how he's still alive," one of the medics said. "His right lung is pulverized. He shouldn't be alive after, what, nine hours. He should have died moments after the injury."

Angus did not reply, and the other men remained silent, though nobody could keep their eyes off the gurney carrying Tom — except for Tank, who stared straight ahead, and Doctor Ng, who stared at Tank.

The rocky giant let out a low rumble as the elevator shaft opened up to reveal the cavernous space surrounding ABRA City's nuclear reactor. The reactor itself was within a large containment bunker at the heart of the immense room. The bunker had concrete walls — with lead and steel plating sandwiched between more layers of concrete — and a steel door twice as large as Tank.

Angus looked up from Tom and spoke to Tank, "Do you recognize this place? You haven't been down in here in a very long time."

"Mm. Lonn time," Tank stated, though nobody could tell whether he was agreeing with Angus or merely repeating the words.

The elevator came to a stop, and the medic began to detach the I.V.'s and sensors from their patient. The nuclear technicians led Ng and Holly toward the entrance to the control room, while Angus stepped closer to rocky giant.

"I need your help, Tank," Angus said slowly. "Are you ready to help?"

"Red-dee, Doc-ta."

"Thank you, Tank. I need you to carry this bed into that big door over there." Angus pointed to the heavy door of the reactor's containment bunker. "Take it inside, then through another door. You will hear my voice, and I will tell you where to place it. Then you can sit down and rest."

"Rest," Tank nodded his great, rocky head. Then he lumbered over to the gurney — the medics all backed away — and looked down at the prone figure. He said, "Mm. Look hurt."

"He is hurt," agreed Angus, surprised by Tank's spontaneous observation. "But if you take him in there, he will get better."

"Bet-ta? Ow-kay, Doc-ta. Make'm bet-ta." Tank slid his right hand under the gurney and lifted. He looked down at Tom before plodding toward the door.

Angus and the medics walked up to the control room. Holly

chatted with the two petty officers at the control panels while the five nuclear technicians explained the systems to Ng. Angus ignored everything but the monitors.

His mind wandered back to when they placed the shrieking, terrified, one-year-old Adam in a Leksell Gamma Knife in the first attempt to empower the clone. Normally, such a device is used for radiation therapy in the treatment of brain tumors; back in 1969, it proved to be an ideal method of flooding the infant with enough energy to kick-start his development. The Golden Home had suggested it, preferring to use human technology and keep its secrets safe from the dangerously curious people of Earth.

For a moment, as he watched the walking monolith on the video monitors, Angus almost wished that the insufferably arrogant Artificial Intelligence had never left. At the very least, it could help save the life of Thomas and help uncover the depth and breadth of the boy's power.

That was the real mystery. How much of this boy was Adam? What could this child do, if he lived?

He would likely be more powerful than any mere Posthuman; even the mightiest of them had only a fraction of Aegis and Adam's ability. Would the boy be so potent? Only time—and testing—would reveal the truth.

And time, Angus knew, was a luxury they did not have.

He'd been shaken by NASA's news—that the Union of Knowledge had sent a probe to Westburg only hours ago. Angus knew that nothing could protect ABRA City from the frighteningly advanced alien machine. The boy's predecessors had repelled the Union's assaults, but was young Thomas capable of the same wonders? How much time remained before the inevitable attack?

The old scientist had so many questions and very few answers. Even if the boy recovered from the gunshot, he was surrounded by threats. Angus could offer little protection from any of them—and the greatest threat of all existed beyond any hope of detection, and far beyond any hope of defense.

Bloodlust.

It was out there, somewhere in the universe. It could be anywhere. It could be on Earth already, for all that Angus knew—

although he doubted such a thing, given the being's disdain for stealth. But one thing Angus did not doubt was that Bloodlust would one day come again. It had promised as much, both before and after the murder of Adam. It would come back to slaughter humans the way settlers had slaughtered the great herds of bison on the Plains—by the thousands, with no conceivable opposition. It would inevitably return ... and find young Thomas.

Would it sense the boy's existence, as it had apparently detected Adam? Had it felt the boy's awakening power this very night?

Angus faced too many questions, and none could be answered. But there were possible solutions.

Underground, below the prison but above the reactor, ABRA City kept its darkest secrets, the hidden laboratories of Doctor Angus. Indeed, the labs had been constructed long before the prison, back when the military had considered forming a brigade of Posthuman soldiers. Down there, amid pirated Gray nano-factories, patchwork Carnivore computers and technology stolen from the Golden Home, Doctor Angus pursued his true work, the birth of a new Independence. For sixteen years, the doctor had been attempting to remake his creation.

However none of the clones survived beyond the blastocyst stage. Some flaw in the technology, some lack of understanding on the part of human science, *something* prevented Angus from duplicating the process.

But now they had the cells of Thomas Fuson, enough for a legion of clones. It was a gamble, but the old man felt that the odds were in his favor. After all, the son of Adam was also the child of a woman. Half of his genome came from Megan, and his mitochondria was by necessity totally human, unlike the synthetic organelles of Aegis.

The half-human DNA of Thomas might survive, *should* survive. And if it did, then perhaps all of Angus's questions would have the same answer—they would be irrelevant.

For if Aegis and Adam could defeat the Union, if both could nearly equal the terrible might of Bloodlust, then the clones might tip the balance of power against such threats. If one Independence could do so much for the world, then how much more could be done by a squad, a platoon, an *army*?

Angus smiled.

Tank finally entered the containment structure and stood motionless, staring at the entry to the reactor. The ABRA City power plant had been designed with several unique features, one of which was that the still-fissioning core could be exposed, and irradiated steam could be released into the surrounding chamber. Many Posthumans could absorb radiation or were simply immune to it, like Tank, and the reactor had been designed for various experiments of Angus's devising. Other Posthumans were invulnerable to all harm *except* for lethal radiation, and in those cases the reactor could serve as a means of execution … if such became necessary. The old scientist knew that killing Posthumans often requires creativity. He'd been doing it as long as they'd existed.

Angus spoke into a microphone, "Now enter that room when the door opens."

It opened slowly and the huge Posthuman trudged forward with Tom's bed balanced on one colossal hand. The vault-like door sealed behind them with a resounding slam.

"Very good, Tank. Now place the bed on the floor and have a seat."

The rocky giant put the gurney on the floor and ponderously sat down, resting his mountainous back against the wall. An unseen hatch slid open, steam filled the chamber like fog, and the blue glow of Cherenkov radiation played on Tank's craggy hide and the ashen face of Thomas Fuson.

CHAPTER ELEVEN

Megan took a sip of water and examined a floating double helix; a glowing, semi-opaque red, green and blue hologram of human DNA slowly rotated above the workstation. She looked younger than Tom had ever seen. Maybe it was just her hair—long and parted in a way that made him think of the late Sixties or early Seventies. She wore a white lab coat over a blue blouse and black trousers, and she carried a notebook, filled with her own dense scrawl. The workstation, counters, cabinets and walls were apparently made of gold; the floor was a white stone, like polished marble.

Tom knew where they were.

He stood with his mother on the Golden Home, like it was the most ordinary place to be. They were in a small room on the six hundredth floor of a tower called City Hall. Megan picked the room because she liked the view.

The Golden Home was built on three connected disks; the middle one was twelve miles in diameter, while the smaller two were merely nine miles across. Countless towers extended from both top and bottom. Great curving bridges flowed among the swooping spires and between the disks. Gardens from ten thousand worlds adorned the white stone streets. The flying city had belonged to Aegis for a billion years, a gift from a grateful race to the benevolent Golden Light. With the hero's death, the Home's

RISING SON | 75

artificial intelligence considered itself an independent entity, but it allowed some humans to live in its innumerable rooms.

Any place in the Home could be used for almost any function, so the researchers and staff chose their quarters and offices out of personal whim. Many of Megan's coworkers shied away from the soaring spires; she supposed that most people just don't like heights. She couldn't make fun of them for it, though—some of her colleagues stayed in towers on the *bottom* of the floating city. They lived upside down compared to the rest of the world thanks to the Home's artificial gravity.

Having the ground above and the sky below made Megan nauseous; she avoided even visiting that side of the Home. She was happy to have a lab here, high above the Earth, safe and warm in the subtly glowing force field.

The Carnivore War had been raging across the globe for nearly four years, and the Home was the safest place to be. The flying city maintained the course of its choosing and allowed only certain people aboard—people connected to ABRA, the Posthumans and, above all, the care and education of the clone child, Adam.

Unwelcome human visitors were turned away. Approaching Carnivores were destroyed. The Home claimed to possess the most advanced technology in the galaxy; the comparatively primitive Squids posed no threat.

The Home floated above Cape Crozier on the eastern shore of Ross Island that day, on a meandering path along the northern edge of the Ross Ice Shelf. Mount Terror's black rock and white ice dominated the view below, rising to a windswept summit at more than ten thousand feet above sea level—but still miles beneath the Home—with Mount Erebus reaching even higher in the distance.

Megan knew that the airspace above Cape Crozier was ordinarily forbidden; it had been made an Antarctic Specially Protected Area in 1966 to protect the native wildlife. But the Home had been freed from such restrictions. It would have just ignored them, anyway. Besides, the silent passage of the flying city did not appear to disturb the clustered penguins or the big, mean seabirds.

Tom didn't understand how he knew all of this, but know it he did. He seemed to be aware of many new things but wasn't sure exactly what or how. He must be dreaming. The clarity surprised him, though. It felt so real; the depth and certainty of everything equaled his conscious perception. He felt more awake—more aware—than ever before.

Megan made a gesture in the air, and a section of the helix expanded. The image focused on a point just above the upper-most twist in the spiral, and several small segments changed color, becoming vibrant gold. Lines of text popped into existence and scrolled before her eyes, labeling sections that had been modified by the Aegis virus. Megan was one the world's foremost experts on Posthuman genetics, and the Golden Home was the only place to study such wonders.

There was a desperate need to unlock the secrets of the virus, especially now that it had somehow begun to spread across the globe. For years, the only Posthumans had been employees of the American government, beginning with Charles Young's transformation into Milk in 1971. Each sample of the virus had to be specifically tailored to the host's genome, and even then it wasn't always successful.

But now the virus had apparently mutated and become airborne. Millions of people had been infected, but the wild strain of the virus was even less successful than the laboratory version. Most infected subjects developed symptoms similar to a mild flu and recovered quickly. But roughly one in a million infected people became Posthumans. Dozens had transformed over the previous few months and more appeared every day.

Megan did not care really about any of that. Unlike Angus, she wasn't worried about the growing Posthuman population. All she cared about was the nature of the virus itself. Being a retrovirus, it altered the DNA of its host. But that did nothing to explain Posthumans or their gifts. Mutation can do great many things, but it cannot allow people to break the laws of nature; there had to be more going on than simple genetic tricks.

This frustrated Megan, a cytogeneticist, a rising star in her specialty. Her personal hero, Barbara McClintock, laid the foundations of the field in the Forties by discovering transposable elements in maize. The Aegis virus was precisely such an element, a unique retrotransposon—or rather a retrovirus that formed a collection of DNA transposons within the host's genome—but it had very little direct effect on the organism's phenotype.

In other words, the virus did not seem to really cause mutations, certainly not obvious ones. The physiological alterations in Posthumans—such as Milk's mass, pigmentation and horns—did not seem to be directly connected to the actions of the transposon. For all intents and purposes, the Aegis virus did nothing.

None of this was very strange; genetic codes all contain vast stretches of DNA that lack any obvious function, such as introns, pseudogenes and telomeres. The human genome is almost entirely noncoding—ninety-eight percent of it, by most measures—although debates rage as to how much of this "junk DNA" is actually nonfunctional.

Megan had begun to believe that she would never understand the mystery of Posthuman abilities. She rebelled against defeatism, but in truth she was no closer to penetrating this puzzle than she'd been a year earlier. Many of her colleagues thought the answer lay deeper than DNA; the best analysis suggested that the Aegis virus showed structure at the subatomic level. Quantum physicists would have better luck at cracking this chestnut than geneticists—at least they *should*. So far no one could even begin to understand the reality-warping abilities of Aegis and the Posties.

The Golden Home had created the Posthumans to protect Earth from the invaders, and allowed research teams to use some of its technology, but it would offer no more than vague explanations about the mechanisms behind the superhuman powers.

"The Golden Light belonged to a species made of spacetime, not matter or energy. As such, they possess remarkable control over physical reality." The Home would say no more than that, leaving Megan and her team alone in their search for answers.

Posthuman abilities seemed more focused and limited than those of Aegis or the child, Adam. Some Posties, like Milk, subconsciously altered their own bodies and became intrinsically different from ordinary humans. Other Posthumans could manipulate the rules of science in various ways—this is how Gloria Stewart moved at hypersonic speed; she altered her course down the river of time.

But this was all a fuzzy area. Milk's strength far exceeded what muscle and bone could do. Even if he somehow had the strength to bench press a locomotive, the machine would fall apart under its own weight—to say nothing about leverage. But he generated a gravitational field that, in combination with his titanic musculature, enabled him to perform technically impossible feats of might.

Gloria also displayed numerous physiological changes, notably utterly perfect cellular regeneration, but also enhanced reflexes, balance and bone strength. Her power involved a lot more than just time manipulation. Every Posthuman was unique, with a unique mix of abilities, and none of it could be explained by solely by genetics.

The whole thing gave Megan a headache. She rubbed the bridge of her nose and exhaled slowly. Her eyes were closed, and her back was to the open door, so she did not notice a guest arrive in the lab. Neither did Tom, until the small blond child walked into view.

Tom stared with a slack jaw, looking at his father for the first time.

Adam was eight years old on that bright day. He was a touch short for his age, with a big, round head, wide, metallic gold eyes and diminutive, immature features. The child carried a flower in his hands, though it did not resemble any flower that Tom had ever seen. He drifted around for a better view, moving to a spot beside his parents.

"Hello, Doctor Megan," Adam said softly; the woman jumped slightly from surprise.

"Oh, hello, Adam."

"Here," he said quietly, shy but trying to be bold. "I made a flower for you."

Adam raised his little hand and offered the flower to Megan. She took it and examined it, feeling a mixture of curiosity and wonder. It felt cool and organic, like an ordinary plant, but she knew that the boy had *created* the flower. He had built it, atom-by-atom, in the way another child might build a house with blocks. It looked like no flower on Earth. The stem was too thick, the perfectly symmetrical leaves were cartoonish spade-shapes, and the five petals were crimson teardrops surrounding a bright yellow sphere.

"Why thank you, Adam," Megan's grin spread wider. She raised the flower to her face, inhaling the fragrance. "Mmm, it smells like bubblegum!"

Adam shifted his weight from foot to foot, and asked in his tiny voice, "Do you like it?"

"I love it, Adam. Thank you very much!" She bent down to hug the boy.

"You're welcome, Doctor Megan," he said, squeezing her neck, beaming with pride and happiness. She stood straight, and Adam took a step back. His head bobbed, and his chest puffed up as he worked up the courage for his question, the real reason he'd come to visit his favorite person. Then he asked, "Will you be my girlfriend?"

Megan's smile softened, becoming patient and maternal. Tom had seen that expression at least a million times during his childhood. He felt a pang of grief, a spike piercing his heart, but realized that he was smiling, too.

"Now, Adam, you know that I can't be your girlfriend. I'm a grownup, and you're still a little boy."

Adam looked at Megan; his expression bore an immeasurable seriousness and *gravitas* that can only be achieved by young children and the moai statues of Easter Island. The boy simply stated, "I can grow up."

"Yes, sweetie," Megan replied. She turned away and stepped over to the workstation to place the flower in her glass of water. "And you *will* grow up. But by then I'll be an old woman and you wo—"

A brilliant light burst out of the child, and an unnatural thrumming noise drowned all other sounds. The blinding glow filled the room; Megan covered her eyes and turned around.

She exclaimed, "Adam!"

Megan couldn't see the event occurring right in front of her; the radiance overpowered her vision. She closed her eyes but that did not help. The glare hurt, even with her eyelids down and a forearm thrown across her face.

But Tom could see the transformation. He watched the boy become a man in only a scant few seconds. Adam's eyes screwed tightly shut, but his expression did not show pain or fear. His clothing burst at the seams as he grew to adulthood. In the span of a few heartbeats, he became a man.

The light dimmed. Megan opened her eyes and blinked against the afterglow, trying to banish the spots obscuring her vision. Then she saw Adam. She gasped, and her eyes expanded to wide circles of shock. Her mouth opened and silently formed the phrase *oh, my God.*

Adam now stood six feet four inches tall, with strong features and a slight smirk. He walked closer to Megan, slowly, for her benefit. She took a step back and blushed. He was nude, shredded clothing scattered on the floor. She tried to not stare at his gleaming smile, his perfectly proportioned, well-defined musculature — or any other part of his anatomy.

"Hello, Megan," he said in a deep, quiet but infinitely confidant voice. He spread his hands to shamelessly display his new form. "What do you think?"

Tom stared in awe and realized that his mind had not created the scenario. This might be a dream, but it was also something more. He had seen the event that gave the world its greatest hero; he had witnessed the moment that would lead to his own birth.

"My God, Adam," Megan whispered, having finally rediscovered her voice, "What have you done? Change back. Make yourself a kid again, Adam. This isn't right! Change back now!"

"No, Megan," Adam replied calmly, that movie-star grin never leaving his face. "I don't think I will. I like being an adult, and I'm not certain that I was ever really a child."

Megan ran from the room and yelled for the Home to call Doctor Angus.

Adam watched her leave and shook his head slightly. He laughed, low and amused. Then he looked right at Tom and said, "That could have gone better. It's okay, though. I have plenty of time to change her mind."

Tom started to reply, but suddenly began to fall into darkness. The vision had released its hold, and Tom screamed as he fell faster and faster into the black.

Then he jerked to consciousness and found himself on a hospital bed in a windowless room. His heart thundered in his chest.

✪   ✪   ✪

"Oh, you're awake," a girl said, from Tom's left. He jumped and let out a yelp. The girl giggled. "Sorry. Didn't mean to startle you."

Tom rolled over and looked at the girl. She was his age, maybe a little younger, with long, wild, red hair, blue-gray eyes, delicate features and very pale skin. He could smell soap and shampoo, her hair looked darkened and damp, and she held a brush in her left hand. She wore blue nurse's scrubs—though she was obviously too young to be on the hospital staff—and appeared to have just finished bathing. She sat on the edge of another hospital bed.

Mist wafted through a partially opened door on the right side of the room; the bathroom, apparently. A squat dresser with two lamps and a clock sat between the beds. Behind the girl, two small chairs and a little table sat next to the room's door. It was closed. There were no windows; two vents in the ceiling moved the air. Under each vent was a small red sticker covered in tiny script; Tom could only make out the five largest words:

LETHAL DANGER!

DO NOT TOUCH!

He shook his head in confusion, "Where the hell am I?"

"Oh, you don't know? What's the last thing you remember?"

"Milk," Tom said.

"You were drinking milk? Milking a cow? What?"

"No, I was *with* Milk. The hero. You know ... Milk? Milk and my…" Tom suddenly saw his mother—prone in the dirt. He felt acidic grief rise up, and something rock-hard seemed to roll up his esophagus. He tried to choke it back, failed and wept like a child for a long time.

When he came to his senses, Tom found that the girl had come to sit next to him and laid her hand on his arm. He sniffled and tried to apologize.

"It's okay," she said with concern in her voice. "Are you okay?"

"Yeah," Tom said. "They... Mom. They killed ... they killed my mother."

"Oh, my God... I don't know what to say."

"It's..." Tom closed his eyes; he could see nothing but his mother.

"You said that you were with Milk," the girl said and walked back to her own bed. She was obviously trying to change the subject, and Tom saw the wisdom in that decision. "*The* Milk. Did you mean that? You know Milk?"

Tom sat up, noticed the box of tissues on the nightstand and removed several. "I met him. Right before... And then *they* attacked. They had a Walker and wore all black. One of them hit me with an Active Denial System."

"What's that?" the girl asked. "Sounds like some kind of computer."

"No. It's a weapon. I saw a documentary about it once. Looks like a big satellite dish on a Hummer, but it's a microwave gun."

"Oh, yeah? I've never heard about that before. What does it do?"

"It hurts like hell. Or it did, anyway ... at first. Then, well, I guess I absorbed the energy and shot it back. I blew the hummer to hell. With an energy beam ... from my hands."

The girl just looked at him and asked, "Oh, that's what you do?"

"I don't know what I can do. That was my first time. The only time. It faded really fast." Tom stopped, remembering the soldier and the gun. "Holy shit. They shot me!"

He noticed his clothing for the first time; he'd been dressed in a loose blue scrubs, just like the girl. He pulled the shirt up and marveled. There wasn't even a scar. He was totally uninjured. "What the hell?"

"No, no. That makes sense," the girl said. "You feel like a vacuum, or a whirlpool. You're pulling in energy from all over, and you can use it to shoot laser beams or regenerate. I've seen this kind of thing a lot. It's a pretty common power. But there's something different about what you do. Your power's fuzzy ... blurry. I can't quite figure it out. It keeps moving around, pulsing like a heartbeat. It's kinda weird. No offense."

"None taken. I don't even know what you're talking about."

"That's what I do," she replied. "I can feel other Posties and figure out what they can do. They call me a power manipulator. I can turn powers off ... or make them stronger."

"No way! You're a Posthuman?"

The girl shook her head and giggled at Tom's cluelessness. "Well, duh. We're all Posties here. You're in ABRA City, in the maximum-security area. They call it MegaMax. It's where they put the dangerous ones."

This did not surprise Tom—actually, it made perfect sense. He wondered how the soldiers had taken him from Milk. What happened to Milk? Was the big guy okay? Of course he was; they couldn't hurt him like they'd hurt Tom. Is that why he was here, instead of with Milk? Did Milk give him to ABRA for medical treatment? Did they heal him? Why? How? He decided to worry about all of that later. He looked at the redhead and asked, "Why are you down here? You don't seem all that threatening."

She frowned and then bit her lower lip. "They keep me here so I can shut down the bad ones when they attack the staff or try to escape. I've been here since I was in seventh grade."

"Is that why you're my roommate?" Tom asked. "To shut me down?"

"Yeah," the girl admitted. "They told me to make sure you didn't destroy anything or try to escape. Sorry."

Tom grunted, unsure of how to feel about it.

"I don't like doing it, okay? And I try not to do it much. People hate it when I do. Even Fiona gets really mad at me for it, and she's kinda like my adopted mom. But I have to do it if they tell me to. You see this?"

She pointed at a metal plug behind her left ear. Tom reached up and found that he had one of his own. It didn't hurt at all, but seemed to go all the way to his skull.

The girl spoke up, "Don't mess with it. It's a bomb. We all have them. That's why I do what they tell me to do. We don't get to say no. You better learn that before your head gets exploded."

"That's fucked up," muttered Tom.

The girl shrugged, "Welcome to the Postie life."

"I'm not a Posthuman."

"You aren't a ... what do you mean? Of course you're a Postie," she said. "It's okay. There's nothing wrong with it."

Tom looked at her and made up his mind. He asked, "What's your name?"

"Tiffany," she replied. "Tiffany Cooke."

"Nice to meet you, Tiffany," he said. "My name's Tom. I'm the son of Independence."

CHAPTER TWELVE

Milk sat on the front porch steps and watched the sun rise over the eastern plain. He had skipped sleep the previous night, sick with worry for Tom and troubled by Mister Moment's call. Rest had eluded the giant but the gentle sunrise brought comfort to his troubled mind. Buttery light flowed over the endless grass — it stretched to the horizon and beyond — a soft breeze stirred the leaves on the nearby trees, and cheerful birdsong filled the air.

Then Gloria called from inside, "Charles! Charles, get in here!"

Milk stood as quickly as his massive frame allowed and walked to the front door. Gloria stood behind the couch, hands over her mouth. Their superfast son zoomed down the stairs and blinked into the living room before Milk could step inside.

"What's wrong, Mom?" asked David, embracing his mother. He blinked groggily, having just opened his eyes when his mother cried out. Gloria hugged her son, stepped back, glanced at her husband and pointed to the television.

All-American News showed a helicopter view of the Fuson's demolished house in Virginia. Milk saw that the DPS had been busy. The ground had been cleared, the house razed; vehicles — from police cars to semis — were clustered around the ruins. Milk knew how Uncle Sam operated. They would try to sweep this under the rug as quickly and quietly as possible. But apparently keeping it quiet wasn't possible at all.

Milk gaped at the headline crawling across the bottom of the screen.

Son of Independence?

He never expected the secret to be revealed, certainly not so soon. Tom's yearbook photo flashed up on the screen, followed by a series of pictures showing the late Megan Fuson and the long-dead Independence. In some of the photographs, Megan and Adam were young, together and obviously in love. Tom's face was placed on-screen next to a close-up of Independence; the resemblance was uncanny. The truth had been laid out for the whole world.

"How did — ?" Milk began to ask, but Gloria cut him off.

"It's horrible, Charles. Those … those monsters!" She grabbed the remote control and began to flip through the channels.

Every station seemed to be running the same story. There was barely even any election coverage; the Fusons were the most talked-about people in America.

Several stations showed footage of a weeping couple, somehow connected to Megan and Tom. The tall, bespectacled, man with iron-gray hair and a thin mustache had an arm around his petite, raven-haired wife. The text at the bottom of the screen identified them as Jack and Lisa Alexander of Westburg, Virginia. Gloria switched back to AAN and raised the volume.

"…body was found by his parents this morning," said Susan Reeves, host of AAN's early show, *All-American Morning*. The screen showed the image of a young dark-eyed man; Marcus Alexander, age sixteen. The label underneath called him the friend of Thomas Fuson, the alleged son of Independence.

"Police reports state that the body had been burned beyond recognition. The photo album was found in his backpack. Marcus Alexander had apparently retrieved it from the wreckage of the Fuson house. In light of his friendship with Thomas, it is reasonable to conclude that he knew the truth. His parents and other residents of Westburg deny having any knowledge about the Fusons, other than to say that they were valued members of the community."

The weathered face of an elderly man appeared on the screen. He wore a battered baseball cap and a week's worth of stubble. He looked at the camera and said, "They was good people an' I won't let nobody say no diff'ernt. That Megan was the kindest lady I ever knew. She come down to my store all the time an' knowed my whole family. She never did nothin' to deserve none of this. An' them boys were good'uns, not like these trouble-makin' youngins you hear about all the time."

Then a round-faced black woman appeared on the screen, identified as Christina Saylor, a teacher at Westburg School. Her soft voice was full of emotion, varying between sadness and outrage as she spoke.

"I have known Tom Fuson and Marcus Alexander for most of their lives. They've been students of mine and were pleasures to teach. I cannot believe that something like this would happen to them, or to Ms. Fuson."

A reporter asked Mrs. Saylor something, but the question was inaudible over the background noise.

"No," she replied. "We had no idea about that. We knew that Tom's father died some time ago but that's it. Tom was just a normal boy, polite and intelligent. His mother was active in the PTA. They certainly didn't deserve this. I'll also say that Marcus Alexander was an innocent bystander. Even if he knew his friend's secret, he did not deserve to be murdered."

"Do you think that the government killed Marcus Alexander?" the reporter asked. "What about the Department of Public Safety's announcement that he was murdered by a Posthuman terrorist?"

Mrs. Saylor shook her head and sighed, "I don't know who killed the boys or Ms. Fuson, and I won't dare speculate. All I know is that this is a horrible tragedy. Inexcusable."

Susan Reeves looked up as the feed switched back to the studio. She said, "Nevertheless speculation abounds … despite a lack of facts. Many of the residents of Westburg are convinced that the government was behind the deaths. Our AAN Live Action Polls indicate that a majority of our viewers feel the same way."

A pie chart filled the screen, with the numbers listed beside. Seventy-four percent of respondents believed that the government had killed the Fusons and Marcus. Eighteen percent believed the official explanation that Posthumans were behind the deaths. The remainder was undecided.

The broadcast cut back to the Alexanders, who stood in front of a crowd of journalists. Lisa Alexander had her arms wrapped around the photo album; her husband rubbed the bridge of his nose then fixed his glasses. Local cops flanked the grieving couple while a crowd of reporters and neighbors surrounded them.

Jack Alexander spoke in a hushed, halting voice, "My son ... died. He died to bring us the truth. My son ... I'm sorry. I... my son is dead."

Sheriff Jeb Ford stepped forward and gripped the weeping man's arm. The sheriff leaned in close and whispered something. Jack replied too quietly for the cameras to hear and returned to his wife's side.

Ford motioned to the reporters and let them know that he was about to speak. His deputies circled around the Alexanders, like a ring of bodyguards. The sheriff was a hefty, bald man with a red face and surprisingly high-pitched voice. He pulled a pair of index cards from his breast pocket, cleared his throat and mustered up all of his courage and dignity to make the announcement.

"Twenty minutes ago the Department of Public Safety issued a subpoena to my office demanding that I hand over Ms. Fuson's scrapbook by three o'clock this afternoon. I offered to give them copies or to have the pictures examined by a third party such as the University of Virginia. The Department of Public Safety refused and informed me that keeping the book would amount to a Federal violation, that I'd be withholding evidence and guilty of a whole list of offenses.

"My response was a prompt and immediate refusal of their terms. The citizens of Westburg won't be bullied or intimidated. Three of our own died last night and *we'll* get to the bottom of this. We are the ones who deserve an explanation, not this vague hooey they call press releases. They will not bury this. Not this time. I believe I have the support of my community, and that matters a lot more than having the support of bureaucrats in Washington."

The crowd cheered.

"Moving stuff," said Susan Reeves as her face reappeared on the screen. "But is he right? Should a sheriff ignore the laws he has sworn to uphold? Does the Department of Public Safety have the right to seal this case shut? And what does it mean that Independence, the greatest hero of all, may have had a son—only for that son to be murdered while still a teen? And how will these revelations affect the election? We'll discuss all this and more after a short word from our sponsors. This is Susan Reeves for All-American News, where we put the nation first. We'll be right back with more of your *All-American Morning*."

"Jesus Christ," muttered Milk as he shook his great head, lowered himself to his knees, and pulled his wife into his arms. "Come here, babe. It'll be okay."

"But, Dad … isn't this good?" David asked, confused by his father's melancholy reaction. "I mean, you saw those people, right? They're finally standing up."

"Maybe they are," replied Milk. "Or maybe they're just upset over their neighbors getting killed. Either way, I don't want to see more people hurt or locked up because of this. That poor kid."

"His parents," whispered Gloria, thinking of the misery etched into the expressions of Jack and Lisa Alexander. "I can't imagine…"

"What about the Posties locked up in Alaska? We could use this to help them. It's like the Boston Massacre. Your friends and that guy, Marcus, they could be like Crispus Attucks." David put his hand on his father's shoulder. "We should go there. We should help them. This is *it*. We've been hiding long enough. We need to act, Dad. Now's the time."

Milk rose to his feet and said, "No and no. You see that?" He pointed at the crowd on television. "They aren't on our side, not yet. They're just angry. And, besides, they aren't going to win. They aren't prepared for it."

"They could win with your help," said David.

"Oh, and how's that?" Milk cocked his head to the side. "You think I can beat Uncle Sam?"

David took a step back and stared, not sure of what to say. Finally, he whispered, "Of course you can. Nothing can hurt you. I can't believe that you're afraid of them. You have the power to make them change! But you're too damned scared to use it!"

"David!" Gloria gasped, her eyes bouncing between her husband and their eldest.

Milk turned toward his son. David took a step back, aware that he had challenged his father.

But the horned giant simply sighed. "Maybe you're right, son. Maybe I am scared."

Milk went to the front window. He gazed out at the gentle hills of his property and the expansive prairie beyond. The grass swayed in the breeze and puffy white clouds drifted lazily against the vibrant sky.

"I gave them a chance last night, the soldiers. I gave them the chance to stand down. Did I tell you that?" The giant looked back at his son. "They couldn't hurt me. All they could do was hurt Tom. They'd already killed Megan, and how much of a threat was she? Then they shot him. They could have let us escape, but they'd destroy what they want before they'd ever let it get away.

"I let them take Tom because he was dying. I knew it was wrong to let them take him, but I'd rather risk it than let him die. I gave them exactly what they wanted. Maybe I should've done that first. Maybe none of this would've happened. Megan would be alive, that neighbor kid—Mark or whatever—he'd be alive. Maybe you think I'm weak for saying that. Maybe you think I'm a coward for hiding all these years. After all, I'm invulnerable, right? You think I'm afraid of them, son?"

David stepped close and put a hand on his father's arm. "Dad, I … Of course not."

"I *am* afraid, son. I'm afraid for you, Nikki and Sean. Even for your mother. You're fast, but can you dodge *all* their bullets? Do you think you can run forever? They can't hurt me, but you?" Milk looked into his son's eyes. "I don't want to think about it. If something happened to you ... I don't even know what would happen to me."

David was shocked to see tears welling up in his father's enormous eyes. He was even more astonished to discover that he'd also begun to weep. His lifelong fantasies of revolution and heroism felt small and petty compared to his father's words. He'd always known that his father stayed hidden to protect the family, but now he *knew* it. Now, he understood.

Milk hugged his son, encasing him in those mighty arms. David stretched his own arms around his father's chest—as much as he could, anyway—and felt like a child again.

The giant stepped back and looked at his son. "You're right about one thing, though."

"What's that, Dad?" David wiped his eyes and blinked until his vision cleared.

"It is time to do something," said Milk.

"What do you mean, Dad? What are we going to do?"

"I need you to go upstairs and wake your sister. I've got a job for the two of you."

"Really?"

"Yeah. Maybe I am afraid for you guys, but I can't let that fear run our lives forever. Besides..." Milk trailed off.

"Besides, what?" asked David.

Milk gestured toward the second floor and said, "If you can live through waking up Sleeping Beauty, then you can probably survive anything."

The family sat around the dining room table for breakfast. Milk, of course, didn't have a chair. He wasn't exactly built for chairs, and they certainly weren't built for him. So he sat on the floor, with his knees under the head of the table and his rear on his heels, *seiza*-style. This had the advantage of allowing him to eat at a human-scaled table, and it put him closer to eye level with his family.

Gloria sat on Milk's right, with Sean to his left. Nikki was on the other side of Sean, with David across from his sister. Breakfast had been quieter than usual; Nikki was upset about being pulled out of bed so early, and David was lost in thought.

Sean was his normal, exuberant self. "Hey, Dad, can we go to the junkyard today?"

The junkyard was owned by old lady Wilder, their closest neighbor. Mrs. Wilder and her late husband had sold the land to Charles and Gloria and kept their secret all of these years. Milk and Nikki used the junkyard as a gym. Neither of them really needed exercise, but it felt good to stretch their limbs and smash old junkers. Sean liked to watch while they played wrecking crew; he dreamed of the day when he would be able to do the same.

"Not today," Milk replied. "I have to visit a few friends with Mister Kobar. And your siblings are going to Detroit."

"Detroit?" Nikki looked curiously at her father. "We gotta go to Detroit?" She turned to her brother who merely shrugged.

Sean pouted silently, and Gloria reached across the table and grabbed his hand.

"I tell you what, Half-Pint," she said. "I'll take you for a run later. Piggyback."

Sean's eyes grew wide and he grinned exuberantly, "Really? Awesome!"

"Yes sir," she replied. "Come help me with the dishes. These three need to talk."

"Okay," Sean sighed melodramatically at having to do the dishes but rose to give his mother a hand.

"Thanks for the grub, babe." Milk leaned forward and kissed his wife's cheek.

"Thanks, Mom," echoed David and Nikki. They carried their own dishes into the kitchen—and they all helped to carry away Milk's four plates, three bowls and the coffee pot he used for his morning Joe.

He stood and walked out into the living room. The TV was still on, with the sound muted, and AAN was running a special program showing photographs from Megan's album. Milk could not take his eyes away from the screen.

He clearly recalled those old days in the late Eighties, with

Megan and Adam hiding the romance from everyone. Well, almost everyone. Milk and Gloria were also youngish lovers back then. They'd been in on the secret along with a few other close friends. Everyone who'd known approved; the couple had been a perfect match.

Adam could go anywhere and do anything but would always be an outsider; Megan had lived most of her life within that amazing brain and often neglected the real world. He brought her out of her shell by sharing the wonders of Earth. She brought him out of *his* shell by giving by anchoring his humanity. They were better people with each other than they'd ever been apart.

Milk stared at an old picture of the couple, a shot of them walking in Paris. Adam—in jeans, a baggy jacket and big Eighties shades—smiled and held Megan's hand as they strolled down the Champs-Élysées. Their old friend Sophia had taken that picture, though the newsies couldn't possibly know that.

Milk remembered that trip. They'd all met in Switzerland; probably the day after that picture was taken. Megan joked that they were going to lose sight of Milk in the Alpine snow.

The next photo was from Adam's funeral. Milk had sat next to Megan on that miserable, godforsaken day. She struggled to remain composed, though nobody had been suspicious of her tears. The entire world mourned the loss of their champion. Even old Angus exuded something that might pass for sadness. Megan's small hand gripped Milk's forefinger throughout the service, and she wept against his gargantuan arm.

After the funeral, Megan had taken him aside and told him the secret.

"I'm pregnant, Charles. About four months along and I ... I don't know what to do." She buried her face in his chest and wailed uncontrollably for a long time.

"Shh," he had said, patting her back as softly as possible. "It'll be alright Megan. I'll do whatever it takes to protect you. Both of you."

Now, sixteen years had passed and Milk had failed. Megan was dead and Tom was in Doc Angus's hands. Yes, Milk had warned her against living under her own name, about not going into hiding when the Public Safety Act passed, but he'd still broken his promise. He'd been unable to protect them.

Tears rolled down his broad cheeks; he closed his eyes and tried to choke back the burning grief and icy self-recrimination. He still had a chance to save Tom. He would have to risk everything—would have to send his own children into danger—but he had sworn to do whatever it took. Now, he had to live up to his word.

"Daddy?" Nikki said, with a tremulous voice, as she stood in the doorway. "Daddy, are you okay?"

He opened his sad brown eyes. "Not really, Goober. But I will be."

His daughter raced forward and hugged him, squeezed him, as only she could—with her own inhuman strength.

David walked on Milk's left, with Nikki on the right. They had gone behind the barn and stood by the small creek that rolled past the rocky hills surrounding their home above the prairie.

"We have to rescue Tom," Milk said simply. "And I'm gonna need your help to do it."

His children stopped in their tracks. Milk couldn't help but snicker at their shocked expressions.

"Seriously?" gasped David.

Nikki narrowed her eyes incredulously. "But you're always telling us to lay low."

"Things change, Goober. I've always tried to protect you both, but it's time to face the truth."

"What truth?" they asked simultaneously.

"The truth that you're my kids—and your mother's—and that makes you a couple of serious badasses."

The siblings laughed and looked at each other, not sure whether their father was joking. Milk motioned for them to follow him and then led them to the side of the hill. He sat down, leaning on the gentle slope to look up at his kids for a change.

"So what do you need us to do," David asked. "You told me that you had a job for us, but you didn't explain what kind of job. I seriously don't think you want to storm ABRA tonight."

"Not tonight," agreed Milk. "But it's going to come to that soon enough."

"But," Nikki planted her feet and crossed her arms over her chest. "You said that kid—"

"Thomas. Tom Fuson," Milk said. "Not much of a kid; he's a bit older than you."

"Well, you said that he got shot in the chest," Nikki motioned toward the house. "The news keeps saying that he's dead. It may be too late to help him."

"Oh, he's not dead," answered Milk. "Matter of fact, he'll be on his feet today. But in about a week or so, they're gonna kill him."

"How could you know that?" David's brow creased in confusion. Then a realization blossomed in his eyes. "That phone call last night."

"Heh, guess you got a brain after all, Dave," Milk smirked. "Got that from your mother, obviously."

"So who was it? Don't make me guess," said David.

"Oh, you'd never guess, son. It was Mister Moment."

Nikki shook her head, as if to clear her ears. David's expression changed from curiosity to amazement.

"Mister Moment? The villain?" he exclaimed. "Wasn't he in that crazy cult back in the Seventies? The one that tried to destroy Washington?"

"He still is," replied Milk. "Least as far as I know. Still got the same girlfriend and she's what you'd call the prophet to his high priest. But never mind all that. That's not too important right now."

"But how can you trust him?" Nikki asked. "Why should you believe anything he says?"

Milk shrugged, "He's got no reason to lie, especially about this. His cult, the Children of Man, they had some ideas about Independence. For a while they thought that he was their messiah, no matter how much he denied it. Now, well, I guess they think the same about Tom."

"Holy shit," Nikki blurted. "Sorry, Dad."

Milk just chuckled, "No, I think that about says it. Moment and his people believe lots of holy shit. But like I said, that don't really matter. That's why I can trust him about this. For him, it's self-serving."

"But how does he know that Tom's alive?" Nikki asked. "I didn't know he could see the future. I thought he could, like, time travel or something."

"Kinda," Milk said. "He can't go backwards. They called it temporal alteration, but Doc Angus liked to come up with all sorts of fancy names for what we do. No, Moment can't see the future … but his girlfriend, Silent Sarah, she can. As much as anybody, anyway."

"Well, if she's silent how does she tell people about it?" Nikki pursed her lips and planted a fist on her hip.

"Hell if I know. Maybe she writes it down. Now quit sidetracking me with questions." Milk scowled mockingly at his daughter and continued. "Anyway, Moment said Tom's going to be alright … for another week. But they're gonna kill him while they still can. Then they'll clone him, and Moment says the clones are bad news. Whatever happens after that will destroy the world. He thinks it will, anyway. Moment's cagey and probably up to no good, but I believe him. Whatever Sarah saw scared the shit out of him. If Tom dies, then the show's over for the rest of us. Well, we're gonna stop that from happening. We're gonna save him."

The siblings glanced at each other again, unsure of how to react. All their lives they had wanted to follow in their parent's footsteps — to use their gifts for something, to be heroes — and now their chance had arrived. The future of the Earth was on the line and it was up to them to help save it. For the first time, they both wondered if they had what it took.

Milk stood up suddenly, and looked down at his children. His face showed a broad, entertained grin, like he could read their minds.

"Oh, yeah," Milk said. "We're not just gonna bust out Tom."

"We're not?" David asked.

"What do you mean?" Nikki added.

"We're gonna tear that place apart. We're gonna free every last prisoner," Milk's grin turned fierce. "We are going to finish ABRA, once and for all."

"Well, we've got a week," said David. "Where do we start?"

Milk motioned to his children and they all walked back toward the house. The sunlight was brilliant and warm, but the wind felt cool and refreshing. The air smelled fresh and alive, and the sea of grass danced under the bright blue sky.

"Detroit." Nikki glanced at her father. "That's what you said earlier, right?"

"Indeed," Milk replied.

"What's in Detroit?" David asked. "Other than bad neighborhoods and old factories?"

"Not what," answered Milk. "Who. You're going there to meet a Postie. A young guy named Michael Dawkins. I want you to recruit him."

"What's so special about this Mike guy?" Nikki raised an eyebrow curiously. She had a hard time imagining that the three of them needed help to destroy ABRA City.

"You'll see," Milk said. "The Old Man said he's almost as important as Tom. All I can say is that he's smart. Really smart."

"Smart?" Nikki wasn't convinced.

"Yeah, smart," rumbled Milk. "He's got brains, something this family seems to be a little short on … except your mother, of course. The Old Man says he can do just about anything with a computer and that's why we need him. Can't teleport through that force field, and even I can't bust it."

"Really?" Nikki was astonished that her dad couldn't break something. As far as she knew, he could smash anything.

"Hey, even I got my limits, Goober. One of the most important things you can do is figure out what you can do — and what you *can't* do. ABRA was really smart when they built that place. The Old Man says Michael Dawkins is smarter. You gotta convince him to lend us a hand. Or, um, a brain."

"Why us?" David wondered aloud. "Why don't you go talk to him?"

"Getting cold feet, son? Figured you'd be eager to get involved."

"I am, Dad. I'm just curious. I mean, you're *Milk*. Everybody knows you. I'd think any Postie would jump at the chance to work with you."

"Yeah, I am pretty amazing. I mean just look at this," Milk laughed, flexing his awesome muscles. His biceps alone massed more than most people. The sunlight danced on his alabaster flesh. "Some people got guns. I've got *cannons.*"

Nikki giggled and David just shook his head.

"Seriously Dad," he said. "Just doesn't seem like something you'd need help with."

"Number one: he's in the middle of the city. Not exactly the kinda place I can reach easily, even with Kobar's help," Milk explained. "Number two: he's eighteen. Figure he'd trust you two more than an old fart like me."

"Makes sense," David said. "Thanks, Dad. We won't let you down."

"You never do, son. Not often, anyway."

"When do you want us to go?" Nikki asked. "It's, what, nearly noon in Detroit?"

"Yeah, almost noon. I want you to go now," said Milk, pulling a sheet of paper from the back pocket of his immense blue jeans. The page was wrinkled but unfolded—the pocket was larger than the eight-by-eleven sheet. "Here's his address and some directions. The Old Man says that Mike lives beneath this building, so you might have to figure out a way in if he doesn't answer the door."

David took the paper, glanced at it, then folded it and placed it in his own back pocket. Nikki grinned from ear to ear and jumped up to hug her father's thick neck.

"Thank you, Daddy!" She kissed his cheek. "This means so much to us!"

"I know," Milk said.

David motioned over his shoulder, and Nikki hopped up onto her big brother's back. She wrapped her legs around his waist, her arms around his neck. David looked back at his father, nodded once, and then they were gone.

The grass parted in their wake, and a cloud like a dust devil rose from David's feet. He broke the sound barrier before they reached the horizon.

Milk kept his eyes on the east for a while. "Means a lot to me too, Goober."

CHAPTER THIRTEEN

Tom found a brand new toothbrush in an opened package by the sink. His keepers had also left an electric razor, although shaving wasn't really a necessity to the mostly beardless young man. However, all of the other personal hygiene products apparently belonged to his new roommate. He shook his head at the strawberry-vanilla scented shampoo but figured it was better than nothing.

"It's okay for this thing to get wet?" Tom called through the door, rubbing the cold steel plug behind his left ear.

"The implant? Yeah, it's waterproof," came Tiffany's soft voice from the other side. "Just don't mess with it or anything."

"I can't believe this little thing stops people like us." Tom muttered incredulously. Such a small hunk of metal didn't seem very threatening.

"That 'little thing' is full of microscopic bullets or something. They say it can mush the brains of even invulnerable Posties. The topside prisoners don't know it can blow up. They're just told it's a tracker. I've only ever talked to the ones who got sent down here, and they didn't know what it really does."

Tom wasn't surprised at all. ABRA and the DPS would do anything to maintain control of the Posties. Marcus had said that exact thing as they walked home from school the previous day, but he hadn't really gotten through.

Now Tom understood all too well. The DPS agents had no second thoughts about making a preemptive strike with heavy weapons, despite the fact that his capture had been their goal.

They introduced themselves by firing at rocket at Milk. They weren't worried at all about endangering Tom or killing his mother.

Mom.

Tom leaned over the sink and tried hold back the memories. But all he could see was his mother, dead in the dirt. He closed his eyes, lowered his head and tried to bury the pain, tried to force it down, lock it away.

He was fine, that's what he thought, what he forced himself to think. He was fine. He'd survive. He just need needed to pull himself together. He needed to think about something else. Just think about something else.

Opening his eyes, Tom looked up at the mirror and gasped at the reflection. His eyes had changed!

They had always been hazel-green, but now they were metallic gold. From a distance, they didn't even seem real—gold-chrome contact lenses, obviously artificial—but up close all of the little details and textures of the human eye were apparent. Tom pressed his face to the mirror and pulled his eyelids apart. His pupil shrank in the light.

"Are you okay?" Tiffany asked. "Is everything all right?"

"Yeah ... I, uh, I just noticed my eyes."

"Your eyes?"

"They're gold now. They look like metal. Like my father's. They weren't like this ... before."

Tiffany responded with a giggle. "I didn't even notice. Guess I'm just used to this stuff. My very first roommate was a giant rock monster ... well, he looks like a monster. Your eyes aren't weird compared to that."

"I guess not," Tom replied. He had already observed that his definition for the word weird needed to be revised.

✪   ✪   ✪

After his shower, Tiffany announced that they were going on a tour of MegaMax. She, of course, would be the guide.

"There are twenty-four inmates," she explained, standing between Tom and the door. "Well, twenty-five, now that you're here. And then there are the three of us — me and the other Posties that help Security when they need it — Tank, Julio and me. Julio was Blackout, a hero down in Miami, but he doesn't talk much. Julio can knock people out and shut down their powers, but that doesn't work with everybody. I can negate *anybody's* powers. Sometimes I wonder how they ever ran this place without me."

She opened the door and motioned for Tom to follow.

Their room was at the end of a short hallway — white tile, metal walls and fluorescent light — with three other rooms and a sliding steel door at the far end. It looked like an elevator, but there was only one button on the keypad. Two of the other rooms were vacant with opened doors; the furthest room was closed. A placard on the door named the occupant McNamara, F., and below the name were several lines of jumbled letters and numbers. He glanced back at their door, and saw a similar board with information about Tiffany.

Tom pointed at McNamara's board and asked, "What's all that?"

"Oh, that's Fiona's room. If the door's shut she's not in there or she's sleeping."

"No," Tom pointed at the nameplate. "All that other stuff."

"Oh. It's for the guards more than anything," Tiffany pointed at the top line. "That's her identification number. She was one of the first prisoners."

"What about the rest of it?"

"I don't know what Protocol Four means," explained Tiffany. "I think it's the plan Security made to stop her if she ever goes off."

Tom asked, "What's she do?"

Tiffany pointed at the middle line and said, "That's what this means; ambient energy absorption and conversion — pretty normal stuff. She absorbs light, heat and stuff. Kinda like what you said happened to you."

"What about that?" Tom indicated a line with larger characters than most of the others.

Tiffany laughed, "Oh that just means she's a career felon with violent tendencies."

"Didn't you say that she's like a mother to you? A career felon with violent tendencies?"

"We're all felons here, Tom. Just by being Posthuman. Fiona, though ... she's got some history. I can't wait for you to meet her."

"You don't have to wait, sweet pea," said a raspy female voice. "I'm right here."

Tom looked up and saw a woman standing in the now-open metal door. It wasn't an elevator at all—beyond the doorway was a large cafeteria, the hub of MegaMax—but he barely noticed. He and the new arrival eyed each other. There was something about her. She was disturbingly familiar, but he couldn't put a finger on it.

Obviously, she was the infamous Fiona.

She wore pale blue scrubs—the inmate uniform in MegaMax—with the pants hacked into rough shorts. She was very tan with short, spiky, brown hair. She was short, too, maybe an inch taller than Tiffany, but had a hard, athletic physique, powerful thighs and rather broad shoulders. She had angular features, oddly violet eyes and appeared to be older than thirty—just how much older, Tom couldn't guess. Posthumans usually age slower than normal people, but it's different with each one.

"Heya, Fee," Tiffany squealed. "This is Tom Fuson, he—"

"I didn't know his name, but I know who he is," interrupted Fiona.

"How do you know me?" asked Tom suspiciously. Tiffany frowned at both of them.

Fiona took a step closer. "You can't hide those shiny eyes, boy, or that pretty face of yours. Not from people that actually knew your father. And—except for kids like my sweet pea, here—we *all* knew Independence."

Tom blanched and backed away from the woman.

"Don't look so surprised, boy," Fiona whispered with a playfully malicious tone. "I danced with your daddy long before you were born. Think I wouldn't recognize his spitting image? Your old man and me, we go way back. Matter of fact, I used to be famous. Maybe you heard of me. Once upon a time, my name was Flamechylde. They used to call me a villain."

Fiona brushed past Tom and entered her room. Tiffany began to say something, but Fiona slammed the door in their faces.

Tiffany pursed her lips and sighed, "Come on. I'll talk to her later."

They walked slowly through the sliding door and into the cavernous space of the cafeteria. Aside from the scale, it resembled any other prison mess hall—not that Tom had ever seen one before, unless TV shows count. MegaMax held less than thirty Posthumans, but there were seats for several hundred and scores of tables.

The ceiling, floor and walls were smooth white-and-blue tile, the buffet counter and kitchen equipment was all stainless steel; the tables and stools were all bolted to the floor. Tom's hallway was one of four on that side of the cafeteria. The far wall also had four identical, elevator-like doors, while on the left was a large corridor with a gigantic metal door—at least four feet thick—retracted into the ceiling. Numerous cameras gazed down from above.

No other inmates were in sight, only a few cooks worked in the back, and eight bored guards stood in pairs around the room. The guards wore something like steel riot armor, with metal helmets and big, reflective goggles. They carried an array of odd-looking gear on their belts and harnesses—a large pistol, a heavy baton and assorted gadgets. Tom thought prison guards didn't usually carried guns, but things must work a little differently here.

"The food's not bad, I guess," said Tiffany. "Maybe I'm just used to it. Wanna get something to eat?"

"No," replied Tom. "I'm not hungry." He suddenly realized that he'd eaten nothing since lunch at school the previous day, but felt no interest in food. *Hmm.*

"Well, if you want something, just ask the staff. There's always something ready. There's breakfast stuff—usually eggs and sausage and pancakes—and sandwiches and salads and fruit and whatever they're making for dinner. They always have the three meals ready since some of us are nocturnal. Dessert kinda sucks, though. It's usually just pudding or these nasty little bricks they call brownies."

"This place is huge," Tom said and motioned to all of the tables. "Do they really need all this space for us?"

"Not really. I think they made it bigger than they needed. You know, just in case. Fiona thinks they're scared the Aegis virus will mutate again and start infecting more people."

Tom pointed at the rows of doors and asked, "Do all of the prisoners live right here?"

"No. I guess you'd call these four halls the prison hospital. But they let some of us stay here, instead of in the cells. I get to stay in there—I guess you do, too—and a couple of inmates earned privacy through good behavior."

Tom snickered sarcastically, "Is that how Flamechylde got her room? Good behavior?"

"I'm sorry she was kinda rude. She's always been so nice to me. I think you'd like her if you got to know her. She's a good friend."

Tom shrugged and remained silent. He knew Fiona's reputation—she had indeed been famous in the decades before his birth—and didn't care whether or not they became friends.

Tiffany squirmed uncomfortably for a few seconds, then squeezed his arm and said, "Come on. Let's go say hi to the neighbors."

She led him out of the cafeteria and down the oversize hall. Several cameras swiveled to keep them in view.

CHAPTER FOURTEEN

The warehouse appeared abandoned, with old planks nailed over busted windows and heavy, rusting chains on the doors. Scraggly weeds poked up from the cracked pavement, and pigeons cooed in their nests on the crumbling facade.

The entire neighborhood showed the same decay. Rotting wasteland was all that remained of this once-thriving center of industry. The low shroud of ashen clouds in the cool October sky seemed fitting, looming over the graveyard of America's past.

The siblings had been in the parking lot for a good twenty minutes. They'd circled the building and tried every door several times. The warehouse was locked up tight, and nobody answered Nikki's forceful pounding on the old metal doors.

"Hello! Michael Dawkins! Is anyone here," she called, and her clear voice echoed in the dead, empty neighborhood. She snarled with frustration and paced back to the parking lot.

David stood, staring at the sheet of directions. The young man seemed to be trying to find something he may have missed — despite having read the scrawl ten thousand times or so in the past few minutes.

"Jesus, Davy, where is this guy?"

David looked up from the sheet and shrugged. "I don't know. This is the place. It's gotta be."

"Or maybe Dad's wrong, and he's not here," she said. "Doesn't look like anyone's been here in years."

"The Old Man gave Dad the directions. They gotta be right."

Nikki scoffed under her breath and scowled at the warehouse. She'd been thrilled that their father sent them on an official mission—more or less—but now it felt like they'd begun a wild goose chase. She grumbled a curse and kicked a rock. The stone flew up like a bullet and shattered against the building, leaving a deep gouge and spider-web cracks in the masonry.

"Come on, Nik, cut it out. Last thing we need is for you to attract attention."

"Shut up," Nikki barked at her brother. "Nobody's around here anyway."

"We need this guy's help. Don't want one of your tantrums to make us look bad."

"One of my... you asshole," Nikki wheeled around and got right in her brother's face—or as close as she could, on her tiptoes and still seven inches shorter. "I do *not* throw tantrums, and there is *nobody* in there!"

"You don't know that, Nik," David replied.

"Like hell," she sneered. She turned and pointed at the warehouse. "That place is as dead as your love life. Nobody's been here since the Twentieth Century. This whole place is a fucking ghost—"

Then Nikki saw something—a brief red flash from within a shadowed cleft on the top of the building. Without a word she leaped—one thrust of her powerful legs propelling her through the air—and landed with a thud in the deep dust on the roof. Dozens of pigeons flew away, startled and chattering.

"Jesus Christ," David muttered and ran up the wall, briefly ignoring gravity thanks to his incredible velocity. He kicked up a cloud of dirt as he stopped next to his sister. "What the hell are you doing?"

But David saw the answer before he finished asking the question. Nikki slammed her fist into the edge of the roof—pulverizing the old bricks—and pulled out a device that had been hidden within. It was a small security camera, with a Wi-Fi transmitter and a power cable that sparked when Nikki ripped it free.

"It looks like Dad was right," Nikki said. "Somebody's here, for sure."

"Told you," said David. "Dad wouldn't send us out here for nothing."

Nikki did not reply. Instead, she glanced around the rooftop. Piles of brittle leaves and grime covered the place. A metal hatch on the far side was the only way up there—for normal people—and Nikki made up her mind to go check it out.

David beat her to it and put his foot on the hatch. He shook his head, "Uh-uh. We're not breaking in on this guy. Dad said—"

"Dad said we might have to find a way in," Nikki bent down and grabbed the hatch. "And I am sick of standing around with my thumb up my ass. Now get out of my way."

"No," said David. He folded his arms across his chest. "Let's try and figure something out before we go busting in. You want down there, you gotta go through me."

"If you say so," Nikki said and ripped the hatch from its hinges. She pulled the heavy metal lid out from under David's foot—he stumbled but steadied himself—and tossed it aside. They both glanced down, past the rusted steel ladder, into the dark interior. Nikki looked up and smiled. "You coming with? Or do I gotta do all the work around here?"

Then she hopped inside and fell to the floor below. David whispered a string of expletives and slid down the ladder.

Dim light leaked through the boarded-up windows, casting silvery beams in the floating motes of filth. Cobwebs covered the old equipment—some kind of conveyor system—and rats scurried away from the intruders.

"So damn disgusting," Nikki hissed as she looked around.

"Hey, it was your idea."

"Please," Nikki replied. "I'm gonna blame this one on Dad."

The warehouse had obviously been undisturbed for years. Thick dust caked the floor, and the air reeked of mold and ancient oil. Nikki thought the place might be abandoned after all, and then David tugged on her sleeve.

"Check it out," he pointed down and to the left.

Footprints in the crud made a path to a small door—Nikki realized that her plummeting entrance would have erased tracks nearer to the ladder. The door bore a faded not-an-exit sign but had no other identifiers.

David tried the handle and found it locked. He began to say something, but Nikki brushed past him and simply ripped the door free of its hinges. Beyond it was a stairway—leading down to the basement

"Well," David said. "That's one way to do it."

"WWMD, Davy," was Nikki's only reply as they walked down the stairs.

"Say huh?"

Nikki smirked at her brother. "I always ask myself the same question, when I don't know what to do. What would Milk do?"

David grinned back, "Knowing Dad? He'd smash something."

"Damn straight. Always works for me."

They stepped into the blackness. The meager light from above barely helped, and the entire room was obscured by the darkness.

"Should've brought a flashlight," David said.

"No joke. Remind me to buy an equipment belt next time we're at the mall."

"You serious?"

Nikki raised an eyebrow. "Maybe. Why not?"

David was silent for a moment. "I want a costume. A uniform."

"Like Mom and Dad used to wear?"

"Yeah," said David. "I'm Shockwave, dammit."

"Oh, Davy," Nikki put her arm around him and rested her head against his shoulder. "You know what Mom and Dad would say."

"Yeah," he said. "But I'm nineteen for crying out loud—old enough to decide what I want to do with my life. I don't want to waste it hiding on a farm. I want to be a hero, Nik. I was born to be a hero."

Nikki hugged her brother and kissed his cheek. "You are a hero."

"Not yet, I'm not."

"Well, you are to me," Nikki said. She walked away from David and took a few steps deeper into the basement. "You always stop me from doing stupid things."

"I always *try* to stop you from doing stupid things."

"Exactly," Nikki giggled. "You face impossible odds, but you never give up. If that doesn't make you a hero then I—"

A heavy weapon fired and struck Nikki's torso. The blast knocked her off her feet.

Then she felt a tremendous jolt and a rush of hot wind. The world blurred and explosions rocked the warehouse. Dust filled the air, and Nikki fell on her back … at the top of the stairs. David stood beside her, covering his ears.

Nikki was used to being zoomed around by her big brother and realized right away that he'd carried her out of the basement at superhuman speed. She rubbed her side—that was the first time she'd ever been shot, and while it didn't really hurt, it sure as hell stung—and looked around. "What the hell was that?"

"Booby trap," David explained, reaching down to help her up. "I took care of it."

"Thanks," she said, climbing back to her feet. "Told you that you're a hero."

David grinned, and they went back down the stairs. Smoke filled the basement, but it wasn't too bad. Small fires helped illuminate the small room.

Nikki saw a crude, multibarreled gun turret by the far wall. David really had taken care of it; the weapon had been reduced to a burning stump. There was another door on the far wall. The siblings looked at each other.

"Think it's a trap?" asked Nikki.

"Of course it's a trap," answered David.

"What should we do?"

"That's easy, Nik. We do what Milk would do."

"Sounds good to me," Nikki laughed. Then stopped and snapped her fingers. "I've got it! You go open the door, and I'll throw that cannon through it."

David shook his head and scoffed; "Now *that's* a plan."

"You got a better one?"

"Nah. Besides, I got the last one. We'll do this one your way."

"Trust me, it's a good plan," Nikki said as she ripped the broken turret from its moorings and raised it over her head.

David walked over to the door and grabbed the handle. He tried it; this one was unlocked. "You ready?"

"Yup."

David turned the handle, and light flooded the room as the door opened. Nikki saw a long, dingy hallway but did not hesitate. She hurled the wreckage with all of her might, and it flew down the hall before blowing through a wall at the far end.

And nothing else happened.

David raised an eyebrow at his sister and snickered. She shrugged and raised her palms.

That's when the robots attacked.

Three speeding forms shot down the hall, aimed at Nikki. One of them sailed through the air like an arrow. It resembled an oversize needle with four blurring, dragonfly wings.

The two on the ground were both the size of little red wagons, with low profiles and three razor-edged wheels that sparked on the concrete floor.

Nikki snorted with simmering fury. All she wanted to do was to find this Mike Dawkins guy and talk to him. Now? Not only had the guy not answered the door—not only had they been forced to creep around in the most disgusting, decrepit warehouse ever— not only had one of this boy's toys fucking *shot* her—now, she was being attacked by killer robots.

Nikki had enough of this bullshit.

She roared incoherently and lunged at the closest bot. They were fast, but she was faster and caught it by the outer wheel. The spinning blade dug into the palm of her right hand, but it didn't break her skin. She slammed the robot against the floor—two, three, four times—until the wheels were utterly demolished and the gyroscopic motors buzzed uselessly.

Right about then, Nikki noticed the second robot heading straight for her. It was about three feet from her face.

David exploded into view. He held the formerly-flying needle in his right hand and stabbed through the attacking robot so swiftly that Nikki only saw an afterimage.

She slipped and plopped down—right on her ass—and started to laugh.

"You okay?" David asked and extended a hand to his sister.

"Oh, yeah. Just look at us," Nikki said as David helped her back up. She laughed again. "Here we are, crawling around in an underground lair, up against killer robots and booby traps—it's like we're in one of Mom and Dad's stories."

David smiled, "This is our story now, Nik."

Nikki beamed at her brother. "Yes, it is. Let's go find the bad guy."

"I'm not a bad guy," said a soft voice from the lit corridor. The startled siblings looked up as the speaker stepped into view.

CHAPTER FIFTEEN

"Are we really going to let him wander around down there? You saw how McNamara reacted," grumbled Captain Holly, his dark face half hidden in the shadows of the surveillance room. He pointed at the wall of monitors. On screen, Fiona paced around her room, obviously agitated. Her body shimmered with a dim, violet luminescence.

"No, Captain Holly, we are not," said Doctor Angus. "*I am.*"

"The other prisoners might kill him, Doctor. With all due respect, sir."

Angus glanced at Holly. The soldier was obviously unconcerned about Tom Fuson's well being; his only concern was the security of the prison. Still, the doctor admired the hulking officer's attempt at tact; maybe there was some hope for the man, despite his stubborn habit of questioning orders. "I do not believe any of the residents are capable of killing him. Particularly with Miss Cooke as his chaperone ... and your own soldiers standing watch."

Holly remained silent, but his broad shoulders seemed to tense. He turned away from the doctor and locked his eyes on the monitors. The lanky young man and the red-haired girl were just approaching the entrance to the cellblocks.

"Is there a problem, Captain?"

"No, sir. I have complete faith in your judgment, sir." The soldier did not look back at Angus as he spoke.

"Of course you do," said the doctor with barely restrained antipathy. "But you do have concerns, don't you? I am not foolish enough to ignore your concerns, Captain Holly."

"I would never suggest that you are foolish, sir," Holly replied through gritted teeth. He paused for a moment and tried to arrange his thoughts so as not to offend the Chief Administrator of ABRA. Then Holly said, "It's the girl, sir. I'm … concerned that it may not be safe to allow them to be alone."

Angus explained, "Miss Cooke has been obedient and helpful since her arrival. I hope that some of that might rub off on young Mister Fuson. At the very least, she can weaken the boy if he gets out of hand."

"If she wants to," said Holly. Then he hastily added, "Sir."

Angus raised an eyebrow and asked, "You feel that she may disobey such an order?"

"It's possible," the captain eyeballed his superior. "They may form a relationship that compromises her loyalty. If she is loyal at all."

"I am counting on that possibility, Captain. Not that she may disobey, of course, but that they may form a romantic or sexual relationship. If the boy is anything like his father, then he is particularly vulnerable to such passions. Why else would I have them sleep in the same room?"

"Sir?" Holly's forehead creased in bafflement.

Angus smiled coldly, "If the boy presents a problem, then she will be our leverage. Believe me when I say that there is only one way to control Thomas Fuson, and that way is through the people he loves."

"Are you saying that we threaten her if things get out of hand, sir?"

"No, Captain," Angus replied. "We will threaten her to keep things *in* hand. She is expendable. He is not. Not yet."

Holly nodded and turned back to the monitor. He didn't want the old man to see his expression.

✪   ✪   ✪

Tiffany led Tom down the main passageway; it was only fifty feet long and ended at a crossing hall. Arrows on a sign showed that the security desk and entrance were to the left, and Cellblock A was on the right. Tom started to go that way, but Tiffany grabbed his arm and pulled him to the left.

A short walk brought them to another corner; this one was marked with directions to the entrance and Cellblock T. Tiffany led him the way toward block T, and they entered the first in a series of hallways. Surprisingly, it was boring, kind of a letdown.

Some of the halls were straight; others zigzagged. Some of them were only fifteen feet long; others stretched on for fifty yards. Tiffany explained that all of them were separated by thick steel doors—as they walked under one. They were nothing more than blocks of steel and weighed at least twelve tons, rigged to fall in emergencies, isolating the cellblocks.

"The big ones are a lot heavier," she said. "The one in the cafeteria is supposed to weigh two hundred tons. They call them blast doors, which I think is all kinds of cool."

There were twenty cellblocks in total, with thirty cells in each block. MegaMax had six hundred cells for less than thirty prisoners. Blast doors blocked the entrances to thirteen of the cellblocks, which still left more than two hundred rooms available.

This abundance of space troubled Tom; there were only about three hundred Posties in America, the majority of which were already in custody, whether down in MegaMax or up above in the town. ABRA would never need this much room. Why didn't they keep all of the Posties down here? There was plenty of space and nearly airtight security.

He didn't ask Tiffany about it; he just tried to pay attention to everything she said—and everything that he saw—while they continued the tour. He thought about Marcus, who always said that the smallest detail is often the most important. Tom wondered what his friend would think about this place.

The cells lined up in long rows on both sides of the long blocks. They had heavy doors with thick, metal bars—though only a few were closed—and an interior wall that blocked the beds and toilets from view.

Libraries, gyms and various recreational rooms were scattered randomly throughout the maze. Cameras stared down from the ceiling at frequent intervals. Groups of guards roamed the cellblocks. Some of them wore enormous, heavily armored exoskeletons that Tiffany called APEs. Those things looked like they could take on Milk—and they all paid attention to Tom.

Some of the prisoners walked around, chatting. Others sat in small groups played cards, board games or even chess. Some watched movies in comfortable-looking entertainment rooms. They barely reacted to Tom and Tiffany, though a few glanced at the passing youths.

The inmates were as varied as only Posties can be.

One little guy had big eyes, bigger ears, and patagia, flaps of skin connecting his thin chest and too-long arms, like a flying squirrel. His name was William something or other, but everyone called him Billy the bat boy. Tom had seen him in the news, but didn't know anything about him.

Another Postie wore something that resembled a spacesuit; a dim, blue light shined in the inky blackness of the dark faceplate. Tom wondered if the suit was there to protect the Postie, or if the guy wore it to protect everyone *else*.

A totally bald, green-skinned woman with glowing white eyes and short, curving tusks strode purposefully down the hall. She said hello but kept walking.

A very muscular man with reflective bronze skin stopped dead in his tracks and stared, but he said nothing. He practically pressed against the wall, gaping as they passed.

Tom only recognized a few of his new neighbors. The tall, skinny black guy with silver hair and eyes was Jace Wyatt, a mercenary known as Razer. He was pretty famous. That crazy survivalist Clive Bingham was in MegaMax, too; his trial had been televised, so anyone would have recognized him.

The former hero Blackout had been the leader of the East Coast Alliance, so of course Tom knew him. The government crowed for a month after they caught him in 2007. He sat on the floor of his cell, alone. He made eye contact with Tom, but turned away.

The round-faced blond, Ashley Lang, had made the news two years earlier—after she destroyed a mall in Houston during a spat with her boyfriend. She'd apparently gotten over it, because Tom and Tiff caught her making out with a towering wall of hair and muscle in one of the libraries. The big fur ball might have been one of the bruisers from Mister Moment's cult, but Tom wasn't sure.

"Where are the real bad guys?" he asked as they entered another long hall. "Like Mister Moment, King Kaos or Miss Information? Where are the heroes? Is Blackout the only one?"

"The strong ones, the smart ones, they never got caught. Heroes and villains, both; they just hid after the crackdown. And lots of them got killed when they didn't hide."

"Like Stonewall."

Tiffany nodded, "Like Stonewall and Invictus, the Blue Berserker, Trebuchet, Bad Girl, Heavyweight, Diomedes Smith, Mister E, Raptoress and a bunch more. I've heard all the stories. Those people are saints down here. Anybody who went down fighting the Department of Public Safety earned a get-into-heaven-free card according to most of the neighbors."

"But not you?"

She shook her head. "No. I think they're pretty stupid for fighting back. Milk knew how serious the government was, so he stayed under the radar where he can do some real good. The guards all say they have weapons that can kill even him. So I think it's better for him to hide. He can actually help people that way. Everyone says that he helps run the underground railroad and keeps lots of us safe and free."

"I think he does. Mom said she knew people who hid Posties, and..." Tom trailed off, He saw soldiers firing their weapons at Milk. He felt the heat of the ADS; saw his mother on the ground. Smoke wafted up from her head.

Tiffany noticed where Tom's thoughts had wandered. She nudged him with her elbow. "Prepare yourself. We're going to Cellblock A, the final stop on the tour. There are only two prisoners there right now, but they're special ones."

"How special?" They rounded the corner to the final cellblock, and Tom walked straight into a boulder that filled the entrance. He yelped, belatedly threw his hands up in surprise, took a too-quick step back and stumbled over his own feet.

"Saw-ree," boomed the boulder in a sluggish, rolling bass. Vibrations of the voice buzzed through the floor.

"It's okay, Tank. It was an accident," Tiffany laughed and put a hand on Tom's shoulder.

"H'lo, Tiff-nee." The stone giant said nothing else. He merely glanced at Tiffany, then tilted his blocky head to the side and stared at Tom with those unnervingly human eyes.

Tom asked, "Your old roomie?"

Tiffany nodded her head and grinned. "Yup. When I first came here. They put us together so I'd be safe from the neighbors. I was only twelve. They told Tank to protect me. He always did, right?"

"Prow-tek Tiff-nee. Mm. Friend."

"Always friends," Tiffany beamed at the craggy colossus and made the introduction. "Tank, this is our new friend, Tom. Tom, say hi to Tank."

"Hi, Tank."

"H'lo, Tom. Mm. Know Tom. *Met* Tom."

Tiffany looked at the young man. He shook his head and shrugged. She placed a hand on Tank's tremendous arm and asked, "When did you meet Tom?"

"Lass night. Made'm bet-ta. Mm. Look bet-ta now."

"Yes, Tank. Tom is better now." She looked at the young man, raising one eyebrow.

Tom shook his head and whispered, "Made me better?"

The stone titan shifted on his feet and knuckles and rumbled, "Blue light. Take'm to blue light. Ree-ak-tow. Make'm bet-ta. Tom bet-ta. Know Tom. Know In-deep-denz."

"Independence?" gasped Tom. "I'm not Independence." He shot Tiffany a questioning look, but she did not notice. She was staring at Tank; this was the chattiest she'd ever seen him.

"Mem-burr Tom faa-thurr. Mm. Was friend, In-deep-denz. Tom is In-deep-denz, now." Tank nodded once and turned away.

He had apparently grown tired of speaking and ignored them until they gave up and entered Cellblock A.

"Jesus, do I really look that much like Independence?"

"I don't know," replied Tiffany. "I think it's the eyes."

Tom saw that these cells had no privacy walls—and also no bars or doors. Then he noticed the subtle sheen of force fields on the faces of the two occupied cells. These were merely class one containment fields, since each cell had independent generators. Tom knew nothing about force fields, but he was about to receive an education.

He started to ask Tiffany about it—why this block used force fields instead of bars—but a sibilant voice from the closer inhabited cell interrupted him.

"I don't need to see your eyes to know who you are, boy. You have the stench of that alien bastard oozing from your pores. You're *his* bastard. I can smell it," hissed the low, breathy whisper.

Tiffany rolled her eyes and snapped, "Shut up, Vaughn."

They stepped in front of the cell, and another strange sight startled Tom. The prisoner was mostly hidden in the darkness of his cell, submerged in a large metal tub that was full of stagnant, brown water. The tub was the cell's only furnishing. A carrion-and-waste stench passed through the ventilation system. It permeated Tom's sinuses and stung his eyes.

"Nice to see you, too, you delicious little bitch," hissed the inmate, who rose from the water. Tom Fuson saw Vaughn Gregory—the most feared serial killer of the Twentieth Century, the Behemoth of the Bay—for the first time.

At seven-and-a-half feet, he wasn't as large as Tank or Milk, but he was grotesquely obese, with a vast, swinging paunch, and jiggling fat rolls at his neck and joints. Green-gray, crocodilian plates and scales covered much of his body, except for his lower face, sagging belly, dangling genitals and swollen inner thighs. At those locations, the disgustingly pink, slimy skin had an uneven pebbly texture and many deep stretch marks. His fat neck and scaled torso possessed disturbing gill slits. His chest rose and fell, and the ragged gills opened with each breath, revealing the moist pink interior and the thorny rakers within.

Vaughn's square head had heavy, ridged brows over pale yellow, serpentine eyes. Instead of lips, he had a short, broad muzzle with shark-like rows of conical, uneven teeth, visible even when his mouth was closed. His nose had devolved to simple holes on the front of his snout; he had no ears. Tom thought that the Behemoth resembled a mash-up of the worst features of men, reptiles and fish.

Vaughn placed his right hand on the force field—his palm was nearly a foot wide with curved six-inch claws on thick, powerful, webbed fingers. The field sizzled at his touch; the Behemoth exhaled with a sound like pleasure as the electrical charge flowed through his body.

"Ooh," he said with an aroused tone to his snakelike whisper. "Maybe I should step out and have a taste. I bet you'd like that, wouldn't you?" A long, forked tongue slithered out of his maw and wagged at Tiffany.

"Back off you fucking freak," said Tom, moving between the Behemoth and the girl.

"Freak? Freak! Call me a freak, you alien motherfucker!" Vaughn's voice rose from a reptilian hiss to a wordless roar of primal wrath. He slammed into the force field—a detonation of sparks threw him backward. He landed on the edge of the tub, yelled again and crumpled the metal lip with his fearsome claws. Some of the revolting bathwater splashed out and spread across the floor. When it touched the force field, the water exploded in a cloud of steam and jagged bolts of electricity climbed the field to the ceiling.

Vaughn's eyes narrowed, his nostrils flared, and a spiteful sneer spread across his feral muzzle. Tom saw the many rows of those savage teeth. The Behemoth raked his claws down the side of the tub, tearing through the metal. Two hundred gallons of filthy bathwater rushed forward, into the force field, vaporizing in an explosion of steam and sparks. The pulsing energy and thick, reeking vapor obscured Tom's view.

Then the Behemoth rushed through the fog, slamming against the force field again—and again, and again. He pressed his entire body against the flashing wall of energy. It clung to him, stretching like a sheet of plastic wrap, as electricity crawled across his scaly hide. The Behemoth bellowed with demonic ferocity and pushed even harder against the wavering field of light.

Tom saw Tank lumbering toward them out of the corner of his eye, but what happened next happened too quickly for anyone to react.

The force field collapsed with an explosive eruption of power. The Behemoth burst through it and struck Tom with a vicious backhand. The blow hurled the boy sixty feet down the cellblock, past Tank, through the doorway and into the corridor. He crashed into the far wall, a meteor of flesh and bone. The impact shattered the alloy paneling, and dust filled the air.

CHAPTER SIXTEEN

JJ Joyce and Sol Beck sat on the roof with Madison, Vanessa and the shapeshifter, Anon. Nobody knew Anon's true name, appearance, or gender. It insisted that it had none. And, yes, Anon preferred to be referred to as *it*, not he or she. Neither term really applied; Anon changed genders far more often than most people change clothes. That day, it had taken the form of some old comedian, a little guy with a big nose. JJ could not remember the guy's name, but it was right on the tip of his tongue.

He'd invited everyone to come up to the roof after lunch. Madi's eavesdropping had given him some ideas, and he wanted to bounce them off the people he trusted. JJ had been surprised that the list—when he thought about it—was so terribly short. And that it included Vanessa.

The others were the only obvious choices. Sol was JJ's best friend, Anon was one of Sol's, and Madi knew everything anyway. Those three were bound to be invited to the conversation.

The more JJ thought about it, though, the more he realized that Vanessa didn't seem to have any friends of her own. She was probably closer to him and Sol than anyone else in the prison; they certainly talked to her more than most. Maybe they were her only friends. If that was true, then he wasn't about to leave her out. Friends stick together; that's just how it is.

He took a can of cola from the cooler, and noticed a guard on the Wall, looking at the roof. He raised the can in their direction and nodded. The soldier waved back.

"Do you think they can read our lips?" Vanessa asked, as cheerful as usual. She opened a plastic bottle of water. "Or, um, is this place bugged?"

JJ adjusted his baseball cap and chuckled. Her concern about being spied on was kind of ironic, given her particular abilities. He caught Sol's eye, and could tell that his stout friend had a similar thought. They shared a silent toast to the inside joke.

"It's not bugged," said Madi. "Trust me. Though I guess they could be listening if they wanted."

"Eh, fuck it," Sol expressed his opinion. "No guts, no glory."

"This is the safest place I know," JJ said. "And we really need to talk about this stuff."

"So the kid's alright?" Sol looked at Madison. He and JJ had returned to their apartments at about three a.m.; Madi had stayed awake until dawn, listening to the staff and soldiers. They'd all slept most of the day.

"Yeah, according to the last thing I heard," she said, leaning forward in her lawn chair to grab a beer. "They took him out of the reactor, and he was all fixed up. Still knocked out, though. I never heard if he woke up or not."

"That's awesome," JJ raised his drink. "Here's to the most kick-ass girl in Alaska."

Madi laughed and tapped his can with her bottle. Then she swallowed a mouthful of the cold beer. She was underage, but only by four months, and the keepers of ABRA city ignored a lot of the resident's bad behavior.

Don't poke the dragon was the unofficial motto of ABRA City Security. Everyone knew that. But they also knew that the unspoken second line went, *because if the dragon wakes up, we have to slay it.*

"I don't get why this kid is that important, anyway," Vanessa shrugged. "You think we should stick our necks out for him? Why should we do that?"

"Jesus, Nessie," Sol grunted. "He's the son of Independence."

"And that matters to me because?"

"Think about it," JJ said, leaning forward, his voice low and serious. "He's probably stronger than all two hundred of us put together. If we can help him escape, then *he* can help *us*."

The rest of the group fell silent. He tried to lock eyes confidently with his friends, but found it was a difficult thing to do. They all knew how serious the roof party had become. JJ had admitted that his goal was freedom. If they took the conversation any further, they were guilty of conspiracy and scores of other crimes. Everyone knew what happened when residents made plans to escape. They disappeared.

"I'll drink to that," said Anon, its first words since arriving.

"Hear, hear," agreed Solomon. He squinted in the sunlight and grinned at the ladies. "What about it? You two in?"

Madi rose to her feet and stammered, "I—I can't. I'm sorry, but I just can't. Listening is one thing, but this? I've been in solitary. I know they'll do worse if they catch me trying to bust out." She was close to crying, and her cheeks blazed red. "I won't tell anybody though. I promise I won't tell. But I just... I can't help you anymore."

And she walked away. Her half-empty beer sat on the plastic arm of the now-empty chair. The group gawked in shock and sat in an awkward silence. Sol and JJ both looked like they'd been sucker punched. Anon showed a total poker face, while Vanessa huffed contemptuously and sneered.

Then she looked at JJ and grinned. "I'm in. Fuck this place."

"Really?" Sol raised one of his bushy, blond brows. "Heh. I owe you ten bucks, Jay."

JJ remained silent for a few seconds. Madi's abandonment was totally unexpected, and it hurt worse than he'd imagined. But he put on his own poker face and managed to grin. "Pay up, Solly. I knew Nessie would sign on. She's too damn mean to stay in a cage."

"You're absolutely correct, asshole." Vanessa gave JJ the finger, and they all laughed. "Give the man his money, Sol."

"Add it to the books, Jay. I'll get back to you on payday." It was an old joke. The residents had no money. Everything was free in ABRA City. Everything except the Posties.

"And so it begins," intoned Anon, mimicking the bold, stentorian voice of a movie trailer announcer. "These brave few will take a stand against the forces of oppression and evil. Long live the Resistance!"

"Hear-fucking-hear!" Sol drained his beer and grabbed another.

Vanessa raised her water bottle and started to take a sip. Then she froze, cocked her head to the side and said, "Do you guys hear that?"

JJ knew how sensitive Vanessa's ears were; his head snapped up and he leaned forward. "No. What do you hear?"

"Something like a hammer," she winced. "Boom. Boom. Boom. And something else. Screaming maybe ... no. A siren."

"A siren?" JJ, Sol and Anon asked simultaneously.

"Yeah, a siren. Wow, they're getting louder. The hammering sounds, I mean, not the sirens. Boom. Boom. Boo—"

Suddenly the entire building shook. No, not the building—the ground itself. Then, with a frighteningly loud rumble, it shook again. And again. And again.

ABRA City rocked, but obviously not from an earthquake. The hard, short tremors came in distinct, sharp, pulses—boom, boom, boom—and each was stronger than the last.

Madi's discarded bottle fell from the chair and spilled on the roof. Vanessa whispered something rapidly in Spanish—maybe a prayer, maybe a mile-wide blue streak. JJ thought it sounded like both. Residents cried out on the streets below, and many of the Wall guards had disturbingly disappeared from their posts. JJ figured that was probably because they had gone to their *real* posts—and were getting ready to kill everyone, if that's what had to be done.

Suddenly, absurdly, he thought that if this was the end, he wanted to see it coming. He climbed to his feet and walked to the roof's edge. The strongest tremors almost threw him off balance, but he made it and looked down.

Most of the residents were in the streets and their screaming was a roller coaster chorus. Soldiers ran through the streets, shouting for everyone to remain calm; they were obviously as confused and afraid as everyone else. A massive tremor ripped through town and sent dozens of people to the ground. Then there was one more hit, not quite as powerful as the last, but still a serious quake. After that, there were no more.

Silence settled on the prison city. The people below milled around, talking frantically. Lucy Dressler and Sam Chandrasekhar looked up and waved at JJ. He saw Madi, walking away from his building, maybe heading to the food court. She never looked back.

JJ turned to face his friends. "That was him. That *had* to be him."

"You don't know that, Jay." Sol stepped up beside him. "We don't really know what they've got down there. *Who* they've got down there. It could be anything."

"We could all be vaporized any second now," added Anon. Vanessa slugged it on the arm. "Ow! I'm just saying ... Sol's right. That could have been anything. Doesn't have to be him."

"No," JJ shook his head. "Too much of a coincidence. Independence's son gets brought here — and this happens! The very next day! It's *gotta* be him. And now we know for sure that there's something down there."

Vanessa spoke up, "There is. The guards talk about it all the time. It's the maximum security section. That's where the big and scary ones are kept."

"Are you sure?" asked JJ.

She nodded. "One hundred percent. I thought everyone knew about it. I've heard you both mention it before."

Sol said, "Well, I always figured something's down there. Been the rumor since before *I* got tossed in this dump. That'd definitely be the place to keep the son of Independence. I think you're right, Jay. It's gotta be him."

Anon asked, "The question is, what do we do about it?"

It took JJ a moment to notice that everyone's eyes were locked on him. For another long moment, he stood in silence. He was the youngest of the four (by quite a lot, actually) but they all seemed to expect him to make the decision. They expected him to know what to say.

The funny thing was ... he *did*. He knew exactly what to say.

He just had to say it. His lips paled, pressing together. His jaw clenched, and he took a breath, a deep one. "We need to find a way down there. We need to find him and make contact."

"How the hell are we going to do that?" scoffed Vanessa.

"I have no idea," JJ said, ignoring the goose bumps spreading down his arms. He still knew exactly what needed to be said. "But we'll figure it out. And we'll find a way out of this place. We have *power*, real power. If we work together, we can learn enough to make a plan. They can't stop us. They're just a bunch of Normies. We're Posthumans. We're the Resistance. Long live the Resistance."

CHAPTER SEVENTEEN

Tiffany screamed as the Behemoth wheeled toward her. Tank slogged down the hall, but he was still fifteen feet and too many seconds away. A clanging alarm started to blare; red lights began to strobe. The stink of decay, excrement and even fouler things overpowered her senses.

She tried to focus her power but the closeness of the rampaging beast drove all thought from her mind. She was frozen, cornered by a towering predator of impossible strength. The Behemoth raised his claws to strike—and a blinding gold light appeared between the man-eater and his prey.

Tom had returned unharmed and stood blazing with raw power. The Behemoth flinched and took a step back. His eyes widened and they met Tom's. The boy smiled coldly; the monster was afraid of *him*.

Tom thrust forward, shoving both fists against the rotund mass of the Behemoth's gut. The beast flew backwards through the air, slamming into the corridor precisely where Tom had hit. He left an even deeper dent in the concrete and metal wall. Vaughn toppled to the floor but leaped back to his feet with shocking speed.

Tom hurtled down the hall even faster—his feet never touched the ground—and collided fist-first with the Behemoth's face, a right-hand smash that pulverized dozens of those horrible teeth.

Vaughn responded with a heavy elbow against the boy's jaw and a powerful shove that cracked like thunder in the narrow space.

Tom was spun around by the blow. He saw stars and tried to shake them away, but the Behemoth lunged in from behind, pinning the boy against the corridor's far wall. His right arm was held down by Vaughn's stinking flab, but his left hand was free. He tried to push against the wall's steel plating, but the impossibly heavy monster didn't budge.

The Behemoth leaned in to chomp the boy's shoulder with savage force. Tom felt the crushing bite, but Vaughn's teeth couldn't penetrate the golden aura.

You're the son of Independence, came the memory of Milk's words, and Tom growled with furious frustration. His left hand dented the wall as he straightened his elbow. It was like trying to do a one-handed push-up with Tank on his back, but Tom did it. He forced the gross giant backward, buying some space to move.

Vaughn snorted in shock at the tiny boy's strength and tried to snake his arms around the boy's waist, but Tom's right arm came free. He elbowed the monster's gut with enough force to break loose and whirled around with a hard backhand.

Vaughn tumbled to the steel-plated floor, rolled to his feet and leaped for the boy. But Tom instinctively released a thunderous burst of energy, hurling the Behemoth into the already damaged wall.

Tom charged forward and threw a wild right cross; Vaughn's head snapped to the side with an explosive crack. Then the boy attacked with ungainly abandon, lost in a surging emotion. His shining eyes saw nothing but a red haze of rage, as his grief-torn heart released its pain on the Behemoth.

Tom threw punch after punch against Vaughn's reptilian face. The heavy hits drove the huge Postie into the shattered face of the wall. Cracks spread across the armored metal plating and exposed concrete, stretching to the floor and ceiling.

Tom didn't notice. He couldn't hear the wailing alarms or see the blazing flashes of emergency lights. He saw his mother. He saw the soldiers. He heard bullets and bombs and engines roaring.

He saw armored guards casting suspicious stares as Tiffany led him through the prison.

They had stolen his life, locked him away and put a bomb in his brain. They killed his mother. His mother! They killed her for no reason, no reason at all. They killed her and shattered Tom's world. But he couldn't fight them, not yet. They had too much power, and he had too little. They had destroyed everything and could just as easily destroy him.

But the Behemoth was something he *could* destroy, something that deserved it. Tom had the power to do it.

Vaughn tottered and went limp. Tom stepped back as the scaly brute faceplanted on the floor. He was out cold, maybe dead.

Tom didn't care. He wasn't finished. He took hold of the Behemoth's shoulder and rolled the corpulent monster onto its back. Then he crouched over Vaughn's chest and started throwing more punches, each hit more powerful than the last. Panels and debris fell from the corridor's ceiling, and all the lights winked out. The heavy alloy floor buckled and shattered, exposing the raw bedrock. Stone crumbled to dust under the force of the beating, filling the air. Every punch drove the Behemoth deeper into the ground.

The blows shook the earth and threw people off their feet throughout MegaMax. Above, in ABRA City, the impregnable walls trembled. JJ Joyce and his friends gaped on the roof, while residents and staff members alike ran futilely in the bucking streets. The tremors came with every impact of Tom's fists. Seismic monitoring stations around the globe detected the artificial quakes, feeling the strength of one boy's pain.

Tom raised his fist and didn't notice the golden aura quiver, dim and vanish. He threw one final punch—and half of the bones in his left hand snapped against Vaughn's mangled face.

He clutched the broken hand and howled from the sudden, sharp pain—but it freed him from the frenzy. Vaughn lay motionless in a grave-deep pit. His hideous face was simply gone, replaced by a bloody lump of meat. Tom rolled off the Behemoth and collapsed at the crater's edge. He blinked against gritty, dust-filled tears and looked around.

The hall was a crumpled ruin of twisted metal, pulverized concrete and broken rock. A settling cloud of dust filled the dark passage; muted light streamed in from Cellblock A.

An earthquake could do this much damage, or an explosion. A *big* explosion. Tom could not believe that he was capable of it, couldn't believe that he had done it. He trembled at the insane outburst of violence and the terrifying scope of his power.

His mother wouldn't have wanted him to lose control like that; his father never *had* lost control like that. If his power hadn't shut down, he might have destroyed the whole place. He could have killed everyone in MegaMax. Maybe he would have killed himself; Tiffany would have been killed, for sure. Tom closed his eyes and shuddered.

And from behind his back came a wheezing rasp. "Not bad, boy. Not bad at all. Your old man never hit me like that. Felt like scrapping with Milk."

Tom rolled over and scrambled backward, as the Behemoth slowly stood. The mutilated face healed before Tom's eyes. The skull regained its shape, open wounds sealed and vanished, and replacement teeth moved forward. Bloody, broken ones dropped to the floor.

"But you got no staying power, boy. You're already burned out." Vaughn licked his lips. "Me? I can keep this up all day. Are you ready for round two you half-breed motherfucker?" He spread his arms and lunged.

Tom tried to roll out of the way, but couldn't match the Behemoth's speed. He couldn't escape. The immense, flabby bulk would squash him flat; fang and claws would tear him apart. He closed his eyes and thought, *This is it.*

And a scrawny, elderly man landed on Tom's chest.

It was Vaughn Gregory … in the sixty-eight-year-old body he would have possessed if he'd never become a Posthuman. Tiffany had shut him down.

Vaughn bellowed and thrashed against the boy. He snapped his jaws, gnashing and trying to bite—but he was toothless. Without his powers, the old man was harmless.

Tom managed to catch both of the Vaughn's stick-like wrists with his good right hand. He wiggled and tried to gain enough leverage to pin the old man to the ground, but there was no need.

Tank's thick fingers suddenly enveloped the elderly man's emaciated chest and raised him off of Tom. The stone titan held the shriveled man suspended in the air.

Vaughn kicked and screamed; his voice rose to a squealing rant. But he wasn't yelling at Tom or struggling against Tank. His watery, red-rimmed eyes were locked on Tiffany, who stood just inside the demolished corridor.

"You fucking cunt! I'll kill you! I'll fucking kill you, bitch," the old man raved, spittle flying from his twisted mouth. "I *will*! I'm gonna kill you slow! I'm gonna fuck your goddamn carcass! Do you hear me? I'm going to eat you alive and pick my teeth with your bones! I will kill you! I will!"

Tank raised his free hand and cracked one brick-like finger against Vaughn's temple. The old man went limp in the stone titan's grip.

Tom climbed to his feet and felt his strength return. He took a deep breath and renewing energy tingled in his limbs. Even the throbbing pain in his left hand became a nearly pleasurable itch. The broken bones had begun to mend, he could *feel* it.

Tiffany ran down the hall and wrapped her arms around Tom's neck. They were both shaking. "Omigod, are you okay? Are you okay?"

"Yeah, I'm okay." He returned the hug; he needed it. "Thanks to you. You saved my life."

"You saved mine first." She leaned back a bit to look at him. "I'm sorry it took me so long."

"It's okay. Don't worry about it."

"No, I should have used my power sooner. It was so fast. He hit you, and I thought he'd killed you, and then he came at me, and I ... I was scared. Then you saved me, and ... and Tank wouldn't let me follow you. He stopped me. Held me in place. He's never done anything like that before. I ran up as soon as he let me go."

Tom thought for a second and said, "Guess he wanted to protect you."

"Mm," rumbled Tank, "No."

Tom and Tiffany broke their embrace, looked at their mountainous friend, and simultaneously asked, "No?"

"Mm. In-deep-denz need fight."

Tom stared, in confusion and wonder, and he put a hand on Tank's pillar of an arm. "You think I needed this? I almost killed him."

Tank slowly shook his head, "No. Not close. Mm. Bee-muth tough. Know'm tough. Fight'm lots. Can *take* it."

At that moment fifteen soldiers and two APE jockeys came charging into Cellblock A, yelling for everyone to freeze. They surrounded the group and began conversing with Tiffany. A couple of them bound the unconscious old man with zip-ties, while another glanced at Tom's hand and Vaughn's face. The rest gave Tom long looks but did not speak or ask any questions. Eventually Tiffany told him that she had to help escort the powerless Behemoth to a special cell in solitary confinement.

So Tom wandered down the hall alone. He stopped in the corridor between the Cellblock A and the cafeteria, where he could be alone, and leaned against the wall. Cradling his throbbing hand against his chest, he closed his eyes and tried to think about nothing.

"Mister Fuson?" said a firm, approaching voice. "I'm Captain Holly. I'm in charge of security here."

Tom lowered his hands and looked up at the beefy Army officer. "I'm Tom Fuson, but I guess you know that already."

"I know everyone in ABRA City, Mister Fuson. And I'm certain everyone knows who you are ... after that little show."

Tom wasn't sure how to respond. "I didn't mean for it to happen. None of it."

"I know," replied Holly. "I watched the entire thing."

"Oh."

"Have you ever been in a fight before, Mister Fuson?"

Tom shook his head, "No. And please call me Tom."

"You lost your temper, *Mister* Fuson. That's understandable given the situation, your inexperience and the provocation. But it was undisciplined. Sloppy. Being sloppy gets people killed." Captain Holly leaned forward slightly and said in a low voice,

"Between you and me, I hoped you'd kill that old bastard. Somebody needs to. But *next* time you fight someone, control yourself. You keep going like this, and you'll get somebody killed. If you're lucky, it'll just be you." Then he stood straight, turned as if to walk away and said, "Come with me, Mister Fuson. Don't worry, you aren't in any trouble."

"Where are we going?" asked Tom, who began to follow the captain.

"Doctor Angus would like to speak with you."

"Oh," Tom said again, but he thought, *I think that counts as trouble.*

CHAPTER EIGHTEEN

The young man kneeled in the dust and placed fragments of his creations inside a large canvas bag. The inventor wore a stained T-shirt, baggy shorts and flip-flops. A cellphone-sized object hung at his hip. His skin was very pale; his large brown eyes were bloodshot and kind of puffy. His dark hair stuck up in random, greasy, bed-head spikes. He had not shaved in many days, sporting a rough goatee and patchy scruff on his cheeks—he apparently couldn't grow a mustache.

David thought that he looked like the kind of guy who stays up until dawn playing MMOs or downloading porn. He wasn't bad looking, but he could learn to take better care of himself.

"Man, you busted the BuzzTrikes," he muttered in a resigned, almost sad tone. "And the SpikeFly. Damn. Do you know how much these little guys cost?"

"Excuse me?" Nikki sneered at him. "Those little guys tried to kill us! I don't give a rat's ass how much they cost."

"Chill, Nik," said David as he stepped in front of her. "Sorry about your robots."

The young man grunted noncommittally and slung the bag over his narrow shoulder. "More upset about the auto-turret, to be honest. Sentimental value. I built that thing when I was in fifth grade." He extended a hand to David. "Sorry they attacked you. If it makes a difference, they're autonomous. Barely smart enough to recognize *me*. I always figured that if anyone came in this way it would be the Feds. This stuff was all supposed to distract them so I could get the real defenses up and running. I never thought I'd need a remote control. I was asleep when you busted in, got up here as fast as I could."

"It's okay, man. No harm, no foul." David shook the young man's hand and said, "I'm David Young. This is my sister, Nikki."

"I know. My name's Mike, but you came looking for me, so you already know that, too."

"How do you know us?" Nikki asked, a little too harshly, but she shook Mike's hand anyway.

"Are you kidding? Every Postie on Earth knows about the Young family. Besides, I keep an eye on the DPS, and they keep an eye on you. Hell, they probably saw you come to Detroit." He chewed on his lower lip and glanced nervously up the stairs. "And now my first layer of security is trashed … just what I need."

"Wait a sec," said Nikki. "The DPS keeps an eye on us? How do you know that?"

"I know all kinds of things," Mike said with an incongruously shy yet proud grin. "I'm Tech Support. Come on. Let's go downstairs."

The siblings followed Mike down the well-lit corridor and into a maze of tunnels. The cinder block walls were a dingy off-white color, and the overhead lighting hummed. The place was old, but downstairs was much tidier than the warehouse.

"One company owned the whole area back in the Fifties. They built all of this," explained Mike. "Leads to a bomb shelter. You know, duck and cover and all that jazz. All the factories connect to it. Or, well, they did. I sealed off most of the entrances a long time ago."

"Who owns the neighborhood now?" asked David.

"Me," Mike shrugged. "Sort of."

"What's that supposed to mean?" asked Nikki.

"Well, it's complicated." Mike stopped in front of a closed door and unclipped the gadget at his waist. He continued to talk while pushing a long series of virtual buttons on its face. "The building you came through belongs to a real estate firm. One of the plants is owned by a business that made ashtrays, but it's been closed for years. Developers from all over own the rest ... according to the paper trail, anyway. None of the companies actually exist. I made them up."

"How did you manage that?" asked David. "Doesn't the IRS catch on?"

Mike shook his head. "Nah. They only know whatever their computers say, and I tell the computers what to say. I have about twenty fake companies, seven hundred fake identities. They all pay their taxes, and Uncle Sam stays clueless. It's all just ones and zeroes."

"Where do you get the money for that kind of arrangement?" asked Nikki.

"Oh, here and there. There's lots of money floating around if you know how to find it, and I can find anything." The device in his hand let out a beep and Mike glanced down, then he nodded and said, "There we go. It's safe to go down."

"It wasn't safe before?" Nikki said and looked up and down the empty hallway.

"For me it was. For you? I'd rather not find out. For my stuff? Definitely not." He opened the door and said, "After you."

David followed Nikki into what turned out to be another stairway. Red emergency lights were the only illumination. At the bottom of the stairs was a large metal door with a wheel instead of a handle. Nikki heard something up above—a scrape of metal on concrete. She looked up and saw movement in the shadows above and a glint of red light on chrome.

Mike walked behind them and said, "Go on in. The place is kind of a mess. Sorry."

"You should see my sister's room," remarked David.

"Shut it, Davy," Nikki said but fell silent as she opened the door and walked into a vast, darkened room.

The huge ceiling was a reinforced dome of rock with a dozen broad columns giving the chamber additional support.

In the center of the room stood a platform, about eight feet high and thirty feet wide, with an aluminum stepladder bolted to one side. The other three sides were bordered by a number of desks, with dozens of monitors and just as many keyboards.

Tool chests, workbenches, crates, drums and other supplies were scattered throughout the space. There were few furnishings. A couple of mattresses, pillows and ragged blankets were piled up in one corner to make a bed. Against the far wall was a small refrigerator, a microwave and a kitchen table, with two rickety chairs.

Machines of all shapes and sizes littered the floor, and numerous bots rolled, walked or hovered from place to place. The largest automaton was the size of an SUV, with a brownish-red, ovoid body, six long legs and four rotating arrays of stubby turrets.

It was a fully functional, honest-to-God Carnivore Walker, and it turned to lock its weapons on the intruders.

David and Nikki both froze in their tracks and stared at the hulking hexapod.

"Don't mind Six," Mike said, "I told him to not kill you."

"Thanks," muttered David. "Where'd you get that thing?"

"Arms dealer in Cambodia was selling him. The Squids left a lot of junk in Asia when Independence and Milk … um, your dad … finally chased them off-world. Figured Six would be safer with me. He's way better than those knock-off, reverse-engineered pieces of shit the Army calls Walkers. Was a bitch getting him here, I'll tell you that."

"Why do you call it *him*?" asked Nikki.

"Anthropomorphism, I guess." He made a motion around the room and said, "None of the bots are AI, but they all seem to have personality—like a fussy car that won't start if you turn the key wrong or whatever. You know how it is."

He led them past the machinery—in addition to the robots there were several vehicles in various states of disrepair and something that might have been a surface-to-air missile launcher with a tarp thrown across it. Then they walked up to the platform where Mike kept his computer.

The "business end" of the mainframe (as Mike described it) was beneath the platform—a patchwork of components from two planets—roughly a third of the hardware was Carnivore tech.

"Squiddies may be dumb as dirt," Mike explained. "But they build some damned fine computers. Programming them took some work, but the real hard part was figuring out how to connect their parts to our parts."

"I've never heard of anything like this," David said with a quiet wonder in his voice.

"That's because there's nothing on Earth like her," said Mike as he sat in the fraying office chair. "This is my baby. Her name's Prima—you know, from the Latin. She's the first of her kind."

"So this one's a she?" remarked Nikki. "Hope she's not your girlfriend."

"No, she is not my *girlfriend*. I like to think of her as my daughter, my pride and joy."

Nikki turned away and looked at the surrounding wall of screens. The displays were piled randomly on the platform's fifteen desktops, and not one of the monitors matched. A couple of them were ancient, yellow-cream bodied fossils with black screens and green characters, most were modern flat screens of various sizes, but the one that caught her eye wasn't a screen at all.

A veritable cloud of fly-sized bots swarmed in a rough, chaotic sphere—at the center floated a three-dimensional hologram of the warehouse above. The color was a little off—too green—but the resolution was amazing. Numbers and icons orbited the hologram, including a large red "Intruder Alert" warning.

Mike glanced at Nikki; saw her staring at the swarm. "I see you've found the PhotoFlies. They're among my favorite inventions."

"You invented this?" Nikki gasped. "I'm impressed, Mike."

"Thanks. They use really fast laser pulses to make the holograms. The hard part there was balancing power demands. The flies are powered by radio waves, microwaves, Wi-Fi, etcetera. It's just enough to keep them flying, transmitting back home and firing the lasers. They hardly ever break, and they're hard as hell to detect. Each one is *really* dumb, but as a network they can be pretty clever."

"Wait. Did you say these things can transmit?" asked David.

"Where do you think the image comes from? That's not a simulation or recording. That's a real-time broadcast from a swarm outside. If you were out there, we could have a holo-chat. Hell, I can bounce the signals off a comsat so we could use the flies to talk to each other if you were in Timbuktu or Tahiti."

"No way!" exclaimed Nikki. "That's badass!"

"No kidding," said David. "Too bad we can't sneak a swarm inside ABRA City."

Mike froze and looked up; his expression had fallen to seriousness. "You want to see inside ABRA?"

David shifted on his feet; he hadn't meant to blurt out their reason for visiting. He said, "Yeah. I mean, kind of."

Mike shot the siblings an inquisitive glare.

"That's why our Dad sent us here," said Nikki.

"He wants to find a way inside," admitted David. "He thinks you can help us. Getting a swarm in there would be a good way to start."

"Really?" asked Mike, as he turned around to face Prima's primary monitor. He looked out of the corner of his eye and smiled slyly. "Today's your lucky day."

He punched a series of keys on one of the keyboards. The hologram dissolved and reformed within seconds. The image showed maybe twenty buildings surrounding a slightly taller tower. A high wall of concrete and steel encircled the town.

ABRA City.

"I've been in there for months," Mike said and swiveled around in his chair. He motioned toward the floating image with both hands, his smile widened and he said, "Ta-da!"

CHAPTER NINETEEN

Tom was surprised when Captain Holly led him out of MegaMax, past the APE-suited sentries and into an elevator. He had imagined that it would be a long time before he left the subterranean penitentiary, if he ever got to leave at all. He asked Holly about it.

"Tiffany told me that nobody from MegaMax goes up. Ever."

The large officer glanced and Tom and replied in an emotionless voice. "Doctor's orders. I guess he thinks you're special."

They didn't speak again during the rest of the trip. Holly told him to enter the office, and had remained in the hall when Tom walked inside.

He stepped into Doctor Angus's office and winced at the light. It was on the top floor of HQ with widows overlooking the small town, the Wall, and the rolling tundra beyond. Rough mountains rose in the blue distance to the south. The overcast sky outside seemed incredibly bright after a day underground.

Angus was nowhere in sight, but a closed door stood on the left wall, so Tom figured the doctor was in there. He wondered if the other room was a private office, if this one was just for show. It looked that way. Photographs of Independence were everywhere, hanging all over the walls, sitting on every available surface.

The pictures came from every stage of his father's life. In one, the hero shook the hand of President Reagan; in another, he posed in the Oval Office with the soon-to-be-assassinated President Wallace. On Angus's desk were two photos of young Adam and one group shot of the clone child surrounded by a dozen smiling, lab-coat-clad men and women.

Tom's heart skipped a beat when he saw that one of them was his mother. She was so young. Her blond hair hung long and straight behind her shoulders, just like in the dream.

The horizon seemed to wobble and Tom leaned on the edge of the desk for support. He closed his eyes and there she was, on the ground. The whole thing came back, just like that, and he couldn't pull away. He swallowed hard, tried to think about anything else and forced himself not to cry.

Once he recovered, he walked to the windows. He looked out over the rooftops of the prison city and saw a small group of people sitting in lawn chairs, on top of the second building to the right. Tom wondered if they were prisoners. They certainly did not look like guards; they were all young. They wore street clothes and at least two of them appeared to be drinking beer.

So this is what it's like topside, he thought.

Down on the street, people talked in small groups. None of the prisoners wore hospital scrubs, and they seemed relatively free to wander around. The place really did look like a couple of blocks in a small town, except for the huge, metal wall and the roving squads of soldiers.

He quickly tired of the view, but wanted to avoid seeing his parents, so he sat in one of the chairs before the desk and looked at his left hand. It still tingled, but the pain was mostly gone. He flexed the fingers with little discomfort, and there were no signs of injury. Tom smiled in spite of everything. He felt a thrill of awe at his developing abilities. It was like he could feel the power growing inside.

No, that wasn't right, he realized. The power wasn't growing within; it was *filling* him from the outside. It was coming to him from every direction.

Tom closed his eyes, feeling the pulse of electricity within the building's walls and an incredible thrum of hot power far below the ground. He felt the gentle rain of telecommunication broadcasts, the ponderous tides of magnetism emanating from the Earth and the stormy grandeur of the sun. The entire universe seemed to open to him. He opened up to it.

Then Tom crashed back to reality as the side door opened, and Doctor Angus entered the room.

"Hello, Thomas. It is such a pleasure to finally meet you, my boy."

Tom looked up but did not reply. Angus was a tall, mostly bald and rather thin old man with wild, dark eyebrows and a beak of a nose. He wore a white dress shirt and tie but no jacket. Tom studied that long, weathered face; the doctor's expression was unreadable. Angus seemed to be examining Tom's face in turn, with interest but no emotion.

"Doctor," was all the boy said.

Angus leaned on the edge of the desk, like a teacher speaking to a student. "How do you feel, Thomas? Is there any pain from the gunshot?"

"No," said Tom. "Not from the gunshot."

"And I trust that you are uninjured from the unpleasantness with Mister Gregory? You seem to be favoring your left hand. May I?"

The old man reached for Tom's hand. Tom let him take it. Angus squinted and flipped it over; he prodded both sides with his bony fingers. "It appears uninjured. Not even a contusion. I hope that you will see fit to refrain from such displays in the future. Your parents would certainly have disapproved."

Tom remained silent. He lowered his eyes and stared at the carpet.

Angus let go of Tom's hand and walked around to the windows. The pair remained quiet for a long, uncomfortable time.

Finally the old man said, "Would you care to talk about it, Thomas?"

"Talk about what?"

"Everything, my boy. This experience must have been

extraordinarily trying for you. I would like to help, if I can."

Tom did not lift his head, but his metallic eyes locked onto Angus. He seriously doubted the old man's intentions.

"I understand how upsetting this must be for you, Thomas. Your moth—"

"You understand *shit*, Doctor," Tom growled through his teeth. His eyes flashed gold suddenly, a pulse of illumination that made Angus blanch. Tom did not notice the brief glow; he thought that the old man's shocked expression came from his words. That only stoked the flame. "You killed my mother. Don't think we're going to be friends."

Angus closed his eyes and rubbed the bridge of his nose. "Oh, Thomas, my boy, I would never hurt your mother. I vocally objected to the military's decision to bring you in by force. I cared deeply for your mother, my boy —"

"I am *not* your boy."

Angus looked into Tom's eyes and, with surprising emotion, said, "Megan, your mother, was like a daughter to me. For twenty-five years she was my dearest student, my trusted assistant and my personal friend. And your father," he waved a hand, indicating the many photographs of the hero. "Adam was the closest thing to a son that I have ever had. I held him in my arms as an infant. I watched him grow and become a man. The day he died was the worst day of my life. Like it or not, Thomas, you and I are family, or at least as close to family as either one of us has remaining."

Tom listened to this speech, but it did not change his feelings. He thought the whole thing sounded rehearsed, like Angus planned the entire exchange. And even if the old doctor's feelings were genuine, Tom could never share them. The silence expanded once again.

Eventually, Angus asked, "What do you think about my little town?"

Tom grunted indifferently, and then he said the first thing that came to mind. "I think it's wrong that Tiffany has to spend the rest of her life in MegaMax. She may be a Postie, but she can't hurt anybody. It's wrong to use her just to keep monsters like the Behemoth under control."

The scientist nodded and said, "That is not the only reason that she's in MegaMax, Thomas. Weakening other Posthumans is a useful tool for us, that much is true, but it sickens me to take such a lovely child and cage her for life."

"Then why do you do it?"

"Because she may be one of the more dangerous Posthumans on Earth." Angus glanced across the skyline and motioned for Tom to come and stand next to him.

Tom did so, and the doctor nodded toward the group of Posties on the nearby rooftop.

"Do you see that boy, there?" Angus pointed at a teenager in a gray hoodie and blue baseball cap. "His name is Jeremiah Joyce. He can manipulate space and time to an exceptional degree. Thankfully, he is what your generation would call a 'slacker' and barely has any idea of his potential. He could conceivably destroy entire cities, if he wanted."

"So why is he sitting up here, while Tiffany's in MegaMax?"

"Because she could make him *stronger*, Thomas. That is the other side to her power. Miss Cooke is capable of enhancing Posthuman abilities, just as she is able to negate them. You see, the residents are assigned to either the city or MegaMax according to their psychological profiles more than their particular abilities. Most people are relatively non-violent, and we take advantage of that fact. This is the reason that so many of the residents are able to live up here, in comfort, instead of in MegaMax. I have made this place less of a prison and more of a quiet village.

Angus waved a hand, indicating the prisoners on the street. "These residents seldom even consider escaping. The consequences are too great, and the conditions here are not cruel enough to justify suicidal escape attempts. They are ordinary citizens, and we treat them well. But if Mister Joyce, for example, were to discover what Miss Cooke can do—what she could help him do—then the seeds of rebellion would inevitably begin to grow. She may be helpful and courteous now … but five years from now? Ten? She may very well use her gifts to help destroy this place, Thomas."

Tom snorted. "Can't have that."

"My boy … Thomas. I do not write the laws. I did not

choose to detain the Posthumans, Thomas. That was the American people, Congress, and the President—three Presidents, at this point. Only the nation can decide to free the people here. Until they do, I can only follow my orders."

Tom's metallic eyes narrowed, and he said, "Like a good Nazi."

Angus shook his head and sighed. "I can see that you are not in the mood to have a civil conversation. We will speak again tomorrow."

Doctor Angus called for an escort to return Tom to MegaMax.

✪　　　✪　　　✪

"Hey, kid. Come here a minute," Fiona sat at the table closest to the entrance, obviously waiting for Tom's return.

He hesitated, but figured that talking to her was inevitable, so he decided to get it out of the way. He sat down across from her and said, "What's up?"

She looked at him and smirked. "I wanted to say thanks."

"Thanks?"

"For saving Tiffany. Everyone says you jumped right in front of Vaughn. You kept him from hurting her … so thanks."

Tom discovered that he was blushing; he wasn't used to praise, and wasn't sure that he deserved it. "She stopped him. I just held him off for a bit."

"You did a lot more than hold him off. We thought this shithole was getting ready to collapse. I doubt that old fucker had his ass kicked so hard in twenty years!" laughed the former villainess.

"He got right back up, though. Tiffany's the one that put him down."

"She didn't risk her neck to do it. You did. Everyone says your powers shut down pretty quick, but you still jumped right in the middle and put your ass on the line. That was either brave or stupid. Either way, I respect it." She stood and reached across the table to offer Tom her hand.

He took it, and they shook. "Thank you, Fiona."

She smiled, and Tom realized that she wasn't evil. She wasn't some psycho killer like Vaughn, or a shady puppet master like Angus. He looked at Fiona and saw a person, not the flame-covered villain from before his time.

"Your father, Adam ... he saved my life once. He didn't have to, maybe he shouldn't have, but he saved me. You've got a lot of him in you, kid. I can tell. And it's not just your eyes."

Tom couldn't respond; he didn't know what to say.

Fiona smirked. "You're not quite as cute, though. Maybe you're just too young for me."

CHAPTER TWENTY

"It's not as simple as that, and you know it." The pasty man in the blue suit and bad toupee made a dismissive gesture. "Independence easily caused as many problems as he solved. Who can forget the Tripoli incident? And of course, Bloodlust—who killed millions of people around the world and promised to return, eventually."

"That was hardly Independence's fault," began his opponent, a somewhat larger man in a slightly better suit, but—even worse than a toupee—he had hair implants that made his scalp resemble the plastic head of a little girl's doll. "And has nothing to do with his son—"

"His *alleged* son," interjected the pasty man.

"So you admit that Thomas Fuson may not even be the son of Independence, but you still defend the child's killers? Explain that to me."

"There is no evidence that the Fusons were murdered by the government. Everyth—"

"Because there *is* no evidence! None!"

The host of the program leaned between the men. "Gentlemen, please. This is hardly time for a screaming match." He mugged for the close-up and said, "We'll have plenty of time for that after a word from our sponsors. This is Carlos Singh of *All*

Opinions with Carlos, only on All-American News, where we put the nation first. We'll be right back."

The screen clicked to another network.

"—in six different cities already. In Manhattan, alone, some three thousand people have gathered around the Memorial of Heroes in preparation for tonight's candlelight vigil."

The screen showed a large crowd milling on the verdant expanse of Sheep Meadow. They clustered around the late hero Stonewall's enormous diorite sculpture of Aegis and Independence. Protesters and counter-protesters waved poster-board slogans at each other.

"They died for us," cried a middle-aged woman. "We deserve to know the truth!"

"This isn't, y'know, like, just about Tom Farston, or whatever," stammered a local college student. "This is about all of us. America's, like, a police state. Totally."

"Independence wouldn'ta stood for it," barked a wrinkled old man with a large nose and squinty eyes. "Now they went and killed his boy! They arrested that Sheriff in Virginia, and they took the scrapbook from those poor parents at gunpoint. 'National security' my eye! It's fascism, that's what it is!"

The on-screen image panned over the crowd and then closed in on the statue—the heroes stood back to back, capes joined as one, arms raised together, crossed at the elbows; the left hand of Aegis and the right hand of Independence balanced a globe, ten feet in diameter, with a deeply-etched inscription: Men may die, but legends live.

Click. The channel changed again.

"Marcus Alexander was obviously murdered by a Postie," said a ravenously thin woman with jittery nerves. "Is it such a stretch to accept that Megan and Thomas Fuson were as well?"

A slick younger man with an expensive suit, perfectly sculpted hair and a fake tan replied, "Why would Posthumans possibly want to kill the son—"

Click.

"Antimatter weapons! Antimatter! This stuff makes nukes look like water balloons! And they have cameras in space, watching us. *All* of us! They have weapons up there. Big metal rods in orbit, pointing down at us! They call it Public Safety! I call it bull—"

Click.

"—time to rethink the internment of American citizens on American soil. Interned, I might add due to an *infection*. Regardless of the effects, the Aegis virus is an infection. Most Posthumans are not criminals. They should not be imprisoned. It is un-Constitutional madness, and frankly, it's un-American," said the soft-spoken elderly man as he adjusted his tie.

"Is that your party's position, Senator?"

"Of course not. If it was, then maybe I could find even one other legislator brave enough to sign my—"

The television clicked off, and a cheer went up through the bar.

Jacqueline Dean held the remote but did not reactivate the television; she glared at the huge hand that had flipped the switch. The owner of the hand sat on the other side of the room, and his arm stretched across the twenty-foot space like living taffy.

"Sorry, Jac," said Alec Morris, as his massive limb dwindled to its normal length. Across his broad forearm, in big block letters, a tattoo displayed his *real* name: Hardcore. He was one of those über-strong, disproportionate Posties. A seven-foot tall brick of a man, he had more muscle than five bodybuilders, short brown hair and a fleshy, rugged face. He wore a black T-shirt, with "No, I Don't Lift" stenciled across the chest, and old, ragged jeans tucked into knee-high engineer boots. He grinned broadly and drained an entire bottle of whiskey—he needed a great deal of alcohol to even feel tipsy. "I love ya, but seriously … fuck that shit."

"You could have just asked," replied Jacqui, a petite blond with an hourglass figure and tanned, flawless skin. The former California Girl appeared to be barely out of her teens but was actually over sixty years old. Decades ago, she'd been an A-list celebrity, a world-class superhero and a very successful entrepreneur. She'd been one of the founders of the Paragon Patrol—along with Milk, Shockwave, Stonewall and, of course, Independence. Jacqui retired from business and adventuring after the Public Safety Act passed; since then, she laid low, managed her investments and ran the Dust Bin.

There were seventeen patrons in the bar at that moment, all Posties, though there was no rule against bringing Normie friends to the watering hole. Anyone was welcome in the Dust Bin as long as they didn't start trouble and could keep the place a secret. The mind-reading bouncer, Quietus, was very good at making sure the rules were enforced. The dimension-hopping Portero made sure that only approved guests entered. Regulars like Hardcore helped out if things got too rough.

And, of course, Jacqui used to be California Girl and, according to reputation, she was one seriously dirty fighter. Strong, fast, tough and very, very smart, she could throw down with the best. Anybody with an active sense of self-preservation knew better than to cross her.

Three former heroes sat at the bar—by tradition only such retirees could. Old Curt "Lockdown" Talmadge shared drinks his former teammate in the old East Coast Alliance, the apparently ageless Hannah "Glimmer" Taft. They had been joined for the evening by their friend Gia Drake, once the leader of San Francisco's former local team, the Riot Act. She blew a stream of flame to light a cigarette for old Curt.

Booths lined the far wall, but only two were occupied. Hardcore and the eyeless telepath Quietus sat together in the usual spot, directly across from the bar. They made an unusual duo—the compact, silent martial artist and the brash, boisterous metalhead—but were practically joined at the hip.

At the last booth sat four guys from Los Angeles, Doctor Delight and his posse. The infamous uniter of half the gangs on the West Coast, he'd risen from being a nobody thug in Compton to become the young prince of the underworld. His imposing Posthuman companions were paid very well to serve as bodyguards. Delight was a serious, twenty-nine-year-old veteran of the streets and wore a tasteful black suit, black shirt and gold silk tie. His head was shaved so closely that it appeared polished; his dark skin enhanced the intensity in his eyes.

A few random visitors occupied the center tables and floor. They were mostly college-age kids who had been hidden from the government by a loose affiliation of Posties and sympathizers. Jacqui was part of that underground railroad, which is why she ran the bar. It helped to have a base, even one so small and informal. She liked giving the youngsters a place to socialize—not to mention being able to wallow in nostalgia with other old timers.

"What do you think, Jacqui?" asked old Curt. "You think they might free everybody?"

"Maybe, but this isn't the first time there've been protests," said California Girl. "I'm not getting my hopes up."

The door opened and the bar fell silent as a titan entered. Every set of eyes in the place locked on the huge figure, but nobody said a word.

Milk stepped up to the bar. "That's a real shame, Cali. I was hoping we could have a little talk about hope. I'll take a keg of Milwaukee."

✪   ✪   ✪

Captain Holly poured two fingers of bourbon into the thick-bottomed glass. He knocked it back with barely a grimace and decided that just wasn't going to cut it. He left the glass in the kitchen and carried the bottle to the living room. The orange and pink light of dusk spilled into the room; Holly closed the blinds and sat down in front of the television.

They called the building Barracks One, but it felt more like a hotel, especially up top in officer country. The rooms were spacious, with soft carpet and plenty of privacy. Even the enlisted men lived well, with no more than two to a room. It was all a part of Doctor Angus's philosophy of control through comfort. Holly took another swig and grumbled under his breath.

Sometimes it seemed like everyone in uniform wanted to volunteer for an assignment at ABRA City—not really surprising considering the glamour of guarding the "most dangerous prisoners on Earth" and the cushy living conditions. Of course this just meant the soldiers grew complacent and soft.

The saddest part, to a career serviceman like Holly, was that the guards were basically unnecessary. The Posties rarely stirred up trouble, and when one of them did—like with the Behemoth earlier—they usually took care of it themselves. The APEs, Walkers, noise cannons and other toys were mostly for show. Only the cranial implants and the city's containment field really mattered against the more powerful residents.

Holly flipped through the channels; every network seemed to be talking about Tom Fuson and the Postie freaks.

Postie freaks…

The captain mentally kicked himself for the thought. His mother had been a boisterous black woman from Ohio; his father had been a moderately successful restaurateur from Hawaii. Holly was painfully aware that he would have been considered a freak in much of the country only a few decades earlier.

Most of the prisoners were decent people, and none of them had asked to be infected by the retrovirus. Holly knew that he sometimes dehumanized the Posties, if only to make the job easier. His duty was to protect the American people and hold the prison together, not sympathize with the inmates.

But what if he was working for the wrong team?

Holly closed his eyes and laid the bottle against his forehead. He tried not to think about things too much; he was a soldier, and it wasn't his job to question his orders—it was his job to carry them out. It was his job to keep the prisoners inside the Wall, plain and simple.

Nothing is plain or simple, he thought, swallowing more of the straight Kentucky.

He remembered the callousness with which he'd objected to Angus's attempt to save the boy the previous night. At the time, all Holly could think of was the danger Fuson might pose after absorbing power from the reactor. The captain had thought Angus was being a sentimental old fool and risking the safety of everyone at ABRA City.

But now Holly didn't know how to reconcile his conflicting emotions.

Thomas Fuson had saved Tiffany Cooke's life without hesitation. He had thrown himself into the fire, squared off against one of the most dangerous creatures on the planet, and Angus had inferred that the kid would soon be *expendable*.

Yes, Fuson was dangerously powerful and suffering from profound trauma, but he wasn't crazy or broken. He could learn to be a force for good, just like his father had been. Holly had watched Fuson all day, had grown to kind of like him.

The boy was thoughtful, serious and grounded. He wasn't flighty or lazy or moody like many teens. The loss of temper he'd suffered while fighting the Behemoth was understandable. The boy's mother had been dead for less than a day; that kind of damage takes a long time to heal. All things considered, Fuson was handling the situation far better than many adults would. He had the markings of a damn fine potential soldier … if Angus didn't expend him first. Holly didn't like it very much when soldiers were considered expendable.

He glanced at the television and saw some old footage of Independence on the news. The hero flew through the air, carrying a cargo ship filled with supplies for victims of an earthquake in Mexico City. In the next shot, he stood in between a line of police and a herd of protesters somewhere in Eastern Europe. He begged them, in their own language, to find a peaceful resolution to the conflict.

Holly suddenly remembered tying a blue towel around his neck—he'd been maybe six years old—and running in circles around the yard, pretending to be the hero. Didn't every kid in America want to be Independence?

"Damn it." He turned off the TV and drained the bottle dry.

"I have never been comfortable with ABRA City, that's no secret," said President Samantha Calhoun to the two men in her office. She made eye contact with both of them before continuing. "I am definitely uncomfortable about lying to the people like this."

"Madam President," replied Zane Jones, the photogenic, young Chief of Staff. "If they find out that he's alive, then they'll demand that we free him. You'll lose the election, and you'll be impeached. At the very least."

"And how do you think they'll respond once they learn that the son of Independence was not killed at all? Look at that." She pointed at the screen on the far wall of the Oval Office. Nearly five thousand people had gathered in Central Park—chanting, singing and calling for the release of the Posthuman prisoners. "We are already being bombed by petitions in favor of relaxing the Public Safety Act. The American people are beginning to rethink their position. Maybe it's time for us to do the same."

"Give them time, Samantha," said the director of the Department of Public Safety, Kevin Givich. The seventy-four-year-old bureaucrat had once been in Congress with her father, the late Senator Ryan Carlson, and still tended to treat the President like a niece, despite the fact that she was well into her fifties and the most powerful political leader on Earth.

The director calmly explained, "We all know that it's only a matter of time before there's another Posthuman disaster. The media has been stirring this up, playing up the hype like always. That's all it is, and it will pass. One or two good scares will remind them why we keep an eye on the Posties."

"There is no such thing as a 'good scare,' Kevin," was the President's retort. "*We* should be scared of what will happen when the public discovers that Thomas Fuson is still alive."

"That's not going to happen, Samantha."

She glared at the older man and shook her head. "Do you really think that we can keep him imprisoned forever? You've gone over Doctor Angus's report. The boy may be just as powerful as Independence and Aegis. You've seen the damage he caused. We won't be able to hold him much longer."

"Precisely," Givich smiled with a flash of white dentures. "That is why Angus is going to eliminate the boy as soon as..." he glanced at Chief of Staff Jones. "As soon as the *other* option is viable."

The President slammed her right fist against the desk. "I did not authorize that. How does Angus think that he has the authority to execute an American citizen? The boy's little more than a child!"

The DPS Director only smiled again. "Actually, Samantha, you did authorize it—last night when you signed off on the cover-up. You should learn to read the fine print, darling."

Calhoun stood so swiftly that her chair clattered to the floor. "Don't 'darling' me, Kevin! I am the President of the United States—at least for now—and it's past time you learned to respect that. I expect to see your resignation papers on my desk in the morning."

Their eyes locked. Jones squirmed in his seat and tried pretend that he wasn't there.

"I don't think so. I have served three Presidents as the head of the DPS, and I do not intend to retire any time soon."

"It was not a request, Director."

"I don't really care, *Samantha*. You can't fire me. You can't afford to make this public. Don't forget that I know where all of the skeletons are buried. Even yours. Be careful not to do anything that might jeopardize your reelection." Givich stood, offered an ironic bow to the President and then turned his back on her. "Good evening, Madam President. I'll see you in the morning."

Calhoun stared in shocked silence as the older statesman walked out of the Oval Office. Jones exhaled with relief and hopped up to lift her chair. He noticed that the President was shaking as she collapsed into the seat.

"Thank you, Zane."

"You're welcome, ma'am."

She sat for a moment; her gaze turned inward, her thin lips pressed together so tightly that they turned white. Her voice sounded harsh and dry as she croaked, "God save us from unelected officials."

Milk downed the keg in one long swig then turned to face the patrons. "I suppose you all heard about Independence's boy by now."

"Of course we did, Charley," replied Alec "Hardcore" Morris. "It's the top goddamn story on every channel. Those DPS fucks fried his ass, may they all die nice and slow."

"You heard wrong. I was there. The kid's still alive, but not for long."

Whispers raced through the room as everyone digested this interesting factoid. Delight motioned for his minions to remain silent. Jacqueline pouted, Hardcore frowned, and Quietus merely watched in his odd, eyeless fashion.

"So why should we give a fuck?" Doctor Delight asked defiantly; his posse tittered and giggled. "It ain't my damn problem."

Milk shrugged, "Maybe it's not. Not yet anyway. But I think it will be your problem when Doc Angus manages to grow himself a new Independence. Using cells from the kid, ABRA will finally be able to make another clone. And this one will be used against us."

The bar seemed to grow colder as the patrons absorbed this information.

"I am not going to let that happen," stated Milk. "I'm forming a team—a new team—and we are going to save Tom Fuson … and we're going to take down ABRA once and for all. Who's with me?"

Hardcore gulped another bottle of whiskey. "Shit, I want to stop those assholes as much as anyone, but we've got good reason to lay low. They already harass my mamma two or three times a month. And, well, it won't just be our families on the line if we do this. It'll mean war, Charley, real war. Lots of people getting hurt, man."

"Not if we do it my way," Milk replied. "We're going to blow the lid off that place, and we're gonna do it with style. I've got a plan, and I'll explain it all once you're on board. Join my team, all of you, and we can make a difference."

Doctor Delight brayed with laughter; he genuinely enjoyed having an opportunity to trash talk the legendary strongman. He scoffed, "You senile old fucker. Think you can just march up in here and start telling us what to do? Attack ABRA? We'll all end up locked up or worse. Sorry, fool, but I'm no fool, see? Besides, I never took orders from a *white* man before, ain't about to start now."

Milk's head whipped toward Delight, and his brown eyes burned with indescribable wrath. His nostrils flared and he snorted, one single time, a great bull ready to charge.

"What did you just say?" he growled through clenched teeth. His deep voice shook the entire room, bottles and glasses tinkled behind the bar. Milk took a step forward.

The small crowd scattered, except for Jacqui and Alec; they tried in vain to stop the horned hero. Jacqui vaulted over the bar and leaned into his abdomen; Hardcore wrapped his arms around Milk from behind and pulled. They pleaded for him to stop; they begged him to let it go.

Milk simply walked on, not even slowed by the preternatural strength of the two mighty Posthumans. He flexed his titanic muscles and they both fell to the floor.

Doctor Delight glanced at his posse — who all backed away from their leader — and realized that he was trapped. The impeccably dressed man's eyes widened and he began to sweat. His back was to the wall; he had nowhere to run. Milk stopped and leaned down, his humongous face mere inches from Delight's.

"You listen here, son," the hero intoned. "I was born in Nineteen Fifty-One, in a small town in Alabama. When I was a kid, I drank from fountains marked 'For Coloreds Only' and started school when it was segregated. You stand there and have the gall to judge *me* based on the color of my skin? You're no different than those bastards at the DPS. No different than the KKK riding through town, burning crosses in my nana's yard.

"Well, I've had *enough*. Both ends of my life have been stained blood red by the work of bigots, racists and scum. And it's way past time for us to stand against it. You want to run back to LA and pretend to be lord of your piss-ant turf? Go right ahead. You're too pathetic to be a villain, and you sure as *hell* ain't a hero.

"And that's what we need," Milk turned away from Delight, rising to face the rest of the crowd. "We need heroes. Not angry rebels who want to hurt the Man for all the times he's hurt us. We need heroes who will fight for truth and freedom. I'm not going to Alaska for revenge or to start a war. I'm going to *end* this war, to save the life of my friend's son, to free the victims of paranoia and show the world what it means to stand against hate and fear.

"We're going to remind people what it means to be heroes. Maybe we can't win, but you know what? It's not about winning —

it's about doing what's right. So what I want to know is this: Are you ready to come with me? Are you ready to do what we should have done fifteen years ago? Are you ready to be heroes one more time?"

CHAPTER TWENTY-ONE

Tom visited Doctor Angus every day. They usually talked for an hour or so, often about Adam or Megan, but their conversations ranged from educational lectures to political arguments. The chats had become so frequent and routine that Security no longer sent an escort. Every day they paged Tom to the front desk, and he'd take the elevator up alone. He knew they watched him, so he didn't even think about taking advantage of the situation. Not yet, anyway.

Tom wasn't very interested in being the old man's friend, but he'd grown more polite and tried to enjoy the talks. Sometimes he almost felt sorry for Angus. Thanks to the Golden Home's treatments, the doctor had outlived his family and friends; he had nothing left in life but ABRA. In a way, he was as much a prisoner of the place as Tom or any of the Posties.

Their fourth discussion had been a bit shorter than usual. They talked about Tom's life in Westburg, his friends and school. Angus suggested working up a curriculum so that Tom could continue studying and one day pursue higher education. The boy shrugged, not really interested in the idea; he doubted he'd ever have a "normal" career, even if the government let him go free.

The meeting wrapped up after that, and Angus walked Tom to the door. Then he stopped, grumbled something about senility and pulled a photograph out of his shirt pocket. Tom took it. He wasn't surprised to see his parents, but the picture was shocking nonetheless.

Megan — in a sleeveless, violet evening gown, with her hair pulled up in an elaborate bun — stood next to Adam. He wore the Independence uniform, of course. He never dressed in anything else when making public appearances. They faced the camera, but their eyes angled toward each other. His lips curled with amusement, and she'd been caught mid-laugh; he seemed to be whispering something that Megan found hilarious. In the background, there were piles of balloons, gaudy, red-white-and-blue decorations and other well-dressed partygoers. His parents held glasses of champagne.

"Your father's twenty-first birthday," explained Doctor Angus. "It was *the* social event of Eighty-Eight. Of course, Adam had been an adult for nearly thirteen years by that point. I suspect that your parents' relationship began around that time."

Tom thanked Angus, left the office, and rode the elevator down. He stared at the small picture the entire time, mostly at his mother. He'd never seen her dressed so elegantly and didn't think he'd ever seen her so happy, either. Her smile was brighter than any he'd ever seen; her eyes shimmered with joy. He wondered, for the first time, how different their lives would have been if his father had lived. How different would the *world* be?

The elevator door opened, but Tom kept his head down and walked past the APE jockeys toward MegaMax. He tried to ignore them.

Something about them made him uncomfortable. Maybe it was just that the Armored Personal Exoskeletons had obviously been designed to intimidate. The heavy, featureless helmets made the soldiers look more like robots than men. Tom had heard that the black visors were just for show, that the operators really saw the world through an advanced heads-up display that was painted on their eyeballs by tiny lasers. The APE's arms were easily a foot longer than normal, with huge, vaguely humanoid, hand-like grippers. Reverse-feedback systems amplified the user's strength and speed to superhuman levels. But Tom wasn't afraid of the

APE's, not after his fight with Vaughn. He simply didn't like them. Turning people into faceless pieces of hardware felt like some kind of blasphemy.

"Excuse me, Mister Fuson," came a synthesized crackle from one of the armored guards. "I need to see that."

"Here." Tom raised the photo.

"Your old man. And who's the looker? She's hot."

Tom took a deep breath. "That's my mom. She's dead."

"Well, that's a shame, but it doesn't change anything. Residents aren't allowed personal property. Hand it to me."

"No." Tom's voice remained emotionless; he felt calm, neither angry nor afraid. He didn't want to argue with the guards, but he wasn't about to lose the picture.

"No? You think you can say no?"

"Doctor Angus gave it to me."

"Oh, Doctor Angus? I don't care if the President gave it to you. For all I know, you stole that from the old man's office. If he wants you to have it, he can let us know. Until then, it stays with me, son."

"I'm not your son."

Servos whirred in the massive exoskeleton as the guard stepped forward. "No ... you're Independence's son. Guess you think that makes you hot shit. Let me tell you something—you're nothing but another inmate. Now give it to me."

Tom lowered his hands, planted his feet on the floor and looked right into the chrome helmet's black visor. "No."

"Hand it over. Or we'll take it from you."

Golden light flared in Tom's eyes. "You can try."

The guard raised both gauntlets. "Well. Looks like it's time for golden boy Fuson to learn what happens to prisoners who step out of line. You're gonna love this, boy. I know I—"

"Lieutenant Collins, stand down." The resonant boom of Captain Holly's voice filled the foyer.

The two APEs immediately snapped to attention. The oversize gauntlets clanged against their thick alloy helmets as they saluted their superior. The large officer walked out of the maintenance corridor into the lobby, scowling. He glanced at Tom and said, "Mister Fuson, go on inside but not too far. Wait for me. You can keep the photograph."

Tom nodded but didn't say anything; he just walked away. He heard the APE jockey, Collins, say something, but the captain cut him off. Holly's voice was a low growl, and Tom couldn't hear everything, but he did hear the officer ask, "Are you really stupid enough to poke *that* dragon, Collins?"

Tom kept walking until the voices faded to nothing. He stood in the empty hall, replaying the conversation in his mind. Maybe the guard was just doing his job, but it sure seemed like he'd been trying to pick a fight. Tom definitely didn't want to fight any of the prison staff, but he wasn't going to let them push him around, either. What kind of asshole tries to take the only photograph a kid has of his parents?

Then again, Tom thought, *none of the other prisoners have anything from home. Was Collins right? Do I think I'm "hot shit" because of Independence?*

Tom didn't know. He had never considered it before, but now that Collins said it, he realized that maybe he did.

After all, he wasn't afraid of the guards or any of the other prisoners. He walked around MegaMax like he owned the place. Only he was allowed to venture above ground, and he alone spent an hour a day talking with Angus. No wonder the guard called him a golden boy—he sure as hell acted like one.

Tom recoiled at the realization. He didn't want to be arrogant, and he didn't want people to think that he was arrogant. When people talked about Independence or Aegis, they used words like humble and compassionate. Nobody ever said that Independence acted like he was hot shit. And Aegis frequently said that his abilities did not make him better than other people. Milk, Melusine, Springheel Jack and all of the other old heroes had the same opinion.

Milk had said, "You're the son of Independence." Tom wondered if he deserved it. He was no hero. He looked at the photo and tried to imagine his parents. What would they say if they saw him now?

He heard Captain Holly's footsteps and turned around.

"Thank you for waiting, Mister Fuson."

"Uh, yeah. Thanks, you know, for helping me back there."

"I'm not entirely sure you needed any help."

Tom grimaced. "I didn't want to fight with them. I should've just gave him the picture."

The soldier nodded. "Yes, you should have. It was a gift from Doctor Angus, and he is in charge of this facility. He would have certainly had it returned. So would I."

When Tom didn't reply, Holly motioned for them to walk down the hall. They entered MegaMax and turned left, heading away from the cafeteria. Tom glanced back—looking for Tiffany—but there wasn't a soul in sight.

"I'm trying to decide if you're brave, foolish or looking for a fight," said Holly. Tom did not reply, so the captain added, "My soldiers mean well, but they can be overenthusiastic. Don't push them. We don't see a lot of action here. The trouble makers either learned to behave or paid the price."

"Is that why you don't wear armor? Even the normal guards wear armor and helmets."

Holly did not look at Tom, but he said, "I have armor, if I need it. I've been qualified to run an APE for a long time. But I don't need armor. I don't need to remind the Posties of what they already know."

Tom asked, "What's that?"

"This is *my* house," intoned the hulking officer. "*I* enforce the rules. *I* handle the problems. Don't push your luck, Mister Fuson, not with my men, not with *me*."

Tom started to say something, "I'll try. I—" but Captain Holly cut him off.

"I want you to listen to this. I am only going to say it once. *I* handle the problems here. So the next time there's a problem, go along with the guards ... and let me know about it. If they are out of line, I'll handle it. And if *you're* out of line ... I'll handle that, too."

"Thanks. I think. I don't want to cause any trouble it's just..."

"You've lost everything, Fuson, not just your freedom. Learning about your father makes you question everything about yourself. And the loss of your mother ... nothing can make up for that. It's not even been a week, and you haven't begun to know how deep the wounds go. Believe me, I do understand. That is the *only* reason you weren't out of line back there." The large man's words were as precise and ordered as his meticulous uniform.

Tom said nothing. They passed through the first cellblock in silence. Other prisoners stepped out of the way and scurried into the cells. Tom could feel their eyes; Holly simply walked. He didn't ignore the Posthuman inmates, but he projected a mien of focused alertness and relaxed confidence that made very clear the fact that every one of them lived in *his* house.

"They're afraid of you, Fuson," said the captain as they entered the next corridor.

"Who? The neighbors?"

"Everyone." The hallway turned sharply to the right; Captain Holly held up a hand as they rounded the bend. They stopped walking. "Your neighbors. The staff. My soldiers. Everyone in this place. We're all afraid of you."

"Even you?"

Holly met Tom's eyes and gave one nod. "Only a fool would feel otherwise. These walls are *strong*. Do you think you're the first person to pound on them?"

Tom slowly shook his head. Several of the inmates had incredible strength—it's one of the most common powers among Posties—and certainly some of them had tried to bust out the old fashioned way. He could just imagine the Behemoth thrashing in his cell, slamming against the walls like a wasp in a jar.

"No one has ever caused that much damage. Milk might be able to do it. *Might.* You're more powerful than any of the residents. My men know it, and you can bet your ass that every last one of your neighbors does, too. They know what it takes to shake the Earth. Can you blame us for being afraid of you?"

"No," whispered Tom. "I'm kinda scared of myself."

"You should be. Now that you know what you're capable of, you can learn to use it, learn to control it. You *need* to learn how to restrain it. It's not enough to have a weapon; good soldiers know that the most important part is learning *when* to use it.

"Lieutenant Collins could have handled the situation

differently, Fuson. That's obvious. He was confrontational and out of line. But let's not kid ourselves; *you* were the bully back there. You were the one with power. You're going to be the one with power every single day of your life. People will fear you; they will be hostile and rude. They *will* push you. It's up to you to rise above that. It's up to you to prove that you aren't a threat—even if you *are* dangerous."

"I don't want to be dangerous. I don't want power. I don't want people to be scared of me. I don't want any of this." Tom looked away and lowered his eyes. "I just want to go home. I want to see Mom again. I don't want to be the son of Independence."

Holly put his right hand on the boy's shoulder. "I know. But we don't get to choose who we are. We don't get to choose what life throws at us. We can only choose what we *do*. What we do is what makes us who we are. Not our blood. Not the circumstances of our lives. Our actions define us. What we do is *all* that matters. You remember that, okay?"

Tom nodded and quietly answered, "Yes sir."

"We'll make a man of you yet, Fuson. Eventually."

✪   ✪   ✪

"She's beautiful!" Tiffany lay across Tom's bed, prone on her elbows, with knees bent and feet in the air, like a girl at a sleepover, holding the photograph in her hands. He sat next to her, looking down at that crazy tangle of deep red hair. He tried to avoid staring at the very enticing curve of her backside, but he was a straight sixteen-year-old male, so his eyes often wandered.

"Yeah. She was. She didn't age a day. Doctor Angus told me that Mom was thirty years older than she looked because of something the Golden Home did to her."

"That's just weird," said Tiffany.

Tom shrugged, "I'm the son of a clone of a billion-year-old alien. Weird's relative. My relatives are weird."

Tiffany laughed and looked hard at Tom's face. "You look like her, too."

"Really? Everyone says I look like him."

"You do. A lot, actually. But there's some of her, too." Tiffany pushed up from the mattress and rolled into a sitting position with a supple grace that no male could ever match. She reached up, lightly tapping two fingers against Tom's chin and tracing a line along his jaw. "There." She touched his cheekbone. "And there, too. And your lips."

Her fingertips seemed to tingle on his face, and he couldn't really think of anything to say. Their eyes met, and they just sat there for a few moments.

She looked down and lowered her hand.

"Tell me about your parents." He took the picture and placed it on the nightstand. "You never talk about your family, or how you ended up here." When she didn't respond, he added, "I'm kind of sick of talking about mine, sick of thinking about the whole thing."

Her entire face scrunched up, like she'd just swallowed something bitter. "I don't ... I try not to think about my family. I haven't talked about them in a long time. It's hard."

"Well, you don't have to. I just ... I want to know you. I mean ... We've been roomies a week, and I know you. I want to know about you. You're my only real friend."

"You've got Fiona and Tank, too. And everyone says you're close to Doctor Angus and Captain Holly."

"Everyone says that?"

She nodded. "Yeah. Everybody was talking about you today. Nobody's ever seen a prisoner take a long walk with a guard before, especially not Captain Holly. And you going up top every day ... well, it may just be jealousy, but they talk about you all the time."

"What do they say?"

"They think you'll end up being let go, eventually. You'll be the first person ever released. They think Doctor Angus wants you to be another Independence. Tank doesn't help. He won't stop calling you 'In-deep-denz' and everybody listens to him. So they think you're going to end up working for the government, like your dad." There was something in her voice, a quiet melancholy. Her eyes dropped again. "It makes sense, you know. You're so strong. You could help a lot of people. You shouldn't have to waste your life here."

"Neither should you," he replied. "But I won't ever work for them. Not ever."

"Well, then I doubt they'll ever let you out."

Tom tucked his fingers beneath her chin and raised her face so their eyes met again. "They won't need to let me out. One of these days, I'll leave no matter what they say. And when I do, I'm taking you with me."

"Don't say that. They might hear you."

He shrugged. "They already know. They can't keep me here forever. That's why Angus is trying so hard to get on my good side. And he already knows that I don't want you to stay down here. I told him the first time we talked."

"You did?" She gasped and looked up at him with shining eyes — eyes that reminded Tom of his mother's glowing gaze, as she looked at Independence in the photograph.

"Yeah." Tom felt heat crawl up his neck and turn his cheeks crimson. An awkward rush of timidity jumbled his thoughts. Finally he said, "You're right. Tank and Fiona are my friends, and I think Captain Holly likes me, too. To be honest, he's not a bad guy at all. So, yeah, I do have friends here. But you're my best friend now. And I'm not leaving this place until you do."

He reached down and touched her hand. She stiffened, but didn't pull away. She blushed, too. Their fingers intertwined. Tom wondered if this was the part where he should kiss her.

But before he could work up the courage, she whispered. "They turned me in."

She said nothing else, but Tom couldn't reply. He didn't need to ask who; he understood.

Tiffany sighed and said, "My parents. They turned me in. They called the hotline and didn't even tell me. They called right after they found out, and then the police came and took me away."

"What? That's insane," whispered Tom, and something clenched in his chest.

The corner of Tiffany's mouth twitched, her eyes took on a wet gleam, and she said, "We were always on the other side. We hated Posties. Went to rallies and stuff. Our preacher always called

Aegis the devil. You know Lucifer means 'light bringer' right?"

"Yeah," replied Tom. "And when the sons of God and daughters of men gave birth to the giants in Genesis ... that was supposed to explain Posties like Mister Moment, the ones who say they were around before Aegis came to Earth. A lot of Fundies in my hometown felt the same way. I heard about that stuff my whole life."

"Well I lived it. That was my family, our church. We stood on the side of the road with signs whenever a politician even mentioned freeing the Posties. We went to revivals where they'd show movies about Posties leading people into sin. I remember one about Melusine turning Europe into Sodom and Gomorrah. That was a popular one. And Vaughn ... well, the Behemoth is in the Book of Job, right?

"So it's kind of funny that everything started in church. It was just a normal Sunday, and the service was about over, and the preacher was leading prayer. And I was good. I prayed, too. He asked God to help us help others, and I started thinking about that. It seemed like the best thing to pray for. I prayed that God would help me help people. And then I felt her."

Tom raised an eyebrow. "Felt her? Who?"

"I didn't know, but I could feel her. I knew she was a woman, and she needed help. She was hurt and just a few miles away. I tried to tell my parents. Mom told me it was God's way of telling me to pray for somebody. Dad thought it was just my imagination.

"But I knew better. The woman was like a star in the sky; I could almost *see* her. So when we got home, I told Mom I was going to ride my bike to see my friend Cindy, but instead I followed the 'star' until I found her.

"She was in this old store on the edge of town. It had been shut down and boarded up forever. It was kinda scary, but I knew she was inside. So I went around back and found where she broke in. She was hiding in one of the back rooms and she was hurt really bad.

"Her name was Clotho, and she said that she'd been a hero once. But the DPS found her in Cleveland, and she barely got away.

She'd been shot like four or five times, and was real weak—even with her powers. I started bringing her food and bandages and peroxide and stuff. I even lied to my parents about it and told them I found a hurt puppy.

"Anyway, Clotho told me that I was a Postie. She said any Postie can spot another one if they try, but what I did was more than that. She knew someone else with my power, an old man who lived far away, and she helped me figure out some of the stuff I can do.

"She stayed around for about a month, but then she left. She didn't even say goodbye. She just left me a note that said thanks, and she told me to keep my power a secret and be happy. She said she was sorry for running away like that, but it wasn't safe for her to stay around.

"I cried the whole way home. And when my parents ... I wasn't strong like Clotho told me to be. I told them the whole thing. Mom started crying and yelling. Praying. She put her hand on my head like she was trying to push the devil out of my brain. Dad went to the garage and wouldn't talk to me. My little brothers freaked out. So did I, you know? I was only twelve, and my parents were treating me like I was a monster or something.

"I went to my room and cried. I wished Clotho had took me with her. I still wish that sometimes. I cried for a long time, 'til I fell asleep.

"And then they came for me, a bunch of cops and some guys in suits. They weren't soldiers like with you, but they had guns. They pointed them at me and pushed me down and handcuffed me. It hurt. They didn't care. And Mom and Dad just stood there.

"I looked back at the house when we drove away, and they had already gone back inside. They didn't even stay to watch me leave. They didn't even say goodbye or tell me they... And I was alone."

With her head down, Tom couldn't see Tiffany's face under the flaming cascade of hair, but he heard the soft weeping.

He leaned forward and wrapped his arms around her narrow shoulders. "You aren't alone anymore."

She sobbed against his chest, and he cried too—quietly, so

she wouldn't hear. He didn't know what to say, so he just held her.

They sat like that for a long time, until she fell asleep in his arms. Then he lay beside her for a while, not thinking, just feeling the rhythm of her breathing, the feather-light touch of her hand on his chest, the warmth of her.

CHAPTER TWENTY-TWO

The medic pushed the new tracker into place with a small hand-held device that looked like a ratchet. He turned a dial on the tool's backside—right three times, left five times, right twice—and locked the tracker into the implanted socket behind JJ's left ear. The same tool had been used to remove the old one. The medic had pulled it from a drawer, where there were at least two more. They were kept right there in the examination room. JJ was paying attention to things, now.

"Now remember, don't fiddle with it. Infection's always a possibility." said the scrub-clad young man. He placed the device on the counter top.

JJ rolled his eyes. "Mm-hmm. I hear that every week, dude."

The medic grinned. "Sorry. Just doing my job, Mister Joyce."

"I know, man. Just playing. But you know what I don't get?"

"What's that?"

"Why do you gotta change them out all the time? You'd think something like this would be good for a while."

The young medic shot JJ a conspiratorial glance. "Want to know the truth?"

"Well, duh."

"It's because you guys might tamper with them. Keeping them fresh cuts down on the possibility that you'll figure out a way to get around them. I know it's a hassle, but we don't make the rules."

"That's actually really smart." JJ stood and stuck out a hand. The medic shook it, and they said goodbye.

The medic watched JJ leave and glanced at a clock on the wall. Then he left the room, too, walking down the hall toward the break room. He didn't notice the tiny man on his sleeve.

Sol, only two millimeters tall, held on for dear life and slowly scaled the swaying mountain of cloth.

"Hear about Lieutenant Collins?" asked Private Geary, looking down at the city from the southeastern tower. He was only nineteen, little more than a year out of Basic and kind of regretted signing up for a spot at ABRA City. Being one of the lowest men on the totem pole meant that he spent most of his time up on the Wall, which had to be the dullest job in the known universe.

"Of course I heard about Collins," replied Corporal Ortiz. He was only five years older than Geary, but he carried himself with the world-weary demeanor of a much older man. Unlike his younger colleague, he didn't mind the lack of excitement. He'd been in Iraq and Afghanistan and preferred boredom to danger. "Ask me? He's an idiot. He got off easy."

"It's gotta sting though, being pulled out of the APE squad. I heard all he tried to do was to keep the kid from bringing in contraband."

"It was a picture of the kid's mom, and the Doc was the one who gave it to him. Phipps was there, and he said Collins really pushed the kid's buttons. You gotta admit that's pretty fucking stupid, especially after what the kid did to the Behemoth."

"Still, the guy trained for years to run a suit. I think the captain's gone soft for the kid. It's bullshit that he sided with one of them over one of —"

Ortiz interrupted, "Captain Holly didn't have anything to do with it. He busted the lieutenant's chops, but that's as far as it went. The colonel's the one who dropped the hammer, but it was the Doc who gave the order. He don't want nobody messing with the kid."

"Jeez, is this a prison or a country club? Sometimes I think Angus is on their side."

"Trust me; the Doc's no fan of the freaks. But he made Independence, so the kid's different. Maybe he's hung up on him, or maybe he's got other plans. I haven't heard anything official, but the word is that the brass wants another Independence real bad."

"You mean they want to recruit the kid?" Geary was shocked; he had grown up in a world without heroes, and the idea of sanctioned ones seemed to counter everything he'd been taught.

"Yup. Don't you say a word to anyone, especially not your buddy Lee. That fuck doesn't know when to shut up. And you can't be too careful. Never know when one of those freaks might be listening."

The corporal's words were wiser than he knew. Vanessa sat beside the window in her apartment and heard every word of the soldier's conversation—from three hundred yards away.

Nobody noticed Anon, but then again, few people bother looking under furniture. A sleek, black rat with a tracking implant sticking up between the shoulder blades, it hid in the shadows and scurried through the maze of corridors within the Wall.

Its biggest worry was that Security would be able to track its movements with the implant, but so far, so good. Three hours into the reconnaissance and the guards showed no signs of noticing the enemy in their midst.

JJ had forbidden the shapeshifter from mimicking any of the guards or staff; it was too risky. They didn't know what kind of checkpoints might be scattered around the business end of the city and, while Anon could simulate clothing, it couldn't make an ID card or anything like that. Besides, Anon didn't exactly know the way around, and a confused soldier would probably be noticed in minutes.

But turning into a rat worked very well, and the best part

was that Uncle Sam had no idea Anon could even do that. They believed that it could only turn into humanoid forms. Angus may be smart, but he'd never figured out a way to really find the limits of Postie abilities, and Anon had never revealed the full extent of its power to anyone. Not until JJ risked everything and made the pitch that began their little rebellion.

Anon figured that if the young man could trust it enough to roll the dice, then it could do the same. It told JJ the gist of its capabilities — Anon could become nearly any vertebrate, but had to at least see an animal once.

"I need to get a read on it, learn how it's put together," Anon had explained. "So I can't do dinosaurs or mammoths or anything like that. But I can do rhinos, polar bears and elephants, if I need to. Tigers, gorillas, you know, zoo animals."

"How small can you get?"

"Pretty damn small," it replied and changed, right there in front of JJ's eyes, into a rat, identical to the form it used to infiltrate the Wall.

It peeked out from beneath a desk; the office was empty, but there's no such thing as too much caution. There was a row of file cabinets on one wall, some books, manuals and folders on a shelf, and a stack of forms on the desk next to the computer monitor. There were apparently no cameras in the room, but that kind of made sense.

Watchers can only be watched so much, I guess, Anon thought.

Anon's flesh flowed and deformed as it changed from a rodent to some kind of gibbon. It hopped up onto the desk and flipped through the papers. It saw nothing of interest, but the military-speak was practically a foreign language, so it couldn't be sure. Nothing related to the gate, though, that was obvious. Then Anon looked at the monitor.

Now that's *interesting*, it grinned. The glowing green text was a timetable, a schedule of arrivals and departures. A soldier by the name of Collins would be leaving today, and a new resident was set to arrive tomorrow but those openings were probably too soon to act on. But a supply convoy was due in another two days, and would leave later that same night. If they could reach Fuson by then, and timed the escape right, they'd have a clear shot out the door. *Bingo*.

✪   ✪   ✪

After more than four hours, Sol had begun to think that sneaking into the hospital was a waste of time. He'd found an elevator that might go underground, but there was no way to open it—the cameras in the hall made getting bigger out of the question, and he was certain there would be surveillance in the elevator. So he crawled through the forest of carpet, trying to make a plan.

It had been his idea, sneaking inside. The way he saw it, no one else stood a chance. Anon had volunteered, but JJ wisely pointed out the flaws in that scheme. Of course, the kid objected to Sol's plan, too, but someone had to find a way downstairs. The only way they'd ever escape would be with help from the son of Independence. That was kind of the whole point of the Resistance, after all.

Besides, Sol was the oldest member of the group (except maybe Anon, who could have been any age), and he didn't mind taking the most dangerous job. He'd rather take the risk than let one of his friends do it. Sol figured it was his job to take care of the others. Especially JJ.

The boy had a rough life, that was for sure, and ending up here wasn't even half of it, but JJ still had an optimistic core, something that no amount of betrayal or bullshit could break down. Sol had recognized it immediately after meeting the kid. JJ's attitude—not movies or music or weed—was the reason they had grown so close, so fast.

The truth of it was, simply, that Sol loved the kid. JJ was like the little brother he'd never had. The kid gave Sol hope that life could be better. It began with hope that life could be better in here, with a good friend to help waste the days. But now, for the first time in years, Sol had hope that he would be free again. He believed in JJ and felt like he could do anything for the kid.

Now it was time to live up to the feeling.

Sol scratched his thick beard and looked around. His

perceptions were very different at such small size. The hallway stretched on to infinity; the ceiling was so high that it barely registered in his vision. People were nearly unrecognizable. But there was a sweet spot—at about ten feet—where he could see them rather clearly, thanks to perspective. Much further away, and they'd be lost in the haze; much closer and they'd be too big to see. His ears seemed to work differently, too. Voices were felt more than they were heard, and it took a lot of concentration to separate the sounds out into words.

So it was dumb luck, as much as anything, that he noticed Doctor Angus coming down the hall with two men and a woman. They stopped in front of the elevator, talking; their voices were muted, distorted and barely understandable.

Sol didn't think—he didn't need to think—he grew to five-eighths of an inch and sprinted across the vast plain of carpet. He leaped, shrunk down to his minimum size in midair, and landed on the back of the old man's wingtips. He climbed the ancient wall of leather, holding on with all his microscopic might. Wherever Angus went, Sol would go; he could think of no better way to learn the secrets of ABRA.

They entered the elevator, and the trip didn't take long. It felt like four, maybe five stories to Sol. Or maybe the elevator was just fast, like in a skyscraper. In any case, a woman in a lab coat waited at the bottom, a tall brunette with stylishly horn-rimmed glasses. She was about forty, tall and thin. Sol thought she was kind of hot, in that librarian sort of way.

"Good evening, Doctor Angus," she said, walking half a step behind as they entered a laboratory.

"Good evening, Doctor Mueller," Angus replied, though he didn't even look in her direction. His attention was focused on a rotating hologram hovering in the room's center. Bizarre diagrams and columns of text flowed through the air, and Sol didn't even try to understand any of it. A man's got to know his limitations, after all.

He climbed to the tongue of Angus's right shoe and lay down, nestled among the laces, kicked back with his hands behind his head, staring with stunned awe at the sci-fi surroundings. He wasn't sure how to feel about the lab, but he had to admit that it was pretty damn cool.

Everything was shiny gold or white tile, and while Sol had the usual trouble with perspective, the simplicity of everything made the room easier to see. There were no screens or computers in sight, just the floating images and the equipment hanging on the walls. Every piece of technology looked like it had been ripped out of the Golden Home.

This stuff on the walls consisted mainly of oblong, glass tanks; each was about the size of a beach ball, cradled in elegantly arcing frames of gold. There were at least forty of them, maybe more in the vague distance of the lab. They were full of cloudy, amber fluid and thick, reddish sediment.

Sol had seen tanks like those before. He recognized them from a *Nova* documentary he'd seen about the creation of Independence.

Artificial wombs. Cloning tanks. They'd been taken from the Golden Home.

Sol instantly understood whom Angus was trying to clone; nobody ever called Gladys Beck's boy stupid. The only question was why would Angus want doppelgangers of Tom Fuson? Why would the government make new pet superheroes?

"They're dying, sir. We have already lost six." Mueller abruptly stated, with agitation, frustration and shame boiling under her crisp enunciation.

"Yes, but eighteen remain viable. Your team has done well."

"Thank you sir, but we have no understanding of the cause. They all appear healthy."

"But, yet again, few survive beyond gastrulation," said Angus. The tone of his voice made it apparent that he'd expected as much. "They will all likely be nonviable before long."

"Yes, sir."

The doctor made a steeple with his forefingers and raised them to his lips. He looked around the room, his expression as inscrutable as ever—not that Sol could see it, of course. Finally, Angus spoke. "Continue monitoring them. Tomorrow, we will try something new."

"Sir? The conceptuses are incredibly fragile," Mueller began, and then noticed the old man's expression. "Which you obviously know, sir."

"Indeed, I do. We have nothing to lose, Doctor," replied Angus. "We can always start anew, if this batch fails. But I do not believe that will happen. We will bring these clones to term. All we need is a sacrifice that will assuredly be missed by no one."

"Sacrifice?"

Angus turned around—nearly causing Sol to roll from his perch—and began to walk from the lab. "Have Lieutenant Baker to leave a message for Captain Holly. I would like the Dark Room to be prepared for Mister Slater."

Mueller remained silent for a moment. "Yes, Doctor."

"Now, if you will excuse me, I have some calls to make."

Sol held on as Angus carried him back to the surface.

CHAPTER TWENTY-THREE

Tom leaned against the cafeteria wall and kept an eye on Tiffany. She stood on the other side of the room, in the middle of a ring of tense guards, listening and nodding. Her eyebrows rose up in surprise and then furrowed with concern. Tom watched her mouth move and tried to discern as much as possible, but he wasn't good at lip reading. She noticed him, and they locked eyes. She gave him a little half smile; he tried to put on a brave face and remind her that she wasn't alone.

She motioned toward him; the lead guard shrugged and said something. Tiffany walked over, looking a little pale.

Tom met her halfway and reached out for her hand. Her soft touch sent a tingle through his body. He looked in her eyes. "Are you okay?"

She hesitated, and then whispered, "Yeah. Um ... I have to go shut down, um, Joey Slater."

"Joey the Exploder! He's here? I thought he was dead." The entire world thought Joey Slater had died with Daytona Beach.

"He's been here since the beginning, but he doesn't talk much. You've seen him. He's the guy in the spacesuit. I guess he tried to kill himself about thirty minutes ago. They said he slit his wrists with some kinda shiv. It's not the first time, either, but he hasn't done it in like five years. I had no idea the guy was suicidal. I didn't even know he could take off the spacesuit. Security wants me to make him weak so he doesn't … you know."

Tom nodded. "Go. You've got this. I'll be here."

"Okay. I'll be back as soon as I can."

They hugged, she walked back to the guards, and he watched them leave.

So Joey Slater's alive. Tom had no idea that the guy in the spacesuit was the most infamous boy in America—the most infamous *man*, now. Joey the Exploder was almost thirty now, but it was hard to think of him as anything other than a thirteen-year-old boy. The skinny little kid was almost as famous as Independence, Aegis or Milk.

He'd killed more people than any single person—other than Bloodlust—in an act that changed the country as much as anything in history. *Why did they tell everyone he died? Especially since they just ended up putting him here.*

Tom was so lost in thought that he didn't notice the approaching group of prisoners. They walked up behind his back and were just a few feet away when one of them cleared his throat. Tom whirled around.

Five Posties stood in a loose semicircle. Tom had seen them all before, but none had ever really talked.

The bodybuilder-looking guy with metallic bronze skin was in the center of the group, in front of the rest, the apparent leader. To Tom's left stood the mall-destroying Ashley Lang and her boyfriend, the eight-foot-tall sasquatch. The hairless woman with green skin stood on the other side, smiling prettily, aside from the tusks; her gleaming white eyes were the brightest things in the cafeteria. An old man with long gray hair and an even longer beard rounded out the group; Tom had only seen him in passing. He thought the old guy looked like Moses, if Moses had been a grungy hobo.

The metal man extended his right hand and bowed his head slightly. He seemed relaxed and friendly, but there was a gleam in his eyes that Tom couldn't place and didn't like.

"Excuse me, Tom—may I call you Tom? I was hoping we could talk."

Tom's eyebrows lowered incredulously. Something was up.

The group had obviously waited until he was alone to approach. Why didn't they say hi when Tiffany was around, if all they wanted was to talk?

"You can call me Tom. What do I call you?"

"I am the Lector, the reader of the written word of Guy the Bastard and Prophetess Sarah, the Speaker from Silence. Allow me to introduce Brother Esau, Sister Ashley, Grim Lynne and the Anchorite. My friends and I are the faithful few. We were chosen to descend to this den of lions, chosen to wait in patient reverence."

"What have you been waiting for?"

"You," said Esau the hairy giant, echoed by his lover.

"Me?"

"You are the Son of Light," said the bearded Anchorite. "Thrice-born of the celestial realm."

"You are the bringer of the new age, the Posthuman Age," said the green woman, Grim Lynne. "The promised hope of tomorrow."

"You are our salvation," finished the Lector. "The salvation of the world."

And with that, all five fell to their knees and lowered their faces to the ground. Then they intoned as one, "He who reigns forever, reigns forever. He is lord of all."

Tom took a step back, his boyish face slack with shock and confusion. The cafeteria staff watched, as bewildered as Tom; the guards along the walls spoke into their microphones but did nothing. The only other prisoner in sight was Billy the bat boy, and he seemed to be trying to repress a giggling fit.

"What?" gasped Tom and understanding dawned in his eyes. "You ... you're Children. You're the Children of Man."

"Yes, they are," said a familiar, welcome voice from behind Tom. Fiona had arrived. "And they're all gonna back off. *Right now.*"

She stepped around Tom, putting herself between the boy and the cultists. Violet wisps of plasma streamed from her eyes and hands. Visible waves of heat rose from her body; Tom's flesh tingled hungrily at the energy's touch.

"That's enough, McNamara," called one of the guards.

She glared at the soldier. "Then do your fucking job. Get these fucks out of here."

The Lector rose to his feet, followed by the others. "We simply want to—"

"You want to shut the fuck up and get out of my face, fuckwad," she hissed, and flame flickered in her mouth with every word.

Grim Lynne shrieked, "You have no right to interfere!"

"I'm counting to three, bitch, then things are gonna get *hot*. One."

The guards stepped closer, weapons raised. "Enough!"

"Two." The purple flame crawled up her forearms; her prison-issue scrubs began to smolder.

"Come on," growled the furry giant. "Let's go. None of us need this."

The lead guard bellowed, "Everyone back to your rooms! That means you, McNamara. And the kid, too. And turn off the goddamn light show!"

The five Children turned around and walked to the main door. Only the Lector looked back, giving Tom a sad nod. The purple glow faded from Fiona's hands and eyes, but she still radiated intense heat.

Tom placed a hand on her shoulder—nourishing, delicious, power flowed up his arm. "Let's get out of here."

"Right." She turned, and they walked back through the sliding steel door of their hall.

"What was all that about?" asked Tom.

"Get used to it, kid. Some of the Children think you're Jesus. They used to do the same to your old man. He didn't like it one bit."

"You don't seem to like it very much, either."

She shrugged and opened the door to her room. "Want a beer or something? Those dipshits ruined my morning."

"Nah," said Tom. He followed her inside. He'd never been in her room before, but it looked pretty much as expected—identical to the one he shared with Tiffany—except that Fiona had a small refrigerator on the far wall. "Where'd you get the fridge?"

"Oh, they gave it to me a few years ago. It's to keep me from going to the cafeteria too much. They're always scared I'm gonna light someone up."

"Yeah. I know that feeling."

She opened the fridge. It contained at least two six packs, maybe three. "Sure you don't want one?"

"Yeah, no. I'm alright."

She sat down on the edge of one of the beds and motioned for Tom to sit on the other one. "When's the last time you had anything to drink? Water? Coke? When's the last time you *ate* anything?"

Tom didn't respond. His eyes slid away from Fiona, and his shoulders slumped. To Fiona it looked like the kid was folding in on himself. She couldn't tell if his body language came from embarrassment, shame or something else, and she didn't need an answer to the question.

She grinned and popped open the can. "Your dad didn't need to eat either, but he usually did. He could put away almost as much food as Milk. Those two guys emptied out more than a few restaurants in their day. But Aegis, now ... they say he never ate at all. Maybe you take more after your grandpa than your old man."

Tom grimaced. "Not sure how I feel about that. Is it good to have a lot in common with a billion-year-old alien? And he's not my grandpa."

"What else do you call the guy your dad was cloned from?" She swallowed a mouthful of beer. "Hell, if he's not your grandpa, who is? Doc Angus?"

Tom let out a noise somewhere between a snort, a growl and a chuckle. "As if. I don't have any family. Not anymore."

"Well you got Tiff, that's for sure. And you got me, too, for what it's worth." She winced slightly, embarrassed at her words. She covered it up by saying, "And the Children of Man. Hell, they love you more than I ever will."

"Gee, thanks. Just what I always wanted ... my own team of villains."

Fiona's head snapped up and her violet eyes flashed. "Shut your mouth, kid. Those losers are *not* villains."

Tom gave her an unconvinced look. "Could've fooled me."

"Listen, kid, if there's one thing I know about, it's being a villain. For fuck's sake, there were only like *two* other villains before me. Those stupid punk-ass losers aren't fit to sniff my tights."

Tom scratched his head "Well they attacked Washington in Seventy-Six. And didn't a couple of them kill some mayor in Kansas or something? They did all kinds of stuff back in the Eighties and Nineties. They're the largest group of Posties in the world and one of the few villain teams. That was on a History test last month."

Fiona emptied the beer, crumpled the can and tossed it into a waste bin. "Half the stuff you learn in school is bullshit; you're smart enough to know that. Some people call the Children of Man a bunch of villains, but that's like somebody calling you a hero just cause you got powers and don't steal from people or whatever. Are you a hero, kid?"

"No."

"Exactly. The Children are Posties, and they used to get off on scaring people, but they're just assholes with powers. Most of them don't have what it takes to be a villain."

"What's it take?" asked Tom. "What does Flamechylde think it takes to be a villain?"

Fiona opened her mouth, then stopped, ran fingers through her spiky brown hair and stood. She went to the fridge and grabbed another beer.

Then she turned to Tom and said, "Style. To be a villain, you need style. *Panache.* You know that word, kid? Confidence. Flair. Whatever you wanna call it. Style is as good a word as any.

"It's not enough to be a criminal with super powers, kid. That just makes you a dick. And Vaughn's no villain either; he's a fucking animal, nothing more than that. To be a villain—a real villain, not just some loser delinquent with a chip on your shoulder, you need style. Individuality. Being a villain is being a symbol. Just like your dad was a symbol for all sorts of things. Aegis was a symbol. Milk does a body good. Shockwave, Stonewall. The names, the costumes, the attitudes—the heroes were all symbols. That's the point. They represent things. They stand for ideas.

"Well, villains are like that too. That's the difference, kid; the same thing that separates heroes from boring, lame-ass, nine-tofivers who just so happen to be Posties. Symbolism. Style.

"Look at King Kaos." She saw Tom's expression and shook her head. "No. Don't think about him like that. Think back to when he was just a villain. Think back to how he was before he went off the deep end, shanked President Fat Bastard and helped get us all free room and board at Hotel ABRA.

"Kaos was a fucking rock star. Did you know his merchandise sold better than anybody's? No shit. Even your dad's stuff wasn't so hot. Kaos may have been a mass murderer, but he could work the crowd. *Time* called him the 'demigod of Madness' and that's *exactly* what he wanted to be. I didn't know him very well, and he's definitely one scary motherfucker, but he had style.

"Me? I was Flamechylde. *The* bad girl. I used to be the freest bird on the motherfucking planet. I did what I wanted and danced with the biggest of the big and the baddest of the bad. I was a blazing star. I was free. A wildfire.

"Most of the Children, they're just sheep, clinging to Moment's ideas like ticks on a dog's ass. They feel special, part of the master race. The chosen of God." Fiona made a masturbatory motion with her right hand. "Those fucks don't have enough personality to be villains. They're glorified henchmen, lackeys, kissing Moment's ass and hoping their savior shows up to save all their asses when the shit hits the fan.

"Moment, though? That man was one of the best villains in the game. I *still* get chills thinking about him up on top of the Washington Monument—the fireworks and all. Happy Fourth of July, mother fuckers!" Fiona laughed. "His cloak all rippling. I could never get one to do that. Well … they always catch fire. But Moment could pull it off. And that pitch-black staff of his… Whatever happened to that thing? Anyway, that man did *everything* with panache. He's French, though; he oughta have style, right?"

Tom shrugged, unimpressed. "Independence took him down real quick. His whole group. In, like, ten minutes."

Fiona laughed even harder. "Who *didn't* your old man take down?"

Tom grinned. "I guess you'd know better than most."

"You're damn right. He caught me eighteen times in twenty-three years. The party was over as soon as he showed up, but that was just the facts of life. Most of us couldn't even touch him. You *know* I could only make him stronger. Don't think I didn't notice you sucking up my heat in the cafeteria, kid."

Tom raised his hands, palms up, and shrugged. He motioned for her to continue talking.

"Anyway, when your old man showed up, we lost. Every. Damn. Time. Even when we managed to get away, we still lost. But you know what? That was the best part, the top of the mountain. Anybody could wind up fighting local masks, like the ECA or the Eight Ballz. And getting Milk or the military boys on your ass just meant somebody called the cops.

"But if Independence showed up ... well, you'd know you made the big leagues. It also meant your ass was going to jail." She laughed again and made a balancing gesture, "Take the good with the bad, you know?"

"So why did you do it?" he asked. "I mean you never really tried to hurt anyone, did you? You just robbed banks and stuff like that. There's gotta be easier ways to make money, especially with guys like my ... with guys like Independence around."

"I didn't want to hurt people, sure. I'm not a psycho like Vaughn. Sometimes people got hurt, even killed, but it wasn't what I usually wanted. Hurting Normies is beneath me. There's not much challenge in fighting cops—or even the military, back before they figured out all this alien stuff and made Walkers and APEs. Though it was always a fucking blast watching those assholes run away screaming when I slagged their toys.

"I guess that's why I did it, kid. It was fun. And it made me famous. Hell, I'm still a household name. Mostly, though," she grinned. "I did it because I wanted to. Life's too short to need better reasons than that."

"Did you ever think about being a hero?"

Beer shot out Fiona's nose as she guffawed. She grabbed some tissues and cleaned her face, still laughing to the point of tears. It took two minutes for her to recover, and she laughed the whole time.

She managed to pull herself together, eventually. "A hero?

Me? Why the *fuck* would I do that? Listen, kid, I'll tell you a secret:

"There's no place for heroes in the real world. This isn't some fucking comic book or movie. For all the good your dad did, most of his time was spent fighting wars for Uncle Sam, and most of *that* shit was pretty fucking far from heroic. The same goes for Milk. Oh, plenty of heroes tried to help people, especially those two, but let's face it, the real problems of the world aren't gonna be fixed by muscle-bound freaks flying in and smashing shit. The only good thing they ever did was stop the Carnivores, and that was *all* your old man.

"Most of the rest of the 'heroes' were just plain useless. What did they do? Punch out gang bangers? Bust drug dealers? Go after people like me? Like *that* makes a difference. Guys in funny outfits can't do shit against the real bastards of the world.

"Think about all the people out there, Tom. Billions of them, held down by greedy assholes, two-bit dictators and armies of thugs. Think about the sweatshops and the people, all over the world, slaving away all day for a few pennies while the assholes live like King Fucking Tut. Think about the girls and women, everywhere, made into whores and slaves by soulless fuckwads. Think what struggling people have to do, every day, just keep their kids alive. Think about the ways people dick each other over and ruin each other's lives for nothing. Think about the starving millions out there, and then ask yourself how much of a difference any heroes ever made. I say they never changed a thing and they never will."

Tom thought about it for a few minutes. Fiona stayed quiet and watched his dancing eyes.

"Maybe you're right," he said at last. "It seems like everyone wants me to put on a cape and start saving the day. Or just sit in here the rest of my life."

"Well, what do *you* want?" Fiona asked.

Tom looked at her. "I don't know."

"Bullshit. What do you want?"

"I..."

"Just answer the question. Don't think about it. What do you want?"

"Independence." Tom saw the look on her face and shook his head. "*My* independence. I want to be free. I'm sixteen. I don't know what I fucking want! All I know is that I don't want anybody else deciding it for me. I want to get out of this place and figure out what I want. I want to take Tiffany and leave, if she'd come with me. I want to live my own damn life."

"Good," Fiona smiled. "Now figure out how to do it."

"I'm not sure I can."

She raised an eyebrow and smirked. "Kid, you can do anything."

Tom started to reply but a knock on the door cut him off. Fiona rose, but before she could take a step the knob turned and the door began to slowly open. Tom stood and balled his fist. Just in case. He and Fiona exchanged a brief glance and a nod. Her eyes flared and she grinned wickedly.

Then Tiffany walked in, head down. She wasn't crying, but she looked like hell. Both Tom and Fiona went to her side.

"Are you okay?" he asked

Tiffany looked up. "Yeah. It's just so sad. By the time I got there, Joey Slater was already in a coma. I drained his energy so the doctors could work on him, but they say he lost too much blood and died."

Joey's eyes were open, but he couldn't see anything. He couldn't move. Even his head was held in place by a thick, leather strap and some kind of padded brace. He couldn't feel his arms or legs; he'd been bound to the gurney for so long. He'd been dressed in ABRA-issue scrubs, and shivered in the chilly darkness.

He knew where he was though—he'd been there before—his keepers called it the Dark Room, and it was one of the many special cells in the solitary wing.

The Dark Room was the place they put people like him or Fiona when they got out of line. It was appropriately named; the interior was unlit and pitch black. The floor and walls were covered by complicated, multi-layered, latticework—heavy black grids made from carbon nanotubes and designed to withstand incredible levels of heat and radiation. The cell had been built to block as much energy as possible. Under the lattice were ten-foot-thick walls of concrete and metal—a layer of water supposedly filled the interior. The whole thing was surrounded by a Faraday cage and buried under solid bedrock more than three hundred feet beneath the surface.

The half-ton door had no window and stood at the end of a narrow hallway with an identical door on the other end. The toilet was little more than a hole on the floor; the only furniture was a simple cot, bolted to the wall.

Joey wondered why he'd been strapped to a gurney. He'd spent a lot of time in the Dark Room, but this was the first time they'd ever tied him down. It was pretty stupid and totally pointless. He didn't need to absorb energy to fuel his power, so whatever they'd done to make him weak wouldn't last long.

Any minute now, he'd start emitting radiation and heat. He'd get hot enough to ignite the cuffs at his biceps and thigh—and wrists and ankles, too, but the straps were so tight that his limbs were numb. He'd be free in twenty minutes … maybe half an hour, if Tiffany Cooke had drained his power, as he suspected. The gurney would go up in flames, as would any bedding on the cot. *They should have left me in the suit.*

Joey missed the suit. He'd hardly removed it in years. The only times he'd ever been without it had been during his stays in the Dark Room. He had trouble imagining life without it. He didn't need to eat or breathe, so the vacuum-filled, energy-impervious armor never needed to come off. Things were better that way. The suit was his protection from the world, and it protected everyone else, too. He felt naked without it.

Well, he'd be naked soon enough. His clothes would be incinerated long before the leather straps burned away. He'd have some light, too. Then the air would ignite, until the oxygen got used up. After that he'd just sit here, throwing off radiation, until they came in with their sappers and their suits. And *his* suit.

It couldn't happen fast enough.

He began to wonder why and how they'd brought him

there. It had taken a few minutes for the shock and disorientation to wear off, for his panic and confusion to subside enough that he could think clearly. The last thing he remembered was going back to his cell after watching a couple of shitty movies with some of the neighbors. How did he end up here?

As far as Joey knew, they'd never thrown anyone in solitary without good reason. ABRA might be a collection of dicks, but they weren't usually mean to the inmates. It was safer to keep people calm and happy. Especially people like Joey Slater. Upsetting the guy who killed Daytona Beach was like playing with an atom bomb.

Joey tried to never think about That Day; he constantly thought about it. He'd been thinking about That Day for fifteen years.

Ralph and Paul had caught him walking alone in the trees near the Museum of Arts and Sciences. They were classmates at Campbell Middle School; both boys were big, mean and not very bright. The always gave Joey a hard time and were worse than usual That Day.

He tried for years to forget about it. About how Ralph called him names and shoved him to the ground. About how Paul—whose face always made Joey thing of that vulture-looking buzzard from *Looney Toons*—laughed and threw a kick. Joey tried to forget the humiliation, the helplessness. He tried to forget his anger. He tried to forget the heat.

The heat had flowed from his skin, his hands and eyes. He tried to never remember Paul's wild, high-pitched scream, and the burning-bacon stink of Ralph's death. He tried to forget running through streets, as the air burned and the pavement turned to smoking slag. He couldn't stop the heat.

News crews got plenty of footage over the next hour, as he ran through the city, scorching everything with his nuclear flame. The police found the remains of the bullies and identified Joey. Reporters managed to broadcast the story before radiation destroyed their gear and health. The entire world saw Joey's face and learned his name.

He ran and ran, but the heat kept growing. He couldn't stop it. Buildings burst into flames, trees went up like matches and cars began to go up in flashes of super-heated fuel and burning plastic. The Halifax River boiled away. Daytona Beach went up in smoke. Cops started shooting at him, but the bullets evaporated yards away from their target. He ran, beyond panic, as the world became hell. The temperature kept rising, until he began to emit so much power that molecules were shredded and atoms bent to the breaking point. Past the breaking point.

And then he exploded.

That's how everyone put it; that's what they named him. Joey the Exploder. The kid who killed a city. Joey managed to put out so much heat that the air itself briefly became a fission bomb. The blast was measured at more than four hundred kilotons, with a fireball nearly five miles wide. Everything between Ormond-by-the-Sea and Port Orange was pulverized. The crater brought the ocean two miles further inland; the river now entered the Atlantic where Daytona Beach had been.

That's where they found him, bobbing in the water among debris and the dead. An energy-absorbing hero named Beacon followed the plume of steam to the unconscious boy. ABRA took him into custody and told the world he was dead. That was a gift to Joey. He hadn't wanted to live after learning what he'd done.

He didn't know how many people he killed; nobody had ever told him, and he had never asked. He didn't want to know. But he knew that he'd killed a city. His city. His home.

Thousands of people were dead, including his family, friends, teachers and nearly everyone he'd ever known. He tried not to think about it. He thought about it every day. Thinking about it made him burn with shame.

Nowadays, he tried to remain calm and relaxed. That kept his body at about five hundred degrees Celsius. If he grew agitated he'd become hotter in seconds. Much hotter. But his base level would be more than enough to get free of the gurney. He just needed to be patient. His body had already begun to grow warmer. Any minute now and he'd start glowing. The Dark Room wouldn't be so dark anymore.

The door opened suddenly, light poured in, and Joey squinted. A single person entered, wearing a HAZMAT-style suit of reflective foil.

"Ah, Mister Slater. We are both right on schedule, I see." The voice belonged to Doctor Angus, which surprised Joey; they'd hardly spoken in years. He couldn't imagine why Angus would be coming in, dressed like that, instead of sending in some goons.

"Why," croaked Joey. The back of his throat felt both sticky and dry. "Why'd you bring me here?"

Angus walked to the head of the gurney, disabled the parking brakes and gripped the handles. "There is no simple way to say this, and I require you to experience strong emotions, so there is no reason to dissemble." He turned the gurney and began to push it down the hall. "I am going to kill you, Mister Slater."

"What?" Joey tried to strain against the straps, but he still couldn't move his sleeping limbs, and his head was bound too tightly to even turn. He could only look up at the reflective faceplate of the doctor's protective suit. He could see the pale blue glow begin to rise from his skin. "No!"

Angus let out a sigh. "It is far too late to turn back now. I have already taken the precaution of faking your death. And, as you shall learn, there are certain *other* facts that prevent your return to the land of the living. No, Mister Slater, you are going to die."

They'd traveled through the solitary wing and arrived at the main corridor. Instead of turning left, toward MegaMax, Angus went right. Joey didn't talk. He tried to focus. No way was he going to just let Angus kill him. He closed his eyes and tried to push through more power. He'd turn this place into a lava pool, if he had to. He'd blow it to hell.

Doctor Angus noticed Joey's concentration. "I apologize, but you are going to have a difficult time actively using your abilities. Miss Cooke was very helpful in emptying your reserves, and the sedatives in your system should prevent any surprises. We require a gradual increase of radiation, not an explosive event."

They reached an elevator, and Joey saw a panel indicating that the hospital was above and some laboratories were below. Angus pushed the gurney inside, and they began to go down.

"Where are you taking me?"

Angus did not reply. The elevator stopped, and they went

down another hallway. The old man spoke, "There is no harm in telling you now. We are beyond all surveillance, and you will never be in a position to reveal the secret. You are going to die in a few minutes."

"Why do you keep saying that?" Joey snapped.

"Because it is true, Joseph. I am going to kill you. Slowly."

"You sick fuck!"

"Now, now," said Angus. They turned into a dark room and stopped moving. The doctor walked a few feet out of view, but continued to speak. "I apologize for the crudeness, Joseph. I take no pleasure in being cruel. However, necessity demands cruelty on occasion."

Bright lights glared on white tile. Gold metal gleamed in Joey's peripheral vision. "Where are we?"

Angus parked the gurney and locked the brakes. He walked away again but immediately returned. It sounded like he was rolling a cart. Something with wheels, anyway. "We are in my cloning laboratory. I acquired the equipment from the Golden Home many years ago."

Joey laughed, "Cloning? Pretty stupid exposing fetuses to me."

"Quite the contrary, Joseph. I do not believe that your radiation will harm these subjects. These conceptuses were created using the DNA of young Thomas Fuson. They are dying, and you hold the key to their survival. I believe that infusing the clones with energy may preserve viability.

"Perhaps you have heard that Thomas arrived with severe injuries. He had received a gunshot wound that was quite lethal. We saved his life by exposing him to the core of our nuclear reactor. I cannot take these clones there, so I have brought a reactor to them. However, we will need more energy than you ordinarily radiate, and to ensure success, I am going to subject you pain and duress. Unfortunately, you are quite dangerous, and to prevent any future difficulties I, regretfully, must end your life."

"Well you better hurry, you son of a bitch, because I'll be free in a minute, and then we'll see who dies tonight!"

"Ah, I suppose that you should know that you are not going

to be rising from that stretcher. Here," Angus reached down and loosened the head strap. "Let me show you."

Joey raised his head, looked down at his body and screamed.

His arms had been amputated at mid-bicep; his legs were likewise cut off about three inches above the knee. Straps held the stumps in place, not that it mattered. He was going nowhere. Blue light streamed from his flesh, and smoke rose from his clothing.

The old man rummaged through a bag on the cart. Joey glanced and saw Angus remove a large cordless drill. He fixed a half-inch auger bit to the chuck and squeezed the trigger. The drill buzzed to life.

Joey screamed again, and Angus began to work.

CHAPTER TWENTY-FOUR

"There are three distinct kinds of force fields," explained Mike. He sat at the patchwork supercomputer, Prima, but had turned around to speak with his guests. "They call them 'classes' but that's a misnomer. They're three very different things with only a few commonalities. I'm surprised your father never told you about all this. The military must have explained it to him during the Carnivore war."

Nikki barked a laugh, "All he'd care about is whether or not he could smash them."

"Two of them, he could. But not a class three."

"And that's what they have up at ABRA," said David.

"Yup. See, a class one field is similar to a plasma window, like what Hershcovitch made at Brookhaven back in the Nineties— but I think the Hershcovitch's windows are more awesome, since they only use Earth tech, unlike the military's force fields which are half alien."

He rotated the desk chair, looked at the main computer monitor and gently patted the frame. "Sorry, darling, I didn't mean anything by that. You're more special than anything."

The he spun around again to face the Youngs. "On the flip side, the alien ones are more useful, since they use a shaped diamagnetic field to do most of the work and the plasma core is mostly just a medium for current transmission and modulation. The magnetic field sustains ionization while the diamagnetic effect inhibits ... what?"

Nikki rubbed her temples. "Jesus, Mike, learn to speak English."

The skinny, scruffy genius smiled shyly. "Believe me, Nikki; I'm trying to make all of this as easy to understand as possible."

"What does 'diamagnetic' mean?" asked David.

"Diamagnetism is an effect that materials generate with exposure to an external magnetic field. It's a repulsive force, and works on pretty much everything, though it's a very weak effect. You ever hear about scientists making frogs float in the air? That's diamagnetism. The level of energy necessary to make it useful is so high that it plays hell with ferromagnetic materials and nearby electronics. The only reason diamagnetic fields are useful is because we have Squiddie omniconductors, and we have no fucking clue how to make those damn things. That's quantum engineering ... centuries beyond anything we can do right now. We're talking about direct gauge boson manipulation."

Nikki shot Mike a glare.

He raised his hands and shrugged, "Sorry, sorry. I really am trying to keep it simple. Let's just say that—here on Earth— diamagnetism is only useful in very controlled conditions or when you've got some alien parts that protect your electronics or if you happen to be specific Posties."

David cocked his head to the side. "Posties use it?"

"Sure, it's a component of most kinds of flying, every damn force field you've ever seen, so-called telekinesis—hell, even your dad's invulnerability. Yours too, Nikki. Everything we do is physics, even if it doesn't look like it."

"But that's just the first kind of force field. The class one type?"

"Yeah. But they're not all that tough, not really. A Postie with decent levels of strength can smash one. Class two fields aren't any stronger, but they use active quantum entanglement to make the entire plasma layer into a single wave function. That effect stops some kinds of teleportation, especially molecular transportation like Kobar uses. The whole beam-me-up-Scotty thing doesn't work through class two fields. They're also more resistant to high-end EM radiation *and* they're Faraday cages, blocking radio communications and microwaves."

"And class three?" Nikki didn't really want to know, but she figured that the sooner he finished explain this crap, the sooner this boring-ass conversation would end.

"They utilize quantum gravity, and we don't even know the intro-math for that kind of tech. The other two types we can mostly build. We just need to plug in a few alien parts to make them work. But every class three field on Earth was pulled right out of a Squiddie ship. The only thing we know about them is how to push the on button. Long story short, they're damn-near indestructible. You can't even through them by bending space. One of the prisoners, a guy named Jeremiah Joyce, can make Einstein-Rosen bridges *at will* and he can't get out. You can't even bypass them by short-cutting through worldlines. That's why Portero can't get inside, and he's the best cosmos-skipper there is."

Nikki sneered and opened her mouth, but before she could say anything, David interjected, "So nothing can get through them? Even by using a wormhole or coming in through another universe."

"Exactamundo. You, my man, get the gold star. Extra credit." Mike leaned forward, extending a fist. David did the same and they bumped knuckles. Nikki's scowl deepened.

Mike pretended not to notice. "Visible light and the low end of the spectrum can pass through, so can microwaves and radio, but other than that, they're impregnable. The only way to pop a class three field is by tinkering with quantum gravity. The Grays can do it, so could Aegis and Independence—most likely the Union can, considering its known capabilities—but that's it as far as I know. If any Posties can, they haven't figured out how yet, or at least they haven't done it to any of the class three fields I've ever heard about. And I'm pretty sure I know the location of every one on Earth."

"So how did you get the PhotoFlies in there?" Nikki asked.

"The old fashioned way. I snuck them in on a cargo truck. Supply convoys travel from Deering to the prison every few weeks, so I hitched a ride. The only way into ABRA City while the field's up is through the front door. They took that off a Squid ship, too; it makes a tunnel through the field for access. Don't ask me how. I don't know — and if I did, I'd have a Nobel. Maybe two."

"So that's it, then. We've got to get through the door while it's open and shut down that force field from the inside." David leaned back in his chair. "I can do it."

"You could, but you won't, and that's that," Milk's resonant bass rolled through the cavernous room. The youngsters all looked at the door. The pale titan strode inside and looked around. Nobody said a word about his clothes.

Milk wore a black suit, thirty years out of style, and a very wide tie. In his defense, it was the only suit he owned. Little Sean rode on his father's shoulders and stared in mute wonder at the robots, vehicles and machines. He carried a backpack full of comics, but they had already been forgotten.

"Sorry I'm late. Took your Mom a while to get dressed. As usual. Nice place you got here, Mike. Gloria apologizes, but she stayed outside with Kobar. Didn't want to risk getting dirty."

"I don't blame her. It's a bit dusty down here," Mike replied. He stood and followed the siblings down the platform's steps. They met Milk and Sean halfway across the floor. Nikki hugged her father, David gave a nod, and Mike reached up for a handshake. "It's an honor to meet you, sir."

"Don't call me sir, I work for a living." Milk laughed when the inventor looked up in confusion. "Sorry, old NCO joke. I used to be a Sergeant. It's good to meet you, too, Mike. I've heard nothing but good things about you." The horned hero tossed a nod in the direction of the Carnivore Walker. "Though I almost didn't believe the kids when they told me you had one of those things."

"I hope it's not a problem. Six is tame."

"It's no problem. The best thing to do with an enemy is make him a friend."

"Well ABRA's not going to be our friend," said David. "And we have to get inside. I can be in there and shut down that force field before the guards can even blink. You know that—"

"I know that we don't know exactly what they've got in there waiting for us. I'm not about to let any of my people run in there alone, son."

"I can do it."

"I know you can." Milk placed two fingers on his son's broad shoulder; there wasn't enough room for his entire hand. "Nobody's faster than you. And we'll need your speed once we're inside. But I wouldn't risk losing you right off the bat, and I wouldn't send a soldier in alone—even if you weren't my son. Okay?"

David gave a slow nod. "Okay."

"Good." He looked at Mike. "So what I need you three to do is go through the roster. We have files on most of the prisoners and eyes behind the Wall. Find me an inside man."

"An inside man?" asked Nikki. "I thought you had a team already?"

"I do. And it's a damn fine team at that—especially this one mean-ass girl and her over-achieving big brother—but we need someone on the inside. Preferably up top, since they have more freedom. We've got more than two hundred people to rescue; we'll need help."

"And how are we supposed to get in?" asked David. He noticed his father's stern glare and smirked. "I'm just asking. I heard you the first time."

Milk returned a smirk of his own. "Yeah, but you didn't listen 'til the *second* time."

"I'll get you in," said Mike. "I can sneak something through the gate on one of the trucks, just like I did with the Flies. There's something I've wanted to try for a while anyway. A real shocker, so to speak."

"Oh?" Milk raised a brow and grinned. "Good. I knew you'd be perfect for the team. Now you three get to work. I need a list of possible contacts by oh-nine hundred." He winked at the youngsters and turned to leave.

Nikki rolled her eyes and tossed up a sloppy salute. "Sir, yes sir."

"You heard me, young lady. Don't call me sir; I've got a real job. So do you. We'll be back in a couple of hours. If anything happens—and I do mean anything—you call Rodrigo and get to the Dust Bin. No excuses."

The youngsters watched as Milk left the room (except for Sean, who stared at Six) and then walked back to the computer.

"Hey," came Sean's voice from down on the floor. "Can I play with the Walker?"

"I don't give a damn," Sheriff Ford held up a pudgy hand and shot a bulldog glare at the cameras. "The cemetery's private property and y'all ain't invited. For God's sake, have some compassion, even if y'all ain't got a bit of sense. Let these people grieve."

The crowd of reporters and photographers groaned and whined, but they didn't press the lawman any further. They stood at cemetery gate and had a clear view of the burial service anyway, so being stuck outside wasn't a big deal. They tossed some questions, but Ford ignored them, left four deputies on guard and returned to the service.

He squinted against the biting, icy wind. A low ceiling of gray clouds slid overhead, and mist hung in the air. Ford considered it proper funeral weather, although there wasn't a thing proper about this funeral. More than half of the mourners were teenagers, kids who'd grown up with Marcus and Tom. They all had the same vacant, stunned expressions. They all stared at the three sealed coffins, trying to make sense of the senseless.

Judge Deborah Brewster had saved a seat for the sheriff and motioned for him to join her in the first row. Lisa and Jack Alexander looked over as Ford sat down, and they shared a meaningful glance.

The Judge leaned close to ask, "Has the hearing been scheduled?"

Sheriff Ford shook his head. The Department of Public Safety had arrested him (and half his men) when they came for the photo album. It was the proudest and most shameful moment of his career—being pulled from his own office, handcuffed, and forced to spend three days in a Richmond jail. All for refusing to hand over a scrapbook. The whole thing was a pissing contest, but public opinion was on Ford's side, and the odds were pretty good that the DPS would drop the charges. He was just waiting for the hearing — waiting and doing his job.

In the meantime, the citizens of Westburg not only kept Sheriff Ford on the payroll, they treated him like a full-blown hero. It was nice but a little embarrassing. He liked the appreciation, but parades and parties seemed like overkill. He hadn't done anything except get arrested; he was no hero. Ford didn't think there were any heroes anymore.

The only good thing about the whole mess was that the Alexanders weren't facing any charges. The grieving parents had become celebrities overnight and even the DPS wouldn't risk a public backlash by arresting them.

That hadn't stopped the black-clad soldiers from pointing rifles at the terrified couple while three of them wrestled the album from quiet little Lisa's iron grip. And it sure didn't stop them from giving Sheriff Ford a hard time. But things could have been much worse.

They could be much better, too, Ford thought and watched the pastor, Rupert Daley, step to the front of the crowd.

The Alexanders were not religious, and no one knew Megan Fuson's beliefs, if she had any, but Daley was also a history teacher at Westburg High and had been on good terms with both Marcus and Tom. He was a studious, balding man with an expanding waistline and a quiet composure, especially when speaking to a crowd. He wasn't a fire-and-brimstone preacher, which was fine by the sheriff, who didn't need another headache.

Ford was surprised by Rupert's talk with the people — for that's how it came across, not as a sermon or a formal address. The preacher talked about the boys, and he talked about Megan. He talked about the little ways they'd touched everyone's lives. He didn't talk about the big story. He didn't say the name Independence even once. This wasn't about heroes or politics. It was personal, for everyone in the community, and the preacher's talk was a personal conversation, an opening of the heart for everyone there. It was a good service. Sheriff Ford wondered if he could get Rupert to speak at his funeral.

And then something happened. There was a sound, like a sizzle and a cluster of low pops, from behind Ford's back. Everything grew quiet all of a sudden—and then the paparazzi began to yell. Ford noticed that everyone had turned around, so he leaned back, shifted his gut and looked over his shoulder.

All he could see was Milk, wearing a black suit and tie. He thought the hero looked even bigger in person.

Then Ford noticed the red-haired woman and realized that she was the retired heroine Shockwave. She barely looked any older now than back in the old days. She wore a long coat and a stylish, but conservative, black suit, skirt and low heels. Ford wondered if she could run at super-speed in those things.

Milk walked to the front and whispered something to Rupert. To the preacher's credit, he kept his cool. He nodded, mouthed the words "of course," and shook the giant's hand.

Several of the mourners pulled out their phones and began to record the spectacle. Ford didn't blame them for it; Milk hadn't been seen in public in fifteen years, and here he was, getting ready to speak at this funeral. The sheriff leaned forward in his seat and listened intently. So did everyone else.

"Hello, my name is Charles and this is my wife Gloria," rolled that resonating voice. He spoke softly, with careful enunciation and controlled emotions. "I apologize for intruding, and I hope that you will understand. We've come here today to pay respects to two brave people, innocent people, who were taken from us far too early."

A murmur drifted through the people. Milk had said two people, but this service was for three. Ford hoped that Milk hadn't forgotten about young Marcus—but how could he? All three coffins were right there.

Milk paused long enough to let that question ferment in the sheriff's mind. Then the hero said, "I did not know Marcus Alexander, but I am a father. The death of someone so young—the loss of all he could have been—is more tragic than I can say. I can't imagine your struggle, Mr. and Mrs. Alexander. I hope that we can speak after all of this is done.

"We do not know the exact circumstances of his death, but

we do know that Marcus chose to face deadly peril in order to bring the truth to light. He took a stand in honor of his friendship with Tom. He stood—no longer a child, but a man—and he made the hard choice. Your son was a hero, as much as any I've ever known. We should all hope to have a splinter of his courage, his integrity and his strength. We are here today to remember Marcus, celebrate his life and consider the example he left for us all.

"And we are here to remember Megan Fuson. Doctor Fuson, when I first met her. She led the research teams under Doctor Angus and worked closely with early Posthumans like me. She was curious, insightful and brave—one of the leading geneticists of her time. But you all didn't know that Megan Fuson. You knew a dedicated mother and good neighbor.

"She chose this town. She chose Westburg, and she chose you. She wanted you to be the neighbors, friends and mentors of her son. You should know this. You should know how much she loved this community. And you should also know how she died.

"Megan Fuson died trying to protect her son from ABRA. She was accidentally killed by a heavy weapon when the DPS forces attacked. I know. I was there."

This statement fell like a meteor among the crowd. The official explanation remained that a cell of Posthuman terrorists had murdered the Fusons. After the scrapbook came to light, the story had been modified slightly, and the terrorists were described as being out for revenge against the late Independence. Uncle Sam claimed to have not known about Tom's parentage until the album's discovery. The public, of course, did not know whom to believe. The mourners and journalists all held their breath in anticipation of Milk's version.

"An assault team was sent by the Department of Public Safety to capture or kill Thomas Fuson. Megan died when a missile exploded against my back. We had been talking in her back yard when the attack came with no warning. The agents continued to attack even after her death. Tom was injured as well, but he did *not* die. Tom Fuson lives!"

Milk leaned forward and looked intently at the crowd. He met Sheriff Ford's eyes and a silent respect passed between them.

The hero gave the lawman a nod, took a breath and then proclaimed—loud enough for the reporters to clearly hear, "The Department of Public Safety lied when they told you that he had been killed. He is in Alaska, at ABRA's concentration camp. There is no body in that coffin!"

Milk turned slightly and motioned with his huge, snow-white hand. Gloria stood beside the casket. She'd broken the lock and raised the lid faster than anyone could react. Her husband reached over and raised the coffin so that everyone could see within. There was nothing inside but a rucksack filled with sand.

The small crowd rose to their feet with gasps, exclamations and questions. People began to shout in the distant crowd of reporters. Every phone and camera focused on the empty coffin. Milk placed it on the ground, on its side, open so everyone could see the truth.

Sheriff Ford didn't recall standing up or walking, but suddenly he was so close that all he could see was the giant hero's suit. Ford reached out and grabbed Milk's forearm and looked the hero in the eye, "Why? Why would they do that?"

Milk somberly replied, "I don't know, but I know what they plan on doing. I know that they're going to try and clone him. I know that they plan to kill him. I think they're afraid of him, afraid that they can't control him, so they're planning on replacing him. They're going to murder a sixteen-year-old boy and use his cells to grow a perfect, obedient soldier. I do not know who made this plan or why. I urge you to call and ask. I urge you to try and help the boy.

"*All* of you please," he raised his voice again. "Call your elected officials. Ask them to free Tom Fuson. Ask them to free him today. He has done nothing wrong. He's just a kid. He doesn't deserve to die.

"And I will not *let* him die," Milk bellowed, and the almost physical force of his voice drove home the promise—and threat—in his words. "If they do not free Thomas Fuson, then I will go to ABRA City, and I *will* bring it down. I will free the son of my friends.

"This is a promise. This is a promise to President Calhoun, Director Givich, Doctor Angus, Secretary Mayes, Congress and the American people. I promise that if you do not free Tom, I will.

"You don't know when I'll come — maybe today; maybe next week. I'll give no deadline, but I'll give you time to release him. I'll give you time to do the right thing. It's up to you.

"I don't want to do this. I do not want to raise my hands against the land I love. I stood by when you called me a criminal. I ran away and hid while you locked up hundreds of people for no good reason but fear.

"My wife and I would not turn ourselves in because we have a family. We didn't want to raise our children in prison. Would you? So we hid. I stood by and allowed this nation to go mad with fear. The DPS has killed many of my friends, people I love — up to and including Megan Fuson — but not once have I thought about revenge. I've never seriously considered attacking the prison or freeing the prisoners. I hoped that this nation would come to its senses and end the madness. I had faith that the American people would come around. I still do. I understand the fear that drove you. I'm not angry with you, and I don't want to be called an enemy. I am *not* your enemy. I don't want to attack a government facility. I'm not a criminal, not a terrorist. Not for anybody or any reason.

"But I can't let the son of my friends be murdered for no good reason but fear. I won't."

He looked down at the crowd and frowned. "I hope that you will be able to forgive me. All my life — since I was a scared kid in Vietnam — I wanted to help people. I wanted to protect people. I never really thought I was a hero, but I'll admit that I liked it when other people called me one. The way I see it, 'hero' is a pretty good thing to be called. I liked that people looked at me, and instead of seeing a nine-foot freak with horns, they saw a friend who would help them out. That's who I want to be — a guy who helps out. I never wanted to be the guy who attacked the American government.

"So please let Tom go. I'm giving you a chance, because I don't want to take action against the country I served for decades. If I go to Alaska, I won't be able to take it back. You'll probably declare war on me, and things might get bad. I don't want that to happen … but I won't let you kill Tom. I will not let an innocent boy die because of some people's fear.

"Please," he said, as Gloria took his arm and they began to

walk through the small crowd. "Please do the right thing."

Every news channel—and many of the regular networks—canceled their scheduled programming to cover Milk's revelation. The Internet went wild and YouTube reached new heights of traffic as hundreds of millions of viewers watched and re-watched recordings of the speech. The government denied everything, but even the most loyal of the talking heads disbelieved them. The world had been told that Tom Fuson was dead; now everyone saw the empty coffin.

All around the country they called their senators and representatives; they called their governors, mayors and even the White House. All around the country people left their homes and gathered in the streets chanting, "Tom Fuson lives!"

The previous week's protests had been dwindling. The news cycle had moved on, and the upcoming election had displaced Tom Fuson and the Posties as the number one story. Only the most dedicated opponents of the Public Safety Act remained. But those activists formed the core of a movement that rapidly spread from coast to coast.

There were less than two thousand protesters in Central Park when the news of Milk's reappearance began to spread. They were joined by another thirty thousand in the next fifteen minutes. By the time the crowd spilled onto 5th Avenue and Central Park West, it was least one hundred thousand strong. It kept growing from there.

NYPD patrolled the angry mass but only interfered to prevent injuries or property damage. There were surprisingly little of both. The people of Manhattan united that day, and the only buildings to suffer the mob's rage were those owned by ABRA and the Department of Public Safety. Nobody really cared too much about those incidents of vandalism. New Yorkers went to bed that night with satisfaction at their good behavior and love for their shining city.

Other cities weren't so lucky.

Los Angeles erupted in volcanic fury, as every group with an agenda stirred up trouble, and opportunists used the madness as cover for looting and the settling of personal scores. Doctor Delight used the riot as cover to assassinate his chief rivals, the Posthuman Colombian gang lord Estefan Morella and the Triad boss known only as Chu.

Washington D.C. experienced full-on battle as residents clashed with heavily-armed law enforcement, the Secret Service and the DPS. Three people died in Columbia Heights when an Emergency Response Team's armored personnel carrier turned a corner and plowed into a crowd. Those were the first protest-related deaths, and while the tragedy was nothing more than accident, it certainly fanned the flame. By the end of the night over twenty people had been killed in the nation's capitol, including six police officers and two Federal Agents.

An entire city block burned to the ground in Knoxville after students from the University of Tennessee were chased away from the City-County Building by a line of armored cops — and ran into an even larger force of police on Cumberland Avenue.

In Cincinnati, more than three hundred people were seriously injured when a teargas-fleeing crowd became a stampede.

The nation convulsed; every city of even moderate size faced hordes of angry citizens. Curfews were put in place to little effect. The governors of one-third of the states called for martial law, though most of the protests remained nonviolent. Looting, assault and countless other crimes occurred in the midst of the demonstrations, but not enough to tarnish the cause. More often than not, neighbors came together and the population united to peacefully demand answers and show support for Milk and the imprisoned Tom Fuson.

In Florida, more than ten thousand people lined the entire oceanfront arc of the Daytona Crater, holding hands in an unbroken chain of compassion, over two-and-a-half miles long.

Photojournalist Raul Banda of the *St. Augustine Record* earned a Pulitzer Prize for Public Service when he captured that moment. Later on, he said that the prize was "not half as beautiful as the people, there of all places, when one era ended and another began."

But not everyone had such a poetic opinion about the day's events.

Not by a long shot.

"The answer is simple. We kill him." Director Givich didn't even look up. He flipped through the stack of paperwork and drummed his pen against the conference table. The rest of the Cabinet stared, wordlessly, but Givich didn't seem to notice.

"We do what?" gasped the Secretary of State. She was a tough, seasoned politician and notoriously pragmatic. "That's insane."

"Is it?" Givich shrugged and appeared to stifle a yawn. "Do you seriously think there's another option? If so, enlighten me."

"I want to let him go," said the President. She pinched the bridge of her nose. "He's just a boy, and Milk is right; Independence was a miracle. He saved the world from the Carnivores. He saved this city from the Children of Man."

Director Givich huffed. "This has nothing to do with Independence. This is about Thomas Fuson. The boy is dangerous. Do you think he's going to forgive us for the death of his mother? *Please*. He's already our enemy. Don't let sentiment get in the way of our duty."

"But if we could turn him," muttered Chief of Staff Jones. He hadn't meant to speak aloud, and blushed when everyone turned to him. He made a dismissive gesture and looked down. Of everyone in the Cabinet Room, Zane Jones was the youngest, the least experienced. He didn't relish the thought of going against a rabid dog like Givich.

President Calhoun tapped a finger against her chin. "Speak up, Zane."

His blush deepened. "Well, um, I agree with Director Givich. Tom Fuson could turn into a threat, but he's so young. We might still be able to win him over. We have to do something to win this election. The last polls put us neck-and-neck against Huerta, ma'am.

The only reason we're even doing that well is because the Republicans are even harder on Posties than our party. The people are angry, and they're lashing out against everyone. Your chances might be ruined, no matter what we do. But if we can talk him into working for us, then maybe he can help turn public opinion around. Imagine how the people would react to seeing Independence again."

The Secretary of State leaned forward and nodded. "If we can get him on our side —"

"That's not going to happen," interrupted Givich. "The boy's a ball of rage right now. He's unstable, violent, and already powerful enough to escape. Am I wrong, Phillip?"

Everyone looked toward the fireplace. Holo-emitters from the Golden Home — gifts from long-dead Aegis — had been installed above the mantel during the Eisenhower administration.

The semi-transparent face of Doctor Angus grimaced. "I believe that Thomas could escape, if he were to try, although I do not consider him to be either unstable or violent. He is suffering and confused. The young man certainly has post-traumatic stress disorder, but with time and counseling, he would likely manage to heal."

"Time is a luxury that we do not have, old friend," said Givich. "In case you missed it, Milk is going to attack your facility. But if we announce that the boy is already dead — that he died from his injuries before arriving at ABRA City — then perhaps we can stop Milk's assault. At the very least, we can make him appear foolish, if not outright treasonous."

Jones asked, "But what about the empty coffin?"

Givich glowered at the younger man. "What about it? I would suggest explaining that the good Doctor has taken the body for study. After all, the entire purpose of ABRA City is to find a cure for the Aegis virus. Fuson's corpse could be a very promising source of information about reversing the Posthuman condition. Of course, we didn't tell anyone about *that* in order to protect the people of his hometown from additional pain. Such facts are distasteful but understandable. The public will buy it."

The President's eyes narrowed. "You've put a lot of thought

into this, Kevin. What should be done about Milk's announcement that we killed Fuson's mother?"

"Nothing. We stick to our story. The Fusons were murdered by unknown Posthumans; Milk had no proof of his claims. If he did, he would have just revealed it in front of everyone. Say what you want about that man, but he is no chess player. We denounce his lies, accuse him of inciting rebellion, and we stick to our guns. We're lucky that Tom's friend was killed by the Union. His corpse appears to be proof enough that Posthumans were responsible for the attack. That's more evidence than Milk has."

"And if Milk does attack?" asked the image of Doctor Angus.

"Then we paint him as a villain, a terrorist and a fool. But— if I'm not mistaken—our good friends at DARPA and the DOD have spent years preparing to deal with Milk."

"Yes we have. And we have always expected him to attack ABRA City," said Andrew Mayes, the Secretary of Defense. The stoic old man was notoriously tight-lipped and had said nothing since the beginning of the meeting. He listened, absorbed the facts, and then made a decision; that's how he handled everything. "I agree with Director Givich. There is no way to guarantee that Fuson would ever come around. We have to act now, before Sergeant Young goes to Alaska. But if he attacks, we are prepared for Milk."

Calhoun rubbed her eyes. She did not want to kill a teenage boy, especially the son of the world's greatest hero, but she could think of no way to refute Givich's points. She had been against the Public Safety Act for her entire congressional career, but after winning the election in 2012, she'd been forced to come to terms with the demands of politics—and her responsibility to the American people. She'd allowed herself to be talked into accepting the common rationale for imprisoning law-abiding citizens. She'd allowed safety to trump liberty and couldn't see a way around it. Posties were dangerous, even if they didn't mean to be. She couldn't allow another Daytona Beach, not ever. And Tom Fuson could potentially do much more damage than that.

Damn.

"Okay," she said. "We're going to try both plans. Doctor Angus, speak with the boy and try to convince him to join us. If that doesn't work..." she breathed in, slowly, and swallowed. "If that doesn't work, then we'll follow the recommendation of Director Givich. And may God help us all."

CHAPTER TWENTY-FIVE

Tuesdays were steak days and the MegaMax inmates all came to get it hot off the grill. It was the social highlight of the week; even the vegetarians showed up. Tom, Tiffany and Fiona had beaten the crowd and sat at the table closest to their hall.

Tom just sat while the ladies finished their meals. He hadn't eaten anything at all in the days since his arrival. He didn't seem to feel hunger or thirst and had no desire to consume the contraceptive-laced food.

They sat around the table and listened to Fiona spin yarns about her career as the notorious Flamechylde. Tom loved these stories—a behind-the-scenes look at the old age of costumed heroes—although he got the impression that Tiffany had heard them all before. Still, she listened attentively as the older woman told her tall tales.

"So Milk storms out of the bank, and the fire's just falling off him. He's all snorting and growling like he does when he gets pissed. He's got me up against a wall, and I look up at him and say, 'Wow, Milk, I didn't know you had *three* horns!'" Fiona snickered and took a sip of her coffee.

Tiffany busted out laughing, but it took Tom a moment to get the joke.

"Oh, no. You mean—"

"Yes sir," the former villain winked at him. "The big guy may be fireproof but his clothes sure as hell weren't. All I could see—swinging right in front of my face—was his big old, pasty white—"

Fiona stopped mid-sentence and stared over Tom's shoulder. He became aware that the entire crowd had gone silent. Even the kitchen staff had frozen in place. Everyone looked toward the main entrance.

Tom turned around and saw Vaughn Gregory enter the cafeteria.

The Behemoth had been let out of solitary earlier that day and was on a sort of limited release program; Tiffany had told Tom about it as soon as she'd heard.

Vaughn was ordinarily not allowed to mingle with the rest of the inmates (for obvious reasons) and remained safely behind the force field in Cellblock A. Fiona had mentioned that the guards let him out every couple of days—the staff thought that some socializing was necessary to help him retain some semblance of sanity—and Tom should have guessed that steak day would be one of those occasions. The fat bastard certainly loved eating meat.

The scaly beast wore massive shackles around his wrists and ankles, connected by huge metal chains. The stone giant Tank and four APE-wearing guards flanked the Behemoth. Security was obviously taking no chances with the prison's most violent inmate.

Vaughn's reptilian eyes met Tom's and a hideous grin spread across his muzzle. The monster's gaze slid over to Tiffany, and his disgusting leer widened.

"Oh, hello there, Red. I know what *I* want for lunch. You smell delicious, bitch." His purple-black, forked tongue snaked out and twitched in the air.

Tom stood and turned to face the monster. The golden light flared around his body. "Shut your mouth, or I'll shut it for you."

The twenty-odd prisoners gasped, and the guards put hands on their weapons.

The Behemoth turned his attention back to Tom. He laughed at the boy, "Go ahead and try cupcake. I think your girlfriend likes the attention. Don't you, slut?"

Tom's aura grew brighter. The light blazed in his eyes. "You say one more word to her and I'll fu—"

"That's enough," one of the guards interrupted. "Sit down, Fuson. Now."

Tom glared at the chrome face of the APE suit and then noticed that every guard in the cafeteria had drawn their weapons—and they all aimed at him. Every single guard. They were more afraid of Tom than Vaughn.

Tom looked around the silent room. Several prisoners ducked under their tables; the kitchen staff scrambled behind the counters. Fiona smirked and licked her lips, Tank watched but did not react, and Tiffany's eyes grew enormous. She slowly shook her head.

"Sit down, Fuson," the guard repeated.

"Fine." Tom turned around and closed his eyes. He exhaled and released his power. The halo vanished, and he returned to the stool. Tiffany reached across the table and took his hand.

Vaughn muttered something, and the guard told him to shut up. Tom could feel the Behemoth staring as the group passed.

"In-deep-denz prow-tek peep-ull," rumbled Tank. No one knew whether he spoke to himself, the guards or the other inmates.

Tom was not surprised when the PA system clicked on and a crisp voice said, "Thomas Fuson, report to the security desk. Tomas Fuson, report to the security desk."

Doctor Angus sat at the desk with his sleeves rolled up and tie loosened. He tense and tired, like he'd had a rough day. The old scientist's watery eyes were rimmed with red and his voice was a sandpaper rasp. He seemed to be troubled by something, maybe exhausted from a sleepless night.

"Hello, Thomas. Thank you for coming so quickly."

"Doctor." He walked to the window and looked at the blue sky. "You wanted to see me? Is this about Vaughn?"

The old man shook his head, "Not at all. I don't blame you for being protective of your friends, Thomas, but do not allow

Mister Gregory to provoke you. It is best to ignore bullies."

"I'll try," said Tom. He glanced at the nearby rooftop where the usual gang of young prisoners sat together killing time. "Don't those guys ever go inside?"

Angus smiled wearily. "Young people need a place to socialize. There are no shopping malls here, after all. Besides, it is good for them to have some small measure of privacy."

"Or the illusion of it," said Tom. "Not really very private, with the guards on the Wall right there."

Angus nodded and replied, "I do what I can to make them comfortable, Thomas. I understand how difficult imprisonment must be, even here."

"You could let them go."

"No, I cannot. You know that. Sometimes, yes, I would like very much to free them. Few of them are really dangerous."

"Then why hold them?"

"Because of Daytona Beach, Thomas, you know that. A single child lost control, and thousands of innocents died. There was no ill intent. That boy was no killer—he did not even know that he was Posthuman—but one emotional outburst was enough to destroy a city."

"Doesn't make much sense. Joey Slater was thirteen, right? But you don't do the testing until we're sixteen. So you aren't really protecting anyone from anything."

Angus shrugged. "Politics, my boy. One cannot expect to find logic in such matters. I suspect that the age of testing was chosen for the benefit of the parents. Voters and legislators follow their emotions far more often than they actually think about the issues."

Tom thought about this for a moment. Then he said, "But there has to be more to it than just that. I mean, how many other cities have been destroyed by Posties? Ever?"

"None," admitted the doctor. "But you may as well ask how many buildings have been destroyed by terrorists in airplanes. The fact that such things are highly unlikely does nothing to alleviate the fear of them happening again, once they have occurred. Human beings prefer to feel safe, regardless of the cost."

"A friend of mine once told me that Ben Franklin said something about that. That people who would rather have safety than freedom don't deserve to have either one," said Tom, thinking about Marcus and their last walk home.

"Yes, I am familiar with the quotation. And while I do agree with the sentiment, the truth is that our founders did not face weapons of mass destruction, extraterrestrial invasion, suicide bombers or Posthuman abilities. Idealism rarely wins in the real world, Thomas."

Tom huffed with disgust, still remembering his best friend. "Lee Harvey Oswald was a man with a gun..."

Angus rose from his chair and stood beside Tom at the window. "A man with a gun might kill a few, or dozens or even hundreds, but a Posthuman could kill millions. Imagine if Joseph Slater had detonated in Manhattan, San Francisco or Chicago instead of Daytona Beach."

"But he didn't. You're taking away the lives of hundreds of people for nothing. It would be like me blaming humanity for Mohamed Atta or John Wayne Gacy. Should Aegis have punished all of you for Adolph Hitler? Should *I*?"

"We have to take steps to defend ourselves, my boy. If—"

Tom interrupted, "But you aren't really defending anyone. You said there are more than a hundred Posties hiding in America; there are at least a thousand worldwide. How many people become Posties every year?"

"Just a few. The wild strain of the Aegis virus is ordinarily defeated by the human immune system."

"And you can't stop that," said Tom. "No matter how many Posties you lock up, there will always be more. There's no excuse for any of this."

"Perhaps there are no excuses. Perhaps there are simply facts. If we do nothing and another Daytona Beach happens, then who will be blamed by the American people? Do not answer that, Thomas, because I *know*. I would be blamed; the President would be blamed, along with Congress and the military. It has happened before. We have sworn to defend this nation, and we bear that responsibility. We must do everything within our power to prevent such a tragedy from occurring again."

"And you think that justifies locking people up forever? I don't buy it. There has to be more to it than that."

Angus took a deep breath and nodded. "Yes, there are other issues to consider."

"Like what?"

"Do you know why they are called Posthumans, Thomas?"

"Because they aren't normal people anymore. They've become something different. More than human. Beyond human."

"A reasonable assumption," said Angus.

"But wrong?"

"Wrong is perhaps too strong of a word, my boy." Angus grew quiet for half a minute and then said, "The word 'posthuman' was coined by futurists before the death of Aegis, originally to describe hypothetical human beings who transcend ordinary capabilities through technology or biological engineering. We later applied this word to our test subjects shortly after the creation of Milk, but for a very different reason. We call them Posthuman because they breed true, Thomas. Do you understand the implications of this?"

Tom looked at the old man and cocked his head to the side. "Posties always have Postie kids, everyone knows that."

"Perhaps. Yet people seldom ponder the ramifications of this fact." Angus motioned for Tom to sit and then returned to his chair. Once they were seated the doctor leaned forward and said, "Genetic traits do not work like this, not ordinarily. With other alleles there are always probabilities to consider, but the Aegis virus is different. The odds of its transmission are one hundred percent."

"So it's a dominant trait?" asked Tom. "I took Biology, you know."

"It is not merely dominant, my boy. It is *invasive*. Even dominant Mendelian features do not propagate with perfect efficiency. The Aegis virus is a parasitic, alien organism that infects the human genome like a computer virus. Each segment of the transposon is duplicated on the opposing locus ensuring that the descendants of a Posthuman will be Posthuman. All of them, Thomas, forever."

"Okay, I get it. I still don't understand why it's so scary."

"It is frightening because, eventually, Posthumans will be the dominant species on Earth. Every generation will have a higher percentage until they outnumber normal human beings. It will take millennia, but it is a mathematical certainty. Inevitably, they will take our place. We named them Posthumans because they will replace us."

"Us versus them," muttered Tom. "It's stupid to think that way. Milk is still human, same with Tiffany or Fiona or Tank. Being a Postie doesn't change that."

"What about Vaughn Gregory? Do you think that he is human?"

Tom thought about it and then said, "He's as human as Ted Bundy or Jack the Ripper. He might be evil or crazy or both ... but he's still a man. What you see on the outside is what he's always been on the inside."

Angus nodded, "A very insightful description, Thomas. We know that the Posthuman transformation is driven by the psychology of the individual. Our friend Milk, for example, wished to overcome what he viewed as cowardice and weakness. He became strong and impervious to harm—and, more importantly, he transformed into something that *cannot* hide. Cowardice is no longer an option for Sergeant Young. Day or night, he can be seen from miles away. Likewise, Vaughn Gregory was a sociopath and a killer long before his transformation. We believe that he became the perfect predator because that is what he has always wished to be. You are certainly correct."

Tom leaned forward and narrowed his eyes. "Then how can you group all Posties together like this? How can you condemn them all?"

"Many Posthumans could conceivably kill thousands— without weapons or hijacked planes—and they could do so on accident. *That* is the reason, Thomas. They possess a potential for destruction that threatens all life on Earth—and that potential cannot be disarmed or removed. Now imagine a world filled with tens of thousands, hundreds of thousands or millions of them. How long could such a world survive?"

"So that's why you keep all of the prisoners on birth control," said Tom; it was not a question. His metallic eyes bored into Angus. "You want to wipe them out."

The old man's lips pressed together and he took a slow breath. "Wipe them out? No. We are simply attempting to control their numbers. We cannot allow their population to increase. The risks are far too great. Believe me when I say that some people wish to see every last Posthuman executed. Compared to that, all of this is humane."

Tom said nothing. He looked over the old man's shoulder, out the window at the young Posties on the rooftop. Finally, he said, "So where does that leave me? I'm not a Postie. And I guess you wouldn't call me human, either. Where's my place in all of this?"

"Your place?" Angus leaned back in the chair and placed his elbows on the desk. "I believe that you are meant to take your father's place. I believe that you were born to be the protector of this world. Perhaps you could eventually convince my colleagues that this prison is unnecessary — if you show them that you want only to help. If you help us contain the threat."

Tom shook his head and glanced around the room at the photographs of his father. Adam had served the American government for his entire life, but Tom could not imagine that the hero would have approved of this slow genocide.

Angus cleared his throat and said, "Come around here, Thomas. I want to show you something — something that I have been ordered to keep from you."

"Ordered?" Tom's eyebrows drew together in confusion. He rose and walked around the desk.

"Yes," said Angus. He stood and motioned for Tom to take the seat. "My colleagues think that showing this to you may not be in our best interest, but I think you have the right to know."

"Know what?" asked Tom as he sat in the large office chair.

Angus laid a hand on Tom's shoulder. "This is not easy for me to say, but it is wrong to keep such things hidden. I have asked for permission to show you, every day, but my superiors will not allow it." The old scientist took another deep breath and said, "Marcus Alexander, your friend, was killed the night that ... the night that Public Safety came for you. I am so sorry, my boy."

A wave of disbelief and disorientation rolled over Tom. He closed his eyes and remembered Marcus—a thousand, a million burning memories.

Side by side, they stepped onto the bus for the first day of kindergarten. Together, they explored the wilderness, navigated the maze of adolescent drama and dreamed about the future. Every memory seemed to be centered on either his mother or his best friend, and now they were gone—gone because of the government, ABRA and the stupid, indifferent laws—gone because of Angus.

Tom's eyes snapped open. He snarled, "What did your people do? Killing Mom wasn't enough? What the fuck did you do?"

Angus shook his head and said, "We did nothing, my boy. Nothing. Let me show you." He reached for the computer mouse, clicked open a folder, and brought up a video file. "You deserve to know the truth."

The footage was grainy, green-and-black night vision, taken from high in the air. It took Tom a few seconds to recognize the land as his mother's property in Westburg; their home was missing, and several large, indistinct objects were scattered in the yard.

Angus explained, "This video was taken by a surveillance drone several hours after the DPS left your property." He pointed at the objects in Tom's old back yard. "They demolished your home, loaded the wreckage into those freight containers and then left. I believe that the agents pulled back to set a trap for any Posthumans who might have come after the … incident. None came. There were only two visitors that night, as you will see. The first was your friend; the operatives knew him and considered him harmless, so they ignored him. Here, watch."

Tom watched, and a tiny blurry figure rode up to the house on a bicycle, dismounted and began to explore. He immediately recognized Marcus in the glowing green distance; the walk was unmistakable—that steady, unstoppable determination. Marcus spent some time wandering around and then climbed into one of the containers.

"What's he doing?" asked Tom.

Angus quietly replied, "Mourning his friend. Searching for clues. Just watch."

Tom continued to stare at the slowly rotating video. Eventually Marcus climbed out of the container—and then, suddenly, a large ovoid object descended past the military drone and began to slowly circle the premises.

"What the hell? Is that a—?"

"Yes. I knew you would recognize it. You have taken History as well, I presume. It is a probe of the Union of Knowledge."

"But..."

Marcus hopped onto his bike and rode swiftly into the forest. Tom realized that his friend had taken the old path through the woods, and the probe followed.

Then it attacked, practically in Marcus's own back yard. It knocked him from the bike, and they faced each other for a long, tense moment. Marcus picked up a rock and threw it at the probe—indomitable to the end—then the screen blazed a brilliant green-white, and he fell to the ground. The probe rose and vanished.

"Marcus... it... why?" stammered Tom.

"We do not know. This is purely conjecture, but we think that the Union scanned your friend's mind in an attempt to locate you. We cannot comprehend its reasons for committing violence, but it has often done such things in the past. I am sorry, Thomas. Your friend's death is a horrible tragedy, but I had to show you. I do not care what my superiors think. You should know about your friend."

Tom wiped his eyes. "But ... if the Union is looking for me..."

"Precisely, my boy. We know little about it, only that it is an alien machine of incredible power. It has come to Earth on two occasions. First it attacked Aegis, and then it came for your father. It seems inevitable that the Union will come for you."

Tom sniffled and swallowed. He could not speak. He covered his face with his hands and thought nothing—his mind couldn't operate under the weight of his emotions.

"Let us help you, Thomas," urged the doctor. "Together we can stop the Union. Work with us, as your father once did. Your place is with us. We will make sure that your friend did not die in vain."

That broke through Tom's pain and pulled him directly to rage. He glanced at the old man and understood that all of this was just more manipulation. This was nothing but another attempt to win him over. His upper lip twitched and his golden eyes flared. He whispered, "Marcus didn't die in vain, Doctor. He died because the Union found me. How did it find me?

"*You* attacked me; that's how! You bastards killed both of them—Mom and Marcus—and you have the balls to ask me to work for you? I'll never work for you, you son of a bitch! Never! If the Union wants to come after me then let it. Aegis beat it. My father beat it. *I* will beat it. I don't need you."

"Thomas, I…"

Tom stood and stormed toward the door. "I'm going back to the prison that you put me in, Doctor. I don't want to see you again. I don't care what happens, my answer will *always* be no. I will never be your Independence. Deal with it." Tom reached for the doorknob but was stopped by the old man's voice.

"And Bloodlust? Have you considered him? He murdered both of your predecessors, Thomas. He will come for you. How do you plan to *deal* with that?"

Tom replied, "Without you."

It was nearly midnight as they prepared to turn in. Tiffany always let Tom shower first, so she could take her time. He lay in bed, wearing only the scrub pants he used as pajamas.

He had been quiet since returning from meeting with Angus; the wounds were too fresh to expose, but Tiffany could still see them. So she had left him alone while he stayed in the room and read an old paperback from the meager MegaMax library. She was obviously worried about him, and his attempts to convince her that everything was fine only increased her concern.

Eventually she tried to draw him into conversation.

"I've never seen anything like it," she said, sitting on her bed, absentmindedly brushing her long red hair.

Tom took a deep breath, trying to keep his voice steady, and asked, "What's that?"

"Your power. It's so different than anybody else's." Her face scrunched up as she sought the right words to describe her perceptions. "It's usually like a whirlpool, like you're just pulling energy to you. But it's also like a fog, too, all hazy and moving around. And when you start glowing, it all changes."

"How does it change?" He could only manage simple sentences, but that seemed enough to cheer her up. Tom found that the storm in his soul was calmed by the light in her eyes.

"Well, um, most of us seem to be one of two things. Posties like Fiona control energy or whatever, but people like Tank seem to have changed themselves. When I look at him, it's kind of like looking at two different people. It's like the giant rock monster is a costume and inside is the person he would be."

"Have you ever turned his power off?" he asked, curious for the first time about Tank's origin and history.

She shook her head, "Uh-uh. I don't like to do that unless I have to. He likes being who he is, and it almost seems ... insulting to turn off other people's powers."

"But if you did, all of the rock would just disappear, like how Vaughn turned into an old man, right?" Talking became easier the more that he did it. He was surprised at the sense of relief that came simply from talking to her, even about trivia like this.

"Yeah. Doctor Angus said that kind of thing breaks some kind of law of conservation of something or other, but I don't really know much about that stuff. I just know that whenever I want to, I can make it collapse — that's how it feels, like the costume folds up and falls inside of the person. When I let go, it just pops right back up."

"And what if you do it to Fiona?"

Tiffany giggled. "She gets *really* mad at me. But I've had to a couple of times. She used to get into lots of fights. If I shut her down, it's different than with Tank or Vaughn. Posties like her don't change, but I absorb all their energy and stop them from touching their power. It's like I drain their batteries and put them in glass bottles at the same time."

"So how am I different?"

"Well, you usually seem like Fiona—like you're a normal guy who sucks in energy and uses it, like she does. It's different with you, but kind of the same. But when you start glowing, it's like you become like Tank. You *change* and don't feel anything at all like a normal guy. It's like you make yourself into something different. Only..."

"Only what?"

Her fine eyebrows drew together and she said, "Only it's like *you* are the costume, and there's this ball of fire inside that's the real person. Does that make sense?"

Tom thought for a moment "Yeah. Yeah, it does."

They sat in silence for a few minutes while Tiffany finished preparing for bed. She wore a pale blue nightshirt that fell to her knees. Tom placed his book on the nightstand and turned his lamp off, then lay on his back and stared at the ceiling.

Tiffany climbed into her bed and shut off her own lamp. After a moment she asked, "Can you do it anytime you want?"

"Do what?"

"Power up or whatever."

"I don't know," he said and rolled over to face her in the dim light. "I think so. Today was only the third time I've ever done it. It seemed to turn on by itself when Vaughn attacked me the first time. Did the same thing when they came after me at home. But today ... I wanted it to happen. I knew I could do it. That asshole can't talk to you like that."

She said, "It was very sweet. Thank you." Tom did not reply, so she asked, "Can you try it now?"

"Now? Okay." He sat up in his bed and let his legs fall over the side. He closed his eyes despite the room's darkness, visualizing the energy that flowed into his body. He stood and clenched his fists, but did not open his eyes.

Over the past week, Tom had grown used to being able to sense power all around. The earth and metal above MegaMax blocked much of it, but he could still feel some wireless broadcasts, the deep pulse of the Earth's magnetic field, electricity in the walls and the immense power of the subterranean reactor.

Then he noticed something else, something new—he felt Tiffany, like a spotlight aimed at his face. He could feel Fiona, simmering in her room across the hall. He felt the distant weight of Tank's steady strength and the slumbering Behemoth's bottomless red hunger. Tom could sense every prisoner, both topside and in MegaMax. He could almost see them. Two hundred forty-one stars twinkled in his mind's eye.

One of the stars was a swirl of gravity, like a miniature galaxy spinning in ABRA City. Another broadcast in tiny pulses like that radio tower from the beginning of old movies. All of the Posties were like that; each twinkling pinpoint had its own pattern, song, and flavor. And they were all connected. Each point of light was connected to the others by filaments of energy; they were all connected to *him*. Lights strung along a line; nodes and knots in a spider web.

The web stretched around the horizon and spread into the heavens and beyond—and there was Tom, at the center of it all. His light pulsed out on the wisps, illuminating the smaller lights, touching every Posthuman.

"What did you do?" Tiffany whispered, her voice quavering. Her power touched his, and they shared a silent connection. "Are you ... are you copying me?"

He opened his eyes and she gasped. His glowing irises lit the room. Tiffany's shadow stretched along the floor and wall. A thrill raced through Tom's limbs; he looked at her and grinned. His golden aura flared even brighter, and his limbs reverberated with power.

"I think I kinda am," he said quietly. He closed his eyes again to focus on this new sense. Her power was like his, connected to the roots of Posthuman power. No wonder he'd so easily mimicked her ability. "I can feel everyone. All the Posties, even the ones up above—"

"Omigod, Tom," she exclaimed, standing and taking a step forward. "You're floating!"

Tom opened his eyes and looked down—sure enough, he stood on air, a foot or more above the tiled floor. He wiggled his toes and laughed despite the day's anguish. He could still feel the floor underfoot—or rather, he could feel a pressure between the tile and his soles; the invisible force reminded him of trying to push together matching poles of two bar magnets. Then he wobbled, descended six inches, hovered for half a second and dropped to the ground.

Tiffany stepped closer. "Are you okay?"

"Yeah. I almost had it." He looked at her—the golden light played on her porcelain skin.

"Here, let me help." She placed a hand on his cheek and closed her eyes. Tom felt a sudden flood of power enter his body. He could feel raw energy tingling in his extremities. He felt stronger than he could have ever imagined.

Tom willed himself to rise, and his body obeyed. It was as simple as that, easier than walking.

He laughed again and floated toward the ceiling. She stared with wide-eyed fascination and a bright smile. He bent down, took her hand and pulled her up.

His left arm slid around her waist; both of her arms wrapped around his neck. She stood on his feet—her little toes on his arches—and she trembled, slightly afraid but only for a moment. Then she looked down at the floor, and they began to rotate. She yelped, clutched his back and then laughed.

"It's okay," he said softly. "I've got you."

"I know." She laid her head against his chest. They began to drift around the room; they slowly danced in the air. Her breath was hot on his bare chest. "I've always wanted to fly."

Tom lowered his face and ran his fingers through her long ponytail. He whispered, "We will one day. We'll fly together for real. I'll take you above the clouds. I promise."

She pulled back with her eyes locked onto his; her mouth opened but she did not speak. She drew in a breath, and he felt the fluttering of her pulse. She blinked once, a spontaneous, innocent gesture that touched his heart. He took a breath and leaned closer.

She did not pull away, and their lips met. Hers were soft and tentative but eagerly pressed into his; the sweet, minty taste of her breath filled his mouth. She rose higher on her toes, her arms tightening around his neck; his arms tightened around her narrow waist. The heat of her body was unimpeded by the thin cotton nightgown. Her firm breasts pressed against his chest.

Then the door burst open and blinding light rushed in, followed by a dozen armored guards. The hulking forms of several APEs stood in the hall. Tiffany gasped and nearly fell from Tom's feet. He tightened his grip on her waist, and she buried her face in his chest. Tom winced against the glare and stared at the soldiers.

"Sorry to interrupt, Romeo," said the closest guard. "But you're coming with us."

"What if I say no?" Tom growled defiantly.

The guards responded by raising their firearms. The leader said, "You don't want to find out, freak. Now put the girl down, turn off the lights and come quietly."

Tom's eyes narrowed and his lips twitched with barely restrained rage. He settled on the floor — Tiffany clutched his hand. She started to say something, but Tom shook his head and floated around, placing himself between her and the guards.

"And what if I don't?" he sneered. The guards all took a step back but kept their weapons aimed. Tom could sense a storm of radio communications, but they said nothing.

Instead, the imperious voice of Doctor Angus broke the silence, and he appeared in the doorway. "Stand down, Thomas. It would be such a tragedy if dear Miss Cooke were caught in the crossfire."

"Don't threaten her!" The glow around Tom's fists brightened, becoming nearly white in its intensity.

Angus coldly replied, "Do not threaten *us*, Thomas. Understand that you cannot win."

"I'm not scared of your guns, Doctor."

The old man sniffed derisively. "Perhaps not, but I imagine that Miss Cooke is rather frightened at the moment. Tiffany, be a good girl and negate Thomas's abilities."

"N-no," she replied. "No, I won't! We haven't done anything wrong! Don't do this to us."

"Shut him down, or I will be forced to—"

"Go fuck yourself," barked Tom.

Angus sighed and nodded; the lead guard stepped forward and announced, "Tiffany Cooke, you will comply. If you don't ... we'll blow both of your fucking heads off. Or did you forget about the goddamn bombs in your goddamn brains?"

Tom's blazing eyes narrowed; Tiffany trembled against his back.

Doctor Angus gave them a look of contempt and said, "You cannot win, Thomas. Fight us and she dies. It is your decision."

Tom's lips pressed together, and he closed his eyes. He knew that he could beat these guards—he could kill them *all*—but somewhere there was a soldier with his finger on a button. Tom had no choice but to obey; there was no other way to protect her.

He inhaled deeply and said, "No, Doctor, it's *your* decision. And you're going to have to live with it."

The golden light vanished, and he looked at Tiffany. Angus stepped closer, and the guards rushed forward, surrounding them. One of them pushed a rifle barrel against the back of Tom's head.

Tears streamed down Tiffany's cheeks and she looked up with limitless pain in her quivering eyes. "Tom, I..."

"It's okay," he whispered, reaching to touch her face and wipe away a tear. "It will be okay. I promise. Now do it. Drain me dry."

She placed her right hand on his cheek and bit her lower lip. "I'm sorry."

The power rushed away in a torrent, leaving nothing but weakness in its place. He felt like a drowning man gasping for air, as every cell struggled to reach the energy it craved. He collapsed on the hard tile and lacked the strength to rise.

Tiffany dropped down beside him and threw her arms around his neck, sobbing and apologizing. He tried to hold her, but the guards rushed in, pulled them apart and dragged him across the floor.

Tom rolled onto his back and raised his eyes to the blurry form of Doctor Angus. He tried to push up on his elbows, but couldn't. He extended an imploring hand to the scientist and croaked with a tremulous voice, "Why?"

The old man looked at Tom with a flat gaze. "I have given you every opportunity to work with us, but you have rejected every one of these chances. You determined this outcome. I truly am sorry Thomas, but you have left us no choice."

A guard slammed the butt of his rifle against the side of Tom's head. Tiffany screamed and struggled against the strong arms that held her in place. Tom could see her, weeping and thrashing — then the guard brought the gun down again. And again.

CHAPTER TWENTY-SIX

David arrived in Detroit two hours before dawn. The wind carried a hint of the coming winter, but he was warm from the run. He pulled out a set of keys, entered a small building on the edge of Mike's neighborhood and descended to the tunnels below. The security systems had been reprogrammed to recognize the Youngs, so David didn't need to worry about being attacked by robots this time. BuzzTrikes and SpikeFlies ignored him and continued their endless patrols, as he walked down to the fallout shelter.

"Mike? Yo, man, are you here?" he called. The alien Walker rotated to face him, but did not raise its many weapons. "Heya Six. Where's Mike?" muttered David, talking to himself. He knew that the war machine possessed only the most rudimentary intelligence.

"Over here … um, under here." The voice came from beneath the computer platform.

"How we looking?" asked David as he rounded the corner — and stopped, astonished, as he saw the genius for the first time in days.

Mike looked like a brand new person. He'd gotten a haircut, shaved the ragged beard down to a neat goatee, trimmed his nails and scrubbed his skin pink. He'd apparently just bathed and wore only a pair of sweat pants with a towel thrown over his shoulders. David was surprised to see the skinny computer nerd's sleek, toned muscles. Being a Postie has definite advantages.

"We're rocking," said Mike, pulling a small flash drive from the patchwork mainframe. "Just finishing up. Hard to believe that today's the big day. Nervous?"

"Terrified," admitted David. "But it's exciting, too. One way or another, everything's going to be different tomorrow."

"Good luck. I almost wish that I could go with you."

"We all have a part to play. Yours is here, nothing wrong with that."

"Well, I won't actually be here. While you guys are having all of the fun, I'll be hacking their systems from a hotel in Gary. Don't want to do it from here in case they manage to track me. Come on, I left the PhotoFlies by the rocket."

"Rocket?"

Mike grinned and raised the flash drive. "Gotta get this up there somehow, right? It's not really a rocket, though. Not at all, actually. It's magnetically propelled, just like Carnivore ships; it pushes against the Earth's magnetosphere and can hit some serious velocity." He looked at David and winked. "Well, long as I don't compare it to you."

David chuckled. "You've really thought of everything, haven't you?"

"Probably not. You know how it is; nothing ever goes according to plan."

"Don't I know it? Last time I tried some hero stuff I got attacked by killer robots."

"Touché," grinned Mike as they walked to one of the hallways in back. "So your dad's really going to try and recruit that Joyce guy?"

"Yeah. Why? Don't think he'll help?"

Mike shrugged, "Mostly I'm just worried that we're cutting it to close to the wire."

"I asked Dad about that. He said he'd rather ask at the last minute. 'Don't want to give Joyce time to chicken out,' is how he put it. Besides, the guy's always up on that roof, so he's the easiest prisoner to approach. Pretty sweet powers, too, according to the files you pulled. He can help us evacuate the place better than Kobar and Portero combined."

"I guess that makes sense. Who am I to disagree with Milk's tactics? Just have to make sure that we get this drive plugged in so we can take down that force field. I hope Jeremiah Joyce has it in him." They rounded a corner and Mike said, "Here we go."

"*That's* your rocket?" gasped David. A small table sat against the wall, and on the table sat a four-wheeled platform carrying a yard-long, flat black triangle that pointed up at the ceiling. An open hatch revealed a small cavity in the body of the rocket. Next to the platform sat a smart phone, a short steel tube and a tiny, six-legged robot with a low profile and the same matte-black finish as the rocket. "Looks like a toy stealth fighter."

"Exactamundo. This baby has it all: micro-fusion power plant, total radar invisibility, hypersonic propulsion and a pretty big brain. I'm going to launch it in a few hours, and ninety minutes later it will rendezvous with the ABRA supply caravan, drop off the bot and come back home. The trucks will unknowingly take the bot inside, and then it will wait for your signal to head to the roof."

"Hell yeah, man. One question, though: how do we signal it?"

Mike picked up the smart phone and gave it to David. "With this; it also controls your swarm." He handed over the metal cylinder. "The Flies are inside, don't lose them."

David placed the items in his jacket pockets. "Thanks Mike. I don't know how we could ever do this without you."

"We haven't done it yet, but you're welcome. Oh, and let your dad know that a friend of mine is going to join you all up there. He should be a big help."

"A friend? Didn't know you had too many of those."

Mike smirked, "I don't. A couple of robots, my computer, one or two guys ... and you."

David smiled and shook Mike's hand. "Thanks, man. I've got the feeling that this is the start of a beautiful friendship."

"Me, too. Just keep your head down, okay? It's going to be crazy intense once the shooting starts. ABRA has a lot of experience taking down Posties."

"Don't worry about me, man. I'm pretty good at dodging bullets."

"Yes, you are. But be careful anyway."

"I'll try," said David. He took a step back and zipped up the front of his jacket. "I'll see you tonight, after we kick ABRA's ass."

"Sounds good. See you then. Stay safe."

"You too, man," said David, and then he was gone. Only a rush of air and a distant boom marked his passing.

The inventor smiled to himself and looked at the flash drive. "Now comes the fun part."

✪   ✪   ✪

Eight-year-old Sean knew something was up. Everyone had been too quiet lately, and if there was one thing that his family was *not*, it was quiet.

Dad and David had gone out nearly every day over the past week, and they wouldn't explain where they went. Nikki spent most of her time down at Mrs. Wilder's junkyard; she seemed even more tense and angry than normal. And even Mom acted strangely, especially toward Dad. Sean had never seen his parents argue—he still hadn't—but lately they always seemed *ready* to argue. It was confusing, irritating and a little frightening for the boy. Something was happening, and they were keeping it a secret. He was determined to get to the bottom of it.

"Where's Dave?" Sean asked his mother, while he fished the last few bites of his sandwich. It was about two o'clock on that cold, overcast day, and he felt stir-crazy and grumpy.

"He's still asleep, honey," Gloria replied. "He had to go for a run very late, so we're letting him stay in bed a while."

"Oh. Where's Nikki? Did she go down to the junkyard?"

"Yes, but don't go bother her. Your sister has a lot on her mind."

"Like what?"

"Like stuff that doesn't involve nosy little brothers." Gloria walked over and took the empty bowl.

"I'm not nosy, just curious. You're all keeping secrets. I can tell."

Gloria smiled sadly and bent down to kiss his head between the stubby horns. "I know, Sean. You're a very smart boy, and it's not fair for us to hide things from you. But sometimes we have to keep secrets to protect the people we love."

"Like how we live here to keep the bad guys from catching us?"

"Just like that, Sean. I know you'd rather go to a real school and have more friends your own age, but the bad guys would take you away. So we have to hide."

"Yeah, but that's hiding stuff from bad guys. Why do you have to hide stuff from me?"

Gloria frowned and cupped her fingers under Sean's chin, tilting his head up to look into his shocking greenish eyes. "Because, if something bad happens, it's better for you to not know about it. That way, if the bad guys come, you can't tell them anything."

"I won't tell the bad guys anything, Mom. Never."

"I know, honey, but you wouldn't have to. There are bad guys who could look right inside your brain and learn everything you know."

Sean began to ask his mother what she meant, but was cut off by a flash of light from the living room and the resounding steps of his father entering the house.

"Dad!" The boy hopped from the table and ran into the living room, skidding to a halt as he turned the corner. His eyes widened into enormous circles, and his jaw dropped as he saw the six figures surrounding his father.

Jacqueline Dean was closest to the boy, wearing the old California Girl costume; a blue domino mask, a skin-tight belly shirt with short sleeves—gold with a blue stripe down the center and a gold star in the middle of her chest—blue short shorts with gold trim and matching knee-high boots and short gloves. Sean had known Jacqui for his entire life, but seeing her in full costume was mind-blowing.

Next to the California girl stood Curtis Talmadge and Hannah Taft, better known as the former crime fighters Lockdown and Glimmer. Both wore similar, black-and-red bodysuits with the stylized East Coast Alliance logo on their left biceps. Lockdown looked a little queasy, but Glimmer smiled and waved at Sean.

On the other side of Milk was a short, thin man with blank flesh instead of eyes and a wry grin on his thin lips. This was Quietus, and he wore a simple tunic of black silk, matching pants and low, soft-soled shoes. Next to the martial artist stood the beefy giant, Hardcore. He was shirtless—tattoos covered his rippling muscles—and wore only blue jeans and tall leather boots. He grinned and looked around, "Nice place, Charley."

Portero, Rodrigo Mendez, was in the back—a tall, handsome man with piercing dark eyes, a well-trimmed beard and long black hair. He wore a long duster over a white silk shirt, black slacks and high leather boots. He lowered his head in a charming bow and whispered something in Spanish to Gloria as she stepped into the hall.

Sean exclaimed, "Heroes!"

Milk looked down at his young son and smiled. "Come on Half-Pint, don't you know? We're all heroes around here."

"No. I'll take him for a walk. He doesn't need to hear this." Gloria turned her back to her towering husband and looked out of the window of their bedroom. Thick, gray clouds rolled overhead, promising rain or worse.

"He *does* need to hear this. There's no point in keeping it from him now. In a few hours, the whole world's going to know." Milk kneeled low, whispering; his resonant voice tended to carry. "If anything happens tonight ... Sean deserves to know why."

"Why? So that he can grow up worshiping you and die wearing a stupid costume?"

"Is that what this is about? If you don't want David and Nikki to go, then say so. You gave me your blessing before I recruited them."

She turned and glared—sad, angry and confused—and replied, "I said yes because I know they would hate me if I said no."

Milk leaned forward and gently wrapped his right hand around his wife's shoulders. "I'm sorry, babe. I just thought ... I need them. I need their help. They're strong and they're good. You know how good they are. They'll do the job, and they *want* to do the job. But if you want them to stay home, then I'll tell them. I'll say it was my idea, and they can be mad at me if they want."

"No ... no," she said and leaned up to kiss him. "You're right ... you need them to watch your back. Nobody's faster than David."

"And nobody's meaner than Nikki," finished Milk.

"They'll protect each other. They always do. You be careful, too."

"Come with us," he said impulsively. "Remember how good we were together? Half of the time you took out the bad guys before I even showed up. Remember that time in Berlin?"

Gloria scoffed, "We nearly started World War III!"

"We *prevented* World War III," laughed Milk. He winked and kissed her forehead. "At least that's how I remember it."

She shook her head and rolled her eyes, but she didn't comment on her husband's take on the old misadventure. "No, I can't come. You know that. I have to stay with Sean. But we'll sit through your pep talk downstairs. I'll have to explain everything to him anyway. Kobar will be here at six to take us to the bar."

"Good. The old base is the safest place in the world. And Sean'll get a kick out of seeing it. Be sure to show him Trophy Hall."

She rubbed her eyes and laughed, "That's just what we need. He'll want to bring home Saurus Rex's ankylobot."

"That's okay, babe. He can keep it in the barn."

They held each other in silence, while Sean crouched in the hall, ear pressed against the door. He was very excited at the prospect of owning an ankylobot. Whatever that was.

"So this is the prison," said Nikki, pointing at the floating image within the cloud of PhotoFlies that swarmed over the coffee table in the Young's living room. The entire family and their six friends watched as the picture rotated to show a bird's-eye view of the complex. "The main gate is over there, but Dad said you'd probably want to use this door here." She indicated the rooftop usually occupied by JJ Joyce and other young Posties.

"This is amazing ... most amazing technology," whispered Portero as he examined the hologram. Then he focused his attention to the roof. "Yes, I can open *any* door ... provided I know its location—and providing that it is not covered by that force field. Are we certain that your genius friend has found a way to bring it down?"

"He invented the PhotoFlies," replied David with a yawn. The young man had just gotten out of bed and wore sweats and a tank top while sipping coffee. "I've got faith in him."

"So do I," added Milk. "And so does the Old Man. He says that nobody on Earth is half as good with technology as that kid."

Nikki pointed at a row of trucks near the barracks. "Mike's robot arrived with a supply convoy about thirty-five minutes ago. It's hiding in the prison's sewer system. As soon as we contact our allies, we'll send it to them."

Jacqui asked, "What kind of allies do we have?"

"We're going to make contact with some of the inmates as soon as we can. We've been spying on them for more than a week, and we think they'll be willing to help."

"And Mike said one of his friends would meet us there," added David—he had forgotten to mention it earlier. "Didn't tell me about him, though. Said he'd be a big help."

"Oh, really?" Milk raised an eyebrow and grinned exuberantly. "I've heard about this guy. Been hoping he'd show up."

Glimmer, the brunette woman in a black uniform, spoke up, "I understand the plan for dealing with the guards, but what about some of the prisoners?" She spread her hands and formed her own hologram between them—a glowing image of Vaughn Gregory bared its teeth and seemed to look around the room. Nearly every hero in America had fought the Behemoth, including the light-manipulating Glimmer and her teammates in the ECA.

"There aren't that many bad ones at ABRA," said Milk. "Other than Vaughn, that is. And that fat fuck can rot in hell for all I care. He's staying in Alaska. The rest of them … they can make up their minds whether to cooperate with us or not."

"And if they put up a fight?" asked Hardcore, chewing on an unlit cigar.

"You know the drill—no guards die. I don't even want us to hurt them. That's the most important part of the plan." Milk looked around the room and said, "I don't want anybody to die, but if it comes down to it I'd rather you put down violent prisoners than let them escape or hurt any of the guards."

"So you're willing to kill our own kind," said Jacqui. "But you don't even want to hurt the guards?"

"Come on, Cali, the Behemoth isn't 'our own kind,'" scoffed Milk. "He's a goddamn psycho at best. He's not going free. Period. We all know that Uncle Sam is going to paint this as a terrorist attack—but if we don't hurt the guards or free any bad guys, they'll have less of a case against us. Simple as that."

Hardcore growled, "There's a thousand goddamn soldiers in there and who-knows-what kind of hardware … Walkers and robots and bombs … shit we ain't even heard about. They sure as fuck won't have issues blowing us to hell. Right, Charley?" The big metalhead stood and laughed, "It's gonna be one hell of a party. That's for sure. I can't wait." He looked at his eyeless companion. "Come on, Q. I need to grab a smoke."

"When are we—you—when are you going to make your move?" asked Gloria. Sean sat on her lap and stared in nervous wonder at the hologram.

Milk said, "Sunset's about four-thirty, that far north. If the Joyce kid sticks to his usual schedule then we should be able to make contact before eight, our time."

"I shoulda brought more cigars," rumbled Hardcore's voice from the front porch.

CHAPTER TWENTY-SEVEN

"Dammit, girl, open the door. I know you're in there!" Violet light shined in Fiona's eyes as she forcefully knocked on Tiffany's door. She was tempted to blow the door to hell with a nice plasma burst, but—while that might be satisfying—it would do nothing except buy a trip to solitary. "Tiff, open up! Jesus Christ, girl, let me in."

The door opened. Tiffany stood there, with her long, coppery hair falling over her face in a tangled mess. The girl's face was red, her cheeks stained with tears. She said nothing to her older friend, could barely even meet her eyes.

"Oh, sweet pea, come here," Fiona whispered, and took a step forward. She wrapped her arms around the smaller girl and closed the door behind them.

"Should we deal with this, sir?" asked Corporal Bonano, one of the newer members of ABRA City Security. The young man nodded to one of the monitors.

Captain Holly leaned closer and listened to Tiffany Cooke describe Tom's abduction to Fiona McNamara. The security chief's face showed nothing more than his habitual seriousness.

The corporal added, "McNamara might cause some trouble, sir."

Holly nodded. "She might. She's always been protective of the girl. Make a note for tomorrow's briefing. Tell everyone to keep a close eye on her."

"Tomorrow, sir? Aren't you worried she might do something tonight?"

Holly stepped back and turned to leave the surveillance room. "I'm going down to have a talk with her. I'll determine if there's an imminent threat. We'll leave the dragon alone for now."

"Yes, sir."

The captain left the room and made his way to the elevator. Nobody knew Holly well enough to read his body language, and for that he was grateful. The weight in his heart had grown heavier every day since Tom arrived and had become unbearably heavy last night.

Angus had said nothing, but the hen house was clucking that the order to do away with Fuson had come from the top—Director Givich or maybe even the President, herself—and the only real trouble was figuring out how to do it. The boy's power had grown to such a degree that bullets or poisons would likely be ineffective. So Angus had chosen to send Tom down to the Dark Room, a special cell designed with energy-absorbing Posties in mind. The plan was to weaken the boy over the course of a few days before trying to finally eliminate him.

Holly didn't know if such a thing was possible or not, but he decided that they weren't going to find out. A dizzy effervescence rose in his head as the elevator began to descend. He knew that any action against ABRA would be treason. If he tried to free the kid, he would be looking at a long prison sentence or an early appointment with St. Peter.

He did not care.

Captain Holly's life had always been defined by duty. For as long as he could remember, he'd wanted to wear the uniform, wanted that total devotion to his nation and its people. The guns, glory, the glamour of military life had never attracted him; what made Holly into one of America's finest soldiers was his passion for responsibility, his desire to serve others, his dedication to the greater good.

And sometimes the greater good was more important than following orders. Holly hoped that the Twentieth Century had taught humanity that lesson. His superiors would definitely disagree, but that didn't matter. The only thing that mattered was that Captain Holly would not allow an innocent young man to be murdered, even if the cost was his own life.

He remembered Granny dragging him to church back in Hawaii. He remembered the old preacher hollering, shouting and crying behind the pulpit. And most of all, Holly remembered the words of Jesus, himself. One verse in particular had stamped itself on Holly's heart before he was old enough to really understand it, but his entire life had been built around it. It was the thirteenth verse of the fifteenth chapter of the Gospel of John.

Greater love hath no man than this, that a man lay down his life for his friends.

Tom Fuson sure needed friends right now, and Captain Holly chose to be one.

✪   ✪   ✪

Tom was surprised to find himself in another dream that wasn't a dream. He was even more surprised to see an alien. He had never seen an alien before, at least not in real life—except for himself, of course. But Tom was human in mind and body, and this short being with silver skin certainly was not. It was a Gray, a male, Tom knew somehow, with huge black eyes and a nearly featureless face.

The alien stood in the hangar door, watching as the wrecked starships were loaded into crates for transport to a place called Nevada. The military vehicles were old, heavy monstrosities; all of the soldiers looked like extras from a World War Two flick. Tom realized that he was seeing a vision of 1947, from right after the aliens crashed in Roswell.

The Gray man's posture betrayed his inhuman nature. His hips tilted back slightly, and his spine curved in a way that pushed out his compact chest and smooth abdomen. His oval, oversize head constantly moved in small twitches and nods reminiscent of a bird; he remained otherwise motionless in the growing light of dawn.

Behind the diminutive alien stood a tall, muscular man in a white bodysuit with a blue cowl and a cape that fell to the ground in heavy, grand folds. It was Aegis, the Golden Light himself, only hours after his public debut.

A large gold shield stretched across the white top, from mid-abdomen to just under his collarbone, the simple, classic icon of the world's first hero. The gloves, boots and overshorts were the same blue as his cape, with golden trim; the belt was gold with an absurdly large, round buckle. The cowl and mask covered his entire head, leaving only his chin and mouth exposed, and Aegis reached up to pull it back over his head, exposing slicked-back blond hair and that all-too-familiar face.

Tom slid through the air and looked closely at his forefather. Aegis was nearly identical to Adam, of course. The hairstyle was the biggest difference—the impeccable grooming of a man from the 1940s, instead of Adam's somewhat shaggier late-Twentieth Century style. Aegis also looked bulkier and more muscular than Independence had been (or *would be*, since Adam's creation lay two decades in the future), but that may have just been due to the broad, flat colors of his outfit.

"What do you think of the humans, Simon?" asked Aegis. His voice was deep and clear, with the same timbre as Adam's, but the formation of his words was different, more precise and formal. Tom knew —through the bizarre certainty that came with these dreams—that Simon was not the Gray man's name, but it was a rather close approximation of his proper title, S'sehm'ahn, and he had chosen to use it while on Earth.

The Gray man turned and nodded several times. "They are behaving most civilly, Golden Light. They have been quite helpful, even kind, and they appear to feel genuine sorrow over the death of my crew. They have stored the bodies according to my specifications. There will be no autopsies, for the humans respect the dead."

The hero nodded, "They are capable of great empathy, despite their often primitive nature."

"Perhaps," said the alien. "Or perhaps they merely understand the wisdom of not provoking a more advanced species."

Aegis smiled slightly and made a dismissive gesture. "Goodness can arise from many sources, my friend, even from trepidation. Actions, as the humans say, speak louder than words."

"An illuminating phrase, Golden Light. What, then, have you heard, listening to this most recent decade? I, for one, have heard little goodness in what they have named the Second World War."

"I remember a time when your species made war, Simon. Do not judge the humans too harshly for sins that your ancestors once committed."

"My people have not made war in more than forty million Earth years. You may recall such distant times, but we do not. I do not believe we ever engaged in such ruthlessly efficient extermination, even in those ancient days. I cannot comprehend a mind that would construct factories for death, as the Nazi regime attempted—or a mind that would use the gift of atomic power to annihilate entire cities, as this nation, America, has done. I fear that my arrival will do nothing but give these primates greater methods to slaughter greater numbers. I fear they will cause irreparable harm to the wondrous and precious Earth."

"Surely your technology cannot be used by the humans," said Aegis. "I already feel the nano-destabilization process. Within hours your vessel will be a mere heap of molecular dust."

The Gray man's head bobbed rapidly. "They will learn nothing from my ship, but the Carnivore vessel is a different matter. The invertebrates are only a few millennia more advanced than the people of Earth, and humanity's knowledge is rapidly growing. They will swiftly unlock the secrets of Carnivore technology."

An expression of sympathetic concern spread over the Golden Light's face. He kneeled on the hangar floor and placed a hand on the tiny alien's shoulder. "You feel guilt for this, Simon?

The Carnivores chose to attack you; this is their fault, if blame can be given in light of such tragedy."

"But it is my fault, Golden Light. It is true that the Carnivores attacked my ship, but they are not responsible for these events. They attacked as I approached the superluminal conversion point and struck at the precise moment of my ship's greatest vulnerability. They are no threat to my people, unless they catch us by surprise. My defensive fields were lowered. Their crude weaponry simply tore through my hull. From the moment the attack began, I knew that my ship was doomed. And I … I chose to destroy them. I turned my ship, faced them and engaged the sublight drive."

"You *rammed* them," whispered Aegis.

"Yes," replied Simon. "I struck their vessel microseconds before conversion, and both ships were pulled through spacetime. Both emerged in low-Earth orbit, with time to do nothing but crash. The repercussions of this event are my responsibility—even the greatest repercussion of all, the revelation of your existence."

Aegis squeezed the Gray man's shoulder. "You are not at fault, my young friend, and I absolve you of all blame. You are forgiven; now forgive yourself. May you and your offspring be blessed with tranquility and wisdom, now and until the end of stars."

Simon looked at Aegis and trembled. "I do not deserve this pardon and blessing. I shall endeavor to aid humanity as they deal with these events."

"As will I, Simon, but remember my words. The Carnivores chose to make war on you, and you made the decision to reply with war of your own. Perhaps your people are more like the humans than you realize."

Those golden eyes slid over the Gray man and focused on Tom. Aegis said, "This lesson, perhaps, is why we are here today. We are all more similar than we tend to believe and, despite our differences, we are reflections of one another. Wouldn't you agree, Thomas?"

Tom drifted backward, shock ripped through his dream-body, and the hangar rippled in his vision. "You can see me?"

"Of course not, I've been dead for decades." The hero rose and walked closer. Aegis brightened with each step, and the dream evaporated in the growing golden light.

✪   ✪   ✪

An entire crowd of inmates gathered in the cafeteria, close to the door of Fiona's hall. They fell silent as she walked out, and few restrained their curious stares.

She just glared at them, with purple fire in her eyes, and they all sank lower in their seats. She didn't need to tell them to back off; nobody messed with Flamechylde.

She stormed out of the cafeteria on her way to find Tank. The big guy never had much to say, but he was a damned good listener, and she needed to vent.

Goddamn Angus and his fascist asshole storm troopers! I could fry every goddamn one of those mother-fucking, ass-licking, chicken shit little bitches, hiding behind their goddamn toys and making goddamn kids do their evil fucking work for them!

I could turn this place into a lake of fucking lava. I should! I should slag this shit hole and kill every last one of those fuckers. I should! I should...

I should find Tom.

Fiona would never admit it to anyone, but she'd been humiliated by her initial reaction to Tom. Coming face-to-face with the spitting image of Adam had been overwhelming, and she reacted to the pain like she always did—by lashing out, carelessly. But now that she'd gotten to know the kid, she genuinely liked him.

He was humble and simple in a way that Adam had never been. He didn't judge her or fear her like most other people. Tom treated her like another person and politely listened to her endless storytelling. Most importantly, he'd earned the affection of Tiffany.

Fiona thought that Tiff was as close to a daughter as she'd ever have, and Tom had been nothing but good for the girl. Over the past two weeks, Tiff had grown out of her shell and begun to develop the poise and power of womanhood. Love can do that, Fiona knew.

Like any parent, she was sort of living vicariously through her young friend. If Tiff and Tom had worked out, maybe it would have made up for some of the stupidity and mistakes of Fiona's past. And now all of that was gone. Tiffany's hopes had been brought down by the senseless actions of small-minded men.

It made Fiona want to burn something.

A deep voice rumbled from behind her, "McNamara, we need to talk."

Captain Holly, she rolled her eyes. *Just what I fucking need.*

She stopped, sneered, took a breath, closed her eyes, counted to ten and turned around to face him. The big soldier took a few steps closer and said, "Follow me, please."

"What's this about, Holly? There are other places I need to be."

"There's *one* place you need to be, and we both know that. Now come on; we don't have much time." He led her down the corridor and through the first cellblock, but stopped at a turn in the hall. "Stop right here. We're in a blind spot, but it's only about six feet wide."

She wasn't sure how to respond to that, so she stuck to the basics. "What the hell is this about, Holly? I've got better things to do than waste time with a screw."

"Damn right you do. You remember how to get to the Dark Room, don't you?" His eyes narrowed. "You've been there often enough."

"The Dark Room? What the fuck, Holly? I haven't done shit to get tossed in the hole."

"No, you haven't. Not lately, anyway. You know who else hasn't? Fuson. But that's where he is right now—down in the Dark Room. They're keeping him out cold until he's weak enough to execute. I don't think you want that to happen. So, are you up for a prison break?"

"Are you shitting me?" Her jaw fell. "Why should I trust you?"

"Because I trust *you.* Fuson doesn't deserve this, and we're going to stop it. I changed the schedule; solitary will be empty for half an hour, starting at seventeen hundred. Doors unlocked, cameras off, and no guards between here and there. Take the elevator down, but use the stairs to come up. It won't be a picnic, but there's no surveillance that way. You'll come out near maintenance. The crews don't work this late, so hide in the shop. We'll meet at eighteen hundred, and I'll help the three of you escape."

"Three?"

"You, the boy and the girl. I'll pick her up before the rendezvous. That should be payment enough for your cooperation. Here." He pulled a small, flat-screen device from his belt and punched a string of icons on its face. "I just disabled your implant, theirs too. Don't make me regret it."

She touched the cold metal behind her ear. "Thanks, but what about getting us upstairs and out of the force field? What about—you know—the whole fucking Alaska thing?"

"The boy can *fly*, McNamara. If he needs some juice, either of you can feed him enough power to get out of here. We'll take the freight elevator up through the hospital and lay low in an empty office. The main gate will be opening later tonight. A supply convoy came in a few hours ago, and they're heading back out. If we time it right, we can get you out the door without my men noticing. Then Fuson can carry you wherever the hell you want to go. It's best if I don't know about any of that."

She stared at the soldier with shock and something like admiration in her eyes. "You ... you're going to try and pull the heat off of us, aren't you? They'll kill you. Angus will have your head on a platter."

Captain Holly surprised Fiona by laughing. "My name's John, so I guess that's a good way to go."

CHAPTER TWENTY-EIGHT

JJ sat in the lawn chair, sipped a beer and tried to avoid looking at Headquarters. It wasn't easy. Sol was somewhere inside on his latest mission.

JJ hated sending his friend into the lion's den, but they really had no other option. Anon had volunteered — since it could take on the appearance of any person or vertebrate — but they figured that was too much of a risk. Nobody knew how the tracking implants worked or what kind of sensors ABRA might employ, so a rodent might not even be able to sneak inside. The ventilation system was protected by lasers, blades, explosives and poison gas — Vanessa once heard some guards describing it to a rookie.

Sol had taken it upon himself to go spying. His impromptu trip to the cloning lab seemed to prove that he could sneak into the subterranean parts of the prison. Over the next few days, he had explored every room of HQ, the hospital and the barracks, and he'd located the elevators to the secret underground facility known as MegaMax.

At that moment, Sol was attempting to enter the underground prison for the first time, and JJ was very nervous. Anything might happen, and there was nothing he could do to help his friend. So he put down the beer, stood up and stretched, walked to the far side of the roof and faced the opposite direction. He looked at the Wall and sneered but tried to calm down and think happy thoughts.

He'd been impressed with his friends and all they had been able to learn. Vanessa and Anon were both excellent spies—between its shape changing ability and her enhanced hearing, they could learn almost anything. The Resistance could certainly have used Madi's wireless reception, but they were doing well with what they had. If they could find a way to contact Tom Fuson, then they could really begin to make plans for their escape.

He figured that they only needed two things to succeed: remove the implants and shut down the containment field. He didn't have a clue how to accomplish either goal, but he knew that they would find a way. Tom might be able to do both, if he was even half as powerful as Independence.

JJ noticed that he had left the beer on the lawn chair and cursed under his breath. He felt tired and lazy—he hadn't been sleeping well, thanks to the conspiracy—and didn't want to walk across the roof for the drink. The worst part was that he could feel it sitting there, taunting him with the slight mass of the glass and liquid. It was like he could feel it in the palm of his hand.

He could feel everything, in a way—the pull of the Earth, the tug of the moon, the subtle mass of every person or object, rippling spacetime like a boat's wake. He could feel his home in Tennessee, around the curve of the planet, thousands of miles to the southeast; he could feel the force field that blocked his attempts to twist holes in the universe and connect here and there.

He felt the bottle, just like it was in his hand, and he thought, *I can connect here and there.*

And the bottle wobbled, slid an inch or two, then flew through the air and slammed into his palm, sloshing beer over his fingers.

JJ laughed and took a swig.

He thought about the subtle curl of space that he'd made; how he'd caused the bottle to surf on a swell of gravity. He could do a lot of things with a trick like that. He laughed again and whooped at the sky, his troubles and fears forgotten, at least for a time, thanks to the thrill of learning more about his power. He cheered and danced—and began to explore this new aspect of his ability.

Twenty minutes later Madison Doyle walked onto the roof. They hadn't spoken in days, so the visit was kind of a surprise. The pixie-haired young woman seemed uncomfortable, maybe nervous, JJ noticed.

"Hey, Madi, check it out." He stood beside the stairwell, arms wide open. A dozen beers floated around his left fist, like a Ferris wheel of bottles. One of the lawn chairs hung in the air two feet from his right hand, slowly tumbling end over end.

"What are you doing?" she gasped. "That's awesome!"

"I think I'm making localized gravitational fields, but I might be wrong about that." He winked, lowered his arms and the chair dropped, the bottles slowly descended. "I kinda dropped out after ninth grade, you know."

"I thought you just made those portals."

"Wormholes, yeah. But it's all the same thing. I can feel it. I can *play* with it."

"I know the feeling," she replied and extended her own hand. One of the bottles began to twitch and then burst as the beer within flash-boiled. She grinned and said, "Oopsie."

"Remind me never to make you mad."

Madi's smile faded and she said, "You're the one who should be mad. That's why I came up here."

"To make me mad?"

"No, because you *are* mad. Or you were mad. Or, um, should be mad ... at me. I'm sorry that I ran out on you guys."

"It's okay. I'm not mad at you. Disappointed, yeah, but not mad." He picked up the chair and carried it back to the hangout spot. He plopped down and motioned for Madi to take a seat.

"Well, I'm sorry," she said, turning her chair to face him before sitting. "You're a good friend, you and Sol both. I feel like an ass for running out on you guys."

"It's okay, Madi. I know they treated you pretty bad when you got here. I don't blame you for being scared of them. And if you want to help now, we won't say no. I'd get down and beg for your help, if that would change your mind. You're one of us. You should be with us."

She looked down and pouted. "I want to, but I … I just don't know if I can. I don't think we can really get out of here, you know? And things aren't too bad up here in the city. It might be worse down below … or they might kill us just to make a point."

JJ nodded and leaned back. "I know. But you remember Patrick Henry, right? 'Give me liberty or give me death.' That just about sums it up for me. I won't stay here. I just won't. None of us deserve a life sentence, no matter how not-bad this place might be. I'd rather die than stay here. But we all have to make our own decisions. I'm still your friend—whether you help us or not—and I know Sol is, too."

"Thanks, Jay. I … I can't really help you escape, but, um … I wanted to tell you a couple of things. Maybe it'll help, maybe not."

JJ nodded and said, "I appreciate it, but don't do anything you're not comfortable with. We're doing alright, so far anyway."

"Good. I'm glad, and I hope you all do make it out of here."

"Thanks. So what did you want to tell me?"

"Well the first thing is this." She tapped on the implant behind her left ear. "I don't think these are tracking devices. At least, they don't broadcast anything I can detect."

JJ reached back and touched the cold metal nub. "Really? Then what the hell are they?"

"I don't know," she answered. "They don't send anything, but they can receive radio signals. I can feel the frequency, but it's encrypted, and I don't know the code. And I'm *not* going to try and break it. I think they're bombs or something like that. Something made to kill us."

He glanced at HQ, then looked away and rubbed the implant distractedly. He whispered, "Goddamn."

"Yeah."

"Well, thanks for letting me know. I'm not sure what to do about them, but we'll figure out how to get rid of them."

"Be careful. They might go off if you mess with them."

"It's a sure thing they would. But I could nab a remover from the hospital. We can beat these bastards, no matter how smart they think they are."

"They're very smart. Which kinda brings me to the second thing I wanted to tell you."

"What's that?"

"There's some kind of new drones flying around in here."

"In here?" He looked around and up at the night sky.

"Yeah. In here, with us," she waved her hand in a loose circle. "They're small, like flies. There's gotta be hundreds of them, but they zoom around all over the place or hang on walls."

"Damn. Security might already know everything."

"I don't know," she said, leaning forward. "I don't think they belong to ABRA."

"What do you mean?"

"Well, it's kinda complicated. They're broadcasting outside, not to anyplace inside. The rest of the drones communicate with HQ, but not these little flies. And the signals are … brilliant. They're always timed to hide in other transmissions. Normal equipment wouldn't even notice them. *I* can barely even detect them. I think someone's spying on ABRA City."

He paused and thought for a moment. "Someone who doesn't work for the government?"

She shrugged. "Maybe, but it's more high-tech than I've ever seen. For all I know the drones might belong to DPS or some other agency that's keeping an eye on us — or on ABRA. Who knows?"

J.J shook his head. "So they spread out all over the place? Like they're checking out the whole prison?"

"Usually. Sometimes they group together, like a flock of birds."

"Do you sense any of them now?"

She nodded slowly and pointed over his shoulder. He turned and could just barely make out a hazy spot against the darkening sky, like a cloud of mosquitoes. "They're right there. All of them. I think they're watching us."

Sol watched the girl from above; he stood on the small lip between the wall and ceiling. Climbing so high had been hard work, but there were few other hiding places in the featureless corridors of MegaMax.

He had waited in HQ for hours, near the elevator, until a group of guards came along. He hitched a ride on a soldier's boot and didn't let go until they entered the cavernous main hall of the underground complex. Abandoning the soldier, Sol scaled the wall and began to explore.

He eventually entered the cafeteria, and that's when he saw her. Her eyes and nose were red from too much crying and her fiery hair was tangled and unwashed. She looked like she'd been awake for days, weeping the whole time.

Sol felt a pang in his heart for the girl. He wondered who she was, why she'd been locked up down here and what happened to make her cry. He hated to see ladies cry, and she was young, just a kid. She couldn't be any older than sixteen … right around Tom's age.

She had to know him, Sol realized. The place was too small for the youngsters to remain strangers. *And teens tend to flock*, he thought, *like a bunch of hormonal geese*. The girl was the closest thing to a lead he'd seen.

She sat alone at one of the tables, not really eating, though she picked at a tray of slop. Few other inmates came to the cafeteria while Solomon was there, and only one approached the girl.

Sol recognized the short, bald, big-eared guy as Billy the infamous bat boy. The tabloid legend scampered into the cafeteria, hopped about nine feet straight up, spread his arms and sailed on the air to the young girl's table.

"Hey, Tiffany. What's up? Where's your boyfriend?"

"Shut up, Billy." She snapped, but her tone was closer to weary than annoyed. She looked at the food on her tray and tried to ignore him.

"Sorry. Sorry. Just curious is all. You two've been inseparable since he got here. Hope you didn't have a fight or nothing."

"Shut up!" She swung an awkward backhand at Billy, but he danced back, leaped up, somersaulted rather gracefully and landed on the table once again.

RISING SON | 255

"Sorry. Sorry. Don't be mad Tiff. We're friends. Friends. Always were. Don't be mad, okay?" He frowned and gave her an exaggerated look of puppy-dog sadness. "Flamechylde was looking for you earlier. You and your boyfr—I mean you and that Tom guy. She said you weren't answering your door or nothing. We were all worrying that something mighta happened to the two of you. I think she went to see Tank, ask him if he knew where you two mighta run off to."

"Just go away, Billy. I don't want to talk right now."

"Hey, hey, don't be like that. We're friends and all. You look like you could use some company. Need to be cheered up and I—"

"I said go away!" Tiffany slammed her fists against the table and stood. Her blue eyes locked on the bat boy.

Billy jerked and twitched like he was having a seizure. Then he rapidly grew to a more normal size, bursting through his clothing. He became a skinny, bug-eyed, totally nude man. He yelped and covered his genitals with both hands. "Tiff!"

"Shut up and leave me alone," she said and turned to walk toward one of the sliding metal doors—directly beneath Sol.

He made up his mind instantly and jumped from the wall, landing in the jungle of her hair. She froze, for an instant, and Sol realized that she'd noticed his presence.

But she didn't say anything. She just walked into a short, well-lit hallway. The metal door slid shut behind them.

The girl—Tiffany—entered what looked like a hospital room with two beds but no real medical equipment. Both beds were rumpled nests of wadded sheets and random pillows. An image of Tiffany passed through Sol's mind—the poor little darling in this room, alone all night, crawling from bed to bed while bawling her eyes out. Bawling her eyes out over Tom.

She closed the door, locked it, and immediately whispered, "Who are you? Why are you here?"

Sol rappelled down the cascade of fiery hair and landed on Tiffany's shoulder. Then he grew to about two inches—tall enough to be able to talk, but short enough to hide in her hair, in case Security had cameras in these rooms—and leaned close to her ear. "My name's Solomon Beck. I'm here to help."

✪   ✪   ✪

Hours passed, and JJ remained alone on the roof. He wasn't leaving until Sol got back, even if it took all night. Besides, it wasn't like he was going to be able to sleep that night. Madi's double bombshell had broken whatever peace of mind he'd had. He couldn't stop thinking about the tiny flying machines. It was only safe to assume they belonged to Security. But if that was the case, then the entire escape plan might fall apart.

He needed a plan. He needed hope.

Then, suddenly, a sound drew his attention—buzzing, a quiet hum like flying bugs. Like bees drifting among flowers. Like a *swarm*.

He jumped from the lawn chair and spun around. There— not ten feet away—floated a cloud of shifting specks, hanging in the air, just as Madi described. He stepped back and stared.

The cloud spun around, collapsed in on itself and stretched into a thin line of motes that slid inches above the roof before coalescing once more in a rough sphere, close enough to touch. He could see the tiny machines, flying blurs. The effect was hypnotic, kind of like watching a thousand-strong flock of starlings whirl and roll, a riot of motion, the elegant antithesis of chaos. He raised his hand and reached out, surprised at the urge to touch the things.

A spark flashed center of the swarm, and a voice—a young woman's voice—said, "Go in the stairwell. Leave the door open, so we can get inside with you."

JJ yelped and gasped, "Who are you?"

"We'll talk inside, just do it, Jeremiah."

"Call me JJ," he said, nodding, and he walked to the door.

He realized then that the drones couldn't possibly belong to the enemy. ABRA wouldn't use such devices to talk to him; they'd send guards or just call on the public-address system. And if these things didn't belong to the bad guys, then maybe they belonged to the good guys.

A grin spread across his face, his steps grew light and energetic, and his heart beat with a new rhythm—a rhythm of hope.

The swarm flew past as he stepped within the stairwell. It formed a sphere again and once more pulsed with light. The light gathered in the hollow center of the robotic flock and became an almost solid thing. It formed an image, took the shape of the young woman's face and changed JJ's life forever.

She was beautiful, maybe even stunning. Her dark brown skin looked a little green in the light of the hologram, but it was flawless. Thick, long lashes framed her almond-shaped eyes; her deep brown irises seemed to draw his gaze like a gravitational pull. She had this adorable little nose with a smooth, round tip and full, immensely kissable lips.

"Who are you?" he whispered again, unable to think of anything else.

She smiled without a hint of shyness. In fact, her grin was more than a little cocky, "My name's Nikki Young but you can call me Powerhouse. How'd you like to bust out of that joint?"

"Wait. What?" The words spun around in his head, but it didn't take long for him to put it all together. He'd heard that name before, and he quickly remembered where. He'd never met her, but other Posties talked about her … and her famous family. "Nikki Young? Like Nichole Young? Milk's daughter?"

"The one and only. Now, are you going to answer my question? You wanna break out or not?" A playfully wicked grin danced across her face. JJ could see the tip of her tongue between her teeth. "Or should I go look for some other sap to recruit?"

"No. I mean, yes. I mean … I'm already working on breaking out of here. A friend of mine is down in MegaMax right now, trying to find Tom Fuson. You know who that is, right?"

"Yes, we do," an improbably deep voice came from off-camera. The holographic image pulled back to reveal the room around Nikki. She was sitting in a chair, surrounded by half a dozen people, including her colossal father and the old heroine California Girl. Most of the other people all looked like heroes, too; they all had flashy styles and obvious attitudes. They were all Posties, for sure, from the big guy with the ink to the little kid with stumpy horns—another son of Milk, obviously.

Absurdly, JJ thought, *The Paragon Patrol returns, coming to a hologram near you.*

Milk leaned forward and asked, "Have you seen him? Do you know if he's okay?"

"I haven't seen him. Well, I saw them bring him here, but that was a week ago, when they flew him in. He'd been shot. They threw him in the nuclear reactor and he got better. They don't let us mix with the downstairs prisoners at all, but my friend Sol's down there right now, trying to find him."

"Sol? You mean Solomon Beck?" asked Milk.

"Yeah. Do you know him?"

"No, but I've read his file. Yours too. He's down in MegaMax?"

"Yeah. We figured that if we got help from Tom Fuson, escaping would be a lot easier." JJ shrugged. "We can't get out of here without some help."

Milk smiled, "Well, you've got all the help in the world right here, son. All we need is a computer. Think you could get into Headquarters?"

A rough voice spoke from low to the ground, "*I* can."

"Sol!" JJ jumped back as his friend suddenly appeared on the steps, growing to his normal height in less than a second. "Dude, when did you get back? What happened down there? You alright, man?"

"I'm fine," Sol replied grimly. "But we need to hurry. Security took the boy away last night. I think they're going to kill him."

JJ ran downstairs and retrieved the little spider-robot from the alley. Milk said a Postie inventor named Mike had made it. JJ thought it was pretty damned cool.

The machine moved with a natural grace far beyond the military's Walkers or even the creations of the Carnivores. It skittered around with a lifelike agility and curled up in his palm like a dead bug. The flash drive popped out with a subtle click, and

JJ stuck it in his pocket. Then he opened a small portal to his bedroom and put the robot in the closet. He closed the wormhole and walked back down the alley, trying to suppress the adrenaline-fueled spring in his step.

He swung by Anon's apartment first; they went upstairs and asked Madi to come hang out. They picked up Vanessa last, since she lived in JJ's building. She glared at Madi, but JJ told her it was cool, and the quartet walked upstairs.

Sol stood at the top of the stairwell, still talking to the hologram. Things got crazy for a minute or two, as JJ's friends all flipped out to varying degrees. Everybody started talking at once, and most of it wasn't good.

Vanessa didn't think an invasion of heroes was the best way to escape. JJ replied that they needed the help. Madi was terrified of Security. JJ's answer was that they had *Milk*, so how big of a threat was the Army? Anon was ready to go to war, but wasn't sure about doing it without more planning and preparation. JJ insisted on moving right now; they had no time to waste. Tom Fuson's life was on the line. Vanessa wasn't sure that breaking out of prison was worth risking her life. JJ asked why she'd even joined in the first place, if that's how she felt. The argument spun around like that for a few minutes, going nowhere.

The holographic heroes remained silent. They'd apparently muted the audio from their end. JJ could see Nikki raging at a mile a minute while a tall young dude—that had to be her older brother, David—tried to calm her down. JJ looked back at his friends. Madi and Vanessa were bickering with Sol, Anon shifted from Betty Page to Woody Allen, looking even more nervous and uncomfortable as it stammered timid excuses.

"Everyone cut it out!" JJ barked, loudly, and everyone stopped arguing (Vanessa was the last, of course). "I'm doing this. Tonight. *Now.* I will not waste one more night of my life behind this wall. And if I die ... then I die. It's better than staying here. It's better than sitting here and letting them keep me under glass. At least I'll have done something with my life. At least I'll have tried to save somebody who needs it. At least I'll have taught those assholes that there's a price to pay for taking away a person's life and freedom and hope. I'm going to make them pay it. I'm going — *now* — and I'm going to bring this place down. Are you with me or not?"

Vanessa, Madi and Anon fell silent. Then Anon nodded and Vanessa whispered, "Yes."

And Madi said, "I'm with you, too. Maybe ... Maybe we can get out of here together."

"We'll get you out of there," came Milk's rumbling voice. "But it'll be dangerous. Any one of us could die tonight — any one of you — but JJ's right. Some things are worth fighting for. Some things are worth dying for. I believe that ending ABRA is worth it. Rescuing Tom is worth it. Your freedom is worth it."

Sol grinned, "Our independence."

JJ walked up the steps and opened the stairwell door. "Tom Fuson's *our* Independence. Let's go get him."

"Let's do it, bro."

The hologram zoomed in on Milk. "Just plug that thing in a computer and keep your head down. You're the best escape route, JJ. Try to gather all the prisoners in one place so we can disable those implants and get everyone out."

"We'll help with that," said Anon. Vanessa and Madi agreed.

JJ looked at his friends and felt a swell of emotion. Tears actually rose in his eyes as he admired them and their bravery. He told himself that they'd be together before morning — safe, free and thousands of miles away. He told himself that destroying ABRA City, saving Tom and freeing the prisoners was worth their lives, if it came to that.

In fact, JJ was totally fine with dying for the cause, but he wasn't sure that he'd trade his friends for it. Not to mention the other Posties, or even the prison staff — who weren't really bad guys, for the most part. Indecision and fear crawled under his skin, and he regretted endangering so many people, but it was too late to back out. He'd made up his mind and had to live with it.

He wondered if that meant he'd suddenly become an adult, instead of the aimless boy he'd always been. If so, then being an adult sucked.

"You ready?" asked Sol.

"Yup." JJ looked at HQ, at the windows of Doctor Angus's office. It seemed as good a place as any. He raised a hand, and a swirl formed in the air at his fingertips. The portal spun open, and they stepped into the darkened room. "We better hurry. They might detect us."

"Wow, check out the old man's collection. Looks like my bedroom when I was twelve," laughed Sol. He walked around and examined the many pictures of Independence while keeping an eye on the door. "Course, I mostly had posters of California Girl."

JJ turned on the computer. He pressed the button on the monitor and the desktop background popped into view. He pulled the flash drive from his pocket and looked at it. The little thing was going to change everything forever, one way or another.

An electric thrill raced through his limbs. ABRA City would fall, and his hand would begin the destruction, just by using the small device. He plugged it into a USB port on the tower. "Here we go."

The computer began to loudly hum. Too loudly. The whirring and rattling swiftly rose to a shrill wail. The smell of hot ozone filled the small room. JJ stepped back and looked at his friend, "Sol?"

"What's the hell's it doing?"

JJ shrugged. "I don't know. It—"

Suddenly a wild spark shot up the tower. The display flared and winked out. Electricity began to crackle all over the computer. The screeching intensified, and JJ covered his ears. Random tendrils of flashing power shot out of the computer leaving smoldering burns on the desk and carpet. Smoke rose from the tower, and the plastic shell began to warp. Tangled sparks enveloped the computer, spread wildly into a rapidly fluctuating sphere of electricity, and then collapsed, vanishing into the machine.

For one or two intense seconds, everything fell silent. JJ and Sol looked at the damage, each other, and the computer. They both wondered if something had gone wrong, if the mission had failed.

Then the computer exploded with a hot flash and thunderous boom.

JJ instinctively threw up his arms and blocked the flying

shrapnel with a push of gravity; Sol was far enough away to be out of the blast radius. They both gaped as a large glowing orb of lightning coalesced above the desk.

The ball of electricity was blue, white, violet, yellow and a dozen other colors. A million sparks twisted and coiled, flashing in and out of view. It reminded JJ of a Tesla coil, firing countless threads of power into the air. It flared painfully bright, faded to near-transparency and brightened again. It pulsed and shifted, shapeless but not formless. It flowed and stretched into a flickering, vaguely human figure—a man of electricity.

It was about seven feet tall, with a head, two arms and two legs, but it was not a human being. It floated two feet above the floor, sizzling with power, a glowing body of pure energy. The man-shape was rough around the edges and indistinct. Sparks shot off at random, striking nearby objects and the floor. Paperclips, staples and other metallic debris orbited the glowing form like satellites. The being was obviously a Posthuman, but unlike any JJ had ever seen.

The head turned toward JJ—the mass of sparks showed only the slightest hint of a face, with no eyes, nose or mouth—and then glanced at Sol. A voice echoed in the room, deep and slightly distorted, with just a bit of static and a thrumming undercurrent. It was an inhuman voice, and obviously came from the inhuman form.

"*You must be Jeremiah Joyce and Solomon Beck.*"

JJ opened his mouth, but his throat was too dry to speak. He licked his lips, swallowed hard and managed to croak, "Yeah, um ... Who are you?"

The roiling sparks of the electric man's face shifted. "*People call me* Overpower. *Want to see why?*"

CHAPTER TWENTY-NINE

"In the beginning, there was potential.

"The nothing within everything *is* and is *not*, as it sleeps beyond time and space. Like the face of a tempest-riled sea, the transuniversal void is both a thing and not a thing, foaming in eternal chaos, taking non-Euclidean form, *being* for unreal duration. This is the substrate of all things. It lies beyond and within, and it is only potential.

"For this is the ultimate law of nature: Potential is real. Possibility exists within eternally unmade creation. Pure potential is the foundation and heart of all.

"So our cosmos was born from raw potential, roiling with untamed potential of its own. The diameter of the universe was as small as can be, although it grew and cooled throughout that first, long epoch. It danced randomly to the rhythm of quantum songs. Uncertainty opened paths unlimited, and the newborn universe followed them all.

"Potential flowed through the tiny cosmos; information arose. As crystals grow with no intention, as fusion automatically initiates in the core of a womb-wrapped protostar, so did the emerging information give structure to the currents of potential, so did this structure bring order to primordial chaos. Replicating patterns inevitably formed in the coruscating possibility. And these self-sustaining patterns became more complex and evolved—not through your animal laws of selection, but through the continual acquisition of ever more data and the ongoing expansion of the cosmos itself.

"Thus life came to be, even in those earliest of times, when one single law of nature rang the heavens like the resounding toll of a cathedral bell—the Great Law of Potential, the one rule of all things. Men know this time as the Planck Epoch; I knew it as the age of my birth.

"I became aware of existence in that energetic, compressed cosmos. I could feel others, like me, from that initial moment of consciousness—billions of siblings, awakening together, the first children of our profoundly fecund universe.

"We were harmless beings with nothing to harm. We require no sustenance. We do not reproduce. We developed from the fabric of reality itself. Energy, as you understand it, did not exist in those times. Matter was unknown and inconceivable.

"We had no need for bodies. We are made *of* the universe, and we grew with it, nestled together in intimate warmth. We sang to each other, an anthem of joy and love. We shared that paradise, a boundless universe, full of potential and life. Full of us.

"And then we became aware of a coming change. The great phase change.

"This was to be the first collapse of our ancient community and the end of a cosmic age. Creation was 10^{-43} seconds old. For you, such a span is incomprehensibly short, but to us—then, in the wild glory of cosmic youth—eras untold had come and gone. And, as new interactions came to dominate all things, our age came to an end.

"The gradual cooling of the cosmos brought about a fundamental, irrevocable alteration of reality itself. We could not stop it. Worse, the effects would be random and, thus, beyond prediction. Anything could happen after the universe crystallized in a new form. We held each other, braced ourselves and awaited the unknown.

"We cried out, learning a new thing called pain. Spacetime shuddered as newborn gravity became distinct from the suddenly-defined electronuclear force. Uncompromising laws were imposed on nature, where once there had been only potential. We suffered in agony and grief, but we lived. We are made of the spacetime fabric of the cosmos and cannot be destroyed.

"Other life came to be during that second epoch, fundamentally different from my kind. New laws of nature bound these younger beings, and their existences were of limited duration. Death had come to the universe.

"But my kind endured. We remained through more cosmic changes—each unique and each uniquely painful. When the second age drew to a close and the next phase change occurred, the electronuclear force shattered. The strong interaction split from the electroweak and added another layer of rules to reality, during that long, third age. And new beings came to be, born from the three interactions of those times, but they were also mortal, though remnants survive to this day.

"At the dawn of the fourth age, the electroweak force was torn apart, becoming the weak interaction and electromagnetic force. Later still, the Great Inflation ripped all of nature apart. And with that expansion came the cooling of our cosmos, the coalescing of reality into bound, stagnant forms.

"Raw energy froze, becoming quark-gluon plasmas. The great clouds further condensed, forming hadrons and anti-hadrons—doomed to annihilate each other. Leptons and anti-leptons came into being and followed the same course. Matter and antimatter warred as only mindless nothings can war—with no quarter, no mercy and no hope for peace until the end. And in the end, matter triumphed.

"Nearly three hundred eighty thousand years later, the swelling cosmos burst forth with the birth of light, illuminating the entirety of creation. The cosmic microwave background remains to this day, an echo of that birth.

"Loose mists of atoms surrendered to relentless gravity, collapsing into the first of the stars. The stars forged heavier elements, died in spasms of instability and gave birth to more stars that came together under gravity, the seeds of modern galaxies. The galaxies danced, merged and clustered, forming a great wispy web of light in the boundless dark. And the web drifts along the current of expansion, in the gentle depths of the ever-growing abyss. Such is existence in this frigid, barren, fourth age, your age, the Age of Matter.

"And still, after nearly thirteen billion eight hundred million of your human years, my people remain.

"We exist beyond mortal frame of reference. We manipulate the laws of nature as you vibrate the air to speak or sing. We are fundamentally tied to the fabric of reality and have spread throughout the innumerable galaxies of this cosmos. We have gone beyond, to other realms. Five came to dwell in this galaxy, though rarely do we meet. Only twice have we united—both times to push the Great Destroyer from our home. Aside from those brief partnerships we remain isolated, free to pursue our individual interests.

"The Burning Helix spins forever around the supermassive singularity at the galaxy's heart, pondering the nature of space and time. The Holy Attendant guides the birth of stars, as a gardener with hands in the soil. The Lonely Seeker wanders as an explorer, scholar and friend of life. The Divine Lord rules his eternal realm.

"And I, the Golden Light, roamed this particular galaxy for seven billion years. During this time, I communicated with the members of three million seven hundred eighty-five thousand nine hundred forty-two unique sentient species—including humanity. I hope that you will match that count, or exceed it, in some distant time, for nothing is more important than life.

"Hear my words: Life has existed in every age, beginning with my own and continuing to the present. Life has formed regardless of the hazards and conditions of nature.

"And yet, the universe did not *need* life. Life is not required. It develops only through the organization of information in cosmic byproducts—whether those byproducts are nonphysical patterns of spacetime, intelligent electromagnetic fields on the crushing face of a magnetar or quivering colonies of warm mud and amino acids on a little ball of stone.

"Life's many iterations developed under ever-harsher laws, but each has obtained greater diversity and numbers. Each strives for survival in the slow-dying explosion of the cosmos. Life unneeded, life uncreated, life that demands existence for no other cause than to *be*. The purpose of life is to live and nothing more.

"And with no other purpose, life's potential has no boundaries, no limits … no end.

"It is on this basis that I came to see the existence of life as the most important facet of reality. Life is free to define its own purpose. Life is able to transcend the limits and laws of nature. Life embodies the inestimable potential that creates worlds. Life is the only thing worthy of worship and love. Only life is *capable* of love. For these and many other reasons, life is precious and holy. Only life — of *all* things — is precious and holy.

"To see life in the empty darkness of the vacuum, to explore that life, take its form, touch it, smell it, taste it — to know and connect with life was my reason. My purpose. This is what brought me to Earth, Thomas."

Aegis appeared, and Tom became aware of himself once more. There was nothing else — no shadow, no light — only the older man in blue, white and gold and the astonished boy with wide, metallic eyes.

"I found Earth — or rather, my Golden Home found Earth — through a casual study of star systems, during the time of the hulking but harmless *Scutosaurus* and the fierce therapsid hunter, *Inostrancevia*, a quarter-billion years ago. The richness of life here, even then, was astonishing. The blessed Earth is among the great treasures of the galaxy, among the most bountiful of worlds. I have returned, from time to time, over the ages since."

"When did you meet us? Them. Humans." Tom spoke without meaning to. The question came out as soon as it formed. He realized that it was the first thought he'd really had in some time — before then, Tom had simply been absorbed in his forefather's words and the vision of times past. Now, he had active thoughts for the first time since the warehouse-vision of 1947, which hadn't been exactly real, either, he knew. This limbo, and the story of Aegis, was a vision within a vision, a dream within a dream.

The ancient being replied, "I first met humanity in Nineteen Thirty-Nine. I had chosen to avoid the Short Spur Route and passed within two light years; my Home detected primitive radio communications from Earth. Learning that a new technological species had developed here was thrilling; we arrived within hours of receiving that first signal.

"The swift advancement of human knowledge and society was too intriguing to resist and I came, joyously, to explore. Leaving my Home hidden in the shadow of the Moon, I dwelt among man and woman. At times, I projected a shell of matter and mimicked human form, but more often I remained invisible to human eyes. I had not been here in over eight million years, and many things had changed.

"My joy, however, was rapidly tainted. Earth was becoming engulfed by war." His voice fell darkly. "I detested war. I detested killing. But I did not judge humanity for their legacy of territorialism and bloodshed. Most species experience war, and many are destroyed by it. Such behavior is all too common among intelligent life, arising as it does from the base impulses of their evolutionary ancestors. So despite the war, I grew to love humanity.

"I found in them a bold, dramatic species, given to extremes of action and a passion for carving meaning from life's formless mass of toil. I witnessed heroism and sacrifice, compassion and generosity, depravity and atrocity. I listened, for nearly eight years, to the stories and tales of your mother's kin.

"And humanity has a love of stories. Most species have stories, in their myriad ways, but humans are of a particular orientation. They are a species that defines its place in the universe through stories. Through myth, legend, literature and song, through *story*, humanity creates and refines their sense of self.

"By Nineteen Thirty-Nine, imaginative individuals in this nation, America, had invented a new type of story—that of the costumed hero with strange and incredible powers, the comic book superhero. Bizarre, often alien beings, these fictional champions were dedicated to using their extraordinary abilities to aid humankind. These tales were simple entertainment—very little complexity or depth—but they touched a chord within me, as a human might say.

"And in these stories, I believed, lay the answer to a problem that has plagued the universe from the beginning."

"What do you mean?" asked Tom, but Aegis did not reply. He simply continued the tale.

"When Simon and the Carnivores came down in New Mexico, I made this form, this body. I placed my mind in the cramped tangle of a human brain, clothed my new flesh in this garish costume and appeared openly before humanity for the first time. I did not simply create a simulacrum of *Homo sapiens sapiens* — I *became* a man. I cast myself in the role of hero, clothed myself in this gaudy attire and brought an end to the Carnivore's first rampage.

"In part, I believed that being a superhero would help mankind accept me. They would be more at ease with my presence if they saw me as a comic book character come to life. I believed that the concept of using ones skills and abilities for the good of others was a laudable goal and, in that way, the costumed champion of comic-book lore was a worthy representation to utilize.

"But more than that, I believed that the archetype of the superhero could serve as a focus for my will. I could become an embodiment and image of the stories of humankind. And through the power and focus of that image, those stories, I would at long last gain the strength to defeat the Great Destroyer."

"Great Destroyer? You mean Bloodlust?" asked Tom, but Aegis had vanished. The young man floated alone in a colorless nothing.

A voice from behind answered the question. "Yes, son. Bloodlust."

Tom recognized the voice and turned to see his father.

Adam smiled slightly and dipped his head in a subtle bow of acknowledgment. His cape rippled, though no breeze blew in the limbo. It was long and solid blue, bordered by fifty small white stars. His two-piece red-and-white uniform had something of a military style, with a clerical collar and a belt cinched at the waist, tall blue boots and long blue gloves. On his chest was the symbol, the white star within a blue circle, the emblem of Independence.

"Aegis was wrong, Tom," said the hero. "But only by half."

"Half? How was he wrong? Wrong about what?"

"Aegis worshiped life, Tom, and Bloodlust despised it. He became bitter and cruel before the stars even existed. He never recovered from losing the happy pre-cosmos at the beginning of time. He hates the cold, dark universe of now. If he were mortal, I'd call him insane. But he's not mortal, and he's beyond insanity. He's driven millions of species to extinction, maybe billions, and he's terrorized even more.

"Remember, right before he killed me, he said, '*But punishment for your creation will be a pleasing game.*' He's played that game with many worlds, Tom. He's been a figure of myth in countless cultures, over billions of years, throughout the Local Group. He is a god of chaos and doom. He kills mortals by the million and takes pleasure in the survivors' grief."

Tom's eyes narrowed and he glared at his father. "And Aegis thought he could stop Bloodlust? But he said that his species—our species—is made out of spacetime and can't be destroyed."

"Exactly. Bloodlust was able to kill *us* because we were bound to our bodies and brains. Aegis wasn't using his body like a puppet or a video game avatar; he *lived* in it. Everything about him took up residence in a human nervous system. I was born in mine and never lived without it. When our bodies died, we died too.

"I thought I could learn to ... I don't know how to describe it. Disperse? Disperse my body. Not leave it or turn it into energy or anything like that. I thought I could learn to let it go and exist without a body at all. I thought I could learn to be what Aegis was. What we really are. Maybe I could have. Maybe one day *you* will. But I think that having flesh is addictive, and letting go of it is a scary thing. It wouldn't have helped kill Bloodlust anyway."

Tom scoffed, "But wearing a cape and fighting crime will?"

Adam said, "It's not like that, Tom. Aegis came to believe that humanity draws strength from their stories. He thought that by becoming human and embodying their heroic ideals he'd be able to triumph over evil.

"That's what most human stories are about, when you get down to it, triumphing over evil. Especially the mythological ones, the ones people turn to for guidance and wisdom. But look at movies, television shows or video games — and, yes, comic books — if the good guy *doesn't* win, you can bet that the creators were trying to make a particular point. The protagonist succeeding is the norm; that's what people want to believe. People need those stories. They're fuel for the hope that drives us forward and the faith that allows us to stand.

"Being human *and* the Golden Light might have given Aegis the edge. In his natural form, Aegis was nothing but will, thought and power. If he could gain the human ability of gaining willpower through hope and faith, then he might become more powerful than Bloodlust, instead of just being equal.

"But Aegis was wrong, Tom. He wasn't human. He could never be human, never draw on the power of cultural narratives for inner strength. His humanity was a weakness not a strength. As he died, Aegis touched the Golden Home and ordered my creation. He thought that through this rough resurrection, he could find another chance to embody the hero of myth. He was wrong about that, too. He could never be the avatar of legend, but neither could I."

Tom said, "I don't understand."

"I was no more human than Aegis. Think about it, Tom. I was born in a lab. The closest things I had to parents were a mad scientist and a billion-year-old artificial intelligence. I never really lived inside of human society. I was trained from the beginning to be their hero. I never really experienced childhood or growth. You saw how I became a man."

"Yeah," replied Tom. "You said you weren't sure that you'd ever really been a kid."

Independence nodded. "Exactly. I never had the chance to be a complete person. I had been made to fulfill a role, and I tried ... but when Bloodlust came, I wasn't strong enough. I was even worse off than Aegis. I not only lacked humanity, I also lacked his experience. I was caught between the two worlds. Bloodlust killed me easily.

"But my dying thoughts turned to your mother and you. I saw that you were a promise to the future. I touched you with the last thought to cross my mind ... and I changed you."

Tom looked at the image of his father. "How?"

Adam frowned and replied, "I duplicated our essence and merged it with yours. Your flesh is half human, but *you* are the Golden Light ... as was I, as was Aegis. Your nature and substance are identical to ours. You aren't simply one of our species; you *are* Aegis, and you *are* me. We are you. You are the union of two indescribably different species, a legend come to life."

"What?"

"You are the child of a mortal woman and a celestial being. You grew to the edge of manhood ignorant of the truth of your nature. You've suffered loss and pain. All of this is a part of the heroic myth Aegis attempted to embody. Even the death of your mother was probably necessary for the needs of your journey."

"Fuck you! Mom's more than a goddamn plot twist! You're supposed to love her." Tom tried to turn his back on his father. It didn't work. No matter which way he spun, they faced each other, locked in a tidal embrace.

Adam's brow furrowed. "Tom, listen to me. I loved your mother, and I loved you, but I am not here. I'm dead. There is no 'me' for me. Aegis wasn't here, either. Your mind created this vision.

"You could do this because you share our essence. The human part of you is a unique person, but the nonphysical, alien part is *identical* to us. Think of it this way: your hardware is different but the software's the same. You're a different computer running a copy of the same operating system—installed from the same disc, even. Your soul is a copy of our souls, in a new body, with a different mind. You're my son, Tom, but what we were lives in you. You made this vision because you need us right now."

"So I'm talking to myself?"

"Kind of," Adam shrugged. "People often do, when they need to figure something out."

Then Aegis reappeared—he was simply *there* again—floating beside Independence. Tom looked at his father and the primordial entity that spawned them both. They were three distinct people, but they *were* the Golden Light. It flowed between them, through them, from them and over them. It filled the nowhere void of Tom's dream.

"You are unique, Thomas, unique in the whole of creation," said Aegis. "That which *was* at the dawn of time survives in *you*; none can claim such an inheritance. No other being is both of the Age of Potential and the Age of Matter. No other being has been born of my race and a younger species. You are the firstborn of the firstborn of creation. You are the child of humanity. This dual heritage is your greatest strength and the necessary fulfillment of legend. Through your journey, through victory and exaltation, trial and suffering—and through your embodiment of the story—you may achieve what we could not.

"You may find, in the human story, the will to defeat of the greatest of all evils. The human story is one of dogged struggle, persistent hope, and the confirmation of faith. You may win, you may rise, and you may prove the validity of faith."

"I don't think I have faith in anything," said Tom. "I've lost everything. Mom's dead, my best friend is dead. I think *I'm* dying. I'm talking to a goddamn nightmare. I'm alone."

Adam smiled, put a hand on his son's shoulder and gave him a gentle shake. "Your mother had faith in you. I had faith in you. Marcus did, too. And *you* have faith in some people ... Captain Holly, our old friend Fiona and, of course, Tiffany. I wouldn't be surprised to learn that they have faith in you, too. My son, you are not alone."

"Wake up, dammit." Fiona gripped Tom's shoulder and shook him forcefully. He continued to sleep, completely undisturbed by her aggressive attempts to rouse him. She had removed the IV from his arm, but old Angus had apparently put Tom on some serious sedatives.

She sat on the edge of the cot, trying to wake him. The poor kid had taken a beating; a scabby gash covered his forehead, and his left eye was swollen and black. Fiona brushed his hair away from the injury and laid her right hand on his forehead. He felt both clammy and feverish. His breathing was shallow, and she could barely find a pulse.

"Just wake up, kid. Jesus." She was worried about him. How bad was that head wound? The boy may look like his dad, but Adam had never been hurt like this—not until Bloodlust showed up, anyway. She didn't look forward to carrying Tom up two hundred feet of stairs, but a gal's gotta do what a gal's gotta do.

"Scram, you big dork!" Fiona had yelled at Independence, outside of that bank on Garden Street, when they first met. She was eighteen back then and had taken up the outlaw lifestyle for kicks. There never were that many villains; the young Fiona figured the career path would lead to wealth and fame. She never expected any heroes to show up, not during her very first gig. Certainly not Independence.

But there he was, floating in the air, big, blond and beautiful, surrounded by that golden light. He looked like an angel wrapped in a flag. A part of her swooned in that first second, but then the *other* part awoke—the part that lived for thrill and danger. She spread her hands and threw a violet ball of plasma at him. She'd used the same move to blow a hole in the bank vault, not five minutes earlier.

The energy splashed against his chest. It didn't even knock him back, and he drifted to the ground in front of her. He grabbed her wrists with his large hands—not roughly, just with firmness— and looked right into her eyes.

He smiled at her, not at all angry, and said, "That's not going to do anything but make me stronger. What do you say we have a little talk?"

From that moment on, she was hooked. The risk and the rush of being the Big Bad Girl, the hilarious way the people ran away, the powerlessness of the authorities and Adam's inevitable appearance. Their dance went on for decades, and she relished every moment of it. She never thought it would end. She wanted it to last forever.

"Okay, kid. We don't have time for this shit," she said, moving her hand from Tom's forehead to his bare chest. She took a breath and made up her mind. "Sorry if this hurts, but I can't think of anything else."

Her hand flared purple, light flickered in the Dark Room, and the sound of screams filled the empty halls.

CHAPTER THIRTY

Goose bumps crawled on JJ's skin. It didn't help that the charged air made his entire body tingle. And, yeah, he was more than a little nervous. There he was, standing in Doctor Angus's office with his Sol and a talking lightning bolt named Overpower. The volume of JJ's life had been turned up to eleven, and it was overwhelming.

Milk and the heroes—including the sarcastic, beautiful Nikki—would be here as soon as the force field dropped. The fight was about to begin, and people would probably die. JJ wasn't a fighter and definitely didn't want to die, but he'd crossed the line. It was sink-or-swim time; there was no going back now.

Overpower hovered in the air with arms extended to the side, a vaguely humanoid mass of flickering electricity. He seemed to be concentrating. Jagged mini-bolts shot from his body at random, but he remained motionless.

JJ didn't understand what was going on but felt too afraid to ask. So he just watched, waiting for the supercharged Postie to finish whatever he was doing. Adjusting his baseball cap, JJ glanced at Sol and tried to not laugh. All he could see was the bulbous tip of Sol's nose peeking out of the mass of static-charged blond hair. The dude looked like Cousin It with a 'fro—nothing but a frizzy fuzzball poking out of a shirt.

Sol noticed JJ's look and leaned closer. He whispered, "You

know, Jay, the way I see it, every story needs a good *deus ex machina.* Right?"

Overpower let out a white-noise screech, like radio feedback, *"Like I've never heard that one before."*

"Sorry, um, Overpower. My friend was just joking," stammered JJ.

"I know, man. So was I. Lighten up," The electric man lowered his arms and drifted closer, but stayed on the other side of the desk. *"I thought you guys were supposed to be the cool kids."*

Sol chortled. "You wish you were as cool as us, OP. That body of yours is what, a couple thousand degrees? Burn my hand right off if I tried to touch you, right?"

The featureless, head-shaped knot of lightning seemed to shake slightly. *"You'd get fried before you ever got close. But it's not my body."*

"Say what?"

"Nope. This is cosmetic, just wasted current so I look like a man. Right now my mind exists as a little knot of electromagnetic fields. My body is in a hotel room in Indiana, protected by the smartest man on Earth and some seriously heavy weapons."

"You mean Mike Dawkins? The guy who made the robots?" asked JJ.

"Yeah. Tech Support. He's hacking this place right now. I just helped him get in the network. We're going to know everything that's ever happened inside these walls."

"Awesome," muttered JJ. Chilly perspiration tickled his neck, especially the area around the implant. That made JJ think. "Hey, is there anything you can do about these things?" He pointed to the black metal knob behind his left ear.

Again, Overpower shook his head. *"No. I could pull them out, but they might blow up. There are too many non-metallic parts and they're made to be tamper —"*

"So they *are* bombs?"

"Oh, yeah. I just downloaded the specs. They're nasty little gadgets; graphene nano-shrapnel and a shaped charge pointed right at your brain stem. I could disarm or reprogram them if I had access to the control system, but it isn't connected to any of the main networks. They might

relay the signals through a satellite from a bunker in Antarctica for all I know. Sorry, guys."

"No worries, man," said Sol. "We'll deal with them. Matter of fact, Jay, why don't you open up a door to the hospital. I'll sneak in and grab one of the remover thingamajigs."

"You sure?"

Sol gave a nod. "Figure we gotta get moving anyway, right OP?"

"Oh yeah. Won't be long before Security realizes they can't see this room. You guys need to leave before that happens."

"What about you?"

"Oh, I've got a few things to do. We'll catch up in — and, there they go." Alarms began to blare and three heavy thuds shook the building. *"They're on the way. Get out of here, guys. Now."*

"Don't have to tell me twice." Sol slapped JJ's back and grinned. "The hospital, if you don't mind my good man."

JJ nodded and raised his hands and a pair of wormholes spiraled open — one showed Madi, Anon and Vanessa huddling on the roof, the other opened in the street beside the hospital. He looked at his friend. "Be quick, man. I'm not leaving without you."

"You better not. You're my ride out. I'll grab the thing and meet you, I dunno, near the food court. Just keep your head down and don't get killed."

"You too." JJ reached for Sol's hand, but the stocky little guy pulled him in for a rib-cracking bear hug. "Ow, fuck!"

"Deal with it, pansy," Sol stepped back, laughed and wiped his eyes. He grumbled something under his breath about dust, looked up at JJ and said, "See you in a few."

"Count on it." JJ's eyes began to water, too. "Fucking dust."

Overpower grew brighter and hissed, *"You guys* really *need to go."*

JJ looked up at the electric man and nodded. He exchanged a glance with Sol but said nothing more. The hairy man hopped through his portal, shrinking as he leaped, and vanished in the dark.

A loud bang shook the hall. Overpower yelled something, but JJ didn't stick around to listen. He stepped through the tunnel of spacetime, closing it on his heels. Alarms and spotlights filled the night, the noise of boots and engines rose from street level.

"Omigod, Jay!" Vanessa ran over and hugged him. "What happened?"

"Did something blow up?" asked Anon, who for some reason had turned into John Wayne in an olive-drab Army uniform circa World War Two. "Where's Sol?"

"He went to the hospital to get an implant remover. And nothing blew up yet, but the night's still young." JJ looked at Madi. "What do you hear?"

She shook her head. "They don't know what's up. They know something went down in Angus's office. We could see lights in the window. So could the guards on the Wall. They think it's an escape attempt but they don't—"

Suddenly the top three floors of headquarters exploded in a blast of shattered windows and lightning. Strobing light flared in the sky above HQ's roof, pulsing down to the top of the Wall. The spot in the air directly above the tower began to brighten; JJ, Madi, Vanessa and Anon all shielded their eyes.

And with an earsplitting bang, the light flashed and died. Arctic wind rushed inside, and the tundra's biting chill flooded the prison streets. The force field was down.

The four friends stared up at the smoking tower, too stunned to move or feel the cold. They glanced at each other, cautious and speechless. They all held their breath for one long second of anticipation and fear.

Then everything kind of happened all at once.

The alarms tripled in intensity, more lights flashed into the sky, distant voices relayed orders and shouted warnings, metal clanged on metal as the soldiers took their positions and armed their weapons, and fierce machinery fired to life on the Wall and in the streets below.

The stairwell door blew to smithereens with the crack of a sonic boom as Milk's team ran onto the roof. JJ numbly wondered if he was in shock, but that worry was blown away by the thrill of seeing the heroes arrive through the flashing transdimensional gateway.

The first one through was nothing but a blur. The flight path of the door's splintered remains was all that marked his passage. He appeared at the edge of the roof, staring down at the street. His outfit had a bulletproof vest and lots of padding at the joints. He didn't wear a mask, but had a beanie pulled down over his ears to guard against the cold. It was Nikki's brother, David. Shockwave.

He popped in and out of view a dozen times over the next half second—on the other side of the roof, on top of a building across the street, on the ground next to HQ, then back to the roof. He appeared—with a pronounced boom—about a foot to JJ's left and said, "What's up?"

The legendary California Girl cartwheeled out of the stairwell next. She flipped through the air and landed in a ready crouch, scanning the sky with her sky-blue eyes. She hadn't changed at all over the years. JJ thought she'd stepped right out of the Eighties in her gold-and-blue costume and big blond hair. He couldn't wait for Sol to meet her.

Behind California Girl came a rather short, totally bald man in black, with nothing but skin where eyes should be. He slid across the roof with unnaturally smooth steps and stepped beside her. The eyeless man's body was half-turned with the left side forward. His slippered feet were spread apart, with the knees slightly bent; his right hand was held at waist level, while the left had been extended and raised higher. Both hands were turned up, fingers pointing at the sky. It looked like some kind of kung-fu stance to JJ.

A huge, shirtless brute with lots of tattoos came through behind the martial artist. He flashed JJ a thumbs up and took position right behind the smaller man and woman.

Another pair jogged out next—a man and woman in matching black outfits with red trim. JJ kind of recognized them— they were from that old team, the East Coast Alliance—but he couldn't remember their names. The lady had a relaxed alertness expression. Sparkles of light danced over her body and red energy glowed in her eyes and around her balled fists. The man looked older, with graying hair and a beard, but moved like a panther with an expression of determination on his narrow face.

Behind them came Portero. JJ had never met him, of course, but the world-famous son of Mexico was unmistakable in that ankle-length coat and expensive shirt. Only one A-list hero dressed like that. JJ thought Portero looked more like the cover of a romance novel than a superhero, but that was the dude's shtick. Every hero had a gimmick; Portero's just happened to be that he looked like a male model. His long black hair waved in the breeze and a confident smirk curled his lips. His piercing eyes slid past JJ and Anon the Duke; they flowed over Madi and came to rest on Vanessa. She noticed and half-posed, half-blushed in response. JJ had to give her credit; she did well, despite the subzero chill.

Then everyone jumped as the stairwell burst apart in a cloud of pulverized brick and flying wood. JJ briefly thought it was an explosion, before the motion of an enormous figure revealed the truth. Milk had stepped through and been too big for the doorway.

When the dust cleared, the giant hero stood in the center of his group. He wore the classic NASA-engineered uniform of his save-the-world days. The government had spent millions of dollars on the suit because everyone had grown tired of Milk's all-too-frequent public nudity. Congress felt that preserving decency was worth the fortune it cost to create an outfit capable of withstanding the hero's undeniably active lifestyle. The bulky armor consisted of smooth white plates, constructed of classified ceramics and alloys, over a black, synthetic bodysuit. It was nearly indestructible but bore quite a few pockmarks, chipped spots, small cracks and scorched blotches from decades of use. JJ thought Milk looked like a walking space shuttle.

The titan glanced around and grinned at the boy, but JJ's attention was locked on Nikki, who must have come through with her father. She stood right next to the nine-foot champion and looked utterly tiny beside her old man.

And damn, JJ thought. *She looks even better in real life.*

She was his age and kind of petite — well, short; she was no skinny young girl. Her figure was compact and curvy with strong, well-defined muscles. Her outfit was loose enough for free movement, but tight enough prevent snagging. She wore kind of a flak jacket over a tight black top, cargo pants tucked into armored boots, elbow and kneepads and those forearm things like old-school armor. Around her narrow waist was a heavy duty, multi-pouched belt.

She was bold, ready for anything, and not even slightly afraid. Everything about her seemed to proclaim that she had been born for this. That confidence impressed JJ even more than her abundant hotness.

He was immediately convinced that he'd never seen anyone with that much beauty, strength and attitude. He was sure in that moment that he'd never see someone like her again for as long as he lived.

Her large, dark eyes scanned the skyline and the Wall — then her gaze fell on JJ. Both teens froze. He could tell that she recognized the interest in his expression. She saw that he was really, *really* into her. A mix of emotions played across her face. Was she embarrassed? Shy? *Her?*

Then she scowled at him, turning that luscious mouth into a taunting sneer. She shook her head, rolled her eyes and pointedly turned away.

JJ didn't mind. If she wanted to make a game out of it, he was more than willing to play. Besides, the backside looked just as nice as the front. Maybe even nicer.

His head cocked to the side and an almost pained expression crossed his face as let out the breath he had unknowingly been holding.

A swift tap to the chest and a firm hand on his shoulder reminded JJ that David stood by his side — and had just watched him unabashedly check out Nikki. JJ swallowed hard, trying to will away the crimson heat in his cheek.

"Dude," David scoffed. "You know that's my little sister, right?"

JJ could only nod, not sure how to react.

"Be careful," the speeder whispered, in a tone of total seriousness.

JJ blinked and took a half-step back. For a second, he wondered if that was a threat. Some big brothers can be overprotective, and the son of Milk and Shockwave was nobody to be messed with, JJ was certain. He tried to speak, found that his throat was too dry and tried again. "Um … I will?"

David's brow wrinkled in confusion as he picked up on JJ's nervousness. He shook his head and laughed. "No, man. I meant that for your sake. Be careful." He winked and raised a fist, bumping knuckles with JJ. "If you're into Nikki, all I can say is … good luck. You'll *need* it."

JJ grinned, "Thanks. I love a good challenge."

Then the gunshots began—from every direction—and lights flared in the sky, briefly illuminating dozens of airborne drones.

"Incoming!" bellowed Milk, loud enough to shake building, as missiles began to fall.

✪   ✪   ✪

The raspy voice of Staff Sergeant Vimes filled the command center. Onscreen was live footage from four APE cameras. The sergeant's squad had entered Headquarters less than a minute after the ninth floor disappeared from ABRA's security systems and were heading up the stairwells. "The computers are not accepting our commands, sir. We initiated manual lockdown and are now proceeding upstairs—"

The sergeant's voice turned into a feedback screech, dissolved to static and disconnected. The screens went black. According to the computers, Sergeant Vimes, Squad Seven and the top three floors of Headquarters had all ceased to exist.

A shrieking alarm began and everyone in the security room gasped—the force field had crashed. The computer chimed an emergency alert, the soldiers shouted in surprise, calls came in from a dozen sources, and Private Lee read a scripted announcement over the comm. Captain Holly didn't pay attention to any of that.

He reached down to Corporal Bonano's keyboard and rapidly tapped out commands, pulling up broadcasts from the overhead drones. The main monitor switched to eye-in-the-sky views of the prison city, showing only green and black. The view immediately focused on one of the residential buildings; thirteen figures stood on that roof. One giant towered over the rest.

Even through low-resolution imaging, the horned colossus was unmistakable. Milk had come to ABRA City.

God damn you, Milk. Captain Holly could not move or speak. He wouldn't risk letting any of the men see his face. His jaw worked, a scowl twisted his paling lips, and he couldn't pull his eyes away from the monitor. *You're going get us all killed.*

"Sir?" whispered Corporal Bonano. The young soldier was the first to find his voice; everyone else had been stunned into silence by the heroes' arrival.

The captain did not reply. His dark eyes searched the screen, analyzing his foes. Heat welled up in his chest; that roof was JJ Joyce's hangout, and four residents had been there when the intruders arrived. Milk and his crew had obviously contacted the youngsters to find allies on the inside.

Holly's mind went to *his* secret ally, Fiona McNamara. She should be in the Dark Room at that very moment.

MegaMax would already be locking down; Holly didn't need to check. The systems were automated, initiated by the sudden collapse of the force field. The immovable blast doors would isolate the cellblocks, automated defenses would initiate, and the guards would receive their shoot-to-kill orders. The captain didn't think that Fiona or even Tom could make it out. Holly's escape plan was doomed the moment Milk arrived. *You son of a bitch.*

Bonano spoke again, "Sir? Um, Colonel Swain is requesting order for evac."

"Agreed. Announce Code Troy," replied Holly, relieved to be rid of his mostly worthless superiors. He peeled his gaze from the monitor and looked around the room. His men all stared, waiting. "Find Angus and round up the doctors. Fire up the Launcher; I want all civilians and techs in the air in three minutes. Every man and woman with combat training needs to be armed and outside in half that time. *No* exceptions. Fire at will; shoot to kill. Call for immediate air support and issue a general alarm. This is Code Troy, people. We've trained for this. Stick to the routine and we might make it out alive."

Holly felt the eyes of his subordinates. Code Troy, they all knew, was likely to end with death from above. All of those young men knew that their lives were probably over. Silence pressed down in the room, a nearly palpable force.

Once more, young Bonano was the first to recover. "What about Milk, sir?"

The hulking officer growled, "What about him? Call the armory. Tell them to prep my suit. I'm going out to say hello to Sergeant Young. You all know what to do. I'll see you outside."

❂   ❂   ❂

JJ threw his hands up and *pushed*. An arcing wave of gravity pulsed out of his palms, detonated three missiles and sent two more spinning out of control. He saw Madi fling her arms wide, but couldn't tell what she was doing. The soldiers could though, and they didn't like it one bit. She was shoving static down the wavelengths, killing radio communications for miles. It took a lot of concentration but was totally worth it. Only the flying drones and the Wall guards had line of sight, and Milk's team easily countered their attacks.

Old Curt ran to the edge of the roof, opened his arms invitingly and stood motionless while bullets pinged off his flesh. Red bolts of brilliant light flew from Glimmer's hands and torched incoming projectiles. David blurred in front of them, blocking bullets with debris from the busted stairwell.

On the other side of the roof, Hardcore rose over Vanessa, Anon, Portero and Quietus. His tattooed torso stretched like putty to shield the smaller Posties from harm. Several shots slapped against Hardcore's bare flesh, but he just laughed and yelled, "Bring it on!"

California Girl and Nikki seemed to share that opinion. They both moved to the edge of the roof to give the guards better targets. The blond heroine stood in a defiant pose, letting everyone see her return—she'd always loved being in the spotlight. Nikki flipped off the troops and shouted her opinions of their characters, hygiene, sex lives and mothers.

JJ thought she had a truly impressive vocabulary.

He winced when she got shot—on her right shoulder, left hip and dead-center of her forehead, all in quick succession. She flinched, grimaced and swore with each impact, but wasn't really injured—though she did tend to stay moving after that. She was learning to dodge.

Milk didn't dodge anything. He thumped his chest, roared with laughter and jumped into the sky—slamming into a missile, detonating it harmlessly above the rooftop. The gigantic hero was thrown down by the explosion, crashed behind the hospital, and immediately leaped back overhead.

He arced above the city, bounced off the side of the Wall and shot back into the air to tackle another missile. He grabbed it in a bear hug and took it down, plummeting into one of the barracks in a ball of flame. Soldiers surrounded the titan, hosing him down in bullets, rockets and grenades.

Milk stood, bellowed a laugh, and stomped on the ground with staggering force. The troops were thrown off balance by the resulting tremor, and the hero used the distraction to jump back to the roof.

Landing right beside JJ, Milk looked down and said, "I think they know we're here."

Then thunder ripped through the night and lightning flashed down from the burning top story of Headquarters—Overpower had arrived.

He was the brightest thing in sight, glaring, pulsing and discharging sparks in every direction. He destroyed five missiles with thunderbolts blasts, tossed electricity at the soldiers below and fried some turrets on the Wall. His sudden assault trashed half-a-dozen Walkers, sent the ground troops running and brought silence down on the city.

The East Coast heroine Glimmer waved her hands in the air; a scintillating dome of flashing sparks spread overhead, blotting out the rest of the world. To distant observers, cameras and radar, the roof appeared empty. Glimmer looked at Milk and said, "Okay, we're clear."

"Good job, Hannah. Thanks."

"Just like the old days, big guy."

Milk grinned, so did Glimmer. JJ couldn't help but smile, too; he was in the major leagues. Overpower flew down and hovered half-a-dozen feet above Milk. Everyone else clustered around the three of them.

"JJ, can you take us somewhere else? Fast."

The youth blinked, thought for a second and said, "Sure thing."

He raised a hand and opened a portal to the basement of his building. Overpower flew through first (JJ thought he was checking for cameras and bugs) and everyone else followed. Glimmer came last, distracting the guards by casting an image of Milk in the sky while dispelling the empty-roof illusion.

"Why the cellar?" grumbled Vanessa through chattering teeth.

JJ walked over to a stack of boxes, "Clothes." He pulled out some heavy coats, sweaters, gloves and boots. "Stocked in every building in case of blackouts."

He passed cold weather gear to anyone who wanted it— Vanessa and Madison bundled up tight, David took a coat, Glimmer and Lockdown took coats and gloves. Nikki shook her head at JJ's offer. She was unaffected by the cold; so were Anon, California Girl and the tattooed brick, Hardcore. Quietus had too much kung-fu to be bothered by the elements, and Portero wouldn't be caught dead in such ugly gear.

"Smart thinking, JJ," declared Milk. "And good job everyone. Especially you, Overpower. That was one hell of an entrance."

The man-shaped lightning bolt hovered in the most distant corner, stirring up dust with ambient static. *"Thank you ... but how do you know my name?"*

Milk waved a hand dismissively. "I know *all* about you, kid. But don't worry about it; your secret's safe with me. Thanks for doing this."

"I should thank you. It feels good to finally be out of the closet. You know how it is. Sometimes you just need to stretch your wings."

"You're damn right about that," laughed Milk. "Do you feel up to playing air support?"

The humanoid mass of sparks gave a nod. *"No problem."*

"Good, that'll free up Hannah to help on the ground. You take out the drones and any bombers or ICBMs or whatever else they throw our way. Don't kill anyone. If they send jets, make sure the crew gets out alive. And don't mess with their evacuation. We're here to free Tom, not go after Angus. Help out down here if you have time, but your job is to own the sky."

"*Will do.*" He motioned to JJ. "*Mind putting me up in the air?*"

JJ nodded, "Sure thing." He opened a portal that showed only black sky. Overpower shot through with booming speed, and the wormhole instantly collapsed.

Milk looked down at JJ and Madi. "You both did well, too—no hesitation and lots of guts. Are you ready to go?"

"Never been so ready," replied JJ. "But I've got to get to the food court. Sol's going to be there with the implant remover. We'll help anyway we can, but getting rid of these bombs is the most important thing."

The surrounding group gasped, and JJ felt his cheeks flush. He could've dropped the news more gently.

Milk's brow rose. "They're *bombs*? We thought they were trackers."

JJ replied, "So did we, but Overpower found the truth in the computers. Madi already had suspicions. It's okay, though. We can get rid of them. It's quick and easy."

Milk nodded. "Then you know what to do. Try to gather the prisoners on your way to the food court. Take out those bombs, then use your power to get everyone out of here."

"Okay, but where should I send them? I kinda need to have been to a place to open a hole. Otherwise it's a crapshoot."

Milk motioned to his daughter. "I know. Powerhouse has a list of safe houses—all in cities you've visited. She'll go with you, protect your ass and hand out directions."

JJ glanced at Nikki. She was not even remotely looking at him.

"Sounds good," he looked at the heroes and his friends. "Let's roll."

Milk looked up. "The rest of you know the plan. Cali has the Wall. Portero, Shockwave and the East Coasters are crowd control. Disarm the soldiers and get them off the field. Quietus and Hardcore, keep them on the west side. Everyone remember to move fast and keep the property damage low. Try your damnedest to not hurt the guards—and keep the other prisoners in line. We're here to save people, not start a war. And never forget rule number one: watch each other's backs. Always."

"All right," said JJ. "Who wants to go where?"

"First, I need to get back to the roof," said Milk. "You all stay here for a few minutes. I'll go and keep them distracted for a bit then head underground. Good luck, stay safe and stick to the script. I'll catch up after my mission's done."

"Wait, um, where are you going?" asked JJ.

Milk looked down and grinned. "Somebody's gotta clear out MegaMax and save Tom, right? That's my job. Now come on, let's get to work."

CHAPTER THIRTY-ONE

Tiffany heard the alarms and immediately ran from the room. She'd learned enough about Security's plans to know that she only had moments before all the doors locked. She didn't know what might have triggered the alert, but she didn't want to be trapped in her room—their room. Besides, it might be *him*, in the process of a daring escape.

Or it might be Sol, the strange little man from up above. His friends were supposedly trying to break out and wanted to find Tom. They might try to save him.

But Tiffany didn't have faith in them; she had faith in Tom. He could escape. They would escape together.

She slid to a halt against the metal door, pushed the keypad's lone button and cheered when it slid open. She immediately jumped through, before it closed for good.

"You! Come with us! Hurry!" A female guard yelled from the other side of the entrance. She stood in the corridor with seven other soldiers and a single APE. Red lights flashed on the ceiling, and the shrieking alarms seemed to grow louder every second. Nobody else was in sight. Even the kitchen staff was gone. The guard waved frantically, and Tiffany ran as fast as she could. The soldier stood in the doorway and pulled the girl into the hall.

Tiffany started to say thanks, but the soldier interrupted by calling over her headset, "Central One this is Bouncer Two-Two

Actual. Site is clear, repeat, site is clear. Drop and lock!"

The hall rang out with a tremendous, ear-splitting thud as the blast door plummeted into place, less than two feet away. Nearly two-hundred tons of metal dropped eighteen feet, and the shocking crash knocked Tiffany off her feet. She landed on her knees and felt the reverberations of other falling doors ringing through the floor. The cellblocks were now isolated — though the guards had secret passages all over the place.

"We were coming for you, Miss Cooke," said the soldier. Her name, Farella, was stenciled on the armored chest plate. She extended a hand and helped Tiffany back to her feet. "Thanks for saving us the trip. Please come with us."

The group walked cautiously down the hall, weapons drawn and ready. The APE led the way, and Tiffany trailed behind. She glanced toward Cellblock A, relieved to see an impenetrable steel door blocking *that* particular corridor. Even Vaughn wasn't strong enough to get through it. He was trapped until the blast doors were raised. Farella gently touched Tiffany's shoulder and pulled her along.

They led her all the way to the foyer, where twenty armored troops and five more walking tanks stood in a tight cluster around the security desk. Julio stood off to the side, the only other prisoner in the room. He glanced her way, gave a terse nod and looked down. But she saw anxiety and stress in his dark eyes.

Julio had been helping Security for almost nine years and was notoriously tight-lipped. Lots of people assumed he was a jerk, but Tiffany always thought he was ashamed to be working for ABRA. He'd been a hero, once — a leader of heroes — but he never spoke about those days. His name had been Blackout, and he could make people pass out; as a side-effect, his power deactivated some Posthuman abilities. If Security had brought them both here, then whatever was happening almost certainly involved dangerous Posties.

There were seven or eight conversations going, and Tiffany couldn't catch them all. Apparently the prison was under attack, but nobody really knew anything. Everyone seemed to be having trouble with their radios. Eight of the soldiers had weapons aimed toward the main entrance; three guys were prone, with large, bipod-mounted machineguns. She didn't understand the point of stationing armed guards. That blast door was fifteen feet wide, twelve feet high and five feet thick; it weighed two hundred twenty tons and sat in a frame that was even heavier. Were they *really* worried that something might get through?

Tiffany opened her special sense, feeling the hundreds of Posties—and nine *new* ones—in the city above. One of them was almost directly overhead, much closer than any others. It was an incredibly potent presence. His power resounded with breathtaking force in Tiffany's perception. He felt *big*.

One of the lightly-armored soldiers yelled, "Oh, God! He's coming!"

"Calm down Geary," barked a lieutenant in an APE. The featureless chrome face turned toward Tiffany. "Miss Cook, come here."

She steeled herself and walked closer. The rest of the soldiers dropped into firing positions, aimed their rifles, pistols and machineguns at the door.

The armored Lieutenant raised a gauntlet and pointed at the door. "You're going to give us some assistance."

She looked at the black visor. She had no desire to help Security anymore, but wasn't suicidal. She knew the answer but still asked, "How?"

"A serious threat is approaching. Shut him down. Blackout here says that he can't."

Tiffany glanced at Julio, who shrugged and looked down. She turned to the door and closed her eyes.

The mighty Postie seemed to have entered the elevator shaft; she felt him dropping like a stone. The floor quaked from his thudding touchdown. Geary yelped. All of the soldiers tensed up.

Then a titanic impact shook the blast door like a burst of cannon fire—but caused no obvious damage. Another quaking blow rang out, and another; they began to fall with relentless regularity, pounding like a heartbeat. The floor shook with each strike, but it wasn't as bad as Tom's fight with Vaughn.

One of the soldiers shouted, "Holy shit, Milk's *here*!"

Tiffany's eyes widened at the news. She knew what she had to do.

The lieutenant's exoskeleton rose to its full height and raised a watermelon-sized, robotic fist and aimed the huge forearm blade at her face. "Are you going to help? Or is this going to get ugly."

"I'll help," she said, turning to face the wall of steel. "You're damn right I'll help."

Milk growled in frustration and hit the wall with the side of his hand. The impact left a dent in the metal, but he could tell (through a lifetime of punching things) that the armor covered solid bedrock. He could dig through, but it would take time and might cause a cave-in. The door was a much safer option. But it was goddamn *strong*. He grumbled under his breath and threw a jab that accomplished nothing.

He punched the door again, and again. His baseball-sized knuckles left deep impressions in the polished steel, but the damn thing was too dense to really smash. Even Milk's strength had limits. He could probably lift it but there was no place to grip.

"Assholes," he rumbled, beginning to suspect that the blast doors had been designed specifically for him.

He reared back and slammed both fists against the steel, crashing like a gong from hell. The floor shook, and ceiling panels creaked at the mighty blow, but he still hadn't damaged the damn thing. He glanced up and wondered about going over the top—and then felt a quickening rush of raw power.

Surging warmth coursed through his body, and Milk experienced *déjà vu* at the sensation. He had felt it before, a long time ago. Someone was giving him a power boost. He *felt* another Postie, beyond the door, magnifying his abilities. Milk had read the files on all of the inmates, including Tiffany Cooke, the young power manipulator. She must have decided to lend a hand.

His rippling muscles expanded, throbbing with vigor as he grew in might and mass. Invulnerable fleshed burst through the space-age armor. The ceramic and steel plating split at the seams;

pieces of the black-and-white breastplate clattered to the floor. The sleeves ruptured when he flexed his titanic arms; the rest of his upper-body armor fell apart. His heavily reinforced boots popped apart, and his huge toes dented the metal flooring. Most of his pants survived the growth spurt. Milk was happy about that; he didn't want to make other guys feel too bad about their shortcomings. He'd gained an extra ton of bulk, and nearly another foot in height—and he felt dizzyingly stronger.

It was like becoming a Postie all over again, like waking up with all that strength for the first time.

The hero raised a still-growing fist and grinned, "Hell yeah! That's what I'm talking about!"

The next hit broke the reinforced frame and knocked half-a-dozen troops off their feet. Metal plates dropped from the ceiling and the ground heaved. The earth staggered at the force and some of the lights flickered out.

The APE-jockey Lieutenant stepped closer to Tiffany. "What are you doing? Shut him down!"

"I-I'm trying! It's not working," she lied, but the soldier saw through it.

"You little bitch!" He drew back his fist. "Shut him down or I'll—"

Another titanic blow shook the tunnel, knocking the APE-armored officer off balance. The massive blast door was actually *pushed* forward by the impact, tearing through the floor, ceiling and walls.

The lieutenant recovered quickly and rose to his feet. He loomed over Tiffany and roared, "That's it! Sta-stand down. Staah…" His voice trailed off and he collapsed in a clanging pile of technology.

All of the other soldiers fell to the ground, too. They'd all been knocked out at once.

Tiffany gasped and her eyes shot to Julio. The older man cocked his head to the side and smirked, "Fuck those guys."

A wide smile broke out on her face, "Yeah! Fuck those guys!"

Then the ground began to shake—the blast door itself was trembling—and the huge block of metal shook with devastating force. Stone and steel screamed, buckled and gave way. The overhead lights winked off, but red emergency strobes began to flash in the darkness.

Julio ran forward and grabbed Tiffany, pushing her into the side hall as the ferocious quaking intensified. He wrapped his arms around her head, trying to cover her with his body, if necessary, but they were at a safe distance.

They felt more than heard the tremendous reverberations as the colossal blast door was pushed from its resting place. The mini-quake lasted almost a minute, and the silence after was like a sigh of relief.

Julio let go of Tiffany. She hugged his waist and said, "Thank you."

"Don't mention it," he replied, and they peeked into the foyer.

Rock and dirt fell from the ceiling in the foyer. Ruby pulses of hazy illumination flared in the dust-filled gloom. The entrance was half-blocked by the crumpled blast door, and debris filled the foyer, but the way was clear. Tiffany gasped at Milk, seeing the giant for the first time—even larger and stronger than normal, thanks to her help. The curling horns nearly touched the shattered ceiling and his herculean muscles rippled in the red emergency light.

"Julio! Good to see you, man," bellowed the colossal hero, when he noticed them peeking around the corner. "And you must be Tiffany. Pleased to meet you, miss. Thanks for the boost."

"You're welcome," she managed to nervously whisper. In her special sight, Milk was a surging mountain of power. He was *strength* in human form. His towering presence moved the world.

Milk looked down at the unconscious soldiers, checked to make sure that none had been seriously injured by falling wreckage and laughed, "Can you believe these guys? Taking a nap at a time like this! Bunch of damn slackers if you ask me."

CHAPTER THIRTY-TWO

"You're goddamn heavy for someone who don't eat," grunted Fiona as she hauled Tom up to the next landing. He stumbled drunkenly, with his left arm flung around her shoulders for support. They'd made it up nine flights—halfway to the top— but his knees gave out every few steps, and she had to keep an arm around his waist to keep him upright.

There were doors at every level, and she'd opened the first two out of curiosity. They appeared to be maintenance corridors, but she was too scared to explore. She just wanted to get up and out. Nothing else mattered. She glanced over the rail, looking at the floor a hundred feet below, and the ceiling a hundred feet above. The stairs wound around the chimney-like shaft and hadn't been built for comfort.

"This would be a whole lot easier, kid, if you'd just wake the fuck up."

"Mm-mm … m'way … m'wake," slurred Tom. His head rolled limply around; those metallic eyes blinked blearily at the fluorescent lighting. He weakly slapped his chest and gently stomped his feet, realizing that he wore nothing but scrub pants. Then he noticed his rescuer. "Fiona?"

"That's right, kid. Come on," she pulled him up another step. "We've got to move."

Tom looked around and steadied himself on the wall. He shook his head to clear away the fog. "How did you—?"

"Captain Holly, believe it or not." She continued to lead him upwards. "He turned off the cameras and our brain bombs—me, you and Tiff—and cleared out the guards. We're headed up from Solitary right now. We'll meet up with Tiff up above. Then we're out."

Tom couldn't help but grin, despite his exhaustion, despite his fear; despite everything. It felt good to smile; it felt right. He glanced down at his bare chest and saw the blackened streaks outlining a small, hand-shaped clean patch of skin. He dimly recalled Fiona glowing like heaven while she filled him with life and power. "Doesn't all this make you one of the good guys?"

Fiona mockingly sneered and let her eyes flash. "Watch your mouth."

"What are you gonna do about it? Charge my batteries?" They both laughed, but Tom stopped and looked at her. "Thank you, Fiona. You saved my life."

"Don't get all mushy, kid. Pay me back by busting us out."

He nodded. "I can do that. Especially with Tiffany's help."

"Good, just don't get cocky. We don't know what—" The ground shook suddenly—two powerful tremors in less than five seconds. Fiona hissed, "What the fuck was that?"

Then a long, tremendous quake rocked MegaMax and the lights went out, drowning the pair in absolute darkness. The violent shaking went on for nearly a minute, made worse by the oppressive shadows. Fiona responded by firing up, and Tom let his power shine. They pushed back the blackness with gold and violet light.

Tom asked, "What do you think?"

"I dunno. Felt like your little tussle with Vaughn."

"Think it's about us?"

"You mean do I think it's about *you*? Only one way to find out. Come on." She turned to resume the ascent, but Tom put a hand on her burning shoulder.

"Let's do this the easy way." He stepped closer, hooked an arm around her waist and they began to rise. He carried her over the railing, and they both looked down at the black depths. He didn't go too fast, but drifting up the shaft was much easier than hiking up those steps.

Fiona quietly laughed and said, "Oh ... if your daddy could see this."

Tom laughed too.

They'd risen about thirty feet when a door opened above, sending garish red light into the stairwell. The light came from a couple of levels beneath MegaMax, but still fifty feet above the floating escapees. A head poked over the rail—a helmeted guard in light armor—then ducked back.

Fiona shouted, "Watch it!" And things happened very fast.

The soldier leaned over the railing again—this time holding a shoulder-mounted rocket launcher. Tom turned to take the hit on the back; the explosion slammed him into the metal railing of the stairs but didn't really hurt. Fiona buried her face in his chest, grunted in painful shock and spat an admirable chain of profanity. A shadow in the flickering red light made Tom look over his shoulder. A soldier in an APE-suit ripped away the railing and jumped!

The four-thousand-pound suit slammed into Tom, wrapping its gigantic legs around his waist. They dropped a dozen yards but remained airborne.

The APE reared back and raised a giant fist to strike—but Fiona attacked first, screaming furiously, spitting purple-white flame. She grabbed the exoskeleton's smooth helmet with both of her burning hands. She held on tight, turning up the heat until the reflective metal faceplate glowed under her white-hot fingers. The APE pilot screamed and pushed back, trying to shake her. He failed, lost his grip and fell, dragging Fiona with him down the shaft.

Tom tried to dive after them, tried to catch Fiona, but another rocket detonated against his back, hurling him into a wall. A torrent of bullets filled the air, pummeling his body from head to toe.

He turned back around and faced the assault. Helmeted guards peeked over the railing, and ducked back for cover. Muzzles flashed, and streaking bullets bounced off his golden light.

In his mind, Tom saw the black-clad DPS troops in his back

yard; he saw the terrified soldier on the ground and the wisp of smoke rising from the pistol. He saw a rocket fly from the woods of his childhood and explode against Milk. He saw his mother on the ground.

Tom snapped out of the nightmare memory and glared up at the attacking guards. He had been helpless back then. He wasn't helpless anymore. He'd never be helpless again.

He snarled and hurled a blast of radiant energy, shattering the stairs beneath the soldiers. One of them fell to a lower level and rolled to the next landing. Another soldier tumbled off the broken edge into the gaping shaft. Tom caught him, instinctively, with his left hand.

The soldier wore the usual light armor with a helmet and reflective goggles. Tom tossed the man onto the closest landing. The remaining soldiers began to fire as soon as their squad mate was clear. Tom heard the thump of a grenade launcher (recognizable thanks to playing First Person Shooters with Marcus and Omar) and the small explosive bounced off the wall, blowing up two feet in front of his face. He drifted backward and blinked, trying to clear the spots from his eyes.

Two more APEs took advantage of the distraction and leaped from above, grappling the flying boy. Their crushing weight nearly yanked Tom out of the air, and he fought to remain in control. He wobbled and dipped but managed to stabilize and even begin to climb, but the soldiers started attacking in earnest. One of them tried to pin Tom's arms behind his back; the other went for the throat.

Tom tried to break the exoskeletons' holds, but they were unshakable. So he spun higher, careening into the stairs and walls. Concrete shattered as he shoved the APEs through every available surface. He crashed into a landing and snagged an I-beam, dislodging one of the soldiers.

With an excruciating jerk, the falling, two-ton APE grabbed hold of Tom's left ankle.

Tom screamed; it felt like his leg was being torn off. They dropped sixty feet down the shaft. The other guard held on for his life, wrapping those massive steel arms around the boy's bare chest.

Tom stopped the tumble with another wrenching tug from the dangling APE.

The soldier tried to use the suit's mass as an advantage. He arched his spine and whipped his legs back with servo-driven strength, swinging out like a pendulum. The arcing return drove the long blade of the exoskeleton's right gauntlet into Tom's crotch. The boy roared at the pain and threw a wild, stomping kick at the soldier's head.

Tom's bare heel left a deep indentation in the armored helmet. The soldier twitched fiercely, twice, and went limp. The robotic hand relaxed, and the suit tumbled out of view.

The remaining APE shifted, scissored his long legs around both of Tom's knees, and retracted his blades. He began to pound one huge fist against the boy's face, while trying to crush his throat with the other gripper. Tom threw up his left arm to block the hammering attacks, grabbed the clutching gauntlet with his right hand — and squeezed.

The metal plating crumpled in Tom's grip and the arm went limp. The APE responded with a lightning-fast uppercut; the boy saw stars, tasted hot pennies. The soldier took advantage of the moment and threw a feedback-enhanced elbow. His arm hooked around the back of the boy's neck in a crushing guillotine choke.

Tom struggled and pushed against the immovable colossus. He felt vertebrae stretching in his neck, felt his throat being crushed. Black haze crawled in at the edges of the world, and he couldn't focus.

He was tired, so tired, and overburdened by more than just a four-thousand-pound opponent. Life and everything … he didn't want to face it anymore. He stopped fighting, stopped struggling, stopped *flying* — and they plunged into the darkness below.

CHAPTER THIRTY-THREE

Old Curt ran beside the apartments with Hannah by his side. The prisoner kids and Milk's girl were going to try to round up all the inmates in the food court, so everyone else needed to pull danger away from the center of town.

Bullets whizzed by, followed by the sharp cracks of gunfire. All of the shots were coming from the Wall, so Curt and Hannah ducked beside some steps to take cover. He heard vehicles, but the street was clear. Explosions and tremors came from the direction of the tall Headquarters building. Milk had gone that way after leaving the basement; it sounded like the whole damn Army was chasing after him. Well good, let the big guy pull the military's attention; he was made to take on armies.

Curt, however, was not. He always thought of himself as a niche hero. His power was neither flashy nor exciting.

He wasn't a force of nature like Jacqui or Milk. He couldn't play with physics like Hannah. He wasn't as versatile as the mind-reading Quietus or even Hardcore, the big, elastic strongman. Maybe Curt could do more in a fight than Portero, but that was an unfair comparison. Rodrigo's ability was profound on an almost mystical level; he routinely visited other *universes*. No, Curt would never say he was more powerful than his old friend from Mexico.

Posties come in a lot of flavors; that's just life. Some are combat machines, others have more practical traits—and some are just plain weird. Some Posties can only do a single thing while others, like Hannah, had wide-ranging abilities.

She was Glimmer; she manipulated light. There are all sorts of tricks one can do with light. She'd been in Curt's life for so long that he knew most of them. After all these years, they could practically read each others' minds. He even knew what she was doing when he couldn't see her at all. Actually, being unable to see her was usually part of the plan.

She squeezed his shoulder and tossed a nod. He peeked above the steps and saw troops run around the end of the block. At least twenty soldiers and two of those big APE suits; the infantry took cover and claimed firing positions, while the walking tanks trudged inexorably closer.

Hannah leaned in and whispered, "You take the APEs. I'll handle the boys."

"Will do. You be careful, *kiddo*." He winked; it was an old joke. Hannah was actually the elder, despite appearances. She'd just stopped aging at some point, whereas old Curt had more salt than pepper in his beard these days.

"You too, *old timer*." She kissed his cheek and rolled into the middle of the street. Shots immediately rang out, but she bent light around her body and vanished. Even radar couldn't detect her when she did that old trick.

Hannah's specialty was visible light, but she had limited control over everything from gamma rays to radio. She wasn't incredibly skilled with the far ends of the spectrum, but she could radiate variable frequency bursts to jam communications over a limited range. The APEs stopped walking and looked around, and the soldiers made confused gestures at each other.

Curt grinned; he knew where this was going.

Several of the soldiers shrieked, jumped and slapped their armor. Hannah was projecting invisible bursts of hot infrared—not intense enough to cause injury, but enough to get a reaction. Her targets felt like they were on fire. One of them actually started rolling on the ground. The unharmed troops looked around suspiciously and raised their weapons.

Then two Carnivores fell from above, landed near the APEs

and rose up menacingly, dripping slime.

They resembled horse-sized squid or cuttlefish, but with multifaceted insectoid eyes on thick, retractable stalks, thousand-fingered mandibles in place of mouths and way too many long, powerful tentacles. The sagging mass of their boneless bodies dangled grotesquely under arcing appendages as they scrambled along the ground. Their wrinkled, pebbled flesh seemed to pulse and shift in the crisp Arctic wind. They wore ranged weapons on saddle-like harnesses and carried particle lances, long, pointed staffs that fired beams of focused protons.

Curt knew the extraterrestrial marauders were some of Hannah's illusions—harmless photons, steered along by subtle electromagnetic fields—but they still took his breath away.

Writhing tentacles lashed in the air, and one of the aliens twirled its lance, firing a white beam over the heads of the ducking troops. Several of the guards were dumb enough to fall for it—popping off a few rounds at the holograms—but most immediately recognized the images as false. One of the big exoskeletons waved an arm through the closest projection and motioned with a heavy gauntlet at his colleagues.

Then Hannah flashed back into view—standing behind the kneeling soldiers.

"Hey there, boys," she said, and they all swung around to face her.

Curt didn't see the next bit because he knew what was coming. He turned away, crouched behind the steps, covered his face with both arms and closed his eyes.

Glimmer's double flash was *still* bright enough to hurt. The first pulse wasn't intense enough to cause permanent damage, but it would make any onlookers blink, flinch or cringe; the second pulse was simply incapacitating. Her flaring brilliance turned the world bright red behind Curt's eyelids—even with his back turned while hiding in the shadow of the banister, even with his eyes as protected as possible.

Anyone looking directly at her risked permanent blindness, but her double-flash technique usually kept that from happening. Instead, her victims would lose vision for a few minutes or hours;

but all of those soldiers—and several snipers on the Wall—were now out of the fight.

Yeah, Hannah was smart, skilled and powerful. She might have been the most talented partner Curt ever had. She could do so many things.

Well, he could only do *one* thing. The trick was being creative about it.

The APEs weren't affected by Hannah's flash attack. Their optics were relayed through a computer, and filtered to protect against such effects. The pair of chrome hulks immediately charged toward her. It was time for Curt to move.

He tumbled clumsily into the street and scrambled to his feet. The tall, lanky man winced at his lack of coordination. "Time to knock the rust off, old timer."

He raised both of his large hands—fingers splayed, palms out—and locked those bastards down. The armored soldiers froze mid-step, becoming motionless steel statues. They couldn't move, couldn't speak—couldn't even think.

They'd been frozen in Curt's stasis field. They'd been immobilized at the quantum level. The power felt like rays of energy from his hands and eyes. The big exoskeletons would remain trapped as long as Curt concentrated, but it didn't take lots of focus.

Back during the Invasion, he'd once held off a legion of Squids by making a barrel indestructible and immovable. He'd crouched inside for three hours, sniping through a small hole with a stolen particle lance. Good times.

He could also lock himself in a field, gaining protection from all threats at the cost of mobility—as a bonus, his mind worked normally in stasis, unlike the APE jockeys. Their brains and bodies had effectively been stopped.

"Thanks, Lockdown," chirped Glimmer. She flashed an "E" with her right hand, and he gave her a grin. "Let one of them go and I'll open him up like a can of soup."

Curt nodded and started to respond, but a sonic boom cut him off. David Young suddenly came on the scene like a roaring whirlwind, and the older man couldn't help but watch. The crow's feet deepened beside Curt's dark eyes. "The more things change…"

The new Shockwave was a tornado, a ripping blur of motion, and the fallen soldiers disappeared.

David had slowed to about three hundred miles an hour. That was very slow for the young speeder, but he had to be careful. He was used to hauling around Nikki, and she was nearly invulnerable. The guards were normal people, mostly around his own age, and he didn't want to hurt them. David didn't consider the military his enemies. They just happened to be on the wrong side this time. He didn't hold it against them.

So he carried them behind the barracks, as far away from the food court as possible. The goal was to contain the guards until Nikki's team got everyone out. The small paved lot between the Wall and barracks was a perfect place to keep captured soldiers.

Hardcore was waiting to take it from there. The muscle-bound Postie ripped the soldiers' weapons apart with his bare hands, stripped off their gear and tied them all up. Most of the guards carried zip ties, so they provided their own restraints. A few had to be bound by the twisted metal remains of their own gear — but Hardcore always enjoyed showing off his strength.

Portero stepped out the back door of the barracks and shouted for Shockwave to throw the soldiers inside. David loved the idea. Their unlucky victims ended up a few thousand miles away. Portero scattered most of them across the lower Forty-Eight, but a few were given free trips to Scotland and two fell out of a barn in New Zealand.

A deep blast rose from the edge of the parking lot. Rodrigo glanced over his shoulder and saw California Girl ripping a leg from a big Scarab-class Walker. The pilot managed to maintain balance on the three remaining legs and tried to back away.

Jacqui tossed the metal beam aside and hopped onto the narrow vehicle's conical nose. The Walker's body looked like the front half of a small helicopter, with a cramped cockpit for two. She tore the canopy from the machine, drove a fist through the console, grabbed both pilot and gunner and leaped aside before the machine toppled. She tossed the captive pair to Hardcore and returned to the fray.

Quietus appeared out of nowhere and helped Jacqui hold back the waves of attacking soldiers and machines, while the rest of the crew whittled away at Security's manpower.

Jacqui saw an idiot with an anti-tank weapon fire a rocket. She tried to smack it away with a blue-gloved fist, but it blew up. The fireball dug a crater in the parking lot and caught a dozen of the captured troops. The heroine was flung into the air by the blast but came down on her feet. She didn't have time to check on the casualties, but some looked dead on the ground.

She gasped at the carnage, and yelled at the attacking soldiers, "Stop! Your own men! Stop shooting!"

She waved her hands overhead and the attacking soldiers actually paused. "Just relax," she said. "We're not here to hurt anyone."

Then Quietus flipped in and tackled the smaller woman. Jacqui had superhuman strength, but she weighed little more than one hundred pounds; the eyeless man easily slung her over his shoulder. He leaped back, carrying her away just as a mortar whistled down from above. The explosion hurled them both into the nearby wall.

Quietus kicked off and jumped down to face the ground troops; California Girl sank her fingers into the steel and pulled up with enough force to hurl her body twenty feet above the concertina wire. She landed atop the Wall, on Security's walkway, with astonished soldiers gaping in the nearby tower. They raised rifles and opened fire. Stinging bullets pattered on her nearly impenetrable skin. She crouched to charge the guard tower, but shots from within pulled the soldiers' attention.

Portero popped up through a hatch in the tower's floor while the guards were focused on Jacqui. The dashing hero had snagged a pistol from somewhere and emptied it in the tower's computer and communications equipment. He dropped back through the aperture before the soldiers whipped around and started shooting.

A pair of men followed, but when they went down the hatch there was a flash of white light. The stink of raw sewage filled the small tower.

The two pursuing soldiers found themselves clinging to an old, corroded ladder in a dark foul-smelling pipe. Portero was nowhere in sight, and the sound of gurgling liquid echoed from below. Shafts of light fell from above, through what looked disturbingly like a manhole cover. They climbed up and emerged in a water treatment facility near Perth. In Australia.

Back in Alaska, Quietus telepathically felt Jacqueline leap into the tower and dispatch the remaining guards. He rather enjoyed her mind; the woman's thoughts were pleasant, positive and precise. She was a dear friend and an admirable person. Even then, in the heat of combat, she felt compassion for the troops and hoped to spare them unnecessary pain.

The soldiers, themselves, generally felt terror and confusion. Every one of them quaked at the presence of Milk—to say nothing about his superhuman partners. The assault had been underway for less than five minutes and the troops were already overwhelmed.

None had ever faced dangerous Posthumans without superior numbers and high-tech support from the prison infrastructure. Now, that very support was failing; the numbers meant nothing. Many of the guards suddenly felt inadequate and vulnerable, but they admirably rose above fear and attempted to defend the walled city. Quietus was proud of them.

He knew that twenty-two individuals were aiming weapons toward him at that moment. A total of one hundred sixteen people were observing him to one degree or another. He felt their attention and focus. He saw through their eyes with awareness of their intentions.

The small man relaxed and allowed events to run their course. His head turned slightly and a fat bullet whipped past his cheek. He bent at the knees and somersaulted backward. Five more slugs pierced the air where his body had just been. Springing off his hands, Quietus twirled above the crowd, spinning through the gunfire.

He came down in the middle of fifteen armored men and women, instantly assuming the classic San Ti stance of his preferred fighting style, Xing Yi Quan—left side forward, with that arm extended, right hand at waist level, knees slightly bent, head in line with his center of mass. He cleared his thoughts and calmly gathered strength for defense or attack, preferably both.

Three soldiers lunged in from behind. Quietus whipped round, crunched the closest attacker's throat with a back-swinging knife hand, rebounded into a spinning crouch, toppled the middle guard with a hard leg sweep, rose with a spiraling uppercut to the final assailant's chin and knocked out the still-prone second one with a swift kick to the temple.

Quietus crouched and whirled to face the dozen remaining guards. He snapped upright, drove his palms into two astonished faces, and ripped the assault rifle from the hands of another young soldier. He flipped the weapon up, caught the disarmed private on the chin with the stock, and slung it around in a circle overhead. Four more guards went down as the butt of the rifle struck their abdomens, thwacked their chests and clonked their skulls. Quietus tossed the firearm aside.

One brave soldier, a young woman from Topeka, lunged at his back with a combat knife. He leaned to the left, allowed the blade to pass by his ribs and wrapped his forearm around hers. With a quick twist of the hand, he snapped her wrist. He regretted inflicting so severe an injury, but such are the ways of battle.

Snatching the knife out of the air, Quietus spun and sliced the chinstrap of the nearest soldier's helmet. He gave a swift tap to the brim of the headgear, knocking it over the young man's eyes.

The telepathic martial artist felt another guard taking aim, so he spun and threw the knife. It sank into the attacker's meaty leg and he fell, clutching at the wound. The other soldier had removed the loose helmet and drew a pistol, but Quietus dropped him with a quick string of fingertip strikes from navel to throat.

The eyeless man in black turned around to face the remaining pair of terrified guards.

He gracefully flowed back to a solid San Ti Shi and tilted his shaven head. The soldiers gaped, lowered their weapons, kneeled on the ground and surrendered.

"Whoa," whispered JJ, watching from half a block away. He had stepped through a wormhole just in time to see the eyeless Postie's massive display of kung fu. Even from a distance, it was one hell of a show. Sol would never believe it.

"Come on, dumbass!" Nikki grabbed him by the arm, pulling him into the alley. Vanessa, Madi and Anon (still looking like the Duke) were already huddled against the brickwork.

"JJ? Is that you?" called a voice from above. It was Lucy, the grandmotherly old hippie who ran the prison's meager black market. She'd peeked outside after hearing the others run into the alley.

"Yeah, Lucy, it's me."

She looked through the window, "What the hell is going on out there? Jimmy said he saw Milk!"

"Yeah, he's here," announced Nikki. "Call me Powerhouse; Milk is my father. We're bringing this place down. Evac's in the food court."

JJ spoke up, "Tell everyone in the building to get outside. I'll open a portal to the big warehouse behind the kitchen. It should be safe. Sol's getting a thing to remove these implants. Then we'll get out of dodge."

Lucy frowned then shrugged. "Alright, I'm in. See you in a sec."

Anon shifted from John Wayne to Errol Flynn's Robin Hood and declared in a lame excuse for an English accent. "Come! Let us make haste in the liberation of our compatriots!"

"Right on," replied JJ. "You three each take a building. Move fast."

"What are *you* doing?" asked Vanessa.

"I'll stay out here with Nikki, keep the street clear and send everyone to safety as soon as they're outside. Then we'll catch up with Sol." He looked at his friends. Nikki turned away. "Got it?"

They nodded, hugged quickly, and moved. Anon and Vanessa bolted across the street, while Madi ran to the other building on this side. Someone fired a weapon from one of the guard towers, but nobody was hit. JJ heard more gunfire from that direction, poked his head out of the alley, looked toward the Wall and watched California Girl barrel through the tower, shattering glass, rending steel and scattering soldiers.

"Let's go, dumbass," said Nikki, brushing past him with a

shoulder bump, striding into the center of the street.

"My name's JJ." He rubbed his upper arm.

"And *my* name is Powerhouse. Learn to use it, noob."

"Pardon me. I'm kinda new at the whole hero thing."

Nikki smirked over her shoulder. "That's a fucking understatement."

JJ opened his mouth to retort, but something moved at the edge of his vision. "Oh, shit!"

Three Walkers stormed around the corner, and they opened fire before JJ finished calling out. The middle one was a heavily armed, four-legged, Scarab-class Walker. The other two were smaller Mantis-class models; they had two legs, narrow frames and only one seat.

The Scarab launched a pair of surface-to-air missiles at Nikki; the smaller Walkers fired ripping bursts of depleted uranium rounds from their twin thirty-millimeter cannons.

JJ thrust his hands forward, casting a ripple of distorted gravity down the street. One of the missiles detonated; the other spun wildly off course and slammed into the upper corner of a building across the street, exploding in a ball of flame and shattered masonry.

A round to the face flipped Nikki head over heels down the street. She landed in a three-point crouch, as flying bullets pocked the road and shattered bricks on the apartment buildings.

Her head snapped up, and she glared at the strutting machines. "Motherfuckers."

Nikki's knuckles dug into the road, and she surged forward at two hundred miles an hour.

The thick soles of her armored boots slapped rapidly on the street, she leaped to the side to avoid a rocket, bounced off the closest building and dove fist-first *through* one of the light Walkers. She landed on the road and instantly jumped back on top of the machine. She ripped off the thing's cockpit, yanked the pilot free and hopped from the burning wreck. She let the soldier run away.

The remaining Mantis clattered around to confront her. Nikki grabbed the demolished one, raised it overhead and heaved. Eight tons of metal flew down the street.

The Walker pilot tried to dodge but took the hit square on the side. The machines tumbled down the street, slamming to a stop against the foundation of the Wall.

Nikki snarled, "*That's* what Milk would do, bitches."

JJ cheered and she looked his way, smiling. Her black outfit was covered in grime and small tears. Her thick hair was all messed up and her right cheek was kind of bruised. She wiped sweat from her face and left black smudges of muck from forehead to jaw.

She was the most beautiful and amazing person JJ had ever seen.

Then a rocket blurred down the street and erupted on the face of the furthest apartment building — right behind Nikki's back.

JJ didn't even think; he wrapped her in spacetime and *pulled*.

She crashed into his arms as the building exploded. The face of the northeastern building collapsed in a flood of flame and debris, as they turned together and leaped for the nearest alley.

When the smoke cleared, JJ was on top of her in the rubble. His cap was gone, and they were both covered by a blanket of pulverized brick. They stared blankly at each other for a moment, too dazed to think. But JJ heard the Scarab-class Walker's heavy steps and knew it was time to act.

He rose to his feet and turned toward the street. Nikki said something he couldn't hear over the Walker's engine, as the huge, four-legged machine lurched into view. The boy stood before the twelve-ton mass of military hardware, exposed, vulnerable and weaponless.

And JJ realized that the thing's mass could *be* his weapon. He raised his hands and bent space to his will. Gravity did the rest.

At double weight the nose dipped, the legs strained. Triple and the machine staggered. JJ pushed down with eight gravities — and the legs snapped under the load.

The Walker's frame slammed down, shattering the pavement, but JJ was just getting started. He pushed harder.

Antennae flexed and weapon emplacements angled toward the ground. Smoke rushed from the engine, as it whined and popped to a sputtering death. Cracks spread across the cockpit windows; the crew within struggled against gravity's unrelenting crush. No amount of G-force training could prepare them for this; they couldn't breathe at nearly twelve times their ordinary weight. They tried to push against the encroaching darkness and failed. They went limp nearly simultaneously.

JJ let go.

He blinked, kind of stunned by his power's effects. The Walker was a broken husk, and the unconscious crew might be seriously injured. He frowned, feeling kind of bad about it. Then again, the soldiers had been trying to kill Nikki, so to hell with them.

Besides, he'd just single-handedly taken down a Walker. How awesome was that?

Pretty fucking awesome.

Nikki coughed, and he turned around. She smirked and walked closer. In her hands was his baseball cap. "Not bad, JJ."

"Thanks." He took the hat and secured it on his head, grinning from ear to ear.

Her eyes narrowed, lips pursed. "But you could've done it at the *start* of the fight, if you actually wanted to be useful."

"Hey now, I'm useful! Very useful! I'm a valuable member of the team."

"Uh-huh," she deadpanned, with a mocking eye roll. "You're a real hero."

He scoffed, "You never know, I might end up saving the day."

Her smirk turned into a smile, deepening those dimples. She nodded to the street, "Well come on, *hero*. Let's go help some people."

"Omigod!" cried Vanessa from the building across the street. She ran down the steps, leading a line of people. They all gasped and the damage and the demolished Walkers.

Everyone immediately moved toward the missile-damaged building. There were already people digging in the wreckage. One of those people suddenly became an elephant, to JJ's relief.

There was only one polymorph in ABRA City. JJ was glad his friend had survived.

Jumbo-Anon used its trunk to clear away chunks of debris. Nikki ran over to lend a super-strong hand. Only two people had actually been buried in the explosion, but there were a number of minor injuries.

Vanessa helped people walk away from the ruin. The residents began to pour into the streets, gawking at the damage, flinching at the not-very-distant battle sounds. Madi came onto the street with fifty nervous Posties. Jumbo-Anon raised Autumn Gerber onto its wide, gray back, along with her quintuplets. The kids glowed with excitement at riding an elephant—literally, they glowed. Bright, shimmering light flowed around their small, huddled forms.

Lucy Dressler hobbled over and kneeled beside Jerry Long, who had a deep gash on his cheek. She grabbed his face with moderate gentleness and put her other hand above the wound. A mist of hydrogen peroxide coalesced under her palm, and Jerry winced. Then she pulled a bandage out of thin air and placed it over the cut. JJ finally realized how the spacey grandma managed to rule the black market; she could *make* things.

JJ clapped his hands to get everyone's attention. A wormhole opened by his side, and he called out, "Come on everybody! Exit stage right!"

Suddenly Madi screamed, "Jay! No!"

JJ followed her gaze and noticed an incoming artillery shell. He could feel it with his spatial sense, arcing overhead; it was coming in far too swiftly for human eyes to see. He realized— during that way-too-long microsecond of stunned awareness—that the guards had aimed the shell right at him, probably for trashing the Walker. He thought it would be worth dying, if his friends won.

Then a bolt of lightning ripped across the sky, a ringing boom hit the city and the mortar detonated harmlessly high overhead. The street reverberated from the thunder as Overpower swooped down from above.

The electric man launched a bolt at an anti-aircraft array on the Wall and fried a group of four Walkers with a few gigawatts of raw juice. Dipping lower, he threw out an electromagnetic pulse that disabled some of the city's computers and blew some lights. Then he zipped above the barracks and hurled an empty cargo truck through the armory with a magnetic shove. He shot a thousand feet higher, swooped down toward the apartments and slowed while passing over JJ.

"*Looking good, my man!*"

JJ pumped a fist and hollered, "OP! Burn 'em down!"

Overpower glanced at the busted apartment building. He didn't feel anyone buried under the rubble—unfortunately, locating people by their electromagnetic field is definitely hit-or-miss. But the team had Vanessa's ears and Anon's animal senses to handle that kind of thing; they really didn't need help from a living bolt of lightning.

So he surged upward, rising higher and higher, spreading his arms to embrace the night. He kept a metaphoric eye on the prison city—in case his friends needed support—and watched the horizon for threats. He was the only thing in the sky.

Vast emerald sheets of the aurora borealis stretched in the heavens, under the great expanse of stars. With inhuman senses, he felt, touched, and tasted it; he dove into the flowing energy, baptized in the celestial current. He drifted with the solar stream's rhythmic crash against Earth's magnetosphere; the source of the brilliant green cascades. The experience *moved* him in a way that he could never describe, connecting him to the planet, the sun, and the endless void.

He felt free, alive and part of *everything* in a way he'd never known. There, out in the open for the very first time, reveling in his abilities, revealing his true face to the world—to hell with the consequences—he was happy. And the aurora was a gift from the universe, echoing his simple joy. It was radiance, motion, and song—and Overpower swayed to the music like a child dancing by the sea.

CHAPTER THIRTY-FOUR

Sol watched the medical staff run down the halls. Some of them fled the building but most were running downstairs. He didn't know where they were going and did not care. An evacuation would just make his job easier. Five minutes of running along the baseboards brought him to the examination room.

He grew with each step, reached full size next to the counter, pulled out one of the ratchet-like devices and looked at it. The backside was a dial—like an unlabeled combination lock—with two tiny lights at the top, one red and one green. He knew that the medics always turned the ratchet in the same pattern—right a few times, left for a bit, right a couple more—but the number of turns seemed random. Sol guessed that the lights indicated the time to turn, which stopped him from using it on his own brain bomb. Well, he'd just move fast and meet up with JJ.

Stuffing three more of the devices in his pockets, he shrank to about a third normal size and poked his bushy head out the door. The hall was empty. Gunshots galore and way-too-close explosions echoed outside. Thunder crashed, lights flashed and the ground thrummed like a constant, low-level earthquake—occasionally punctuated by hard tremors.

Sol scratched his beard and muttered, "No guts, no glory."

He took off down the hallway, staying about twenty inches tall—since running at that size wasn't too slow—and sprinted toward the exits.

Luck, more than anything, saved him from bumping into Doctor Angus. Sol rounded a corner and stumbled into a crowd of about thirty people — just as something very large exploded right in front of the hospital.

The blast rocked the building, fire and smoke filled the shattering windows. The soldiers and scientists all ducked and covered their faces. None of them noticed Sol.

He went down to an eighth of an inch, cussing under his breath the entire way. There were sixteen soldiers manning hand trucks — and strapped to the dollies were the gold-framed cloning tanks from Angus's underground laboratory. Alongside the manual labor were nine more military dudes and four doctors, including the attractive Mueller and Doctor Angus. The old man was working on a tablet computer, Mueller and the other science-types were fussing around with the cargo.

The soldiers were anxious to move; some of them hustled to the damaged entrance and shouted something. Sol guessed they said something like "all clear" because the group began to go down the hall. He followed them out the front door and down the steps. They took a right and walked toward the military side of town.

Sol assumed they were trying to run away, but there was nothing he could do about that. He had places to be. So he turned around to head to the food court, and gasped upon seeing the town.

Broken glass and shattered brick littered the streets, the two closest apartment buildings were on fire and one of them had been blown to hell. He looked up at the burning top floor of Headquarters and saw lightning flash across the sky.

A squad of soldiers ran down the street, firing rifles at the old heroes from the East Coast Alliance. Lockdown just stood there, impervious to the attacks. The old black man's teammate, Glimmer, appeared with a flash and disarmed the guards with laser beams, heat bursts and old-fashioned fisticuffs.

Looking the other way, Sol saw the big shirtless guy, Hardcore, storming down the road, straight at a Mantis-class Walker. Thirty-millimeter bullets bounced off his tattooed flesh.

The Walker shot a rocket; Hardcore swatted the projectile

out of the air with a casual backhand and barreled into the walking machine, shoulder first, and stretched those thick, malleable arms around the carriage. He raised the vehicle overhead and brought it down hard on its side. Retracting his elastic arms, Hardcore drove a fist through the cockpit glass and crumpled the control panel with one huge hand. Then he turned from the wreckage to find something else to smash.

Sol shook his head and walked the other way. He started jogging down the street, by HQ, and noticed a bunch of people in blue scrubs. Prisoners from MegaMax! He recognized the green-skinned tusked lady from his trip underground, and Billy the bat boy was there, but Sol had never seen the rest. There was a huge bigfoot looking guy, a youngish woman, an old guy with a bitching beard and one dude made of polished bronze—who seemed to be staring down the street, in the direction of Angus's departing group.

Sol grew to full size and called out, "Hey! Yo, come with me!"

The inmates turned and the metallic man stepped forward, "You're working with Milk?"

"Yeah, my name's Solomon. Let's go."

"Hello, Solomon, I am the Lector."

"Lector?" Sol thought about fava beans but shook it off. "We're meeting up in the food court. My friend can get us out of here, come on."

"Was that Doctor Angus?"

"Yeah," replied Sol. "I think he's trying to get his cloning equipment out of the city."

"*Cloning* equipment?" The Lector raised a brow.

Sol nodded, feeling uncomfortable all of a sudden. He wished that he hadn't opened his mouth. Being fellow prisoners didn't make them good guys.

"We'll stay here for now," said the bronze-skinned man, in a confidential, friendly tone. He pointed at the door to HQ. "We'll spread the word to others and tell Milk about Angus. Where is the food court?"

Sol tossed a nod down the street. He still wasn't sure what to make of these guys, but catching up with Jay was more important.

"End of the block, around the corner. Can't miss it. Just hurry."

"We'll move fast," promised the Lector with a smile.

⭐   ⭐   ⭐

Tiffany slowly walked through the demolished corridors. She followed Milk, along with a handful of prisoners and about thirty disarmed guards. The inmates kept watch on the soldiers while she tracked down other Posties. So far, everything was going well. Milk ripped away blast doors, knocked gaping holes in the walls and demolished Security's toys.

They'd wrecked MegaMax in minutes and told everyone how to get to the surface. Only these brave few—led by the former mercenary, silver-haired Jace Wyatt—stayed behind to help. Earthquakes rumbled continuously, and the empty labyrinth echoed with the sound of battle.

Tiffany's pulse grew rapid as they entered a devastated corridor. The hallway to Cellblock A.

The ceiling panels had been replaced, but the crater in the floor remained. Bare stone showed through the corridor's mangled armor. Both doorways had been damaged during the fight so the blast doors had been disabled and hadn't dropped with the rest.

Tiffany swam in memory for a moment; Tom protecting her and losing control, Tank insisting that Tom needed to fight, Tom holding her close for the first time.

Milk walked a few steps in front of her and looked at the damage. The extra power had faded, and he'd shrunk to the usual freakish dimensions. Now that the heavy lifting was done, he no longer needed the boost. He waved a hand at the wrecked hallway. "What happened here?"

"Tom," whispered Tiffany. "He beat the Behemoth."

"Can you feel him?"

"Tom? He's down … way down below. Him and Fiona both." Tiffany closed her eyes. "I think they're being attacked."

"No," said Milk, motioned to the end of the hall. "Do you feel Vaughn?"

"Yeah," a slight smile grew on her face. "Tank's with him."

"Tank? Who's Tank?" Milk turned, ducked to pass through the broken doorway—and stopped dead in his tracks. Amused surprise lit his face. "*Sherman?*"

"Mm. H'lo, Milk," rumbled Tank. "H'lo Tiff-nee."

Tiffany entered the cellblock behind the huge hero. The force fields were down and Tank stood in the middle of the floor with an arm on Vaughn's shoulder. The Behemoth was restrained by his oversize shackles, and Tank's boulder-like hand gripped the chains. Vaughn's pale yellow, lizard-slit eyes flickered from Milk to Tiffany and back.

Milk put his face inches from Vaughn's and growled, "Try anything—*say* anything—and I will put you down." Then he turned to Tank and grinned. "Jesus, Sherman. Just look at you, all grown up."

"Mm. Good see you."

"You too, kid. I never even … how long have you been here?"

Tank shrugged, "All-wayz. Watch'n bad guyz."

"Your name's Sherman?" asked Tiffany.

"Mm," rumbled the craggy giant. "Faa-thurr's name. Mm. My name. Hek-tor Shur-mann Jack-sonn … duh Thurrd."

"Hector Sherman Jackson the Third?"

"Mm."

Milk looked down at Tiffany and chuckled, "His father was Stonewall, one of my best friends."

Vaughn's huge jaw dropped, showing those rows of blunt fangs, and he gasped, "No fucking way!"

Milk glared and raised a finger, "I'll give you that one, Gregory. Say or do anything else and I'll rip you apart til you stop coming back together." The Behemoth closed his maw and looked away. The hero continued, "Anyway, I've known Sherman his whole life. He's part of the family."

Tiffany gazed up at her old friend and protector; she'd never imagined that he was the son of Stonewall. She'd never known that the late hero even had children. "Who's your mom?"

Tank looked down, with a glimmer in his soft brown eyes. "Lonn stor-ree."

"Well, let's get out of here. We need to find something to do with this piece of shit," said Milk. He waved a huge hand at the Behemoth.

"Tranz-port," explained Tank. "Spesh-ull. Take'm to frayt el-vay-tow. Launch-urr."

Milk nodded, "Okay, but I want you to come with us."

Tank shook his head, "Watch Bee-muth. Mm. My job."

"Well, if that's what you want. You've grown into a fine man, Sherman. Your father would be proud. I am."

Then a quiet voice came from one of the cells — the only other inhabited cell in block A. "I want to go with you. Can I come?"

Tiffany remembered telling Tom that the two A-block residents were special, back on that very first day. Vaughn was a horrible kind of special, but the other guy was special because he wasn't special at all.

He was just a normal, non-powered man, the only Normie in ABRA City. Nobody knew his name, or anything about him, but he'd been there since the beginning. None of the guards seemed to know anything about him. He was average in height and build, maybe in his fifties, but she couldn't tell for sure. His graying hair was still mostly brown, but there was something about his eyes. Tiffany thought he seemed old.

Milk recognized him and did a double take, "Doctor Banks?"

"Hello, Charles. You look well," said the older man. He spoke softly, with a Midwestern accent. He sounded tired, maybe a little sad.

The giant stepped closer to the man. "Why are you here? How long?"

The man frowned, "Angus and I had a falling out."

Milk's eyes narrowed. "You've been gone forty-two years."

"It happened a long time ago."

The horned hero looked at the smaller man with suspicion. Tiffany didn't understand. *Who is he?*

Apparently other people had the same idea. The silver-haired Jace raised his voice. "Yo!" He stood in back of the crowd, guarding the captured soldiers. "Who is this chump?"

The doctor winced and turned away.

Milk looked back at everyone, "This is Doctor Zachary Banks; he helped make us. He used to be partners with Angus, but they obviously don't get along now. Or for a while. He kept you prisoner here all of these years?"

Banks didn't turn around, but he nodded. "A lot of them."

"Why?"

"Do we really have time to talk about this, Charles?"

Milk's lips pressed tight. He obviously didn't want to drop the topic. "No, I suppose we don't."

He walked over to the cellblock's blast door. Tank moved right behind him, leading Vaughn by the chains. The three titans formed a wall between the other prisoners and whatever lay on the other side. Tiffany smiled. It was just like Tank—Sherman—to protect everyone.

Milk grunted and hunched over, pushing against the fifty-ton block of steel. His bare feet cracked the floor and his fingers pressed into the cold metal. He flexed those rippling marble muscles and leaned into the reinforced mass. The heavy frame began to creak, the cellblock rumbled from the pressure, and metal began to squeal.

Then, with a terrifying roar, he shoved blast door from its moorings. Tons of rubble fell on Milk's invulnerable hide, but he cleared the way. Tank and Behemoth went through the gap first, followed by the other prisoners. Tiffany stayed behind with Milk.

"Who is he? I mean Doctor Banks. I don't trust him."

The hero looked down at the earnest young lady. "Neither do I. Angus is a bastard, but he wouldn't keep Banks here without reason."

"But he's not even a Postie."

"I think maybe..."

Tiffany looked up at the gentle giant, "What do you think?"

He paused for a moment and motioned for her to go on ahead. "I think it's time you head topside. Hurry now. Don't worry. I'll find Tom and bring him back."

"Oh no," she pointed. She'd been distracted by Doctor Banks

and Vaughn and even Tank, but now she opened her perceptions again, feeling Fiona's blazing rage and Tom's overwhelming golden power. She saw flashes of energy from both her distant friends, felt their panic and pain. She stared at the far corner of the floor and gasped, "We need to help them!"

She took two steps before a powerful tremor shook the city, a short, violent quake from deep underground. But the shaking quickly ceased; it must have been an explosion. A big one. Tiffany swallowed hard

Milk put a finger on her tiny shoulder. "I will. But you need to get somewhere safe. This whole place might cave in."

She shook her head, but never stopped looking at that spot on the floor.

"Tom would want you to be safe. He and I can handle the guards. You can't help against them."

She brushed the hair out of her eyes, exhaled and slowly nodded. Doctor Angus had threatened her last night in order to make Tom back down. Milk was right. She looked up at the giant, "Okay. Tell him…"

"I'll tell him." Milk smiled, leaned down and gently touched her cheek. "Go on, now."

She turned, stepped through the half-collapsed doorway, and jogged toward the entrance. Milk walked behind her through the strobe-lit corridor, waited for her made it up the emergency stairs, and turned back down the hall. He knew from the blueprints that the maintenance stairway was the fastest way down and ran straight for it, but the hero wasn't prepared for what he found.

The door had been blown off its hinges. Smoke seeped along the ceiling. Inside, the stairwell was hell. The top few flights of the stairway remained mostly undamaged but below that the shaft had been demolished. Broken cement, twisted rebar and shattered blocks hung over the black depths.

Glowing rivulets of molten red slag dimly lit the distant bottom. And in the darkness, over two hundred feet down, Milk saw a soft golden glow and a dim, purple flicker.

With no hesitation, he leaped over the railing and fell.

CHAPTER THIRTY-FIVE

"I killed them," whispered Tom, looking up with those eyes of glowing gold. "They were just normal people ... and I killed them."

On his knees, at the bottom of the dark shaft, he sounded like a lost kid. A pair of mangled APEs lay around him. The one on the right had a horrific dent in its helmet that had surely pulped the pilot's brain; the other lay in a twisted pile of bent and broken limbs. Tom's light played on the chrome exoskeletons, illuminating the lowest level of the prison.

"You didn't mean to," replied Fiona, walking up to him slowly. Of course, *she* had totally meant to kill the armored guard who'd carried her to the bottom. She'd cushioned the fall with exploding plasma and turned the APE into a molten puddle. She'd been jogging up the stairs when the dead one fell, clanging. Tom tumbled down seconds after that, tangled up with another one. She'd raced back to the bottom and found them like this.

She kneeled beside him, put a hand on his shoulder, and said, "You didn't mean to kill them, kid. And they were trying to kill you. Don't get all teen-drama on me. Let's go."

Tom slowly nodded, climbed to his feet, took one more look at the first people he ever killed, and stood with his friend. "Okay. You're right. We need to —"

A fragmentation grenade fell from above and tinked on the concrete floor. Tom jumped and tackled Fiona. The small explosive detonated behind his back; shrapnel ricocheted off his glowing aura.

A dozen soldiers rappelled down the shaft; firing bursts of rounds and grenades from their rifles. The lowest level's exit blew in and troops barreled into the stairwell, led by two more hulking exoskeletons. The air filled with whizzing bullets.

Tom spun around, threw a wild punch at the closest APE and blasted the other one into the wall. Fiona ignited her flame, and flung a roiling arc of energy at the descending soldiers. Bullets melted in flight, evaporating in the air, inches from her face; her feet left glowing prints in the cement.

Tom heard a noise and glanced through the doorway — just as a small RPG shot down the hall and hit him square in the chest. The blast hurled him through the lowest level of steps, burying him under the collapsing structure.

He immediately pushed through the debris, stood up, and saw more soldiers pile through the door.

Dozens of shots hit him in that first second, driving him back against the wall. Another APE lunged forward, swinging the long forearm blade at Tom's face. He blocked the attack with his arm, but didn't see the follow-up knee. It slammed into his gut with shocking, mechanical strength; the impact flung him six feet straight up. The armored soldier jabbed Tom's torso with his right gauntlet blade, then the left — then he began throwing jackhammer strikes to the boy's limp body.

Tom fell back, winded, dazed and losing focus. The hits kept coming, faster and faster. A smashing steel elbow cracked against his face, and he tasted blood. More body strikes landed and Tom went down. The APE loomed above, rearing back for a crushing, two-fisted blow.

Brightness flared behind the APE jockey's back. The soldier stiffened — and his chest plate began to glow. It went from red to orange to white in half a second; it puckered out in the middle, and Fiona's white-hot fist burst through, dripping slag. The hand retracted, and light shined through a gaping hole in the armored torso. A burnt-bacon stench filled the air, and the body fell.

Looking at Fiona was like looking at the sun. She was a woman-shaped, white core of blazing light in the middle of a purple-tipped inferno. Her eyes were dim lavender ovals, and cooler licks of violet flame flashed against the white heat when she opened her mouth. "Get up, kid! This shit's getting real!"

Tom stared in horror for a second, barely registering her words. She'd just plunged her fist through a man's chest. He'd never imagined seeing anything like that, and she'd done it for *him*. He blinked and slowly looked up. He felt numb, dazed and hollow.

Dozens of soldiers stood in the hallway beyond the door, firing everything they had. Sparkles fizzled in Tom's vision, and he wasn't sure what was real. The pinging bullets hurt, even through the golden light. His mind crawled along slowly, muddled and reeling, and his clearest thought was oddly about Aegis.

You worship life? Well, this *is life.*

Fiona turned to face the troops. Bullets streaked in, leaving trails of evaporated metal in the superheated air. She twitched suddenly, and Tom thought he saw a flash at her left shoulder. She jerked again and doubled over, dimming slightly as she grabbed her stomach.

Tom climbed to his feet and took a step toward his friend. He saw a guard aim an antitank weapon. It happened in slow motion, but much too swiftly for him to react.

But it wasn't too fast for Fiona.

She threw her arms up and launched a pulse of plasma that slammed into the far wall, blowing through the door. An explosion filled the stairwell, Fiona screamed, and Tom saw fire.

"Fiona?" croaked Tom, laying on his left side in the scorching darkness. The fingertips of his right hand were dipping into a warm stream.

Then he opened his eyes and saw that his fingers were half-submerged in a puddle of glowing slag. He sat up and looked around with awe and fear in his golden eyes.

The scorched walls dripped molten metal; blackened

326 | MITCHELL ARCHER

concrete radiated visible ripples of heat. The doorway was gone, replaced by a ragged hole. The shattered corridor on the far side was full of smoldering piles of ash and charred bone. Half-melted APE suits flowed into each other like obscene monuments to death.

He looked up; the stairs were just gone, heaps of cooling wreckage filled the surrounding space. Fire flickered here and there in the darkness. And lying in the middle of the floor, in a pool of lava, was Fiona — naked, motionless and bleeding.

Tom ran to her, barely feeling the liquid metal's heat, and picked her up. He carried her to the clearest, least-damaged corner and kneeled down. He cradled Fiona against his chest and cried. He looked at his friend — the freest bird on the planet — and knew she was dying.

Her clothing had been disintegrated; blood and soot covered her limp body. She'd taken bullets to the shoulder, abdomen, chest and legs. Cuts and scrapes marked her from head to toe. A big piece of shrapnel, maybe part of the rocket, had torn through her side; her blood dripped down Tom's belly.

He couldn't feel her breath, couldn't find a pulse. "Oh, no. Fiona ... no."

A spasm rocked her body, heat rolled off in visible waves, and she coughed. She wheezed, mumbled something, and tried to raise her head. She managed to whisper, "Tom?"

"Yeah, Fiona. Yeah, I'm here." He tried to lay her comfortably on his lap and looked down at her paling face.

Purple light shined through her half-closed eyelids; she grimaced in pain. "Listen, Tom. You gotta ... make. Gotta promise..."

"What, Fiona? What do I need to promise?" Tom bent down and kissed her burning forehead. "Fiona?"

Her eyes opened, glowing with painful brilliance, and violet flame engulfed her body. "Don't let go," she whispered. "Don't."

"I won't let go." He wrapped his arms around her small, baking hot frame. Her scorching hands weakly gripped his face. The flow of tears boiled on his cheeks. "I won't let go."

She brightened by the second, heat throbbed in the air. She coughed and convulsed. "Promise me ... you'll stay."

"I promise. I'm here. I'm here."

Then something heavy crashed to the floor behind Tom's back—a resounding thud, followed by slow, heavy steps. Something big had dropped down the shaft, and it was coming closer.

Tom figured it must be another APE jockey. He didn't care. Let them come.

Fiona moaned, bright fire shot past her lips, and she shuddered, growing ever hotter. The air began to burn, roaring like a gale, rushing from her unleashed heat.

"Tom," said an inhumanly deep, reverberating voice. A familiar voice.

The boy looked up through tear-blurred eyes, too deep in shock be surprised at Milk's arrival. The huge Postie was shirtless and barefoot; purple and gold light gleamed on his ivory skin. Tom opened his mouth, but there were no words. His eyes went back to Fiona's face.

Milk kneeled beside the weeping boy and the burning woman. He wrapped them both in his arms. "You're not alone, son."

Fiona looked up at Milk in slow confusion. She smirked weakly and sighed, "Oh, God … not you two. Milk and Independence. T-together again. Never take me … alive."

Milk rumbled gently, "You're always so damned sassy. It takes the both of us to handle a tricky gal like you."

"Got … one more." She coughed; blood simmered on her lips. "One. More. Trick."

Light streamed from her eyes and mouth, rolling plasma formed a shell around them, and the tortured stairwell began to glow from the spiking temperature. Her head moved around, panicky, like she couldn't see, "Tom? Tom?"

"I'm here, Fiona! I'm here!" He held on tighter; she'd know he still wasn't letting go. "Fiona!"

She squeezed back and gasped, "Tom! Don't … don't..." Then her eyes moved over his shoulder, like she saw somebody else standing over them all. She sighed, "Oh, Adam … you big dork."

Then everything blazed white; there was nothing but heat.

CHAPTER THIRTY-SIX

Tiffany kneeled on a patch of frosty grass next to Headquarters, sobbing through chattering teeth. She ignored the biting wind; she tried to shut out the battle on the edge of the city.

Two heroes in black and red were fighting a bunch of guards on the corner. There was a muffled boom in the street to her right. She paid no attention to it. She simply looked down, through three hundred feet of icy ground, and watched as Fiona died. Hot tears rolled down her cheeks, freezing before they reached her chin. She didn't even notice. "N-no..."

She saw Tom in her special sense, his warm glow wavering and raw with pain. Fiona's presence was right on his, but it was so weak, so dim, like a single match in a midnight storm. Milk was down there, too, and he moved so close to the others that they all had to be touching.

Tiffany groaned and dropped to the ground. Her trembling hand closed on the dirt, as she reached out to her friends beneath the ground. "No..."

She could feel the older woman stoking the flame, building up heat, barely able to contain it. Tiffany had never seen anything like it—Fiona was pushing to unimaginable heights of power at the very edge of death.

"No..." She could feel Fiona's fear, pain and defiant humor. Flamechylde was leaving on her own terms. Tiffany touched that bittersweet warmth. She felt the surging firestorm in her friend's heart. She felt love.

And the tiny flame winked out. Fiona was gone.

"No, no, no!" Tiffany pounded the earth with her icy fists—and then came the blast.

Unbridled power erupted from Fiona's embers, like an explosion—like a nuclear bomb. Tiffany could see the terrifying scope of the blast, in the fraction of a second before it reached the surface.

Suddenly, a violent force slammed into her lithe frame. She screamed—

"Mm," rumbled Tank, as the freight elevator descended. He held Vaughn's chain in his left hand; the rocky appendage was larger than the Behemoth's oversized head.

They slowly descended to the bottom of the prison. Tank would lead the prisoner from the reactor chamber to the Launcher, where the techs, scientists and doctors were gathering for evacuation. Few prisoners were even aware of its existence; only Vaughn and Tank would depart with the staff. The Department of Public Safety wouldn't risk allowing the Behemoth to escape and had constructed a special escape capsule for the monster and his stone-skinned keeper.

Tank was looking forward to the ride. He had never traveled at supersonic speed, and had only ever flown once—in a C-130, when he came to Alaska nearly fifteen years earlier, alone with all the cargo—but the Launcher was something completely different.

It was essentially a railgun, a mile-long magnetic cannon, with a class-one force field over the end and vacuum in the barrel. It began at the lowest level of ABRA City and extended through the bedrock, reaching beyond the wall, buried under a few feet of topsoil. The dirt would be blown away by shaped charges seconds before the first launch. The escape pods were blunt cones, similar to the reentry vehicle of old Apollo-era spacecraft. The capsules would be pulled forward by powerful magnetic fields, accelerating rapidly in the airless void. A scaled-up version of the system could throw objects into orbit, but the Launcher wasn't that powerful. Still, the escape pods would fly out at triple the speed of sound and arc over the horizon to land in the frigid water of Kotzebue Sound. It would be thrilling, Tank was certain. Thinking about it helped keep the craggy giant from worrying about his friends.

He would rather be with them, would rather leave with them. He wanted to go with Milk, to protect Tiffany, Tom and Fiona, but someone needed to keep an eye on the Behemoth. And Tank was one of the few people on Earth capable of that particular job. There's a reason that Vaughn didn't cause too much trouble during his long incarceration, and that reason was Hector Sherman Jackson the Third.

An even stronger rumble rolled through the walls; it sounded close. It sounded low. Could somebody be fighting on the bottom level? Was that Milk, breaking Tom out of Solitary?

Tank had no way of knowing. He wished that he could have spoken to Milk for a longer time; he'd always idolized the hero, and thought of him frequently. "Part of the family," Milk had said, and Tank agreed. His only family was the people he loved, and he hoped to see them soon, but that was not to be.

The rock exploded outward, and a resounding detonation blotted out all other perceptions. Suddenly, Tank was falling; the heavy steel elevator had given way. The living megalith dropped like a stone as the caverns of MegaMax crumbled.

He saw Vaughn, briefly, before debris obscured the view. The Behemoth clung to the quaking wall with his shackled hands and feet. His long, wicked claws hooked into the rock. He appeared to be chewing on his restraints.

Then the landslide blocked everything else. Tank slammed to the floor of the reactor chamber, and ten thousand tons of bedrock came down on his head.

"Now, here, take this," said Hardcore, stuffing five bucks in the tied-up sergeant's pocket. "My mamma didn't raise no thief."

The massive Postie rose to his full six feet ten inches and put a cigarillo in his mouth. The fight was going well, and finding the soldier's smokes only made it better. He glanced at the two-hundred-and-some bound guards and almost felt bad for them. Being steamrolled in less than ten minutes by such a small group Posties had to be a real kick in the dick, especially after fifteen years of ruling the roost.

Portero and Shockwave were still off throwing guys through doors, Quietus had run down the block to take the fight to the enemy, and Jacqui was inside the Wall, probably kicking lots of ass. So Alec had gone back to guard duty. There were no bad guys in sight; it was time to light up.

He scratched the stubble under his jaw line, rummaged through his pocket for a lighter, and wondered how the numbers were really stacking up. Q had warned (well, signed) about a second wave of troops, and Hardcore didn't know if it had hit yet.

He cupped a hand around the tip of the smoke, flicked his lighter and took a nice, long drag.

Then Quietus came running around the corner, waving his arms. The bald, eyeless Postie pulled his fists to the center of his chest—left on top of right, with a quick squeezing motion—and flung them apart, opening his hands while spreading his arms.

Alec saw the sign; his eyes went wide and the cigarillo fell from his lips. "Aw, shit!"

The little guy was Hardcore's best friend; they were bros, plain and simple. So while Alec would admit to lacking a bit in the formal education department, he'd learned more than a little sign language for the sake of his friend. Quietus couldn't exactly see the gestures, but he used ASL to express himself. Hardcore liked knowing what was on his silent buddy's mind.

And Q just dashed across town to sign, "Explosion."

Hardcore didn't hesitate. He threw himself to the ground and stretched as far as possible, trying to make a wall out of his body. His thick fingers sank into the pavement and his feet wrapped around a streetlight. Q flipped over the expanding flesh, crouched, and motioned for the confused prisoners to duck.

A whirlwind battered Hardcore's elongated, fifty-foot frame, and seven figures thudded to the ground beside Quietus. Alec had time to realize that it was Shockwave, throwing people to safety—as the city exploded. Hardcore screamed as the blast wave hit, chucks of ABRA city slammed into his tattooed back, and raw heat scorched his flesh.

❂   ❂   ❂

Portero was in an alley, between the movie theater and food court, at the moment of Flamechylde's death. He was too far from a door to step somewhere else; the explosion was a fraction of a second away. Pressing his body against the brick wall, Rodrigo prayed.

Then something rapidly filled the cramped space between the buildings—a mountainous barricade grew from nowhere, sheltering the debonair adventurer—as the explosion shook the world.

On the other side of ABRA City, Lockdown and Glimmer were in the middle of a firefight. Old Curt was playing human shield for Hannah while she shot invisible lasers at the surrounding guards. All of the combatants were unprepared for the detonation— it happened nearly directly beneath their feet—and even David couldn't reach them in time.

Julio, the former leader of the East Coast Alliance hid next to HQ, close to his former teammates. He was trying to work up the courage to go to them, to help them, to apologize for all the bad things he'd done for ABRA. But he never had a chance. He died in the explosion before he even knew what hit him.

Within the Wall, California Girl was running after a small crowd of guards. They had learned there was no point in using weapons against her; their only options were to run or to get knocked out by the knockout (copyright JCG Heroics, Ltd., 1976). The explosion hit with enough force to throw her off her feet; the soldiers stumbled into each other, some fell. Jacqui had been on the receiving end of just about every kind of explosive over the years, and this was a *big* one. She turned away from the stunned troops and raced to the closest guard tower.

And in the sky over ACRA City, Overpower could only watch the blast. The epicenter was beside Headquarters, near the corner of the street. A rough column of earth and debris shot high into the air. The wave of destruction rippled out from ground zero, swallowing the tower, the hospital, a few of the outer military structures—and the apartment buildings.

JJ and company stood in the road as residents filed through the wormhole. Not everyone stepped through the portal. Some wandered off on their own, despite being warned. But most of them had been smart enough to want to get rid of the brain bombs. They listened to JJ and agreed to lay low in the food service warehouse until Sol showed up.

There were only about twenty-five people left in line, and he wished they'd pick up the pace. Everyone seemed dazed, though, and they were all moving slowly. JJ didn't blame them; the night had turned out to be very eventful.

But things were looking good. Milk's team had successfully pulled the military to the other side of town, and California Girl had cleared the Wall. JJ hadn't seen any guards since Overpower's flyby. The warehouse appeared secure, and everyone seemed to share a good—if shell-shocked—mood.

Even Nikki looked almost happy. She stood about ten feet to his right, over by the squashed remains of the Walker, with Madison, Vanessa and Anon (who'd become a tall Asian woman in a fur coat). JJ couldn't help but notice that they were whispering to each other. They all glanced at him simultaneously; red warmth crawled up his freezing cheeks.

He adjusted his cap, tightened the hood of his coat and turned his face away. That was exactly what he needed—Nikki learning all about him from the peanut gallery.

That's when half the town exploded.

The blast ripped down the street, destroying everything. There was no time to think—but JJ somehow found time to act.

He closed the portal and flung a sideways pulse, shoving his friends and several inmates behind the demolished Walker. He anchored the wreck to the ground with one hundred times Earth gravity — making it an immovable buffer to protect the others — and pinned himself down under nearly as many G's.

Out of the corner of his eye, he saw the blast wave rushing closer. The rolling storm of debris had to be moving at nearly the speed of sound, but time slowed to a crawl before JJ's eyes. Thrown earth, pulverized brick and hot shrapnel flew down the street, swallowing everything.

JJ saw a flicker of motion that could only be David racing along the advancing edge of the explosion, pulling people to safety. He thought he saw the Headquarters tower crumble, in the quarter-second before the growing cloud filled the sky.

Then Nikki leaped from behind cover and pulled JJ to the ground. She grunted under the extreme gravity field, but her incredible durability and strength could handle it. Squatting in the street, she pulled his head against her chest and pressed her cheek against the top of his cap. The blast hit as her limbs wrapped around his body.

He thought, *There are worse ways to die.*

The explosion slammed into them with a bone-jarring impact, deafening boom and unrelenting heat — but they did not budge. JJ saw the others huddle behind the immobile Walker, in the instant before light vanished.

He couldn't see during those long seconds of hot darkness, and the only sound was an apocalyptic roar. But he held them all, firmly planted in place, and Nikki was his shield. A violent hail of rubble crashed against her back, something huge smashed into her and spun away, her body was battered by a force that could level a city — and she *took* it.

And, just like that, it was over. Fading echoes rumbled in the darkness.

JJ and Nikki collapsed in the street as dust drifted down like snow. Thunder bellowed above and the Earth grumbled below. An eerie silence blanketed the stunned city, broken only by their pounding hearts. He couldn't see anything, but neither could she. The bright aurora and countless stars had been replaced by ash and gritty blackness. He raised face from her breast, he pulled her close. They embraced, filthy, trembling, exhausted and happy to be alive.

"It's okay," he said, patting her back. "It's okay. I've got you."

Her trembling stopped. She stiffened, holding her breath. He winced.

"You've got me?" She playfully slapped his arm, just hard enough to sting. She straightened his cap and gave him a hug. "Dumbass, I've got *you*."

They laughed, weakly, and held each other, crouching in the ruined street.

JJ said, "I'm cool with that."

—and hit the ground, thumping hard against her spine. Her insides seemed to slosh around and *everything* hurt—but the explosion hit before her brain could register what had happened. She bounced painfully on the wildly bucking earth; the pressure wave shoved her several feet across frost-covered grass. The thunderous blast felt like an all-over punch, leaving her with aching bones, a pounding head and a high-pitched tone in her ears.

Tiffany blinked, shook her head and ran half-numb fingers over her face.

She was on a small field next to the Wall, near the garage complex, almost as far from the explosion as possible. A helicopter was starting up, not too far away. People were screaming in the murky distance. She had no idea how she'd traveled so far so fast, but apparently she wasn't the only one. There were eleven people nearby, including Billy the bat boy and several unarmed guards. Everyone looked around, stunned and shaky; nobody seemed to be in a hurry to rise.

Then she remembered.

Tiffany sat up and cried out, as her widening eyes fell on the destruction. She climbed to her feet, arms outstretched. She reached for Fiona and Tom.

A mushroom cloud surged into the sky. Billowing dust and

ash covered half of ABRA City, swelling but dissipating. Lightning struck near the center of town.

Tiffany began to shake. Folding in on herself, she fell to her knees. She felt naked, exposed, raw and freezing.

Fiona was gone, just gone. And Tom? Where was he? She couldn't focus enough to search with her power; she feared what might be seen.

All of a sudden something like a gunshot went off nearby. She jerked back and looked up. A tall young guy, with a dark skin and a friendly smile, had appeared not two feet to her right. He wore a black outfit and heavy coat, like a SWAT officer in a parka, and had a pile of blankets and winter clothes in his arms.

He looked around and asked, "Is everyone okay? Does anyone need help?" He looked around and vanished in a sharp bang. The wind roared and a tornado zipped around the field.

Tiffany felt a jolting vibration—and suddenly she was wearing a winter jacket. A glance around the field showed the others had also been dressed in cold-weather gear during the roaring tumult. The few guards had also been disarmed and bound.

The young guy met her eyes, gave a nod and raised his face to the small crowd.

"First thing first," he announced. "I'm the new Shockwave and, yeah, my parents are who you think they are. My dad's here, leading our team. We've come to free the prisoners and save Tom Fuson. We don't want to hurt anyone. Whatever happened back there, it wasn't us."

"It was ... it was Fiona," whispered Tiffany. She wiped her nose on the coat's sleeve.

Shockwave did a double take. "Fiona McNamara? Flamechylde?"

Tiffany nodded and lifted the coat's hood. "She ... she was my friend. The guards killed her, and she..." Sobbing muffled the rest.

"How do you know that?" asked David. The redhead had been in the middle of town, crying on the ground, when the explosion happened; he'd found her milliseconds before the blast. She'd been the first of the thirty-three people he'd been able to rescue in that horrible moment. He wondered if she could see underground. Did she have x-ray vision or something?

Instead of responding, she covered her face and wept.

"Tiff can feel us Posties," chattered the bat boy. The parka fell to his feet; two heavy blankets were draped over his miniature frame. "She can make us strong or weak."

"Really? You're the power manipulator?" David kneeled beside the girl. "My father is down there, can you feel him?"

She looked up, nodded, sniffled and wiped her face again. "I was with him down there in MegaMax. Then he went down. He … He was with her. So was … so was Tom. I…" She tried to open her unique sense — but the ground shuddered again.

Every eye in the city turned toward the center of town as more soil was thrown into the sky. Tiffany held her breath. David tensed and prepared to run. The rumbling tremor rapidly strengthened. The tortured Earth roared.

A shaft of radiance burst upward, piercing the dense haze with warm, golden light.

And Tom rose above the city, blazing like the dawn.

CHAPTER THIRTY-SEVEN

He looked down from a place of darkness and ash, fire and ice. Nothing was real. A ringing emptiness pulled at his heart; throbbing numbness filled his mind. Death and loss, power and heat; he still felt the heat of her death. His body pulsed with the power she'd given.

He languidly examined his hand, gazing with a dull sense of detachment. He felt separated from everything—his body, the shadowed ruins on the ground and the endless sky above. The hollow ache behind his ear was a vague curiosity; he absentmindedly touched the spot and felt the tender flesh of fresh scar tissue. He seemed to remember something, but raw lethargy muddled his perceptions and erased curiosity. He forgot the pain and looked down.

Dust had begun to settle on the slow lower world. He blinked drowsily, drunkenly, and tried to make sense of it all. He wasn't a part of this place; he couldn't be. The ash couldn't touch him; fire could only empower him. The frigid night fled his touch. Even gravity released its hold. The world had run away, and he was alone, high above ABRA City and the guards.

He looked down at the once-powerful prison. It was so small. It was broken.

All that remained of MegaMax was a rough subsidence crater, over six hundred feet wide. Nothing was left of

Headquarters other than shattered foundations, twisted girders and heaps of rubble. The sinkhole had swallowed the hospital and two of the apartment buildings.

The rest of the city looked like a warzone. Small fires burned here and there among the battered buildings. Dents and cracks covered the armored plates of the Wall; smoke drifted from smashed weapon emplacements and demolished towers. Empty exoskeletons and pieces of Walkers littered the ground.

ABRA City was dead.

And those little men, with their little weapons, they could never hurt him. They were nothing. They had already lost. What were they to him? They may as well have been ants. They were less than ants; they lacked even a sting.

A memory teased the corner of his mind, but it quickly vanished. Something about ants, something from long ago … he shook it off.

The soldiers looked up at him, most raised their hands against his light. But he did not care about any of them. They didn't matter. They could do nothing. They were powerless.

Tom was the one with power now.

Angus clutched the tablet computer and slowly walked down the helicopter's ramp. The fat CH-53E Super Stallion growled, its rotors chopping through the air. The cloning equipment had been securely strapped in place, Mueller and the staff made preparations to depart, but the old scientist ignored all of that.

His watery eyes were locked on the flying boy. In his mind, the old man saw Adam as a small child, learning to fly before he could even tie his shoes. He saw Adam, the man, floating over the grand boulevards of the Golden Home, wearing red, white and blue.

He heard Tom's voice; *I will never be your Independence.*

Angus stared at the sky, at lifetimes of decision and error culminating in this moment.

The boy hovered over the smoky city, looking down at the world. His clothing had been incinerated. Angus thought Tom resembled Cellini's great bronze, *Perseus with the Head of Medusa*, at the Loggia dei Lanzi in Florence; young, powerful, almost divine, triumphant but weary, with an unreadable expression that could mean anything. Warm illumination flowed from the boy's body, gold, orange and red in the dusty gloom.

"Glorious isn't he?" said someone, off to the side, out of view. The voice was deep and calm, but beneath the surface was a current of rapture.

Angus knew that voice.

He turned to face the approaching Children of Man. The Lector gazed skyward; his polished bronze skin gleamed in the rich light. The Anchorite's weathered old face was also raised, tears streamed into his wild beard. Grim Lynne lifted her arms and sang a rhythmic Greek chant through her tusks. But the shaggy giant Esau looked right at the doctor, and Ashley Lang sneered with fire in her eyes.

Angus backed up the ramp; he glanced at the tablet and tapped through some menus. In the helicopter, Doctor Mueller gasped and a soldier said something. The Children walked closer.

"'And I saw one like the Son of Man dwelling with men and in the world. And they did not recognize Him. And I saw Him ascending into the firmament,'" declared the Lector, the Reader of the Written Word. Angus was all-too familiar with the post-Christian, pseudo-Gnostic hodgepodge of theology espoused by Mister Moment's disciples.

At that moment Tom dropped from view; the golden light flared and dimmed. Night resumed on the tundra, but the Lector's metallic eyes still glinted in the dark.

"'The earth, the sea, the mountains, and the hills shall tremble together. Then shall be revealed the sign of the Son, and all tribes of Earth shall mourn.'"

He blinked, still in the sky, still looking down; his mind found sluggish release from the stunned fugue. The frozen numbness faded, replaced by a prickling return to reality. His daze settled into clarity as the mental fog evaporated. He remembered everything, all at once.

He saw Tiffany, struggling against the soldiers last night, reaching. He saw Marcus on the computer screen; nightvision green flashing to white as he died. Tiffany, standing on his feet as they floated around the darkened room. He saw the rocket flying from the woods, hitting Milk, killing Mom; Mom, dead, forever dead. Tiffany running through the half-collapsed doorway of Cellblock A, throwing her arms around his neck. He saw Vaughn laughing; Tiffany laughing. He saw Angus and the soldiers; the soldiers and Fiona. Fiona and the fire. Fiona and Milk. Fiona and Tank and Tiffany. He thought of the explosion, the destruction of MegaMax, and Tiffany. Tiffany and Tiffany and Tiffany.

Tiffany! He needed nothing else, not air, not water, nothing. He needed her.

He opened his perceptions to the Posthumans, feeling their connection to his power. He visualized the golden web that joined his quantum essence to theirs. He ignored the dozens of sparkling presences, seeking only one. But Tom instantly realized there was no need to search for her. She had already found him.

She was behind him, down near the Wall, looking right at him. Her radiance washed over him, renewing and warm. He was not the light; *she* was. Tiffany illuminated everything.

He turned and closed the distance in a heartbeat, dimming as he approached to avoid hurting her eyes. He touched down a few feet away, ignored the bystanders, and walked to her.

She stood stiffly, arms wrapped across her chest, shivering in the rising wind. Her face was red, especially the tip of her little nose; streaks of half-frozen tears ran down her cheeks.

He stepped closer and bathed her in warmth. She inhaled sharply and exhaled slowly. They pulled each other close; Tom lowered her hood and kissed the top of her head. She wept against his chest.

They didn't talk for a while.

✪   ✪   ✪

"Are you okay?"

The voice came from everywhere, rough and deeper than even Milk's *basso profundo*. It came up through the hard soles of Rodrigo's leather boots; it rattled the roots of his teeth. It was the voice of a giant. A towering colossus crouched down, filling the alley.

"Portero!" it boomed, looking down with huge blue eyes. The titan's head was larger the Mexican champion's entire body; Rodrigo could see little more than dense, wild, blond hair. The yard-wide lips moved, and teeth like cinderblocks clattered; the breath was a heavy, humid gust. Was that smell Doritos?

The giant exclaimed, "What the hell was that? Someone pull a Joey Slater?"

"I ... I do not know, my friend. You are Solomon Beck, yes?"

"That's right, call me Sol. It's a real pleasure to meet you, sir." He shrank while speaking, back to his usual five-and-a-smidge feet. "We need to find JJ and start getting people out."

Portero started to reply but was interrupted by a door on the building to his right, part of the food court complex.

"Sol, thank heaven it is you! What has happened? Was that a bomb or was it one of us?" asked Sam Chandrasekhar, standing at the head of a crowd. It looked like all of the prisoners were hiding in that building.

"I don't know, but we're getting out of here," said Sol, pulling a bomb remover from his pockets. "Come here and—"

A gunshot cracked and Portero's head snapped forward; heavy wads of bloody meat, hair and bone hit the wall. Sam tried to catch the falling body but multiple bursts caught him in the chest. At least twenty guards crouched in the alley, and they all opened fire at once.

And Solomon grew.

Oh, he knew more about the process than he let on. He knew that not a single atom of his body changed because of his power. No, Sol merely altered information. He temporarily changed his relationship with little things like mass and the spatial dimensions. He tricked the universe into thinking that he was small or large. Very, very large.

Bullets pelted his swelling flesh, but he grew too fast for them to do damage. Go ahead and shoot a rhino with a BB gun; good luck with that.

"You little pieces of shit! Try picking someone your own size!" roared Solomon. He charged down the alley, growing with every step. "King Kong ain't got shit on me!"

The guards could do nothing but run.

CHAPTER THIRTY-EIGHT

JJ stared across the prison. His eyes turned glassy, and his jaw went slack with awe. None of the night's insane events could have prepared him for this. Meeting Milk and the other rebel Posties, especially Nikki, had been incredible. The fighting had been intense and surreal, but it felt good to finally stand up to the Man. Kicking that Walker's ass had been epic. Surviving that explosion, working with Nikki to save his friends — it had been like a baptism. JJ felt reborn, he couldn't describe it. *Everything* had changed in the past ten minutes.

But this moment topped them all, as JJ watched his best friend become a legend.

Solomon towered over the buildings; they didn't even reach his knees. Five hundred feet tall at the very least, his upper body vanished in the night. He crossed the city in four strides, and each step resounded like God's timpani, like the drums of doom.

Missiles shot into the air, detonating all over his titanic body. They scorched his clothing but barely scratched his flesh. He walked forward, scattering the terrified soldiers. He kicked aside Walkers like Hot Wheels on a playroom floor. Bending down, he brushed a score of guards from the street with a slow sweep of his building-sized hand.

JJ tried to speak, but could only manage, "Whubba, uh ... he, um..."

Nikki's hand was on his shoulder. She muttered, "Whoa."

"Sol..." whispered Vanessa while Madi cried out in wordless astonishment; Anon flickered between a dozen appearances, before settling on a wide-eyed child.

Through the demolished buildings, JJ saw a mass of soldiers emerging from the base of the Wall. He figured there were three hundred of them, maybe more. Most of them fired weapons up at Sol.

Jesus, can't this just stop?

In the distance, California Girl dropped down from the Wall, landing amid the troops. She charged through the crowd like a bowling ball. Rapid blasts of lightning crashed around the heroine, as Overpower appeared, orbiting Sol like an electron. Hardcore and Quietus ran through the crowd, disarming and incapacitating soldiers around Sol's enormous sneakers.

JJ looked at his friends. "Come on guys, let's find some cover."

"Fuck that," scoffed Nikki. "It's time to show those ass—"

A very loud bang cut her off; everyone whipped around toward the center of town in time to see a plume of rubble shoot out of the crater—and Milk leap into view. He landed thirty feet down the street, white flesh covered in ash and grime. He stood, saw Nikki, JJ and the crew, and jogged toward them.

"Dad!" Nikki flew forward and jumped into her father's arms. They embraced firmly and he kissed the side of her face.

"Hey, Goober. You been behaving yourself?" He glanced toward the sound of combat and gaped at the skyscraper-sized Sol. His square jaw went slack and he blinked. "Well, you kids sure grow up fast. Guess the fight's not over."

"Not yet," agreed JJ. "What should we do?"

Milk grinned, put Nikki on the ground and said, "Smash something."

But a deep voice rolled through the ruins. "First Sergeant Young, stand down! You are under arrest."

Milk turned around; JJ, Nikki and the gang looked toward the speaker. Vanessa and Nikki both spat expletives; Anon and Madi gasped. Neither Milk nor JJ made a sound.

At the edge of the crater stood a line of APEs and fifty or more soldiers—they must have worked their way around Sol and the heroes—but all eyes were on the leader.

His suit was like an APE, but larger, especially around the torso and head. Thick plating had been added to the armored chrome, with obvious reinforcement along the limbs, spine and chest. The helmet was wide, heavy and immobile—locked between a pair of forward-facing, shoulder-mounted tubes; the short cylinders appeared to have grilled speakers at the end, like old boomboxes. The suit's gauntlets were smoother and shorter than the mechanical appendages of a standard APE suit. They looked like actual gloves instead of robotic grippers, apparently so the soldier could use weapons.

The soldier held an extremely large firearm, it didn't even look real. It was a long bulky rifle made of gleaming chrome, with a wide bore aimed right at Milk. A thick, segmented cable connected the gun to a shell-like extension of the exoskeleton that resembled a bulky, metal backpack. The soldier held his weapon at the ready, with perfect posture and steady hands. On his breastplate, stenciled letters spelled the name Holly.

"Stand down, Sergeant Young, or I *will* open fire."

Milk laughed, "You expect me to be scared of a gun?"

"No," replied the soldier.

Then he pulled the trigger.

The shot exploded against Milk's right shoulder with the sound of thunder and a glaring burst of white light. The horned hero flew back, tumbling down the road.

Captain Holly took a single step forward and did not lower his weapon. "You should be afraid of the *bullets*."

Captain Holly thought of the dead and did not regret pulling the trigger. Oh, he understood the reason behind Milk's attack; the soldier was glad that Tom had survived and escaped. But hundreds had been underground, and they were all dead. This clumsy assault had turned into mass murder, and all that blood was on Milk's hands. Holly could have blown the horned bastard to hell.

The massive Postie rolled to a stop in the street. That single shot had blown him back a good thirty feet. It had *hurt*, too, judging by how the hero clutched his shoulder. Infrared showed a pretty little bloom; Milk was bleeding.

Holly thought, *We just made history.*

All of the techs would get promotions, if he lived long enough to file the paperwork. People said it could not be done; the American military had *done* it. They'd drawn blood from the indestructible man. The antimatter bullets did the trick.

The silver pellets were simple things, according to the trainers; each contained a few grams of antiprotons within a magnetic field. They had been salvaged from Carnivore ships and were ordinarily used to produce power. Rupturing a pellet would expose the contents to regular matter with predictable results — total annihilation of equal amounts of mass, and an extremely hot burst of pure radiation. The energy didn't affect Milk, but the knots of antimatter simply tore through his impervious body.

Inside the armor, Holly felt both cut off and deeply connected to his surroundings. All of his senses had either been eliminated or replicated by machinery. Everything in view was drawn on his retinas by lasers; system menus hung in his field of vision, controlled through blinks and specific eye movements. Sight and hearing were artificial and enhanced; he could perceive both sound and light beyond the range of normal, human senses. At that moment, he used a hybrid mode — with infrared highlights over the visual spectrum — to observe the field of battle.

Five young residents stood on the road, stunned, looking at Milk instead of the soldiers. Holly appraised them at a glance.

Madison Doyle, Vanessa Martinez and Anon were in the back; Jeremiah Joyce stood closer, with an unknown young female, believed to be Milk's daughter. Reports indicated that she was physically powerful and highly skilled, but JJ Joyce was the deadliest person in sight. The shapeshifter, the human radio and the scream queen were negligible threats, and the strong girl could prove challenging, but Joyce was nearly unmatched in offensive potential.

Holly had memorized every prisoner's file and paid close attention to scientific analysis of their abilities. Multiple physicists had written about the astounding implications of Joyce's power. Much of that data was beyond Holly's understanding, but he got the gist; the kid was a walking black hole. He *had* to be, in order to make those portals. The level of power and control required to make a wormhole was terrifying. Joyce commanded gravity, manipulated space and could likely travel through time, but the boy was ignorant of his own potential. He could destroy the planet and didn't even know it.

They needed to handle this one carefully. If Joyce became injured—with all that power and adrenaline—he might destroy everything. Better to play it safe and subdue him, quickly.

The captain quickly glanced at the communications menu and selected Command from the list of options. He calmly said, "Non-lethals on Joyce. Heavies take the strong girl. Other targets are secondary. Go."

Three soldiers immediately fired tasers at the boy. He stiffened, convulsed and fell to the ground. Milk's daughter turned and lunged, but most of the APE's converged on her. The other Posties ran toward cover beside the remaining apartment building, pursued by two squads. A pair of APEs and nine men remained behind their captain, to protect his vulnerable and deadly rear.

Captain Holly turned his attention back to Milk.

The shot had left a gaping wound in the giant's dense shoulder muscles; the blood was bright and unreal on that snow-white flesh. The captain aimed for a headshot; the horned hero's expression was one of shock and pain. The first Posthuman hadn't really been injured since 1971, and the sensation had to be psychologically devastating.

Holly eyeballed the com to Voice, slowly stepped closer, and kept the rifle ready. "Stay on the ground! Tell your people to surrender and you'll all live. Resist and you *will* go down."

The horned hero stood. His large brown eyes narrowed and he replied, "It'll take more than that."

Holly responded with another shot, clipping the giant's left hip. The powerful eruption of light and energy spun Milk around and sent him tumbling another twenty feet down the broken street. This sanctimonious prick thought he could wreck Holly's house and be smug about it?

"I've *got* more than that," growled the captain. "This weapon fires antimatter bullets, Sergeant Young. Do you know about antimatter? It will destroy *anything*. I'm carrying two hundred thirty-eight more shots, and I *will* kill you, if you don't stand down."

Milk rolled onto his knees and began to push up, slowly. Holly was astonished at the old brute's resilience. The brass thought Sergeant Young would be overcome by experiencing pain after forty-five years of invulnerability. One shot, they'd believed, would remind the rogue titan of his mortality. Apparently, the old man was tougher than that. Admiration and indignation warred in the captain's heart.

"You're supposed to be a hero! How many good people did you kill?" roared Holly. "How many of my people are dead because of you?"

Milk remained crouched but looked at the soldier, "Don't you think I know that?"

Within the bulky helmet, Captain Holly sneered, "I don't think you care."

"I didn't want to hurt anybody," said Milk. "I let your people take Tom, and you tried to kill him. I'm sorry this went to shit, but I won't surrender. Me and my people—*all* of my people— we're leaving."

Holly said nothing; he was done talking. Glancing at the com, he switched to No Ears. Within the helmet, all background noise dropped. The captain could hear nothing aside from his pulse and breath. He looked at the systems menu and selected Noise Cannons/Max.

The heavy, speaker-like tubes on the armor's shoulders immediately began to emit a pulsing, hundred-and-ninety decibel shriek. The sound hit Milk like a truck. He grabbed the sides of his head and fell to the ground. His thick fingers dug into the pavement, face contorted with pain, but he crawled to his knees and shot a fierce gaze at the armored soldier. Sonic weapons were one of the few ways to hurt the invulnerable man, but they were stop-gap at best.

Holly fired the rifle again, but the big bastard leaped out of the way with surprising speed. A thirty-foot hole was blown in the street by the wayward bullet, knocking Holly back a few feet. The armored soldier shook his head and recovered — in time to see Milk charging right at him.

Grimacing against the unearthly volume, the hero pushed forward. Blood streamed from his right shoulder and left hip, but neither wound was mortal. There was only one way to stop him.

Holly raised the rifle and squeezed off another shot, but the bullet only hit Milk's right horn. The heavy coil shattered, but the titan did not slow down.

Captain Holly barely had time to brace himself. Milk's left fist hit the metal breastplate and knocked the captain off his feet. Then, with a violent lurch, the giant crushed the speakers, ripped away the helmet, wrapped his right hand around the suit's torso and lifted the armored soldier into the air. Those enormous fingers pressed against the metal shell on the captain's back.

Holly did the only thing he could do; he shoved the barrel of the gun under Milk's massive jaw line and grunted, "Stop!"

Without the helmet, the arctic chill stabbed Holly's skin. He heard gunfire and explosions throughout the city. Out of the corner of his eye, he saw Milk's daughter toss an APE toward the crater, as she stood over the semi-conscious JJ Joyce. Some soldiers were running from Anon, who had become a rhinoceros. Lightning ripped across the sky and the tremendous thuds of Solomon Beck's distant steps shook the earth.

But Milk's face dominated the view. The albino giant wasn't afraid, not at all. The antimatter bullets would blow off his head at point-blank range, but the hero made no move to dislodge the gun. He looked Holly in the eye and bellowed, "You stop! This is insane!"

"If you damage the containment housing, you'll kill us all," said Holly. "Surrender while you still can."

"If you pull that trigger, my hand might spasm and do the job on its own," replied Milk. "*You* surrender."

The two big men glared at each other. Their dark eyes locked together; each one looked for an opening, for some way to end the fight. Neither could risk backing down, neither would ever yield.

Holly thought, *It'll take a miracle to get out of this alive.*

Suddenly, almost as if in response, golden light filled in the darkened street. Tom had arrived.

The young man's voice came from above, with a firm confidence that permitted no refusal. "That's enough! Both of you, back off!"

David blurred onto the street, but few people noticed; he rushed to his sister's side. She kneeled over JJ, who slowly recovered from the tasers. The soldiers stopped attacking, and Anon changed into a red-haired man, while Vanessa and Madi stumbled out of the rubble. The fighting ended as everyone raised their eyes to the light.

Tom hovered overhead, with Tiffany by his side. His right arm held her waist, her arms wrapped around his neck. She wore a bulky jacket over MegaMax scrubs, but the boy was clothed only by blazing golden power. "Let each other go. *Now.*"

Milk released the captain; Holly stepped back and lowered his weapon. They looked up at the glowing son of Independence.

Tom drifted closer to the ground. "Too many people have died already. I won't let you kill each other."

Holly looked at Tom, then at Milk. "Sergeant Young has to answer for the deaths he caused."

"He didn't cause the explosion," replied Tom. "I was there. Your men killed Fiona. She was trying to free me and they killed her. I think she tried to give me all of her power, but it was too much for her to control, too much for me to absorb. So blame her, blame them, blame *me.*"

Holly swallowed and could barely meet Tom's eyes. The boy's words were a punch to the soul. The weight of understanding was too much. "McNamara? I... This is my fault."

Tom's feet touched the pavement. Taking Tiffany's hand, he stepped close enough to whisper, "No, it's not. This isn't anyone's fault. You tried to free me, so did Milk, but neither one of you could control what happened after it began. Now don't say anything that might get you thrown in jail. You make a better guard."

Holly blinked and nodded. Tiffany and Milk were both stunned by the notion that the stern soldier had somehow helped Tom escape. None of the others could hear the quiet speech — except Vanessa, who acted like she'd heard nothing.

Tom cast his gaze over the Posthumans and soldiers. He raised his voice, "Listen to me. We need to stop this. It's pointless. We aren't enemies. You can't hold us anymore, but that doesn't mean we have to fight. We should be looking for survivors, not killing each other. Let's work together and make things right."

Milk gave a weary smile, "That sounds like something your father would have said."

Holly looked at the towering hero, "I was thinking the same thing."

Tom frowned slightly, "Maybe that's why we're here. Maybe we needed to be reminded that we aren't all that different. We're reflections of each other. That's what *Aegis* would say."

CHAPTER THIRTY-NINE

Screaming soldiers ran as the warehouse-sized sneaker slowly came down. Sol made sure they had time to flee; he *really* didn't want to step on anyone. He wasn't a murderer, unlike these jackbooted storm troopers, but he'd make sure they paid for killing Sam and Portero. He turned around, to check out the helicopter on the north side, when a bolt of lightning flashed by his humongous eyes.

Overpower swung by, buzzed something that Sol's gargantuan ears could not decipher, and shot across the sky. The electric man flew over the center of town, where the apartments used to be.

Only one remained standing, though all of its windows had been shattered. Another building had been blown to hell; the back half remained standing, but the front was totally demolished. The other two were now part of the MegaMax crater.

Sol was about two blocks away and five hundred feet higher, but he could see a golden glow down on the ground. Tom Fuson was down there! Sol scratched his beard and squinted, trying to look at the shadowed ruins. He shrank another hundred feet to get a better view.

Milk stood down there, standing next to a buck-naked Tom Fuson. They seemed to be talking to a helmetless APE. Nobody was fighting; that had to be a good sign.

Tiffany Cooke was with them, too. Sol was glad she'd made it out of MegaMax, and he grinned at seeing her hold Tom's hand. Those kids deserved a happy ending.

The armored soldier said something to the nearby troops; most of them turned, jogging away.

Then Sol spotted JJ, Madi, Nessie and (presumably) Anon, along with Milk's kids. Overpower came down on the other side of Tom. Maybe happy endings were going around tonight.

The fighting seemed to be over. Sol looked down and noticed that the guys nearby had stopped shooting. Most of them stood around, still staring up at the colossal Postie, but a few were walking closer, with their weapons put away. Closer to the Wall, a small group of soldiers approached California Girl.

The soldiers spoke to the heroine and pointed in Sol's direction. She turned around and waved her arms, motioning for him to stop and shrink. The battle had ended.

He dropped back to normal size and found himself standing close to the movie theater. A bunch of residents were huddled around the bodies of Portero and Sam. He called to them, "Hey! Come with me if you want to live!"

Booming laughter rose behind Sol's back, and a deep voice said, "Really? You're gonna go there?"

Sol turned around and saw Hardcore and Quietus approaching. He hadn't met them, but he'd seen them over the PhotoFlies and caught glimpses of them during the battle. They were part of Milk's new team; with a start, Sol realized that *he* might just be part of that team, too.

The big tattooed guy carried six shivering prisoners, including Autumn Gerber and her five glowing boys. Billy the bat boy crouched on his shoulder.

Sol chuckled, "If you're gonna steal, steal from the best. And by that, I mean Michael Biehn."

"Hell yeah. That dude's the man," laughed the tattooed biker. "I'm Hardcore, this is Quietus. You kicked some major ass back there."

"We all did," said California Girl, walking beside a tense officer and a gaggle of nervous soldiers. "This is Lieutenant Baker.

We've all agreed to stop fighting for the time being. Some of us are going to help out here, but they won't stop us from leaving. If we can find Portero, we'll start evacuating the prisoners."

Sol looked down, felt his cheeks burn, and said, "I'm sorry, ma'am, but he ... he didn't make it." He glanced toward the alley and winced when the hero cried out.

Her blue eyes went wide beneath the small mask. "Rodrigo... No..." Her hands balled into fists and she visibly stiffened.

Sol stepped closer and touched her forearm, "I'm sorry. He was a good man. If it helps ... he didn't suffer. It happened fast."

"Thank you," whispered the hero. She wiped her eyes and exhaled. It wasn't yet time to mourn. "Well ... let's get started. Where's everyone else?"

"Milk, Tom Fuson and my friends are in the middle of town."

"Along with my commanding officer, Captain Holly," added the stiff Lieutenant.

"We should go there, then," said Hardcore. He looked at his small partner. "What do you think, Q?"

The bald man nodded but frowned. He pointed at the crater and shook his head.

"Nobody?" gasped the shirtless brute.

Quietus responded with a single finger, followed by a flurry of sign language.

Hardcore nodded and translated, "There are injured all over, but not underground. He says there's only one person alive down there, some guy named Tank. That dude's almost as tough as Milk, so it's okay, I guess. Q says most people are over that way, but we'll have to look around to be sure."

"Alright," said Sol. "Let's go meet up with the bigwigs."

Everyone agreed, and they began to walk.

"You know," said California Girl. "Technically speaking, *I'm* one of the bigwigs."

✪   ✪   ✪

Nobody argued when Holly gave the order to cease fire. His people seemed eager to end the mad, deadly night. The battle sounds stopped within thirty seconds of his command.

The captain told his people that they were stand down and let the Posties do what they wanted. He realized that allowing the prisoners to escape would probably be called treason, but he was willing to take that fall.

"You're one hell of an officer, Captain," said Milk. A third of his right horn had been blown away, but the antimatter wounds no longer bled. He was as unyielding as ever.

Holly couldn't help but be in awe of the living legend. "Thank you, Sergeant. I've always respected you ... as a soldier and a hero. I hope that we never do this again."

"But you can't promise it," rumbled the giant.

"Well, my career is probably over, so if they send someone after you, it won't be me. But you'll be criminals until the people decide otherwise."

"I can live with that. It's just a shame the kids have to live with it, too." Milk inclined his head toward the knot of young Posties. Nikki, David, Overpower, JJ Joyce and his friends were introducing themselves to Tom and Tiffany. "You really tried to free him?"

Holly nodded. "Wish I'd done it yesterday."

Milk saw the dead in his mind's eye. David had described catching a glimpse of Hannah and Curt, standing right above the ground zero of Fiona's explosion, and Captain Holly had explained that Portero had been shot moments after the blast. Three of Milk's oldest friends, three of the bravest people he'd ever known, and they were gone, just like that.

He looked and Captain Holly and muttered, "You know ... So do I."

Angus glanced down and tried to thumb through the tablet computer's menus as surreptitiously as possible. Fortunately, the Children of Man were distracted at the moment. The Lector was in the middle of a rant. He intoned some invective about blasphemous mockeries and divine retribution. Angus ignored the sermon.

He selected the desired application, entered a general access code and his personal identification. A garish popup window warned of the legal prohibitions, linking citations to half-a-dozen laws, treaties and guidelines; Angus checked three boxes and brought up the menu for Level Three Containment Systems.

The guards and assorted military personnel were classified as Level One Containment Systems. They were valuable on a day-to-day level, necessary as tools of control. However, the guards were hopelessly outclassed by the Posthumans, as demonstrated by the night's events.

Level Two indicated the physical fortifications of ABRA City, a far superior layer of security. The outpost had been designed for a much different purpose, but it adequately served as a prison. The housing and recreational facilities helped keep the potentially deadly prisoners complacent. Systems that had originally been designed for defense worked wonderfully for containment. The Wall was intimidating, the continual display of military force even more so, and the force field was impregnable. But now even those systems had failed, catastrophe was at hand.

There was only one Level Three Containment System, the cranial implants. They were reliable, tamper-resistant, and instantly lethal. Each device was packed with jagged shards of graphene — one of the strongest materials ever created by mankind. The miniature shaped charge was enough to launch the shrapnel through nearly anything. Milk would likely be immune to such damage, but few Posthumans possess his level of invulnerability. Doctor Angus believed that of the two hundred forty-two residents only Vaughn Gregory, young Thomas and Tank could survive detonation.

Of course, the old man would never put that to the test. With his supreme security clearance, he could detonate every such implant on Earth. But Angus only needed to kill the Children of Man.

Executing any single inmate was extremely simple, little more complicated than using a television remote control. Angus, however, needed to strike all of the Children simultaneously. They could not be allowed to react, not with their powers. All had to die at once.

Unfortunately the menu for selecting multiple targets was bizarrely complicated. He was shown a crude map of the local area, with rows of unusual icons along the bottom edge. The map displayed the location of nearby inmates, listing them by identification number. The clustered five were obviously the cultists, but a dozen more stood very close to the helicopter pad.

Angus glanced up. The Children were still listening to their leader's oration.

The doctor returned his gaze to the tablet. For a moment, he could not recall the meaning of every icon, but two were familiar. One resembled a sun-like rosette of arrows, while the other was a set of concentric circles. After a brief reflection, he remembered that the circular symbol represented a localized effect, indiscriminately exterminating any resident within a dozen yards. It would suffice, although it may affect the nearby group of inmates.

That did not matter. Angus would sacrifice anything to save the sixteen clones.

"Calling for help, Doctor?" asked the Lector. His acolytes looked at the golden towers and liquid-filled glass bulbs. Ashley Lang placed her hand on one of the tanks. The bestial Esau stepped closer. The bronze man kept his eyes on Angus. "Your army has fallen. There will be no salvation. The end has come."

Angus looked up, thumb hovering over the icon, "I suspect you are correct, for once in your wasted life. The end, indeed, has come."

Without breaking eye contact, Doctor Angus pushed the button.

"Hold still," said David.

There was a boom, a blur, and Tom winced; it was like being in the middle of a tornado. Deafening bangs, powerful vibrations, and violent winds assaulted his body for half a second. Then it stopped and he had been *dressed*. Although, Tom realized at that moment, he hadn't even noticed the nudity.

He wondered if Milk ever had that problem.

David stood as though he'd not moved an inch. "That's better."

Tom looked down at the new outfit. The speeder had dressed him in a gray T-shirt, black pants and combat boots. No socks or undergarments, though, but that was fine by Tom. Being clothed by a new acquaintance was uncomfortable enough.

"Um, thanks."

Tom looked at the young Posties and thought about his father's words. He wasn't alone, after all. Maybe he had never been alone.

JJ Joyce and his friends had tried to save him. David, Nikki and Overpower had come to free him. Others he hadn't met yet—the recently-gigantic Sol and the rest of Milk's team—had risked everything to rescue him. Captain Holly had tried to sneak him out. Fiona had given her life. So many people had done so much. Tom blinked tears from his golden eyes.

Tiffany reached over and squeezed his hand. She nodded toward David and said, "Don't mind Shockwave. Apparently he goes around dressing strangers all the time."

"He just likes showing off," said Nikki. She sneered playfully at her big brother. "He could have just brought you the clothes, but nope. He just *had* to put them on you."

"*There's nothing wrong with showing off,*" commented Overpower. "*We've got power, we should* use *it.*"

"Heard that," agreed Anon. Madi and Vanessa laughed.

"Maybe," grumbled Nikki. "But he's still obnoxious."

"You're just jealous," replied David. He looked at Tom, "It takes her two hours to get ready for a trip to McDonald's."

"Oh my God," groaned Vanessa. "I've been craving a Quarter Pounder for years. I'd go in sweats. Wouldn't even brush my hair."

Madi laughed, "Well, Nessie, we'll hit up Mickey D's tonight."

JJ stepped closer and put his hand on Madi's shoulder.

"Sounds like a plan, though I'm a little short on cash."

"Hey check it out," exclaimed Anon. "It's Sol!"

Tom, Tiffany and JJ turned to see.

Sol was at the end of the block, walking around the corner with Hardcore, Quietus and California Girl. A mixed group of prisoners and guards followed the quartet; Hardcore carried the Gerber family and Billy the bat boy. Behind them came dozens of Posthumans, hundreds. The prisoners of ABRA City walked toward freedom.

Madi and Vanessa broke into applause and began to chant, "Sol-o-mon! Sol-o-mon!"

Sol blushed at the praise and scratched his beard. California Girl said something that made him turn even redder. That time, he scratched the top of his wooly head.

Anon became a bombshell blonde in a San Francisco Giants T-shirt and let out a whoop. It took off, sprinting toward the newcomers.

JJ grinned, "Come on, let's catch up with Sol."

He began to walk down the block, dragging Nikki. David, Madison and Vanessa followed, laughing and still cheering for Sol.

Tom looked at Tiffany. Their eyes met; a thrill shot through his heart. He wondered if it was right to feel happiness so soon. It had to be. She made it right. She cocked her head to the side and reached up to touch his face.

Her eyebrows drew close and she whispered, "What are we going to do, now that we're free?"

"Anything," was his reply. "There are no limits. Not for us."

Tiffany opened her mouth to speak but was interrupted by a shout. Madison Doyle felt a tingle of radio waves, recognized the frequency and screamed, "No!"

Two hundred thirty-six implant bombs detonated at once.

CHAPTER FORTY

Tom wrapped his arms around Tiffany. She buried her face in his chest, but he did not look away.

The two hundred explosions combined into one wet, rippling pop. Madison's scream echoed over the wind.

Anon's corpse flopped to the street under a red fountain. Only a mangled stump remained where its head should have been.

The crowd of Posthumans fell as one beneath the bloody haze. Autumn Gerber and her glowing little boys died in Hardcore's arms; Billy the bat boy tumbled from the tattooed giant's shoulders.

Stolen implant removers clattered on the pavement, as Sol's body toppled.

California Girl's eyes went wide; her lips moved, but no sound came out. Hardcore dropped to his knees, struggling to breathe through the sudden flood of tears, cradling the dead to his massive chest. Quietus stumbled back, burned by the telepathic touch of so many dying minds. He quickly composed himself, stepped behind his friends and placed a hand on each one's shoulder.

The soldiers reacted with shouted curses, shapeless cries and vehement denials. Blood and brain covered most of them from head to toe; several of them retched, doubled over and vomited.

Milk bellowed while Captain Holly growled through

clenched teeth. David pulled his little sister close, sheltering her while closing his own eyes.

JJ, Vanessa and Madison stood in stunned silence on the street. Tom couldn't see their faces, but didn't need to. JJ froze mid-step and tilted his head to the side; he began to tremble but made no sound. Madi gasped and covered her face. Vanessa let out a stream of Spanish and turned away from the bloodbath.

The little black plugs behind their ears had not detonated. Tom saw fading radio waves stream from pixie-haired Madi, and he understood how they had survived.

She had felt the activation signal, preparing the bombs for detonation. She'd used her power to pulse a jamming wave, milliseconds before ignition. The signals had been nearly simultaneous; Madison managed to save herself, JJ and Vanessa, but she could not defeat the speed of light. Every other implant received the command; every other detonator triggered.

JJ reached out and staggered forward, but his knees buckled. He collapsed on the pavement and howled. He stretched a trembling hand toward Sol then folded in on himself, sobbing.

Nikki and David kneeled on his left, wrapping their arms around his trembling shoulders. Vanessa and Madi hit the ground to his right, joining the embrace. Milk walked to the huddled group, while Captain Holly remained motionless, his fists balled.

"I tried," cried Madison. Tears washed down her face; the groaning plea was barely comprehensible. She gasped and moaned, "I tried! I didn't … couldn't … I tried to save them."

"You saved more lives than anyone else," answered Milk. His arms went around the cluster of bawling youths, holding them all.

Tiffany wept against Tom's chest, shuddering in his arms. He held her tightly, ran fingers through her hair and kissed the top of her head. Damp warmth permeated his shirt as her tears soaked through the thin cloth.

His heart ached for her; it was the only emotion penetrating his almost clinical detachment. A vague sense of grief and a low throb of anger stirred somewhere at the base of his consciousness, but the sensations were distant, more like something from memory than an immediate reaction to such a massacre. For a moment, he contemplated this lack of feeling; this night of visions and violence had left him numb. Then something else rose to the surface: curiosity.

Who pushed the button?

Sniffling, Tiffany raised her face. She wiped her eyes and glanced toward the others. Catching a glimpse of the carnage, she recoiled and clutched at Tom's arm. She looked up at him and whispered, "Everybody's ... gone. They're all gone. Tank's still alive down there ... but nobody else made it."

"I know." Tom brushed a rogue strand of hair from her wet cheek. "Here, let me do something."

His fingertips slid behind her left ear. Closing his eyes, Tom extended his perceptions and touched the little bomb with his golden light. In his mind, he could feel the individual parts the device—the circuitry, the tiny ceramic bits, the shaped charge and packet of microscopic shrapnel. Miniature locks spun, clicked into place, and disengaged. The detonator popped out of its socket and floated to Tom's palm.

He drew his hand away; his fingers curled around the implant an instant before the fist flared white. Tiffany gasped and leaned away from the welling heat. The light faded to soft gold, the high temperature surrendered to the frigid northern chill. Tom's grip relaxed and the little bomb was gone.

"That's better." He leaned down and kissed her cheek. He stepped back and said, "I need to go look around. Want to come with me?"

"Are you going to look for who did this?"

He nodded, "Yeah. Come on."

Tiffany shook her head, "No. You go. I don't want to see ... I can't..."

"Okay. It's okay." They kissed, holding it for a second before Tom pulled away. "I'll be right back."

Their eyes remained locked as he took flight, until she was a speck on the ground.

✪   ✪   ✪

Vaughn figured that he'd been dead for about five minutes. He'd been dead before, though this was a rough one. There he'd been, sneaking around the crater, trying to find an inconspicuous way past the Wall, and then—bang! The implant bomb had blown away a fifth of his meaty head and killed him outright.

Everything hurt. His head throbbed and his jaw still ached like hell. But he was alive again and closer to freedom than he'd been in years. Now he didn't even have a brain bomb to worry about.

He crouched on the crater's edge and wondered if he could scale the Wall without being seen. There were few lights in the city, but the aurora and stars were bright.

He glanced at the sky just as a golden flash streaked overhead. Little half-breed Fuson. The boy never looked down.

Vaughn peeked over the rubble and watched the sparkly bastard land near a helicopter on the far side of town. Closer were the remains of the apartment buildings and a big brick movie theater. He saw Milk, bunch of other people, and a fucking platoon of soldiers—all less than a hundred feet away, down a blown-to-shit street.

The Behemoth ducked and began to crawl.

"Christ," grumbled the scuttling monster. "This night just keeps getting better."

Tom found Doctor Angus wandering on the small field where Tiffany had been, after Fiona's death. Several headless corpses sprawled on the grass in black puddles of blood. The old man stumbled among them.

Fifty feet away, near the helicopter, more bodies littered the concrete. Some soldiers were hauling the giant Esau's hairy carcass down the ramp.

And Tom understood.

Angus had been trying to flee when the Children of Man caught him. The old doctor's anxious body language and desolate expression revealed the rest of the story. The detonation of the implants—the extermination of two-thirds of all known American Posthumans—had been an accident, not murder.

"I did not want this," muttered the doctor in a hollow whisper. "I never wanted this. I *made* them, Thomas."

He looked at Tom and reached out. The boy drifted out of reach but did not respond.

Angus cleared his throat and whispered, "I made a mistake. It was the other button; it was the arrows, but I was confused … frightened. I tried to stop the Children from killing us. I did not want to harm anyone beyond that."

Tom remained silent, hovering five feet from Angus.

"It was a mistake," the doctor stammered and began to ramble. "Mistakes, Thomas, there have been so many … so many. I never wanted this. I never wanted to harm you; I never wanted to harm Megan. She was my pupil, like a daughter to me, and your father was like a son. You are my family, Thomas. I tried to save you. I never wanted this. I wanted to contain them, protect them … never kill them. So many mistakes, Thomas, there have been too many."

The sad lines of the old man's face drew tight. He looked at the boy, seeking … seeking what? Forgiveness? Comfort?

Tom did not care. He hovered higher, illuminating the scientist and the bodies. "You think that matters? Your mistakes killed them, Doctor; the Posthumans, my mother, Marcus. You killed them all. I don't care what you wanted. What you did—what you let be done—was evil."

The old man's left eye twitched. "Judge me, then. I have earned it."

"No. Let the humans and Posthumans judge you for this." He turned his back to the old man and rose into the air. "I'm through with you."

Doctor Angus watched for a moment, until the boy became a golden star in the heavens. He slowly nodded to himself, walked back to the helicopter and left ABRA City behind.

✪   ✪   ✪

Tiffany raised the coat's hood and shivered.

She felt kind of awkward, drifting at the edge of the group. But she didn't really know anyone, and everybody looked busy.

Overpower had thundered into the sky right after Tom left; California Girl, Hardcore and Quietus stood at the crater's edge, having a tense conversation with Captain Holly. Two hundred dead Posties lay on the ground nearby, with soldiers coming from all over the base to cover the bodies with blankets, tablecloths and tarps. But they could not hide the blood.

Tiffany turned away from all the death.

Milk was sitting on a flattened Walker, still comforting the five younger Posties. Tiffany thought about joining them, but feared that she'd start crying, and she didn't want to cry. Not yet. Too many things had happened, too fast. It was too soon to cry.

Besides, she was free, and Tom was free. This wasn't a happy ending, but maybe it wasn't an ending at all. Maybe ABRA City would be where their lives began.

There were sounds behind her back, pulling her from the thoughts—a deliberate footfall and a not-too-quiet cough.

Tiffany whirled around, blue eyes scanning the distance. At first, she didn't see anyone; the road and the Wall were directly in front, but the shadows of night obscured the intersection.

The darkness rippled and a lone figure stepped into view. She saw a short, thin man, wearing MegaMax scrubs, but he was totally unfazed by the lethal cold. Tiffany squinted, trying to make out his face—and then she saw it. She saw the white-flecked brown hair and plain features. It was that strange man, the second high-risk prisoner, the one Milk called Doctor Banks.

They said he was a normal man. She could tell, by simply looking at him, that he was just a normal man. But he stood in the subzero wind with no sign of discomfort. If anything, he seemed to be smiling.

It wasn't exactly a friendly smile, but it wasn't threatening either. His thin lips barely turned, his expression didn't noticeably change, but he still appeared to be smirking. In fact, he seemed to be giving her a little challenge, a dare.

She almost felt the question inside her mind: *Curious, kid? Why don't you come and ask?*

One of his eyebrows rose, almost tauntingly, before he resumed walking down the road. He disappeared around the corner without making a sound.

Tiffany had walked nearly twenty feet before realizing it. Her steps faltered—she hadn't meant to start following the mysterious man—but inquisitiveness pushed her forward. She knew better than to wander off, tried to stop herself. But she needed to see where Banks was going. She had to trail the strange doctor so she could tell Milk about it. *That* was it.

Milk needed to know that Banks had lived through both blasts—Tiffany tried to recall if the older man had a brain bomb but couldn't remember—and she had to at least see where he was headed. She wasn't chasing the guy or anything. She wouldn't even go around the corner; she'd just look.

But when Tiffany reached the corner, she saw nothing. The dark street was empty. No one stood on the road, as far as she could see.

She walked along the side of the building and noticed the alley up ahead, between the apartment building and a recreational facility. She stopped; no amount of curiosity could make her take one step closer to the pitch-black recess. Banks might be important, be he wasn't *that* important.

Tiffany turned around to walk away. A chill raced up her spine—the undeniable touch of eager eyes on her back—and she nearly broke into a run. But she inhaled deeply and slowed her pace. Maybe old Banks was some kind of pervert; she wouldn't satisfy him by fleeing.

But the sensation of staring eyes pressed deeper, and a foul stench rolled through the air. Her prickling skin crawled and bile rose in her throat. She covered her mouth and nose with the coat's musty sleeves to guard against the stink. It smelled like a broken sewage line.

And those damned eyes wouldn't stop boring into her body. Yeah, they were probably just in her head, but being eyeballed by imaginary monsters is no more fun than the real deal.

She was less than ten feet from the corner, and maybe that fed her anxiety. Safety was so close that the make-believe danger felt worse. Her heart fluttered and her muscles tensed; she balled up her fists and took another step.

Then she stopped, let out the breath she'd unknowingly held, and shook her head.

She just had the heebie-jeebies, that's all. She was freaking out like some petrified little kid when the worst things that could happen had already happened. If she looked back right now, all she'd see would be an empty street. There was nothing to be afraid of, she convinced herself, and she turned to look down the road, to invalidate her fear.

Tiffany saw dripping fangs, hooked claws and a rushing avalanche of scaled flesh. Hot, moist air washed over her body, carrying the stench of filth, blood and death.

CHAPTER FORTY-ONE

"Of *course* it wasn't nuclear," grumbled Director Givich, tapping his thick fingers on the desk. He let out a derisive snort and scoffed into the telephone. The NORAD officer on the other end was as thickheaded as ever. "We received Code Troy twenty minutes ago. We know what caused the explosion. We've lost all communication, even our eyes in the sky. You know the protocols for such an event. Why are you stalling?"

"We think it wise to wait for the President, sir," replied the shaky voice of a particularly thick-headed colonel. "Using weapons of mass destruction on American soil should be authorized at the highest level."

"Authorized? You don't need the President's permission for this," spat the heavyset bureaucrat. The President was meeting with envoys from Russia and couldn't get away for at least five more minutes; the timing couldn't have been better. Givich merely needed to act while the opportunity remained. "The authorization is *there*, in the protocols, directly in front of your face! And you know good and well that orbital bombardment is not a weapon of mass destruction. WMDs aren't allowed in space, Colonel. That's why we put the rods up there to begin with! They are perfectly legal."

"Are you giving the order the initiate orbital bombardment, Director?"

"I don't have to! The order is in the protocols. In the event of

Code Troy and a loss of communication, ABRA City is to be destroyed. Some of those prisoners can obliterate the *world*, Colonel. You're concerned about WMD. WMD! The Posthumans are the ultimate weapons of mass destruction. We must act while we still can. We *cannot* sit back endanger the future of humanity. Now, will you obey the orders in your possession, or will you continue to risk every life on Earth? Do your job."

"Yes, Director," replied the nervous officer, sounding almost relieved, released from his burden by the bureaucrat's assurances. "Initiation is commencing, sir. Bundle delivery is projected to occur in six minutes."

"Thank you, Colonel," said Givich. "You may have just saved the world."

✪ ✪ ✪

High above the planet, in an odd polar orbit, a satellite received the command and stirred to its long-awaited purpose. The machine was merely one platform in a network of space-based weapon stations, part of a defense system that covered more than ninety percent of the globe. The satellites had been launched during the waning days of the Cold War, though the concept had existed for more than half a century.

The satellite was little more than a space-based railgun, similar to the doomed evacuation system beneath ABRA City, powered by electromagnetic fields. It carried a payload of large metal shafts in varying sizes and designs; all had been forged of dense, nearly indestructible alloys. Stubby stabilization fins adorned the rears of the otherwise featureless rods. The smallest were twenty feet long, about a foot in diameter, and could level even the mightiest fortifications. The larger ones, however, had been made to annihilate cities.

Launched in the frictionless vacuum, the heavy rods would fall to Earth at hypersonic speed, carrying tremendous kinetic force. The effects of impact would be similar to an atomic blast, without the hazards of radioactivity or fallout. Nearly any location on Earth could be devastated in a matter of minutes; the system was far faster than intercontinental ballistic missiles, almost impossible to detect or counter.

The Department of Defense referred to the weapons as hypervelocity impact bundles; the media liked to call them Rods from God. They were weapons of the future, used for the first time that day.

The platform's computer loaded the chosen rod into the launch tube. It was ninety-eight feet long, three feet in diameter and weighed nearly thirty tons; the force of impact was projected to exceed twenty-five kilotons of exploding TNT. Everything within several miles of ABRA City would be destroyed.

The satellite spun into position and stabilized high over the northern Atlantic. It pointed west, toward the sparkling beads of light on the terminator between night and day. A silent flash illuminated the satellite's launch tube, and the rod shot into the airless void. Gravity and the laws of motion did the rest.

"Wait a second," interrupted Milk from his seat on the smashed Scarab-Class Walker. He patted the vehicle's warped armored plating and looked at JJ with a raised brow. "*You* did this?"

The young man adjusted his cap and looked down. He wiped his eyes and nodded.

He stood with David and Vanessa, in a tight cluster around Madison Doyle. She'd figured out how to use microwaves to generate warmth, which they greatly appreciated.

"I couldn't believe it either," commented Nikki. She was unfazed by the icy temperature, and casually leaned against the Walker. She glanced at her father and nodded toward JJ, "Who would've thought this dumbass could actually be useful?"

JJ smirked a bit at that one. He appreciated what she was trying to do, despite being nowhere near ready to laugh.

"Hey, he saved us all during the explosion," remarked Madison.

David nodded and muttered, "It's true. I saw it."

Nikki scoffed, ignored her brother and looked at the pixie-haired girl, "He maybe saved *you*, but I seem to recall protecting his scrawny ass when everything went boom. So *who* saved everybody, exactly?"

Nikki winked and Madi chuckled. David, Milk and JJ shook their heads.

And Vanessa looked over her shoulder, toward the far end of the block. "What was that?"

JJ looked over, "Hear something, Nessie?"

She nodded, with a look of concern on her face. "Didn't Tom's girlfriend go down that way?"

"You mean Tiffany?" asked Milk. "She may have. I thought she went with Tom."

Vanessa shook her head, "No, I heard her walk away, and I..." She trailed off, distracted by the sound, and began to walk toward the end of the block. Her skin crawled at the guttural noises. She couldn't figure out what it was.

Milk looked questioningly at JJ and Madi; they both shrugged and turned to follow their friend.

Then Madison stopped dead in her tracks and turned around with wide eyes. She looked at the sky and gasped, "Omigod..."

Thunder cracked as Overpower dropped from above. The glaring energy of his body pulsed from anxiety. "*Milk! We have to get everyone out!*"

"Omigod," repeated Madison. "We have four minutes."

"Four minutes until what?" bellowed Milk, rising to his feet.

Vanessa continued to walk toward the corner, focused on that disturbing, rhythmic, moist sound. She ignored her panicked friends, overwhelmed by dreadful curiosity.

"*Orbital strike,*" replied the supercharged Postie. "*They're going to obliterate this place.*"

In the distance, soldiers began to run and shout. Once more sirens began to wail in the fallen city. A helicopter chopped its way into the sky and raced out of view.

"JJ," exclaimed Madi. "Open a portal, get us out of here!"

"Not without everyone else," replied the young man. His fists clenched and he looked at David. "Find California Girl and the others. Tell Captain Holly to get the soldiers together. Shit, we need to look for survivors."

Milk gently touched JJ's shoulder, "You're on the right track. If we stay calm and work fast, we can get—"

An unearthly shriek drowned out the hero's words, a banshee's wail that split the night.

Vanessa had reached the corner and could only scream at what she saw.

CHAPTER FORTY-TWO

Tom soared a few hundred feet above ABRA City. He needed to cool off after confronting Angus. He needed the darkness and silence after so much fire and noise. He needed to release some tension before returning to Tiffany, before telling Milk and Holly what the old doctor had done.

So Tom flew up, spiraling high in the night. The world fell away, without walls or limits, and gauzy light from the emerald aurora borealis flowed across the firmament. Tom listened to the thrumming bass of the Earth's electromagnetic field. Stars sang in chorus from the depths of the infinite void; he heard the music of ancient days.

For one shining moment, he found peace. He found it in the liberating effortlessness of flight and in the stirring awareness of his bond with all things.

Then he heard Vanessa scream, and he knew what it meant. Instantly, he knew.

The ungodly screech hurt his ears, even there, so high above the ruined city. His heart tumbled and his stomach dropped. Icy needles pricked his spine, and he knew. Somehow, he knew.

He knew why the young woman screamed; he understood the desperate meaning of her cry. He heard Vanessa's absolute horror and helpless rage and knew exactly what he would find on the ground below.

Vaughn.

The words of Aegis and Adam echoed in his mind. Loss and pain. Trial and suffering.

Tiffany!

He plunged toward the scream, unconsciously adapting to the volume as he closed in on the source. Vanessa stood near the Wall, at the corner, letting out a high-pitched roar of incredible destructive force.

Tom had been unaware of this aspect of her power, but now he could see the way it worked. Her body was enveloped by a mostly-permeable magnetic field, but the energy was tuned to a precise level and only interacted with sound waves. It manipulated and conducted noise, effectively turning the young woman's entire body into part of her inner ear, giving her the ability to hear far beyond human range.

And she could subconsciously use the field to focus and amplify the sound of her own voice. Vanessa was a living weapon, orders of magnitude more powerful than the noise cannons of military design. She was capable of toppling buildings or instantly killing normal people. But her target was not a normal person.

She screamed at the Behemoth, just as Tom had known.

The disgusting rolls of Vaughn's belly rippled under the force of her sonic attack. Those fat, webbed, *bloody* hands vainly covered his reptilian ear holes. His grotesque gills opened and quivered; he thrashed and stomped like a wailing child.

Vanessa noticed Tom's arrival and fell silent. She stammered something, but he did not hear her words. He'd forgotten she was there. All he saw was Vaughn.

The Behemoth stumbled backward, uncovered his ears and opened his lizard-slit eyes. A slow, bitter smile stretched across his inhuman features. Thick gore and clotted blood dripped from his leering maw. With an exaggerated swoop of his arms, Vaughn gestured toward the ground. An artist, he seemed, displaying his masterpiece with joyous pride.

On the ground... *No!*

Tom looked away, clenching his eyes. It didn't help; he'd seen everything. Tiffany's unmistakable hair waved in the bitter wind.

Red; everything was red.

Red; it was nearly black where it puddled deep, so bright everywhere else. He saw tiny slippers, shredded blue scrubs and threads of the military-issue coat. A small, pale hand lay on the pavement—he would never forget it—the little fingers half-curled to the sky. He saw steam rising from little bits of white, purple, gray and yellow, shapes no one should see, all of it soaked in glistening blood, all of it illuminated by Tom's golden light, all of it impossible to deny.

Red covered everything.

He saw Tiffany, alive, only moments earlier, so small on the distant Earth.

Red everywhere.

Tom opened his eyes, those burning eyes.

Red.

His lips quivered, and his features flicked between hopeless despair and absolute wrath. His entire body stiffened, fists clenched tight; the light around his hands burned with white heat. His eyes grew brighter than a pair of suns.

Vaughn winced at the glare but did not look away. The proud smile never left that hideous face. He felt sated and strong, basking in the joy of killing—of feasting—after so very long.

Oh, the thrill he'd felt upon discovering her, by happenstance, as she walked near the edge of the alley. His skin tingled at the memory of the beautiful terror in her sparkling eyes. The way she'd tried to scream … simply precious, that sweet little thing. Vaughn could have ravished her for days.

But he'd finished it in an instant. He'd ripped out her throat and only been able to have fun after she'd died. It had been too quick; the girl couldn't be allowed to use her power—*God damn her for spoiling the moment!*—but she'd tasted like heaven, and that made it worthwhile. He decided to tell the boy all about it, "She—"

Tom flew forward and slammed into Vaughn at nine hundred miles an hour. The sonic boom cracked the pavement and the apartment building's brick face—and sent Vanessa flying into the arms of a suddenly-there David Young.

Tom and the Behemoth shot a thousand feet into the air and dropped back to the city in a flashing arc. They crashed into the Wall with devastating force, shaking the prison city once more. A large section collapsed, burying them beneath a hundred tons of metal and concrete.

David arrived half-a-second later, with his own small boom. There was no movement in the rubble pile.

Overpower swooped in and hovered near the son of Milk. *"Anything?"*

David shook his head.

Across the city, JJ grabbed Nikki's hand and pulled her through a wormhole to the broken wall. He looked at David and turned to stare through the gap. The frozen tundra stretched beyond sight, and JJ's heart fluttered at the first glimpse of freedom.

Nikki had time to take a step toward the mound and say, "What the hell—" before the debris burst apart and golden light erupted in the night.

Tom rose from the heap of debris, holding the Behemoth overhead. He threw Vaughn to the ground, but the monster rolled with the impact and came up on one knee, still smiling.

Something stirred in his hungry old soul. The first time they fought, the boy's power had caught him off guard, but this time he was ready. This time, he'd teach a few things to the son of Independence. The kid wasn't pulling his punches, but he'd wear down soon enough. This time, there'd be no Tiffany to save the day.

The Behemoth leaped up with astonishing speed, tackling the floating boy. Vaughn pulled them both into the ground with savage might and pinned Tom beneath his grotesque bulk. He leaned down to whisper, "Oh, she was *sweet.*"

Tom fought against the foul flab and took hold of Vaughn's densely muscled forearm. The Behemoth shook him off and threw a string of quick jabs to that pretty-boy face.

Tom's head bounced on the shattering pavement. He writhed and flailed against the blows, stunned but still glowing. The golden light streamed through the Behemoth's webbed talons as he tried to take hold of the boy's throat.

He couldn't get a grip and settled on grabbing Tom's torso.

He rose to his feet, lifted the glowing boy up, slammed him into the ground three times and flung the limp body across the city.

Then—with a deafening thunderclap—a jagged shaft of lightning speared the Behemoth. He roared and dropped to his knees.

Overpower floated above, a supercharged riot of sparks with the shape of a man. He hung overhead, flickering electric blue-white against the wispy green auroras and star-filled northern sky. "*Stay down!*"

The Behemoth did not obey. He pushed upright and took a step. Overpower raised both arms and dumped five hundred megajoules on the monster. The mingled scents of hot ozone and roasting meat filled the freezing air.

Vaughn crawled through the surging current, groping blindly. Raw energy seared his flesh, pierced his bones and boiled his blood. Spasms wracked his body, and his demonic heartbeat randomly staggered, but he pushed through the pain, pulling himself across the ground.

Then his claws clicked on something hard—a six-foot chunk of concrete and steel from the Wall. He grabbed the half-ton block with one massive hand and hurled it at the electric man.

Overpower stopped throwing bolts and caught the debris with a magnetic field—just as Vaughn had hoped.

The Behemoth used the distraction to attack. He leaped into the air, slamming into the wreckage and *through* Overpower's body. The radiant being's humanoid shell flew apart with a crack of thunder. Dissipating sparks writhed in the night sky.

The Behemoth turned to jog away. He figured the electrical man would recover quickly; he'd fought that kind of Postie more than once. But it didn't matter; Vaughn was fifty feet from freedom.

He was stopped in his tracks by a machine-gun burst of flying fists across his abdomen, followed by a roaring barrage of supersonic punches to his muzzle—all in a fraction of a second.

Fifty more hard blows battered the back of Vaughn's ridged skull, knocking him to his knees. He tried to clear his head—and took a thousand-mile-an-hour fist to the face. The blow spun him in a full circle. He landed prone, with a mouthful of dirt.

Vaughn spat a wad of soil, teeth and blood. *A fucking speed freak.*

He knew how to deal with one of those, too.

Oh, he'd never see or hear the attack; he could never react in time. But speeders are predictable. Vaughn's reach, strength and reflexes made close combat too risky for squishy little speed freaks. Out in the open, they usually run to a safe distance between attacks. A real speeder—like that old whore Shockwave—would sprint in, strike, and flee faster than he could even perceive. But the Behemoth wasn't helpless, oh no. He could listen and prepare. He could set a trap.

He jumped toward the breach as if making a break for freedom—accepting a flurry of supersonic strikes from the unseen attacker—and landed at the base of the Wall. He threw a heavy backhand and whiffed, but that was the plan. His fist crashed into the nearby structure, cracking the steel face. A light cascade of debris rained down from above.

Vaughn kneeled, slid his left hand beneath the pile of rubble, set the sole of his right foot against the Wall, and pushed. He kicked back with his full, monstrous strength, leaped upright and tossed a ton of loose wreckage into the air—all in one rough motion.

The Wall crumbled; pulverized concrete and twisted steel poured down. It bounced off Vaughn's thick skin and filled the air. The junk he'd thrown upward mingled with the falling fragments, filling the gap with a cloud of debris and dust.

And—thwack!—a falling, fist-size block smacked David's shin. He'd been trying to race across the uneven ground while dodging the airborne fragments—but didn't see that one small piece. The little chunk of cement shattered his tibia.

Vaughn saw the speeder's fluttering tumble and it was like Christmas had come early. His right hand flashed out and caught David by the chest with a cobra's striking speed. The boy tried to wiggle free; his hyper-fast struggle was an arm-numbing blur.

But the Behemoth held on, squeezed, and dug his claws through the fluffy coat, tough clothing, hot meat and splintering ribs. He raised David overhead to finish off with a mighty smash against the ground—but a small figure leaped into the fray and caught the downward swing with unyielding strength. David slipped from the clawed grasp, thudding to the ground as Vaughn's massive arm slapped against two small, powerful hands.

Nikki stood beneath the Behemoth's outstretched limb, holding it above her head. She pushed against the gargantuan monster's overwhelming weight and power. His disgusting flab was only inches away, heaving, undulating.

Her thighs flexed; rubble crunched underfoot. Her arms began to tremble; his strength was so much greater than hers. She looked up at Vaughn's face — the blood-covered maw, uneven rows of busted teeth, ragged nostrils and pale yellow eyes — and fought to hold him back. His forked tongue flicked out; his eyes slid from her to David and back.

Then his left fist swung in like a wrecking ball and sent her sailing over the Wall.

"No fucking way!" Vaughn sniffed the air, recognizing their scents. "I thought you little shits smelled familiar. So the Great White Hope and his speedy little bitch had some puppies!" He looked at the motionless boy and leered. "I *love* puppies."

"Love *this*, motherfucker!" JJ stepped out a wormhole beside Vaughn. He knocked the Behemoth fifty feet away with a booming pulse of spacetime and kneeled beside David. "Come on, man. Time to go."

"JJ?" mumbled the injured young man through bloodstained lips.

"Yeah, bro. Can you move?"

"Yeah, I…" he tried to rise, grabbed his chest and groaned. "Ahh! Gimme a … gimme a minute…"

Vaughn hopped to his feet and roared. His lizard-slit eyes locked on the boys.

"We don't have a minute, bro."

The earth rumbled as the Behemoth charged forward. JJ put his left hand under David's head and flung the right one out, opening a spinning portal overhead. He made a fist and the hole dropped, engulfing the young men and sending them to the far side of the city.

Vaughn slid to a stop, astonished at the disappearing act. He sniffed the air and looked around. Free and clear; time to get moving.

Then Nikki returned, leaping over the Wall, coming down hard on Vaughn. He fell flat on his back but shoved her into the air. She crashed against the Wall, pushed off its cold steel face and landed on her feet. The Behemoth stood, and she lunged—but he sidestepped and drove a wild backhand into her spine.

She used the impact to roll out of his reach, growling a string of expletives through clenched teeth. Vaughn spun around to pounce, but she whipped around and drove an elbow into his meaty skull, following up with a solid right cross, a snapping left jab and a quick knee to the chin.

He staggered backward and Nikki pressed the advantage. She started throwing quick combination strikes with random kicks thrown in for good measure.

"My *father* taught me how to fight, motherfucker," growled the teenage Powerhouse. "What do you know?"

Vaughn flinched under the raining blows. The hits kept coming, too rapidly to counter, and damn they stung. The little girl wasn't in her old man's league, but she was strong, fast and scrappy as hell. She could maybe beat him down, if he let her keep wailing on him. But Vaughn wasn't afraid. All he needed was an opening.

She popped a sweet uppercut that made his head snap back and sent another four teeth flying in a spray of blood. It was a real beauty of a hit, but didn't do too much damage. Vaughn decided to make a play and cried out as if in pain. He cupped both hands over his face and dropped to his knees.

It worked like a charm.

"Piece of shit," sneered the girl. Then she drew back for a haymaker—and Vaughn rushed forward, catching her narrow waist in his snapping maw.

A dozen blunt fangs pierced armor and flesh. The girl was nearly invulnerable, but *nearly* wasn't enough against the Behemoth's bite. She screamed, and Vaughn simply loved it. Hot, tangy blood—the mingled blood of Milk and Shockwave—trickled down his throat.

Nikki flexed the solid muscles of her abs and back. She tried to pry open his jaws with her hands. When that didn't work, she smashed the side of her fist against his face. He savagely shook his head from side to side in response, loving her yelps and moans of pain. The teeth dug deeper.

Oh, the things he'd do with this little one. He liked the way she struggled; he liked her sass. This night really *did* keep getting better.

Nikki slapped his face and almost panicked. How could she get out? She had to get out! Then she slapped him again and found his eye. She did not hesitate.

Her fingers stabbed into the warm jelly; his thick eyelids squeezed tightly, but her hand plunged deeper. Vaughn squealed, thrashed and bit down harder. She growled against the pain and *hooked* her fingers in the gushing eye socket. Finding a grip on bone, she pulled with all her superhuman might.

The Behemoth roared, dropped his prey and stumbled back. Nikki hit the ground and rolled away. She rose with determination, let the pain stoke her burning rage, and faced the monster.

His head whipped around. Blood and gore rolled down his cheek, oozed in fat drops from his heavy jaw. The cloudy, already half-healed eye pulsed in its misshapen socket.

Nikki raised her fists and growled, "Bring it, bitch!"

Vaughn snarled, flashed those nasty fangs, and lunged.

And Tom rocketed across the city, crashing into the Behemoth at Mach three, with a deafening impact and explosive flash. Nikki was blown back by the shockwave as Tom and Vaughn punched through the Wall and went sailing into the night.

They corkscrewed across the sky before plowing into the permafrost outside. The crash sliced a half-mile trench across the tundra, ending at the base of a low hill. Vaughn lay on his back, a mangled mass of broken bone and chipped scales. Tom straddled the stinking slab of flesh, chest heaving, fists clenched.

He'd been there before, on that very first day. He should have killed the Behemoth then; Captain Holly was right. But Tom had been too weak.

This time, he was strong. This time, his power would not fade. This time, he would do what had to be done.

He snarled like a beast—like the Behemoth, himself—and drove relentless fists into the dense meat of that hideous face. His metallic eyes locked on Vaughn, but they saw Tiffany, nothing but Tiffany.

He saw Tiffany smiling; Tiffany shivering in the cold. He saw Tiffany in their room, sleeping in her bed; Tiffany on the ground, so small, so far away. Tiffany, and what they could have been, what life could have been. Tiffany and Tiffany and Tiffany.

His fists continued to fall. Harder and harder, faster and faster; he wouldn't stop, not this time. He wouldn't stop. This was the end.

Then Milk arrived, crashing into the ice-hard dirt. He landed on the ditch's edge and rose, towering over the helpless monster and broken boy.

"Tom, listen to me." He stepped closer and touched the young man's shoulder. "We need to—"

Tom yelled incoherently and threw a wild pulse of ten-thousand-degree plasma at Milk. The giant was blown back but rolled to his feet unharmed. Threads of smoke rose from his chest; hot mists of his exhalation condensed in the subzero air.

"Thomas James Fuson," rumbled the titan, with a calm and serious tone. "You can't listen, and we don't have time to talk, so *look*."

Milk raised an enormous fist, index finger extended, pointing over Tom's shoulder. The horned hero raised his face to eastern sky.

"Look, Tom. *Look*! You have your father's eyes."

The words broke through Tom's mindless fury. He breathed deeply for a few second then lowered his bloody hands. The world came back into focus, and his gaze rose to the stars.

He saw the object, not in light but in the grainy not-red of radar, a rod of dense metal. It was so small, so far away. It was tiny in the endless night—bigger than a telephone pole, but not by much—coming in at nearly twenty-five times the speed of sound. It soared in a perfect arc toward ABRA City.

Some ancient part of Tom's mind ran the numbers, calculated the time until impact and measured the force it would bring. The rod was just over two hundred miles away, piercing the outermost layers of the atmosphere. Impact would occur in forty-two seconds, with enough kinetic energy to wipe ABRA City from the Earth.

"Save them, Tom. You're the only one who can."

Tom's jaw worked rapidly and his teeth ground together. He looked at the still-breathing mound of Vaughn Gregory. The boy's lips pressed together in a bloodless sneer, quivered with disgust and hate. A low growl began in the back of his throat and grew into a scream, an unbound roar. And he shot into the sky.

His speed burned the night, scratching a pillar of fire toward the stars. The rod was falling at nineteen thousand miles an hour; Tom passed that velocity and continued to accelerate. There was no time to think, only time to feel.

Despair pulled like gravity, like the four-million-sun clench of the galaxy's central black hole. Hate burned like the fusion-fueled heart of a star. If he wanted one thing, it would have been for Tiffany to live. But he couldn't have that; so he just wanted it all to end. Let it end.

Tom screamed and power rushed into his body, pulled from throughout the cosmos—and he let it out. He let it burn away everything. His light flared brighter, and night became day in the frozen world below. People throughout the far north raised their eyes and cell phones to the blazing golden gleam.

The rod sparked on the bending horizon, a twinkle at the world's edge. The cross-section was tiny but Tom locked onto it with every possible sense; he would *not* miss. He felt the rod's mass and shape, its electromagnetic signature and motion in spacetime, and he surrendered to the inevitable collision. Their relative velocity was over sixteen miles a *second*; there was no time to think, only time to aim, only time to hope for the end.

And then, impact.

An expanding sphere of brilliance lit the night, brighter than a dozen suns, bursting like an atomic blast in the heavens.

Down on the frozen tundra, Milk stood with his eyes locked on the explosion. He did not look away; he barely even noticed a wormhole cycle open at his side.

Hardcore, Quietus and California Girl came out first, followed by David and Nikki; they'd nearly healed from their wounds, though David still had a limp. Madison, Vanessa and JJ walked out last and the portal closed. Overpower thundered over the distant wall and touched down a few yards away. Every face turned up, toward the fading golden light.

"Can you see him?" asked Milk. He stepped out of the ditch and glanced at the others before raising his face again. "Can you feel him? Any of you?"

Overpower shook his head-shaped appendage. Vaughn's attack had taken a lot out of the supercharged Postie; the tangled electricity of his body appeared faded and dim. His voice had developed a hollow sound, with a buzzing distortion around his words. "*No. Not at this-zz distance-zzt.*"

Madi closed her eyes and threw radar into the sky. "I don't feel anything. The sky's so big."

"God *damn* it," growled Milk. He walked away from the ditch and everyone followed. Nikki stepped closer and placed a hand on her father's huge forearm.

"What a shitstorm," muttered Hardcore. The shirtless brute's broad shoulders slumped and his beefy face sagged with misery. He turned to face his best friend. "You got any ideas, Q?"

But the eyeless man had walked away. He seemed to be heading toward the three surviving prisoners. Quietus closed in on the scrawny boy in the baseball cap.

JJ's eyes were closed as he tried to locate Tom. He didn't think it would work—people are small and hard to spot, especially from far away—but he had to try. He didn't notice Quietus approach and jerked back with a yelp when the martial artist touched his arm.

The mind reader gripped the boy's bicep, cocked his head to the side and touched JJ's mind.

The young man gasped, catching a glimpse of the world through the telepath's tranquil, compassionate personality. He felt the tangled worry, fear and exhaustion of his friends, and the distant alarm and fatigue of the soldiers, but Quietus turned JJ's attention to the sky.

Both Posties raised their faces. They touched Tom's weakened mind, as it sailed toward the horizon. He was ninety miles up, going a few thousand miles an hour, unconscious and helpless.

JJ grinned. He raised both arms, and a wormhole formed at his fingertips. He made this one parallel to the ground, about waist high. The whirl of spacetime opened. Wind rushed down *into* it, like a drain, as thick sea-level air flooded the sparse upper atmosphere.

Tom's limp body flew through the portal with a thunderous crack of speed. Momentum hurled him upward and he swiftly disappeared in the black sky.

JJ closed the wormhole with one hand and used the other to catch Tom with a gentle tug of gravity. He gradually slowed the uncontrolled ascent, until the son of Independence began to fall back to the ground. Then JJ guided the lifeless form, carefully, to Milk's outstretched arms.

"Holy shit, dumbass," remarked Nikki. She remained at her father's side but looked at JJ. She half gaped, half smirked at the dawning realization. "You actually *did* save the day."

"No kidding," added Milk. "Good job, kid."

JJ blushed, "Thanks, but Quietus did the hard part."

The smaller man bowed and let loose a flurry of sign language. Hardcore stepped up and placed a hand on his bald friend's shoulder—then stretched his other arm a couple of feet to pat JJ's back. The metalhead grinned, "Q says it's easier to look than to act, so you can take the credit. But it was a team effort. We all played our part."

"Sergeant Young," a booming voice rolled over the plain. It was Captain Holly, marching forward at the head of a loose band of exhausted troops. "Is he alive?"

Milk nodded, "It'll take more than that to take down Adam's boy."

"Good. One of our medics should take a look at him."

"No thank you," replied the horned hero. "We're leaving now, Captain. I'm sure you understand."

Holly met Milk's eyes. "I understand. Tell him … tell him to do what she would want him to do, not what grief commands. Tell him I said … tell him that I apologize. For everything."

"I will, Captain. Thank you."

The soldier looked at Tom. His dark eyes focused on the boy's face, like he wanted to memorize every feature, like they'd never meet again. His frown deepened for a moment before he turned away.

The horned giant glanced at his team, his children, and the three surviving inmates. He looked down at Tom and swallowed the hard regret. Had they won? And if so, was victory worth the price? Everything had gone wrong—from Megan's death in her own back yard to these final moments on a windswept Alaskan hillside—and the old hero saw no way to make things right. He could think of no way to heal the wounds they'd taken.

"Come on, Dad," whispered Nikki. "Let's go home."

"Yeah," agreed her father. "Let's go."

Captain Holly watched the Posthumans gather. Jeremiah Joyce said something to the one called Quietus, who nodded in response. The pair stepped to the side and lowered their heads for a moment. Then Joyce straightened up, raised his right hand and created a whirling portal through space.

And the tired group of legends, outlaws and teenagers trudged through the wormhole and disappeared.

Holly wished them well, especially Tom. He hoped the boy could recover from this night of tragedy and death. He hoped Fuson would grow into the man he was meant to be. He hoped they'd meet again.

"Sir!" called a shivering young soldier. "Sir, he's gone!"

The captain blinked, confused for a moment. Who was gone? Then he understood.

"The Behemoth," growled Holly. He pulled the antimatter rifle from its mount and thumbed the activation switch. He bellowed to his men, "The night's not over yet. Call all active squads. I want every functioning Walker and APE on this field in two minutes. Find that bastard and end him! We're not stopping 'til he's a corpse!"

"Yes sir," came the chorus of replies.

"It's time for a monster hunt. *Move!*" Captain Holly raised his gun and led the soldiers into the dark, frigid night.

But Vaughn was a canny beast, the deadliest predator alive, and all hunters know how to hide. He vanished on the tundra and was never seen again.

CHAPTER FORTY-THREE

"We have no words to describe our pain. We have no way to express our shame," said President Samantha Calhoun. She stood on a flag-draped stage in Central Park, before the titanic monument to Aegis and Independence. It was Friday, the Twenty-Fifth of November, the day after Thanksgiving. Yesterday had been one of positive thoughts and celebration of family; today was a day for mourning, remembering and reconciling. Exactly one month had passed since the destruction of ABRA City, and the great memorial service was being held in Manhattan.

Calhoun's political opponents derisively called it the Great Apology, but she publicly belittled that opinion. The American people agreed with her new policy of reconciliation, not Huerta's call for strikes against Milk and the Posthumans. Even Congress managed to work together on the legislation. Only a fool would ignore such a shift in public opinion; Samantha Calhoun was not a fool. Apologizing for the mess in Alaska had won her a second term. She wasn't about to walk back on it, no matter what the other guys said. As a matter of fact, she'd rub their faces in it.

"There is no shame, however, in admitting that we have erred. There is no shame in seeking to correct past mistakes. For more than fifteen years, we have allowed fear to guide us, we have forgotten our ideals. We have allowed innocent people to be stripped of their freedom and locked away on the frozen edge of the world. We have made mistakes, and we have learned from them. We are even now beginning the process of ending an age of fear and beginning a new age, an age of hope.

"The Public Safety Act has been rewritten; the Department of Public Safety has embraced its new role as defender of all our citizens, Posthuman and human alike. No longer will we subject our children to genetic screening; no longer will we imprison our friends and neighbors. Together, we will repair the damage done by fear and hubris. We will work to ensure the liberty of our Posthuman sisters and brothers, and I have faith that we will stand together. Together, we have no limits. We will prove to ourselves and to history that the United States of America remains, now and forever, the land of the free and the home of the brave."

The speech went on for a while after that; Calhoun wrapped up with a big, patriotic finish and wasn't surprised by the enthusiastic applause. She'd tapped into the zeitgeist and knew it.

She followed the escort from the stage and noticed Director Givich huddling with the Governor backstage. The President didn't hide her disdain for the head of the DPS, but had been unable to move against him. He managed to avoid any repercussions from using the Rod; the law had been obeyed to the letter. Givich had not given any order—he *could* not, in fact—he'd merely adhered to the protocols and encouraged others to do the same. His allies protected him and everyone bought the excuses. The smug bastard showed no remorse for encouraging orbital bombardment. After all, as Givich frequently mentioned, nobody had even been hurt by it.

In fact, the public celebrated the moment. Hundreds of videos had been taken by people throughout Alaska and northwestern Canada. The thirty-second flight of Tom Fuson replayed endlessly on television, viewed by billions online. The son of Independence had become the biggest celebrity on Earth, and everyone wondered when he'd make a public appearance.

The President knew the boy had taken up residence at the home of Charles and Gloria Young. The house in Wyoming had always been known to the upper levels of government, but no administration had been foolish enough to order an attack against that family.

Calhoun had debated reaching out to them, though. Milk was the unofficial leader of the Posthuman community, and the situation demanded that they speak. But she feared the Posties would vanish upon learning that their whereabouts were known, and keeping them under surveillance was too important to risk.

Especially young Fuson; Samantha Calhoun was very interested in the future of that particular young man.

So was the entire world.

✪   ✪   ✪

More than a month had passed, and Tom pretended to be fine, but everyone knew better. He never spoke about Alaska, and nobody knew how to approach him.

Gloria and Milk hoped he would bond with their children and the other orphans of ABRA City, but it hadn't happened yet. The other kids had begun to develop deep friendships while Tom just drifted around the farm—usually outside, always alone.

David spent a lot of time in Detroit, hanging out with Mike Dawkins. Nikki had to deal with JJ constantly following her around, but she didn't seem to really mind. And all of the Youngs had grown close to Madison and Vanessa.

But Tom never ate, rarely slept and seldom spoke. He'd respond if approached, but usually in a monosyllabic mutter. Then he'd just float away. Some days he was nothing but a golden twinkle in the sky.

Milk found the boy sitting alone on the hill above the house, oblivious to the winter chill. The trees were mostly bare; leaves crunched underfoot as the titan walked. Tom had to notice the approach but didn't acknowledge it. He didn't even open his eyes. Golden light blazed from his right hand; a small rock rested on his palm.

Like a living thing, the stone twisted, writhed and deformed. It looked like a piece of clay being molded by hand, not cold rock being shaped by willpower. Milk thought it resembled a crude face—hollow eyes, a triangular slab of a nose and a straight gash for a mouth.

Then the movement ended; Tom had stopped concentrating. His glowing hand dimmed, and he looked up at the horned giant.

"When did you learn to do that?" Milk asked as he kneeled beside the boy.

Tom raised the stone for a better view. "Just now. It's my first try. I've been trying to learn new things. Stuff Independence could do."

Milk smiled slightly and said, "Your father could do almost anything, but we had a friend who was even better than Adam at shaping rocks."

"Yeah. Stonewall. I remember him. I wasn't even five when they killed him, but I saw it on TV. Mom was sad. So was I. I didn't understand."

"What didn't you understand?"

"Why the heroes kept dying. What's a kid supposed to think, when the good guys keep getting killed on live TV? I didn't get it back then."

"But you do now?"

"Yeah, I get it now." Tom looked over his shoulder and tossed the rock over the hill, out of sight. "Good guys die because they stick their necks out. They aren't naive or stupid, at least not most of them. They're just always in the middle of stuff. It's not really tragic when a hero dies; it's bound to happen. No offense."

"None taken. I think I understand. Us getting killed is our own damned fault, even if we are usually decent guys. It's just the odds in our line of work."

"Something like that. The tragedy is when other people get hurt."

Milk softly whispered, "People like your mother or Marcus … people like Tiffany."

It wasn't a question; it was a solemn acknowledgment.

Tom winced, stiffened and paled. The corner of his mouth twitched; he nodded slightly but did not speak. He held his breath for a moment, and then released a long exhalation.

"I'm sorry, Tom. I don't know what to say."

"Then don't say anything!" Tom's eyes flashed briefly, but he clenched them tight and took a deep breath. He held it for a moment, counting the beats of his heart, and then let it out. He opened his eyes again. "I'm… Listen, you don't need to be sorry. It wasn't your fault."

The gigantic hero sighed and replied. "It wasn't yours, either."

"No. No, it wasn't. I should have stayed with her … I shouldn't have gone off without her. But that doesn't make it my fault. You may've started the whole thing by attacking the place, but it's not your fault. And it's got nothing to do with the government or Angus or anyone else. What happened to Tiff—" His voice caught on her name. He took another breath. "What happened was Vaughn's fault … only his."

Milk thought for a moment. "Hate's a dangerous thing, especially for people like us. Be careful. Hate makes people destroy things, usually themselves. Don't let it destroy you."

Tom snorted and looked away. He had no reply.

"I can't fix this, Tom, but I'll be ready to listen when you're ready to talk."

The boy didn't look up, "What's there to talk about? She's gone."

"You'll need to talk eventually. And when you do, I'd like to listen. It's good, you know, to remember the people we love."

"That's just it." Tom stood and slapped the dirt off his jeans. "We never had the chance to love. Vaughn took that away." The boy rose a couple feet off the ground; the golden light began to shine. "I need some air … but thanks. Maybe we can talk later."

"We will." Milk stood up, eye-level with the floating boy. "Watch out for trouble."

Tom's shining gaze slid over Milk's face. "Trouble should watch out for me."

And with that, he shot skyward like a rocket.

One night, at about midnight, JJ walked around the hill to the creek. It wasn't even the middle of December, but winter was already in full force. It had stopped snowing a few hours earlier, but the ground was covered by the thick white blanket, as far as the eye could see. JJ wore the bulky military coat from ABRA City, with the hood up and a beanie under his cap. The snow was kind of nice, and the cold wasn't bad at all, not after the tundra.

He was alone for a change. Nikki had gone with David to hang out in Mike's basement. The rest of the Youngs were already sleeping, while Madi and Vanessa had both gone to visit their families, so JJ had the night to himself. He planned on enjoying it.

JJ would have gone to Detroit with Nik and Dave, but he wanted to blaze up and spend some time thinking about Sol, Anon and everyone else from the doomed prison. It was his private ritual. Every few days, he'd sneak off somewhere and get high in memory of his friends. That's what Sol would have wanted, just some quiet, happy reflection.

JJ looked at the sky and scanned the horizon, kind of hoping to spot that golden glow, but Tom was nowhere in sight. It was almost a shame. JJ really wanted to talk to the guy; he hated to see anyone be so withdrawn. Everyone wanted to be Tom's friend, but he was just never around. He didn't talk for days at a time and spent most of his time flying, isolated from everyone else. Nobody should be so alone.

But JJ was all alone in the night, and it wasn't necessarily a bad thing. He walked around the hillside, looking for a decent seat, ultimately settling on reasonably comfortable log. Then he lit the joint and raised it in a solitary toast, "To those we've lost."

"To those we've lost," said someone from behind JJ's back.

He yelped and almost dropped the joint, despite recognizing the voice. He turned around as Tom came walking down the hill. The son of Independence wasn't glowing, but he wasn't dressed for the weather, either. The skinny blond boy wore jeans and a T-shirt, like always, but didn't seem to be affected by the cold.

"Sorry. I didn't mean to startle you."

JJ waved it off. "No worries, bro. I was just thinking about you." He raised the joint and took a hit. Then he thought about it. "You mind?"

Tom shook his head. "Nah, it's better than drinking. What do you mean, thinking about me?"

JJ swallowed. He hesitated. "You know … everything. Those we've lost."

"Yeah." Tom walked over to the log and took a seat beside JJ. Then he motioned toward the joint. "May I?"

"Absolutely, my good sir," said JJ, passing the doob. "It'd be good to have a smoking buddy. Nikki hates weed. Just plain hates it. And David says it won't work on them, anyway."

"Might not work on me, but I'll try to keep my metabolism down," muttered Tom before inhaling. His face turned red and he choked back a cough, forcing himself to hold the hit. It took him a second to recover. "Then again, it might."

JJ chuckled and took the joint. He put it back to the lighter's flame and asked, "So if you can turn your powers off, why aren't you cold?"

"That's not exactly how it works. I'm trying out Madi's trick now, microwaves. I don't need to glow for that. Some things *only* work if I'm glowing, like flying or strength. Some stuff takes concentration to work, other stuff I don't even have to think about. It helps to spend time watching you all, learning what you can do."

"That's nuts, man. I have a hard enough time figuring out what *I* can do."

"So do I."

JJ cocked his head to the side, puffed on the joint some more, then handed it back to Tom.

"I can't seem to do some of the things you do. I can play around with gravity, but I can't make wormholes. I try, but it makes me feel kinda sick. Can't figure out why."

"But you try? You practice?"

Tom nodded, coughing, and gave the spliff back to JJ. His eyes were red and watering. "Yeah, I try all the time. It turns my stomach, makes me want to puke. Gets worse and worse until I have to stop. One time, I even passed out."

JJ took a nice long hit. He couldn't help but grin; Tom was already high as balls, and it was working wonders. The guy was opening up for a change, even if they weren't really talking about anything important. "Man, that's crazy. I'm sure if you work on it…"

"Maybe," said Tom, reaching for the doob. "Brute force stuff comes easy ... strength and flying and channeling energy. Telekinetic stuff's easy, too; the light's like a second skin. But complicated things take some figuring out. I don't think anything's more complicated than making wormholes. Milk says I should be able to do anything, just about. 'Anything any Postie could do and then some,' he says ... but it doesn't matter."

"It doesn't?"

"Nah ... I'll just ask you, if I need a wormhole."

JJ reached over, squeezed Tom's shoulder and retrieved the joint. It had gone out in the cool, damp air, but they'd smoked enough. He opened a small portal and reached in with both hands. "Mike lets me keep it in his bomb shelter. See?"

Tom leaned over and looked through the spacetime tunnel. On the other side was a row of mason jars on a shelf in a dark, cinderblock room. JJ put the roach one of the jars and screwed it shut. Once he finished, he pulled back and closed the spiraling portal.

"I haven't met Mike. He's the computer guy, right?"

"Yeah, he's really cool, man. But he's a homebody, and you never go anywhere, either."

Tom shot JJ a taunting look, not quite a smile. "Want to go somewhere? Right now?"

"What? Where?"

"You're from Tennessee, right? Can you take us to Bristol? Or somewhere in western Virginia. Don't suppose you've ever been to Harlan, Kentucky, have you?"

"Bristol, I can do; Virginia side, just outside of town. Easy and discreet. You want to go to your home town, right?"

"Yeah, it's in Wise County, about sixty miles from Bristol. I can fly us the rest of the way in a couple minutes."

"Let's do it." JJ stood and opened a big portal. "After you, bro."

With one step they were in Virginia. It was warmer, though still cool, and the air smelled differently. They'd come out on a bare hill, overlooking the highway.

"Don't panic, okay?" said Tom as the golden light flared. He extended a hand, and the glow surrounded JJ. Then they rose into the sky, accelerating rapidly toward the stars.

"Holy fuck, this is fucking awesome!" JJ gaped down at the shrinking landscape. The streetlamps and towns looked like Christmas lights. Safe in the bubble of light, he laughed and whooped at the experience.

Tom did smile that time. "You know, man, you could learn to fly."

"Really?" JJ hadn't even thought about it, but it made sense. He controlled gravity, so of course he should be able to fly. He'd have to practice.

"Yeah, you can do all kinds of things. Flying should be easy for you. Just don't go too high. You run out of air faster than you think."

"But that's not a problem with you, right? I don't even feel the wind."

"You won't. The light will protect us. But it's automatic, it just adapts to stuff like that. It keeps me warm and makes air ... well, it brings air to me."

"Ever gone to space?"

Tom shook his head. "No, but I could. I ... I'm not ready. Maybe I just don't want to admit that I'm not human."

JJ blinked, "Dude, you're human. Our abilities don't change that."

Tom didn't reply. He just kept flying. After a few minutes, they slowed down and descended until they were above the thick forest and rugged hills of Appalachian Virginia.

Tom pointed toward the ground. "See that hill down there, by the cemetery?"

"Yeah, man." It was a small rise just within the graveyard's fence; the sides were too steep for it to be used for anything. The top was bare, but no paths went up to it.

"I'll need you to open a portal there in a minute."

JJ nodded and got a lock on the place. "No problem, man."

"Good. Now let's try to be quiet." Tom's light dimmed as they dropped through some trees and touched down on the ground. He released JJ and they both looked around.

They were on a path in the woods, behind a small house. There was a pile of flowers and a makeshift memorial to Marcus, Tom's best friend. JJ had heard the story from the Youngs and the news. This must have been where Marcus died.

JJ looked at Tom's face; his expression was unreadable, seemingly emotionless, except for a slight tightness to his lips. JJ lowered his hood, pulling off the cap and beanie to scratch his head. He didn't know what to say.

Surprisingly, Tom spoke first. "You lost your best friend, too, right in front of you."

"Yeah, I did. It still hurts. I'll miss Sol forever."

Tom hesitated. He wasn't comfortable talking, that much was obvious, but he apparently needed to speak. "What about your parents? I'm sorry to ask, it's just…"

"Don't be sorry, man. We can talk about anything. We've lost a lot of the same stuff. You want to know how I feel about my parents? I miss them every day, man. Some days are worse than others," JJ gripped Tom's arm. "But it does get better, trust me on that. Just remember one thing: they'd want you to be happy. Your mom, Marcus and … and everyone else, they'd want you be happy. They really would. It's cliché for a reason."

"Clichés usually are," Tom nodded again and walked toward a large boulder, at the edge of the path. The facing side was flat and covered in graffiti. He looked back at JJ. "Go out into that field. That's the Alexanders' yard. They won't mind you being there, even if they wake up."

Then those metallic eyes turned back toward the rock. Opening his arms, Tom hovered a foot above the path, glowing softly. The light spread over the rock and down into the earth. There was a small tremor, but it wasn't bad. JJ thought it was like standing next to a busy road.

"Damn," muttered Tom. "It's bigger than I thought."

And the earth opened, almost silently, as the boulder rose above the trees. It was as long as a bus, but a lot wider. It slowly tilted, until the flat side faced the ground. Tom got underneath, holding it overhead with his hands.

JJ gaped and shook his head. "Jesus, man, how heavy is that

thing?"

"*Heavy*," grunted Tom. "Open a hole to that hill."

JJ stretched his arms up and opened a portal in the sky. Tom could fly, and the hole would have to be big, so putting it in the air seemed like the best idea. Once Tom made it through, JJ shrank the wormhole and brought it down low, close enough to enter. He stepped out just as Tom placed the boulder on the graveside summit.

The huge rock settled into place, flat side down, rumbling as Tom sank the base in the earth. Then he drifted backward in the air, away from the hilltop. Without a word, he closed his eyes, lowered his head and raised his arms.

JJ watched, astounded, as the huge stone swelled, roiled and shifted inside the golden light. It was hypnotic, like ocean waves dancing in the dawn, but this was rock, pulsing in time with Tom's thoughts. The process wasn't quick, but it never got boring. The boulder heaved and stretched, and nine humanoid figures began to take shape, sculptures of the mind.

"Like Stonewall," whispered JJ.

Tom didn't turn around or open his eyes. He seemed to be concentrating harder, focusing on the detail work and facial features.

In the back, facing away from the cemetery, Tom had formed six life-size figures. On one side was Sol, with his bushy hair and big Van Dyke, standing next to a smooth, featureless figure, apparently meant to be Anon. Beside them stood Portero, with his long coat and hair, along with Lockdown and Glimmer, the fallen heroes of the past. The last sculpture on that side was Fiona McNamara, Flamechylde. She faced away from the rest, with smirking lips and a fierce gaze. On the base beneath their feet was one simple phrase. "To Those We've Lost."

On the front side, overlooking the graveyard, were three large figures. The biggest was in the center, obviously Tom's mother. She was a pretty lady, with a veil-like tumble of long hair and a gentle smile. Her face was turned down, looking toward the graves below, and her arms were spread slightly, as if opening for an embrace. By her side stood Marcus, feet firmly planted, eyes pointed straight ahead. His expression was angry, his posture defiant. His left hand was a fist, and his right held a rock. And finally, on the right, was Tiffany, frozen in the act of stepping forward, with one hand reaching for the sky. She looked up at the stars, with open joy on her face.

"To Those We've Loved," was etched on that side of the base.

The statues weren't perfect, but that only made them better in JJ's opinion. They were works of art, pure emotion given solid form. He stared silently for a few long moments before whispering, "It's beautiful, man."

"Thank you," said Tom in a low, tired voice. "I hope nobody gets mad about this."

"Dude, be serious. This place will probably turn into a tourist attraction."

"I hope not. Mom and Marcus are buried here." Tom landed at the base of the hill and stepped into the cemetery. JJ followed but said nothing as they walked among the tombstones; it wasn't time to talk just yet.

Marcus Alexander and Megan Fuson were buried close together, with Tom's empty plot in the middle. Tom walked forward and stood on the ground where he could have easily been buried. He lowered his head and took a deep breath, holding it for a time, unable to let it go.

JJ stayed a few steps behind, giving Tom time to think, time to feel. He'd stay there as long as necessary, as long as Tom needed to stay.

Eventually, when Tom started to cry, JJ stepped close and put an arm around his friend's trembling shoulder. They stood like that for a long time.

The only thing JJ ever said was, "I'm here, Tom. You aren't alone. You and me ... we're brothers."

"Half-Pint, get inside right now," barked Milk. "It's Christmas, son. Get in here and open your presents!"

"But Dad," groaned the boy, "I've got a *robot!*"

Tom actually smiled at that one, Gloria noticed. They were sitting together on the front porch, looking through Megan's old photo album, the one that changed public opinion, the one that Tom's friend Marcus had died for. She was happy for the smile. He was doing that more often but still not often enough.

The album been left on the porch before dawn, in an unmarked box with no postage or return address. Nobody had noticed its deliver, but it could have only come from the government. That had really freaked everyone out, learning that Uncle Sam knew where they all were, but Gloria considered it a peace offering and told everyone else to relax.

After breakfast, she'd asked Tom for a look, and they'd gone outside to get away from the Christmas morning chaos. Gloria had seen most of the pictures on the news but acted otherwise in an effort to draw the boy from his shell. It didn't really work.

She pointed out specific people in the photographs, like Hector or Sophia, and Tom would silently nod. He solemnly looked at every page and asked no questions. She worried that the pictures were depressing the boy, but he looked at the youngest of the Youngs, in the front yard, and he grinned. Gloria did, too.

Sean rode the robot like a pony in the snow—a gigantic, steel pony that weighed close to twenty tons—but it certainly didn't look like a horse. Gloria thought it looked like a bus-sized armadillo.

The ankylobot had been built by a bizarre wannabe villain back in the early Eighties, modeled on armored dinosaurs of the ankylosaur family. The robot was simply a great curving dome of gleaming metal on four stumpy legs, with a wrecking-ball club on a powerful tail and a blocky battering-ram head. It was a walking tank—and the eight-year-old boy claimed it on first sight. It was half toy, half pet, and the scrawny kid with the stumpy horns considered it a friend.

"Huh," muttered Tom. His attention had returned to the album.

Gloria looked down; it was a picture from Adam's twenty-first birthday party. It had been a fantastic celebration—well, until they all had to leave to stop Blue Berserker from wrecking Times

Square—and Gloria saw herself in the crowd behind Adam and Megan. She cringed at the big hair and revolting, lime-green gown—but Megan had been simply gorgeous in that violet satin and Adam looked so happy just standing with her.

Tom, however, did not look happy at all. The corners of his mouth twitched and his eyebrows drew together. He inhaled deeply and held it. His golden eyes rapidly blinked, as if struggling against memories and tears.

"What's wrong, Tom?" whispered Gloria.

He let out a slow breath and touched the photograph. "I ... I had a picture like this. Doctor Angus gave it to me."

Gloria did not reply. The wounds from ABRA City were still too fresh to expose. She placed a hand on the young man's shoulder and gave it a gentle squeeze.

Tom turned his face toward Gloria. He opened his mouth to speak, but Sean came bounding up the steps.

"Come on," grumbled Half-Pint with flat intonation and deadpan delivery. "You *heard* Dad. It's time to open presents ... yay."

"Yeah," replied Tom. He stood and playfully knuckled the space between the boy's mall horns. "Let's go, Half-Pint."

Once inside the house, Sean remained a party-pooper and showed no enthusiasm for his gifts. That was to be expected with clothes and toys, but even the virtual reality gear elicited only the mildest joy.

Gloria realized her son had robots on the brain, and wondered if that could turn into a good thing. Maybe he could spend some time with David's reclusive friend Mike and learn about technology. Sean had really been impressed by the inventor's underground workshop, and they got along very well. She made a mental note to pursue the idea later, and continued to officiate the holiday proceedings.

The rest of the kids were happier with their gifts. To begin with, Nikki and David finally received costumes.

"Oh my God, this is awesome!" exclaimed David, as he vanished in a sonic boom.

There were three seconds of riotous wind and a few dozen

quick bangs shook the house. The windows were reinforced Plexiglas and, by necessity, the Youngs own few breakables, so the superhuman speed caused little damage, but Gloria, Milk and Nikki all shouted, "David!"

But JJ, Vanessa, Madison, Sean and Tom all cheered. Powerhouse and Shockwave stood next to the semi-ruined Christmas tree in their brand new duds.

David grinned and said, "Ta-da!"

Nikki began to repeatedly slap at her big brother—who dodged every blow. "I told you to *never* dress me! Never! Do! That! To! Me! You … you … ugh! I give up."

"*You* give up? First time for everything, I suppose," laughed David. They hugged each other, and their parents, before posing in the new outfits.

Both uniforms were mostly black, with recessed trimming— blue for David, red for Nikki. The synthetic material was knife, bullet and fire resistant. They'd been made by the same folks who provided California Girl's wardrobe of choice, with plenty of input from Gloria and Milk.

David's outfit was a form-fitting bodysuit with sleek blue lines, a multi-pouched belt, extra padding at the joints and reinforced boots. The name Shockwave ran down his left arm, and an outlined letter S adorned his back. There was no mask, but Mike had sent some goggles, with a built-in communicator, nightvision and more features than a smart phone.

Nikki's costume was bulkier than her brother's, but the sleeves were short. Fingerless gloves, armored guards on her forearms and legs, Milk-style sci-fi boots and a heavy utility belt completed the ensemble. The red inlays were fewer in number than on Shockwave's costume, but also thicker and bolder. The most obvious embellishment was a line drawing on the back—a circle containing an emblem that could be either the back of a fist or a capital letter P. She loved it immediately. JJ said she was gorgeous; Milk laughed his ass off at that one.

Everyone spent a while gawking at the duo before moving on to Vanessa, Madison, JJ and Tom in that order.

Milk and Gloria had given Nikki and David a few thousand

dollars and told them to pick out whatever the other kids might like. They'd bought lots of clothing and jewelry for Vanessa, clothing and a pile of books for Madi, and some fancy electronic music equipment for JJ. They bought Tom some clothes, including a dozen T-shirts in various colors with the Independence logo on the chests. They didn't know what else to get him and were relieved that he seemed to like them.

He shook his head, and laughed, but put one on at the group's insistence.

That made it easier for Gloria to give him the box.

"We thought you might want this, Tom," she explained, as the boy examined the contents.

"Your father left it at the old base," added Milk. "You should have it. The Smithsonian already has one."

Tom nodded but didn't reply. The box contained one of Adam's old uniforms. The boy raised it, staring in silence at the red, white and blue. He looked at the white star within a deep blue circle, identical to the emblem on his shirt.

"Thank you. This means a lot," said Tom, looking up at Gloria and Milk. He smiled slightly and returned the uniform to its box. "But I think I'll stick with T-shirts for now."

There were nearly a hundred people in the Dust Bin, and they burst into applause when Tom stepped through the wormhole. The roar grew louder when the Young family and the ABRA City trio entered. Then everyone in the crowd cheered, "Happy New Year!"

Everyone, that is, except for one nervous young man in a long dark coat; Tom noticed the guy right away. He stood near the bar, beside a photograph-covered memorial to the victims of ABRA.

Tom quickly scanned the pictures but only recognized Portero, Jace Wyatt, Sol Beck and Billy the bat boy; the rest must have been topside residents, not prisoners in MegaMax. His golden eyes went back to the anxious stranger.

The guy was pale and thin, college age, with wide eyes and

spiky brown hair. He looked almost terrified, but met Tom's eyes and awkwardly approached.

"I know you," remarked Tom, realizing the stranger's identity. "You're—"

"Mike Dawkins," blurted the tense young man. He gave Tom a jittery handshake and rapidly chattered. "Sometimes I use the name Tech Support, but, um, you might already know that. I'm, uh, the inventor guy. You've probably seen the stuff I made. Let me know if you ever need anything. I mean *anything*, because if you need it, I can make it. Um... Happy New Year and all that jazz."

"You, too," replied Tom. He gave the fretful Postie an understanding smile. "I've looked forward to meeting you."

"Thanks," the shy genius sheepishly grinned. "Sorry ... I'm just not used to being in public places."

David walked over and put an arm around Mike, "Relax man. This is the Dust Bin. It's *totally* not a public place."

Nikki stepped up and rolled her eyes. "It's a dank hole in the ground, Mike. Just like home."

"Ha ha," was the inventor's flat reply. "My dank hole's not full of drunk Posties."

"Nah, *your* cave's full of killer robots," laughed Milk, walking past the kids with Gloria at his side and Sean perched on his expansive shoulder.

"Hey, only a few are actually *killer* robots," protested Mike. He looked back at Tom, "We should talk later ... but California Girl wanted to see you guys."

Tom nodded and followed the group. Pretty much everyone greeted Milk and Gloria. A few people hugged the Youngs, more offered handshakes. One lady—with pale blue hair and fuzzy moth wings—hovered above the crowd and drifted over to Sean; he called her Aunt Nancy. She offered to take him to the gymnasium, where the other children were having a party of their own.

"Can I go to the armory instead?" groaned the boy, but he climbed down his father's arm and followed the flying woman away from the celebrating adults and teens.

Nobody really spoke to Tom, but everyone acknowledged his presence. Lots of people said hello or wished him a happy New

Year, but nobody tried to make conversation. Everyone looked at him, though. Every time he turned around, someone's eyes darted away.

That was fine by Tom; small talk didn't seem appealing at the moment. The crowd and the decor had thrown him off balance. Images of the Paragon Patrol covered the walls, with scattered pictures of other old heroes. Tom supposed that Milk and Gloria were used to that sort of thing—Jacqueline Dean surely was by now—but the young man found it disconcerting.

His father's face looked out from a score of photos, posters and magazine covers. There were pictures of Aegis, too, including a display of dusty old newspapers. It was like being in a hall of mirrors.

Even stranger were the keepsakes. Carnivore weapons had been mounted here and there. The Imperator's gleaming helmet hung between the restrooms. Various other pieces of supervillain apparel were scattered about. A large display held a collection of ray guns and gizmos. Mister Moment's onyx staff was fixed to the wall by the bar.

Tom stared at it, stepping close enough to see his reflection in the polished black surface. Goosebumps crawled up his arm. Fiona's voice echoed in his memory, rambling on and on about villains and heroes. She'd wondered what happened to the staff, never guessing that it gathered dust in the Paragon Patrol's former base.

Tom wondered what she'd think of the place, what she'd say about the motif. He could just picture her at the bar, grumbling, cussing and trash talking every hero in sight. Fiona would have complained about everything, but deep down, she'd have loved it. She'd have basked in the atmosphere of heady nostalgia. This place was a shrine to the glory days; she would have fallen in love with it. She would have never admitted it, though. Tom certainly could never have gotten her to admit it. But Tiffany would have tried.

He closed his eyes and stopped the rising thoughts. He wasn't ready to confront those memories, especially then and there. Lowering his head, he listened to the celebrating crowd and tried to forget.

Then a gentle hand touched his arm. Startled, he jerked back and opened his eyes.

It was Quietus, the silent martial artist. He bowed slightly and gave Tom a sympathetic smile. They'd never met, not really. Tom had only seen him near the end, right before Angus pushed the button. Right before…

The eyeless man inclined his head and squeezed Tom's arm.

It occurred to the young man that Quietus could read minds. He knew the direction Tom's thoughts had gone. He probably knew most people better than they know themselves.

Quietus nodded, pointed at Tom, motioned toward the crowd and shrugged. He knew what everyone was thinking, more or less.

Tom thought for a moment, "That must be hard. There are some ugly things in people's brains."

The small man tapped his own shaved scalp and gestured around the room. He raised a hand, with thumb and forefinger pinched close but not touching. There were ugly things in *his* mind, too, and in everybody's. But just a little bit, in the telepath's opinion.

"Yo, Charlie!" a booming voice rose over the general din, and Tom looked toward it.

The tattooed brute, Hardcore, was coming out of the back; his thickly muscled arms were stretched around a pile of fresh kegs. He walked behind Jacqui, lowered the stack of beer and passed one to Milk.

"Don't mind if I do," said the horned giant. He bit through the aluminum and drained the keg dry in one superhuman gulp. He crumpled it like a can as the crowd went wild.

"Dammit, Alec, put that beer where it belongs," snapped Jacqui. She'd been talking to JJ and didn't appreciate the interruption.

Tom thought she looked a lot younger without the California Girl outfit. She seemed more like a sorority sister than a bartender but clearly ran the place. She saw him and waved. "Grab a stool, Tom. I'll be with you in a minute."

The boy turned to Quietus, who smiled and motioned toward the bar. His head dipped again and he squeezed the boy's shoulder. Then he walked away, into the crowd.

JJ leaned across the bar to ask Jacqui, "Like a 'job' job?"

"Yeah," replied the blond heroine. "Only three nights a week and I pay well. Kobar's a big help, but he's always busy. I need someone reliable."

Tom kept walking. Gloria turned around and smiled at him, and Milk shot him a wink. Nikki sat next to her father, with David and Mike further down. There were three empty stools on the other side, so Tom made his way to one of them.

He heard Mike ask, "What do you mean jetbike?"

David laughed, but Nikki shushed him. She leaned in front of her brother and looked at Mike. "You know ... like a motorcycle, but it flies. I need something to get around."

"Why do you need a jetbike?" scoffed David. "You run like three hundred miles an hour."

Nikki scoffed, "That'd be fine if we were a local team, but we're too badass to be anything but global."

"That's true," agreed Mike.

"Yeah, but jetbikes are *so* Nineties," explained David. He looked at his sister. "Listen, I can carry you or JJ can make a wormhole. You don't need jetbike. Tom's probably faster than me, and Overpower's definitely supersonic. Hey, where is OP anyway?"

Mike shrugged, "He's with his family. Or at least the people he considers family. He's kind of a homebody."

"No wonder you two are such good friends," commented Nikki. "I bet you guys sit around and talk about magnetism for fun."

"Sometimes," admitted Mike.

Tom left space for JJ beside the genius and took the middle stool. He looked at the wall of booze and obligatory mirror. Light glinted on his metallic eyes.

Suddenly Jacqui hollered at Hardcore, "Alec! Where the hell do you think you're going?"

Hardcore had walked around the bar and was making his way into the crowd. He blinked in confusion and pointed toward the booths. "Just taking my seat, Jac. Need something?"

The California Girl smirked, "I need you to sit your big ass on one of those stools. You, too, Q! Welcome to the club, boys!"

The beefy strongman gaped, "You serious?"

"Things may have gone south, but being a hero's not always about winning, right Milk?" Jacqui looked at the titanic hero.

"You're damn right, Cali," replied the titan. "Being a hero is about taking a stand, and you all did that. Like the lady said, welcome to the club."

Hardcore whooped and laughed. He strutted over, accepted a bottle of Jack from the lovely bartender and took the seat to Tom's left. He playfully slapped the young man's back and barked, "Damn, kid, I've been waiting for this for years."

Tom didn't quite understand and asked, "Why?"

"Why? Why do you think? Only heroes sit at the bar." His broad smile widened. "And we're all heroes now! Hell to the yeah!"

Tom blinked and tried to swallow. "But I didn't... I'm not..."

He lurched to his feet and pushed away from the bar. Hardcore said something. Mike looked over his shoulder; David and Nikki both spoke, but Tom didn't hear them. He staggered back a few steps and bumped into someone.

Milk turned and put a hand on the boy's shoulder, "Are you okay, Tom? What's wrong?"

The boy shook his head, "I'm not... I can't... I need some air."

He stumbled toward the door and ignored the gawking crowd. Few people were permitted to use the door—and risk exposing the base's secret location—but nobody made a move to stop Tom.

He left without looking back. He didn't know where the stairs led and didn't care. He could fly back to Wyoming from anywhere. It didn't matter. He just had to leave. He couldn't take it anymore.

The Dust Bin was his father's place, not Tom's. He was no hero.

Tom left Niobrara County the next morning, the first day of

2017. He needed to be alone for a while; he had never been alone before. Or maybe he was already alone. The overcrowded house just made it obvious.

He wasn't sure; he'd been thinking about it over the past few weeks. Perhaps he'd never really understand the reason, but he had to go. He just couldn't stay there anymore. He couldn't pretend anymore.

He hovered over the house for hours—all night really, though he would never admit that to anyone else—with a backpack thrown over his shoulder, waiting for the day to come. There had been no stars. Snow drifted down in lazy swirls, occasionally sailing on stronger gusts. Black sky concealed the horizon, forming a bubble universe. A few square miles of snow-covered land, with the Young's farm at the center, nestled in a wintry abyss.

Wind babbled in the leafless trees; sometimes, it screamed. It screamed like Vanessa had screamed, piercing the sky over ABRA City with her voice.

Tom struggled against the looming memories and focused on the present. Marcus always used to say that the smallest details were the most important. So Tom tried to pay attention to the surrounding world, not threatening ghosts.

Silvery light swelled on the eastern horizon, revealing the intricately layered flowing clouds. The day would soon arrive. Tom closed his eyes and concentrated on other senses. He listened to the growing electromagnetic song of the rising sun. He tasted the intensifying rain of light. He felt stirring minds within the house and knew the time had come.

He drifted lower, stopped four feet above the long gravel driveway and waited. It wasn't long before Gloria caught sight of him through the kitchen window. The front door opened less than a minute later. Snow crunched under heavy feet, as Milk walked to Tom's side.

The giant wasn't surprised by the boy's backpack, didn't need to ask about it. He knew Tom would be leaving, had known it for weeks. Last night at the Dust Bin had just sealed the deal. At first, Milk had struggled with it. He'd tried to figure out ways to prevent it and ultimately come to terms with it. He wouldn't attempt to force Tom to stay, even if he could; few people ever had so many reasons to run away. Out there, in the world, the boy might find peace. Milk hoped so.

Tom opened his eyes but did not look at the hero. They faced the dawn with no urgency to speak. The wind carried excited melodies of winter birds. The day stirred to life around them.

Finally Tom said, "I'm sorry."

"Don't be sorry, son. I understand."

"It's just… I can't do it. It's like everyone wants me to be someone else." Tom looked down and whispered, "I don't even know who I am. How can I know what I'm supposed to be?"

"You're Tom Fuson, the child of two of the finest people I've ever known. But who you become, what you do with your life … you have to figure that out. Nobody can choose for you."

"Captain Holly said something like that. He said that we don't get to choose who we are … what life does to us. We only control what we do, and what we choose do is all that matters. That's what makes us … us."

"He's a very smart man," replied the horned giant. "For an officer."

"So you think he's right?"

"Definitely, but *why* we do things is also important. That part's easy for soldiers like us—me and the captain, that is—it's easy for us to forget about the why. We know our reason. You've got to figure out yours. But if you never *do* anything … well, intention doesn't count for shit. The kind of mark you leave on the world definitely defines us, and you have to choose what kind of mark to make."

Tom thought about it. He turned his face to the horizon. "I hope he's right. I don't want to be … I'm not Aegis. I'm not Independence."

"Listen, Tom … back then, that night, you could have flown away. You could have let us kill ourselves. You could have done a million things that made the situation worse. But you didn't. Your father would have locked us all in force fields; Aegis probably would have turned all the guns into air *and* put us in force fields. But you? Your instinct was to reach out, to talk us down. You ended

412 | MITCHELL ARCHER

the fight with your *heart*. I've got faith that you'll do the right thing, no matter where you go from here, because you've got that heart."

"Thank you." Tom hovered over and placed a hand on the titan's broad shoulder. "And thank you for coming to rescue me, for being there ... with Fiona and ... after. Thanks."

Milk half smiled, "Tom, we'll always be here for you. We're your family, and that's never going to change. I hope you come back soon, if only to visit. But this house will always be a home, whenever you need one."

The boy drifted away and said, "I'll be back. But there's something I ... I need time to think."

"Well, be careful. Lots of people will try to find you. Not all of them will be friends."

Tom floated higher, "If I need help, I'll let you know."

"You'd better. Be seeing you around, kid."

Tom's head dipped in acknowledgment but he said nothing. Without a word, he drifted up and flew away. He climbed into the sky, arcing to the east, racing toward dawn. Milk's dark eyes remained locked on the golden glimmer until it vanished in the clouds.

The front door slammed half-a-second later, and the hero heard his daughter's footsteps on the concrete porch.

He turned around; Nikki stared at the horizon with an expression of contempt and fury. Milk half smiled as she marched down the wide steps and onto the snow-covered lawn. He had to give her credit; she was always open about her feelings.

"What the..." She gestured and the sky and scowled. "He's just flying away? And you *let* him!"

"He'll be back," replied Milk. He stepped past Nikki and began to walk toward the house.

"But that's bullshit. It can't end like this."

Milk looked back at his daughter and chuckled, "Nothing ever ends, Goober. This is just the beginning. Now let's go help your mother with breakfast."

EPILOGUE

Half a year passed and life had been good to Vaughn.

He lounged in a hollow on the riverbank, mostly submerged in the cool, brackish water, luxuriating in the soft light of dawn. He rested against the base of an old mangrove, hidden among the dense roots and twisted brush. His drowsy, reptilian eyes followed the flimsy boats and simple rafts of the nervous, superstitious fishermen. They had come down to the river for sustenance but were wary and afraid. Two people had vanished by the water over the previous week. They'd heard rumors from other villages.

Their eyes scoured the river but could not see the Behemoth—only the very top of his scaly head and the swollen curve of his grotesque paunch broke the surface, and the tangled vegetation kept those parts out of view—but he imagined that the people feared him and maybe even worshiped him. How could they not?

He didn't plan on staying much longer. He'd been in the area long enough. Over the previous few months, he'd grown addicted to the nomadic lifestyle. He wasn't even sure where he was. He was close to the sea, but totally clueless about his location. Maybe Thailand or Cambodia, but he might still be in China. He didn't know and didn't care. The only things he cared about were his long-denied freedom and ravenous hunger. And for the first time in too many years, he could satisfy both.

He had been surprised to wake up on the scarred hillside outside ABRA City. The last thing he remembered was Tom's sudden attack—the crash of thunder, the blast of heat and the blur of flying fists. The golden boy left him bleeding in a hole. Again.

Getting his ass kicked like that was humiliating, but he'd come to view it as a victory.

Tom was too weak to kill him. The fact that he'd survived the assault was proof. Vaughn knew what taking Tiffany had done to the boy. He'd seen the look in the half-breed's golden eyes. The little bastard certainly *wanted* to kill him but obviously couldn't.

Vaughn guessed the sparkly fucker had burned out, like during their first fight. Maybe the kid had some of his father's power, but he was too weak to be a threat to the mighty Behemoth.

The bastard had been nowhere in sight, when Vaughn regained consciousness on the tundra.

He'd peeked over the crater's edge and seen Milk talking to Captain Holly—with half the goddamn Army coming up behind. Vaughn saw Tom at that point, dozing like a baby in the big white asshole's arms. A bunch of sweet little morsels were standing with Milk, too, including those tasty Young children and that stuck-up cunt, Jacqueline Fucking Dean, the goddamn California Girl.

Vaughn didn't even need to think about it; he took off and never looked back.

It had taken a couple of days to make it across the Seward Peninsula, mostly because he wasted time hunting caribou and yaks, or whatever those big hairballs were. He didn't really know much about animals; they were nothing but food. Boring food, at that.

The entire trip across the Bering Strait and through Siberia had been the same way; nothing to eat but fish, seals and the occasional bear—stupid, mute animals. He preferred meals that cried and struggled, like that tasty little redhead bitch.

He licked his lips at the memory of juicy little Tiffany; he'd wanted her for so long. He often wondered what the best part of her death had been: satisfying his own desires or hurting the boy. He supposed there was really no need to answer the question—both facets added to the pleasure.

And it had definitely been one of his most pleasing kills,

maybe the best one ever. He only regretted that it happened so fast. It had ended far too quickly. Vaughn would have loved to spend days with her, nibbling on her yummy digits, stretching out the consummation of his desire. However, the endless buffet of Asia almost made up for having to rush through his enjoyment of the girl.

This, he discovered, was the good life. He wondered why he'd never tried other countries before. Back in the day, he'd always stayed in America, but Asia was a far better place to live. There were so many tiny towns, so many labyrinthal waterways and so very many, deliciously helpless people.

He could hunt at his leisure; there were always people on the water. Men cast nets and lines for sustenance day and night. Women came down to fill buckets or do some washing. Children came to play. Some never returned.

After the feast, Vaughn would hide beneath the surface and laugh at the frantic search parties. He savored their fear and pain almost as much as the taste of fresh meat. But inevitably the noisy mobs grew so frenzied that he could no longer rest—his cue to swim away and find virgin territory to despoil.

He wished to know the people's thoughts of him but couldn't understand a word of their chattering language. They surely knew that something prowled their waters. Did they think him a mere beast, like the crocodiles or giant catfish? Did they imagine a human predator stalked them? Or did they know that a god had come to visit?

It didn't matter what they thought. These succulent little people existed only to satisfy and nourish the Behemoth. Tonight he would take another—maybe two or three others—and then leave. He planned on traveling south and west through Asia until he made it to India. Then he would turn around and forge a different path back to the northern Pacific. He could stalk this circuit for decades—centuries—and never hit the same town twice.

Life had been good, indeed. Vaughn expected it to only get better.

He dozed under the gentle waves, lulled to drowsiness by the soft current and burgeoning sunlight. Small fish darted around his bulk, nibbling at parasites on his scaled hide and bits of flesh caught under his thick, curving claws. He didn't mind; all great carnivores have such attendants. As the apex predator of all the Earth, the pinnacle of the global food chain, this was his place in life. He'd earned it.

His thoughts began to drift toward dream, the tranquil dreams of a man at peace with the universe. The indecipherable babbling became a lullaby, distorted and mellowed by the water. He smiled and scratched his pebbly paunch. His mouth opened in a submerged yawn, and he settled in the silky muck of his river-bottom nest.

Then the light abruptly brightened, and Vaughn's eyes clenched tight against it.

He thought for a moment that he must have fallen asleep, only to be disturbed by the growing brilliance of day. He grumbled underwater and rolled over to resume napping.

Cries of shock and shouts of amazement rose from the men on the river.

Vaughn opened his eyes and saw a glowing figure above — a levitating young man in jeans, old sneakers and a gray T-shirt bearing a star in a circle. A blazing aura of golden light surrounded the intruder.

"Well, lookie there," hissed Vaughn, rising from the water. He ignored the exclamations from the locals and locked eyes with the hovering intruder. "If it isn't little Tommy Fuson?"

Tom said nothing. His eyes burned; a scowl twisted his still-boyish features into a mask of disdain. He did not move; he did not react. He breathed slowly, deeply, as if every inhalation required total concentration.

Vaughn refused to be intimidated. All he needed to do was survive until the golden boy ran out of juice — then the Behemoth would taste an alien. His tongue flicked out, past the rows of teeth; he licked what passed for his lips and sneered. "What took you so long, bitch?"

Tom didn't reply for half a minute. When he finally spoke, his words came in a low near-whisper. "I just found you. Been looking for a while. You're good at hiding ... bitch."

Vaughn's eyes widened with anger and narrowed with

amusement. He chuckled, a rasp of cold humor. "You really think you're man enough to take me in?"

Tom's low voice sounded almost weary, "I'm not taking you anywhere. This is where it ends."

"Is that so?" laughed Vaughn. The young man replied with one firm nod. The Behemoth shifted his stance into a half-crouch and bared his claws. "Then I guess it's finally time for round three."

"This isn't a fucking *game!*" Tom roared and threw a high-energy laser. The ray severed Vaughn's left leg above the knee, a thick chunk of his bulbous flank and the left arm just below the elbow.

The massive man-eater bellowed an earthshaking cry and toppled face-first toward the water. Tom caught Vaughn in with a diamagnetic tractor beam and hurled him back to the riverbank. With one extended hand, he pressed down on the Behemoth with everything he had. The tangled mass of roots splintered as the young man's power pinned the monster to the hillside.

Vaughn squirmed under the relentlessly crushing power, sprawling on his back, squashed by many tons of pressure. The stumps of his amputated limbs had begun to heal instantly — but regenerating flesh pulped and growing bone crumbled under the weight of Tom's golden light. Vaughn tried to raise his head, but the best he could do was turn his eyes toward his assailant.

Tom hung in the air above the river, throwing off waves of infernal heat. Vaughn winced as the water — six feet beneath the hovering young man — began to seethe, churn and boil. Steam rose around the son of Independence, as he blazed in the air.

The crushing beam of light disappeared when Tom lowered his hand. The Behemoth flopped on the ground, finally able to move but incapable of escaping the stabbing light and baking heat. The young man drifted closer, his face obscured by the luminescence.

Vaughn whimpered and writhed, his flesh began to blacken and char, smoke rose from his scales. The oily, sweet aroma of scorched meat wafted on the wind.

"Look at me," said Tom in a flat voice. Vaughn winced, screwed his eyes closed as tightly as possible and turned away like a petulant child.

Tom grabbed the Behemoth's face with his right hand—the hellish heat searing through meat and muscle, all the way to bone—and wrenched the heavy head around. "*Look at me!*"

Vaughn's thick eyelids flickered open. He grimaced, terrified and weak, helpless and overwhelmed by pain. Bits of him turned to ash and floated off on the wind; blood boiled on his cracking skin. His power struggled keep up with the damage, but flesh baked away as quickly as it healed.

Tom looked at the cowering fiend and realized that he didn't know what to say, didn't know what to do. For so long he'd thought of nothing but this moment. For months, he'd dreamed about finding this bastard and doing what should have been done long ago. But now, perhaps for the first time, Tom understood his true power and the burdens that came with it.

Vaughn was nothing but an animal—a deadly one for sure, but still just an animal. Tom held the Behemoth's life in his hands and could end it right then. Nothing could stop him from doing what he'd come to do. He was so far beyond Vaughn it was like ... it was like taking a magnifying glass to ants on a hot summer day.

A memory rose to the surface; Tom and Marcus doing that very thing—incinerating ants in the yard, maybe six years earlier, a lifetime ago. They'd felt horribly about it after. Even at so young of an age, they'd understood that carelessly ending lives, even the lives of vermin, was wrong. The strong have no right to harm the defenseless, and Tom cringed at the realization that, compared to him, the Behemoth was defenseless vermin.

Then images of Tiffany surged across his mind.

He saw her laughing at Fiona, smiling at Tank. He saw her gazing up, eyes glittering with hope and promise, as they drifted above the cold floor of their darkened room. He saw her crying as the guards tore them apart.

He saw her remains on the ground at the Behemoth's clawed feet.

His hand tightened on Vaughn's jaw, teeth splintered and bone cracked. Blood seeped around the boy's fingers.

"You *killed* her," whispered Tom. "*You* killed her," he

repeated, as if nothing else mattered. "You killed *her*." Nothing else did matter.

Vaughn sputtered through his mangled, charred, lipless mouth. "B-but you ... you won't kill me. Your father never—"

"I am *not* my father," snarled Tom. He slammed Vaughn's head down, shattering both the thick, steel-hard cranium and the stone underneath. He rose over the limp monster, raised both arms and screamed.

But the cry was lost in a thunderous blast of superheated air as roiling plasma flew from his hands, engulfed the shore and did not stop.

Trees went up in a violent conflagration on both sides of the river. Waves of heat burned the air. The light intensified until nothing could be seen but blinding whiteness.

Then it was done.

Rock glowed lava-red and cooled to black on the bank, clouds of steam and vapor rolled over the river, and Tom floated to the ground. The soles of his shoes began to smoke and melt as he stood over the remains of his enemy. The Behemoth's gray-white, carbonized skeleton lay scattered and twisted on the smoking hillside, half-buried in the scorched earth.

Tom bent down and took hold of Vaughn's ridged, saurian skull, ripping it free from the spine and blistered soil. Fragments of jawbone and shards of ruined teeth clattered on the rocks. The back of the cranium was missing, with jagged cracks extending forward to the ragged eye sockets. Tom looked into those blank holes and frowned.

Shouldn't he feel satisfaction? Shouldn't the pain go away? Shouldn't killing Vaughn feel good?

It didn't. Tom suddenly felt small, just a tiny thing in an imperfect cosmos. Everything was broken, and this made nothing right.

"I am not my father," he whispered again, wondering what he meant. His hand glowed, and so did the skull—red to orange to white—brighter and brighter until Tom seemed to hold the sun.

Molecules of bone and ash unraveled. The skull disintegrated and scattered, dust in the morning breeze. Tom wiped his palm on his jeans and took one last look at the splintered bones of the Behemoth. He shook his head and turned away.

The people on the shore and men in the boats couldn't see Tom's uncertainty. They did not know him. They only knew that the strange, gleaming boy had slain a monster. He'd avenged their missing loved ones and undoubtedly saved others. They waved and cheered as Tom took flight. They watched him shrink against the sky, watched until he disappeared in the golden light of the rising sun.

POSTSCRIPT

Marcus awoke in a coffin. He couldn't see a thing, so don't ask how he knew it was a coffin, but he did, even before touching the smooth, cold, lid. He pushed against it, but it didn't budge. The walls and bottom of the coffin were also smooth and cold. They felt like metal or maybe plastic.

No, he thought absurdly. *The coffin's made of glass. Black glass. Obsidian.*

There was no light, but Marcus realized that things had been dark for quite some time. He had been *dead* for quite some time.

He remembered the alien probe, hovering in his back yard; he remembered the light flashing in his eyes, blinding him. He remembered pain. He remembered falling on the ground under the pressure and heat of the probe's unblinking gaze.

He remembered dying.

Then he started to scream. He thrashed and yelled and pounded his fists against the lid. His efforts were all for nothing. The lid did not move at all. It must weigh hundreds of pounds. *Or maybe*, he thought, very clearly, *Maybe it's the weight of the soil where they buried me.*

"Let me out! Somebody! Goddamn it!" He screamed and pushed with all of his might. "I'm not dead! I am *not* dead! I am not—"

The upper lid opened suddenly and light rushed inside,

causing Marcus to flinch. He had no idea how long he had been in the dark, but the brilliance was too much for his eyes. Hot, dry air washed over him. He heard the sound of wind and distant voices, the thrum of machinery and the hum of power.

And giggling. Above everything else, Marcus heard giggling.

"Well ... get up, silly," exclaimed a girlish voice from the left side of the coffin. The open lid hid the speaker. The ceiling of the room seemed to pulse with color, illuminated from within.

"Get up, get up," implored another voice — an identical voice — from beyond his feet. The still-closed lower lid was blocking his view of that direction. He couldn't tell if there were two speakers or just one; the voices continued chattering, "You've been in that thing, like, forever."

"At least a couple of days," said the first voice, the one to his left.

So there were at least two other people in the room. But what room? Why was he in a coffin? What happened after the probe found him and ... shot him. Was he dead or not?

Was this heaven or hell?

Marcus sat up and blinked. There was light everywhere; it came in through the windows, it shimmered from every surface. And everything was glass. The walls, floor and ceiling were all made of glass, as was the meager furniture, even the mattresses under the windows. The coffin was the only thing in sight that wasn't glowing, but, just as Marcus had imagined, it was made of heavy black glass.

He immediately realized that, wherever here was, it wasn't any place on Earth.

Maybe he was dead, after all, though the place didn't look either bad enough to be hell or pretty enough to be heaven. And the giggling girls — one, right next to him; the other sitting on a pile of mattresses, smoking a pipe — were *certainly* not angels.

They were identical, shorter than Marcus, with exaggerated curves and slender, petite bodies. Their hair was cherry red, and glinted like optical fiber, but it also looked soft and fell naturally, like real, human hair. Like everything else, their skin was made of glass. The twins looked smooth and reflective but moved and flexed normally; it didn't crease unnaturally at the joint like plastic tubing would. But their flesh was not flesh.

They glowed with a pulsing warm pink-white color, as if the girls breathed light. They had perfectly smooth, china-doll faces, violet, smirking lips and solid-black eyes with no iris or pupil. Their cheeks, eyelids and fingertips faintly glowed purple and matched their lips—the equivalent of make-up, Marcus realized. They were lifelike sculptures of college-age young ladies—but they were certainly not ladies.

The fabric of their clothing was made of a fine weave of glowing glass fibers, as were the curtains on the windows and the ratty old blankets on the mattress pile. They wore identical, red blouses, unbuttoned, rolled up and tied just below their perfectly round breasts. This exposed more than a little cleavage, their flat bellies (with thumb-size depressions instead of navels) and curving hips. They wore very short black skirts, knee-high socks and Mary Janes.

Their cluttered, filthy apartment looked like something out of a 1970's New York crime movie, despite being made out of glowing glass. The city outside seemed to be a chaotic jumble of lights and motion, but Marcus could only stare at the twins.

"What are you?" Marcus gasped, as he climbed out of the coffin and stared at the girls.

They giggled and replied in unison, "CherryBerry Sin, at your service."

"Huh?" Marcus wondered if this was how insanity felt.

"I'm Cherry Sin," said the girl on the mattresses. She lit the pipe with a bright light from the tip of her finger and inhaled. The bowl looked to be filled with marijuana, but the glowing buds were made of glass like everything else in sight.

"I'm Berry Sin," added the slightly happier sister on the other side of the coffin.

Marcus saw that the coffin was bolted onto a table and attached to a very tall headstone. Only two words were carved in the obsidian face:

The Grave.

There was no name, no date, no indication as to whose grave

it was meant to be. Marcus stared at the coffin and said nothing.

Berry Sin leaned against the headstone and smiled. Her teeth were straight and perfectly white as she said, "We're the Sin Twins."

"Or the Twin Sins," Cherry laughed. "Most people just call us CherryBerry."

"They can't always tell us apart," explained Berry.

"Neither can we," Cherry admitted; she stood and joined her sister as they stepped closer to Marcus. "Not all the time."

He took a step back and glanced at the door beyond the Twin Sins. He shook his head and asked again, "What are you?"

The twins giggled some more; they didn't seem to understand the question.

"What *are* you? You ... aren't human."

"Of course we're human, silly," they said together and laughed.

"We're every bit..." began Berry

"...as human as you are..." continued Cherry.

"...Buster." They finished together. Then they both poked him, hard, on his chest. Marcus looked down and saw two surprising things that he probably should have noticed earlier.

First of all, he was naked. This wasn't a bad thing, as he was also in absolutely perfect shape now, with lean muscles and washboard abs. He'd always been stout and strong but also a little pudgy—not anymore.

Secondly, he was made out of reflective, flexible glass just like the glowing pink twins; only his cast a soft white light. Marcus raised his hands and looked at the palms. His flesh lacked the tiny folds and wrinkles of normal skin; his fingers didn't even seem to have fingerprints. He *did* have nails on his fingers and toes. Marcus looked down; he was anatomically correct, thank God, if somewhat lacking in fine detail.

The girls gently turned him around, and Marcus found himself facing a mirror. The reflection was startling, but he could not pull his eyes away from it.

He looked like a marble statue under a spotlight; the features were his—the same blunt wedge of a nose, same square jaw and small, angry mouth—but with smooth, totally poreless, shiny glass for skin. The hair on his head shimmered subtly, threads of soft ebony. His eyes were simple, black ovals, just like those of the Twin Sins.

"See?" One of the girls said; Marcus wasn't sure which one. The other one stood on her toes and kissed his cheek with her smooth, cold lips. "We're all the same."

He realized that the twins generally spoke as one being. Sometimes they spoke together; the rest of the time they finished each other's thoughts.

They explained, "We're all the same. It happens to everybody who comes here. But we're still human. You'll see."

"See? Where am I? Are we dead?"

"No," said Berry, while Cherry said, "Yes."

The twins gasped and looked at each other.

Then Berry said, "Yes," and Cherry said, "No."

Then they shrugged and said in unison, "Maybe."

Cherry took Marcus by his hand while Berry went to the window and pulled open the curtains.

"We might be dead," began Berry.

"But we feel alive," Cherry explained, and she kissed him lightly on his lips, to prove the point.

"We were all brought here by the Union. Just like you. We've been here for almost a hundred years," CherryBerry said, too fast for Marcus to tell which one said what, "Some of us have been here longer than you can dream. And there's lots more here than just us humans!"

The Twins motioned to the window with theatrical waves of their dainty hands. "We all call it the Glass World."

He stepped forward and looked through the window at the city of light.

It made no sense. It was a riot of styles and schemes, with buildings randomly scattered about. There was no concept of city blocks or any sort of planning visible in the chaotic urban sprawl. Marcus could see plenty of straight lines, but not very many right angles.

The streets zigzagged and curved among the buildings and

were full of activity. People walked in the middle of the narrow roads. People were everywhere; people in conversation, people making love and people fighting. But not all of the people were exactly people.

There were carts being pulled by various animals: horses, elephants, giant sloths and dinosaurs, to name just a few. Not all of the animals were exactly animals. There were a wide variety of vehicles—some of them looking like modern taxis, others were classic muscle cars, and some bore no resemblance at all to any automobile. All of them were surrounded by the swirling mass of pedestrians, and the traffic crawled down the crooked streets.

All of the *ground* traffic crawled, anyway. Something like a large jet ski flew by the window at about fifty miles an hour. It had three seats; the driver leaned forward in the front, while two passengers lay prone behind him. They yelled and threw obscenities at CherryBerry as they raced up and away into the wild skies above the city.

Marcus figured the guys knew the twins—as far as he could tell, all of the shouted vulgarity had been accurate descriptions of his identical hostesses.

Small vehicles of all shapes and sizes flew about erratically. Cheesy flying saucers with ridiculous antennas zoomed between buildings. Marcus blinked when he saw winged animals of titanic size soaring through the orange and purple clouds of twilight.

He realized that they were about twelve stories up in what appeared to be an apartment building (with red bricks molded from glass, like the rest of this ridiculous world). The nearby architecture was all urban, but each building clashed with its neighbors. Some had been thrown together out of spare parts; others looked medieval or older; a few appeared to be futuristic, gleaming elegant spires. There were skyscrapers, usually clustered in small groups, scattered here and there amid the vast sprawl. But the largest building in sight was an enormous Roman-style monstrosity that looked like a cartoon. It was ridiculously out of proportion, with dozens of white columns, each as tall as any skyscraper in sight, and golden dome that could have covered several football stadiums.

The city stretched for miles, threaded by glowing orange

rivers and etched by the countless, meandering streets.

"What is this place?"

"It's the city," CherryBerry stated flatly. "This city anyway."

"There are more cities?" Marcus asked.

"Yeah, lots and lots more," said one of them.

"But only four of them are human cities," completed the other.

"And this ones the biggest."

"By, like, a *lot*."

"Nova Roma, Caesar calls it."

"But it was here before him, even."

"There's people here from all kinds of times and places and stuff."

"Lots of alien peoples live here, too. They've got all kinds of names for the city like Hk'gl'arph'uhnk'pa…"

"…and Oouoaueouwawawa…"

"…and Vree-*eet*! and—"

"I don't even want to know," said Marcus, but the explanation continued.

"There are the cities ..."

"... and then there are the deserts."

"And the ocean. And the jungle."

"But mostly it's all desert, except what makes the cities. There are people here from all over outer space. It's Glass World. Do you understand?"

Marcus could only nod. He figured out at least something of his new position. He clearly remembered feeling his body burn under the space probe's gaze. Somehow—he couldn't even imagine how—he'd been downloaded (or *copied*, a scary whisper suggested) into the Union itself. He was in a computer program. He was part of a virtual-reality space zoo.

Fuck.

CherryBerry smiled and pranced around. They were very proud for explaining everything so coherently. They hugged and congratulated each other. Then they noticed that Marcus had dropped to the mattresses, head hanging low.

"Hey ... guy? Are you okay, guy?" said CherryBerry, as they

sat beside of him. They hugged him and cradled his head between their breasts. They cooed soothingly and ran their fingers through his hair. "What's your name, even?"

"Marcus," he replied quietly; he thought that maybe being dead wasn't so bad after all. "My name's Marcus Alexander."

"No, that'll never work. We already gots us a Marcus, and he's not what you might call the friendly sort. He's the Caesar. He would *never* share a name with you."

"Well, it's my name." Marcus said, standing up. He immediately remembered that he was naked ... and rather obviously excited. The girls didn't seem to notice, but they were lost in deep thought.

A few millimeters, anyway.

"You should change it! Shouldn't he change it?" Berry hopped up and nudged her sister.

"He should change it! You should change it," Cherry agreed, and then she slumped to the mattress, downcast and glum. "But what should he change it to, you know?"

Berry glanced around the room with an exaggerated pouting concentration, and then exclaimed, "Ooh!"

"Oh!" Cherry joined in, leaping up and grabbing her sister's hands. They hopped around in a circle, cheering for a moment. Then they hugged each other again and looked at Marcus, beaming.

He just sighed. The Twin Sins were obviously a few cards short of a deck, but they were apparently his only guides. Wonderful.

Marcus shook his head and asked, "What do you suggest?"

The twins giggled and chattered. Then they ran around his coal black coffin and threw their arms around the headstone. "You are, from now on, known only as ... drum roll please ... The Grave!

"Now we just need to get you some clothes. *Black* clothes!"

Made in the USA
San Bernardino, CA
15 November 2015